HAVEN

KAREN LYNCH

For my family

You've always been my haven.

ACKNOWLEDGMENTS

As always, I thank my family and friends for their unwavering love and support. Thank you to Melissa Haag and Ednah Walters for being the best beta readers and friends a girl could ask for. I can't imagine doing this without you. Thanks to my PA Sara Meadows for putting up with me, and to all my readers who make this worthwhile.

1

Roland

"She's finished?"

I smiled broadly at Pete as I cut the engine and got out of my newly restored sixty-eight Mustang GT. "What do you think?"

He whistled and walked around the car. "She's beautiful, but I thought you were going to paint her red."

"I changed my mind." I ran my hand along the Acapulco blue paint job. "Every Mustang in town is red. I wanted mine to stand out."

I'd bought the car from Dell Madden's uncle back in January for fifteen hundred dollars. He'd kept her in a shed all these years. What a crime. I'd spent the last six months working on her in my cousin Paul's garage in my spare time. The car had needed a ton of work, and I'd used up my share of the money Sara had given me in California, but man, this car was worth it.

Pete nodded appreciatively. "Well, I don't think you'll have to worry about blending in. I take it you're driving us to Justin's?"

"Yeah, unless you want to take your car."

"My car?" His eyes widened when I pulled a set of keys from my pocket and tossed them to him.

"The Escort is all yours, as promised. I even gave her a tune-up for you."

Technically, the car Jordan had given me before we left California in January had belonged to both of us, but Pete had agreed to let me keep it until the Mustang was ready. It wasn't like we'd had a lot of places to go since we got home anyway. Between school, training, patrols, and working at the lumberyard, there hadn't been a lot of time for anything else.

"Sweet!" He grinned and twirled the keys. "But I'd rather take your car this time."

I laughed. "I thought you'd say that."

"Nice ride, man," called a new voice.

I turned to see Kyle and Shawn Walsh walking up the driveway toward us. The two men were cousins, but they looked enough alike to be brothers. Both of them had straight black hair and matching smiles – or scowls, depending on their moods.

"Dude, who'd you steal this baby from?" Shawn joked as he checked out my ride. "Hey, is that the original interior?"

"Looks good, huh?"

Kyle patted the hood. "What do you have under here?"

The front door to the house opened, and my cousin Francis stuck his head out to scowl at us. "You guys going to play with Roland's new toy or join us for the meeting?"

Pete and I exchanged a look and followed Kyle and Shawn into the house. It wasn't Francis's sour mood that got us all moving; it was the knowledge that Maxwell was waiting for us inside. Our Alpha didn't like to be kept waiting, and the last thing I wanted was to piss him off today. I'd been on the receiving end of his temper enough this year to last me a lifetime.

Maxwell – Uncle Max – was sitting in his usual chair by the fireplace when we filed into the large living room. Uncle Brendan, his Beta, sat on the other side of the fireplace next to Pete's mother, the Alpha female. Every other seat in the room was occupied and so were most of the places to stand. Pete and I leaned against the archway where we could still see and hear everything.

"Now that everyone is finally here, let's get started," Maxwell said in his deep, rumbling voice. He stood and pinned me with a hard stare before his gaze swept across the room. Tall and broad, and built like a grizzly with reddish-brown hair to match, he was the toughest and most intimidating man I'd ever met. But then, it took a strong man to be the Alpha of a werewolf pack, especially a pack as big as ours. I didn't envy him that job one bit.

"First order of business is the pack gathering. We're going to have more wolves than usual visiting this year, and we need to make sure there is room for everyone. Anne?"

Aunt Anne stood. She was short next to Maxwell, but she could be as fierce as her mate when she wanted to be.

2

"The guesthouses have been cleaned and aired out, and we have enough beds in them for forty people, with air mattresses for the children. Plus, we have a dozen RVs they can use, and some people are bringing their own. It'll be a tight fit, but we should be able to accommodate everyone who shows up."

I tried to ignore the pit that opened in my gut every time someone brought up the annual gathering. Pack members from all over Maine came for the month-long gathering to discuss pack business and socialize. That wouldn't be so bad if it wasn't for the fact that every unmated female in the state would be here, hoping to find a mate.

The last few years, I'd hidden out at Sara's place during the gatherings, but that was out of the question this year. Pack meetings were mandatory for all wolves eighteen and older. Not to mention the Knolls would be very crowded for the next few weeks, making it impossible to avoid every female. All it took was for one of them to get my wolf's attention, and it was game over.

Maybe I should ask Sara if I could rent her place for the summer. I needed my own space, and I could afford it with my job at the yard. The pack provided homes for its members, and we had half a dozen new houses under construction now. I could ask for one of those since I was an adult now, but that wouldn't help me with my current dilemma. Living at Sara's place couldn't get me out of every pack activity, but at least I'd be able to escape from the Knolls when I wasn't required to be here.

"...and we'll spread out the patrol rotations with all the extra wolves on hand."

Maxwell's voice jerked my attention back to the meeting, and I glanced around, wondering what I'd missed. My eyes met Pete's, and he gave me a warning look before he turned his head toward his father again.

"Now that business is taken care of, I have an announcement to make." Maxwell crossed his arms, looking even more imposing, if that was possible. "We haven't had much trouble in Maine, at least until last fall."

A murmur went through the room at his words, along with a few low growls. No one would soon forget the vampires invading our territory last year, or the crocotta attack less than a mile from the Knolls. Things had been quiet since Sara left, but the pack had been on edge since last fall.

"If recent events have taught me anything, it's that we've become complacent in the last few years. We must always be ready to defend our territory and the humans who live here."

"Damn right," muttered Francis, who was a few feet from me. If my cousin had his way, the pack would probably be living off the grid in some remote part of Maine and killing anything that crossed our borders.

"Over the winter, I've thought a lot about this and how to ensure we are never caught off guard again," Maxwell said. "The last Alpha, my uncle Thomas, ruled the pack with an iron fist, but he and his enforcers kept our territory safe."

Whispers spread through the room again, and I got a sinking feeling in my gut. He couldn't possibly be thinking about bringing back the old ways. Enforcers were the strongest fighters in a pack, and next to the Alpha and Beta, their word was law. A lot of packs still had them, but we'd all heard the rumors of brutality and abuse. It was one of the reasons Maxwell had abolished the role when he became Alpha. He was a tough leader, but a fair one, and he abhorred unnecessary violence.

He held up a hand, and the room went quiet again.

"Let me put an end to the rumors before they start. There will be no enforcers in my pack, not as long as I am Alpha."

I let out the breath I was holding.

Maxwell continued. "I'm going to reinstate an older tradition used before there were enforcers, something the European packs still do. Instead of a single Beta, we will have as many as I deem necessary. This will spread the responsibilities around, especially for the groups that live separately from the main pack. The new Betas will have the same authority Brendan has now."

Pete and I stared at each other. More than one Beta? I wondered how Brendan felt about this. I looked over at him to find him nodding, seemingly happy about the whole thing.

"Who will the new Betas be?"

I wasn't surprised that Francis was the first to speak up. If there was one thing he wanted in life, it was more authority in the pack.

"Brendan and I will choose the Betas over the next month or so," Maxwell said. "The gathering will give us a good opportunity to observe candidates. I'll send word out to the rest of the pack, and anyone here who is interested in being a candidate can let Brendan know after the meeting."

I saw Francis, Kyle, and Shawn exchange smiles, and I had an image of the three of them as Betas. Francis was four years older than I was, and he'd been trying to boss Pete and me around since we were little kids. I didn't even want to imagine how life would be if he outranked me.

Kyle and Shawn were tight with Francis, and they used to look down on us, too, until Pete and I killed a pack of crocotta last fall with Nikolas and Chris. Since then, the Walsh cousins were a lot friendlier. That didn't mean I wanted them telling me what to do, though.

As soon as the meeting ended, Pete came over to me. "Multiple Betas? Wonder what that will be like."

I looked at Francis, Kyle, and Shawn who were the first ones to go to Brendan. "Not good if those three are in."

He lowered his voice. "Dad and Brendan know how Francis is. They won't choose him if they think he'll cause trouble. And you have to admit, he does care about the pack."

I let out a puff of air. "Well, all I care about right now is a boat and a certain redhead I'm meeting up with at Justin's party. You ready to head out?"

Maxwell had pulled strings to get Pete and me back into school after we'd been gone for a month, and the two of us had put in a lot of nights working on makeup assignments for credit. On top of everything else, it had left no time for dating. When Justin Reid had invited us to spend the afternoon on his father's sailboat, followed by a party at his place, I knew it was the perfect opportunity to make up for lost time.

"What redhead?"

"Taylor White. She's been trying to hook up with me since March."

Pete shook his head. "Lucky bastard."

I grinned because I *was* feeling pretty good today. I had my Mustang, I was no longer under house arrest, and I had a gorgeous redhead waiting for me.

We headed for the door, but I came up short when a heavy hand landed on my shoulder. I looked back to see Maxwell and sighed inwardly. I'd been so close to escaping.

"Where are you two off to in such a hurry?"

"Going out on Justin's boat," Pete said.

I half expected Maxwell to tell us we were still grounded. Instead, he said, "You forgot to tell Brendan you want to be considered for the Beta program."

My mouth fell open, and I didn't try to hide my surprise. Me, a Beta? I'd just graduated from high school. Not to mention, Maxwell had spent the last six months telling me I had to grow up and start behaving like an adult. Was this another one of his tests?

Pete scoffed. "We don't have a shot at being a Beta over some of those other guys."

Maxwell motioned for us to follow him into the kitchen. He was wearing his lecture face, and I bit back a groan.

"You two have Alpha blood in your veins, and one day, one of you could take my place. Being a Beta is a good way for you to start learning to lead this pack."

Whoa! Back up. Alpha? Lead the pack? What the hell was he talking about?

I couldn't hold back the laugh that burst from me. "Are you serious?"

Maxwell's brows drew together. "Do I look like I'm joking?"

"Last month you told me I was so slow in training that my grandmother could outrun me, and now you think I could be Alpha?" I shook my head. "No offense, but yeah, I think you're joking with us."

He crossed his arms. "I didn't say you'd be ready for that job anytime soon. Neither of you have shown many Alpha traits, but you're still young. There's hope for you if you don't screw up again."

I looked at Pete, who seemed as shocked as I was by his father's statements. Obviously, this was all news to him, too.

"What if I don't want to lead the pack?" I had some ideas about what I wanted to do with my life, and none of them included being Alpha of the pack. Or Beta, for that matter.

Maxwell shrugged. "Some of the best leaders are the ones who don't want it. They do it because they know they are the right person to do the job. They do it because their pack needs them."

He turned to go back to the living room. "I expect to see your names on the Beta list."

"Great," I muttered after he left the kitchen. "Let's go, Pete."

Most of the members had cleared out when we went to find Brendan, except for a few stragglers talking about Maxwell's announcement. Brendan didn't appear surprised when we grudgingly asked him to add us to the list. If anything, he looked amused. I was glad someone was enjoying this.

"I wouldn't mind being a Beta," Pete said after we'd climbed into the Mustang. "But Dad's probably making us do this as some lesson about responsibility. No one is going to pick you and me over the older guys on that list."

I relaxed a little. "You're probably right."

Turning the key in the ignition, I smiled at the smooth rumble of the powerful V8 engine. Satisfaction and pride filled me at the work I'd done on the car. Until I'd started restoring the Mustang, I'd never given much thought to working on cars. But now that she was done, I felt a little pang of disappointment that I wouldn't be working on her tomorrow. There was nothing like bringing a classic car back to life.

There was also nothing like being free for the first time in months. Tonight was all about having fun. Tomorrow I'd worry about the Beta program, the pack gathering, and the unmated females who'd be hoping to snare a mate.

I suppressed a shudder at the last thought and put the car in reverse.

Emma

"Here you go, miss."

"Thank you," I said quietly as the shuttle driver set my suitcases on the landing at the top of the steps. I reached into my carry-on for my wallet, but he waved it off.

"The woman who arranged your ride took care of it all," he said before he headed back down the stairs. "Have a nice stay."

I watched him get into the blue airport shuttle van and drive off before I pulled a set of keys from my bag and faced the door. Taking a deep breath, I unlocked the door and pushed it open. My hands trembled from nervous excitement when I grabbed the handle of my biggest suitcase and rolled it into the apartment.

My new home.

I dragged the second suitcase inside and closed the solid steel door, sliding the deadbolt home. Dropping my carry-on beside the luggage, I went to explore the apartment.

The first room I found was the kitchen, and as soon as I saw it, nostalgia filled me. The pale-yellow walls and white cabinets took me back to the kitchen in the house my family had owned at Virginia Beach. We'd go there in the summer, and every morning, I'd make French toast for my sister Marie and me, and then we'd go hang out on the dunes. She loved to collect shells and play Robinson Crusoe while I painted. I wondered if she still...

My throat closed off as I ran to the window. It looked out over a bay that was nothing like the view from our old summer house. My fingers clutched at the granite counter as my heart began to race and the dizziness threatened.

Relax. Deep breaths, I told myself, inhaling slowly, breathing from my diaphragm as Margot had taught me.

It took long minutes before my pulse returned to normal and the room stopped tilting. I relaxed my grip on the counter and closed my eyes for a moment.

You knew this would happen. Every day it's going to get easier.

One more deep breath later, I opened my eyes, feeling in control again. The panic attacks used to happen all the time in the first month after I was healed. Margot and the other healers at Westhorne had helped me learn the signs that an attack was coming on, and how to stop it. It also helped me to know my triggers, which mostly centered around my family and my old life. The life I could never go back to.

Okay, none of that.

If I'd learned one thing over the last three months, it was that dwelling on things out of my control never changed anything. It only made me sad, and I'd had enough sadness for two lifetimes.

I turned from the window and looked around the kitchen again. It was a nice room, warm and sunny, and I could see why Sara loved it. I pictured me cooking meals and eating at the small table, and I smiled. Yes, I could do this.

A sheet of paper on the counter caught my eye, and I picked it up, knowing it was from Sara before I read it.

Emma,

Welcome to your new home! I hope you'll love it as much as I do. I can't believe you're living in my old apartment and I'm on my way to Russia of all places. Life is full of surprises, isn't it?

I know you said you wanted to do everything for yourself, but I couldn't help myself. I stocked the kitchen with some of your favorite foods to help you feel at home on your first day. I also bought a few other things I hope you'll like, such as the cool new espresso machine in front of you. I know how much you love your mocha lattes. They told me at the store it was pretty easy to figure out. The manual is in the drawer by the fridge.

I left a number on the fridge in case something in the building breaks. Brendan is a friend of mine, and he can fix anything. He'll send the bills for any repairs to me. No argument. It's my responsibility to fix things. Brendan is part of the pack, but don't worry. I didn't tell them about you. I also left Roland's number in case you change your mind about meeting him. I hope you do. He's a great guy and a lot of fun.

Okay, I have to go before Nikolas throws me over his shoulder again. That's becoming a bad habit with him. I'll call you in a few days to see how you're settling in. Bye!

Love, Sara

I chuckled, feeling lighter after reading Sara's letter. She was the best friend I'd ever had. I wished she was here, but she and Nikolas were on a plane right now, flying to Russia to visit his family.

I'd never seen two people as crazy about each other as she and Nikolas were. I'd thought that kind of love existed only in romance novels until I met the two of them. Before I was taken from my old life, I used to dream of a love like theirs. Those dreams had died long ago, along with the girl I used to be. Now, I only wanted some semblance of a normal life and a chance for a little happiness.

I shook off the sadness stealing over me again and went to explore the rest of the apartment. On the first floor, I found a cozy living room, the master suite, a bathroom, a laundry room, and Nate's old office. I shook my head when I saw the shiny new laptop sitting on the desk. A few things, indeed.

At the end of the hall was a flight of stairs to the loft where Sara's bedroom used to be. I ran up the stairs, eager to see it for myself. At the top, I stopped, unable to believe my eyes.

"Oh, Sara."

Tears blurred my vision, and I blinked them away as I walked over to the large easel set up in the middle of the room that had been transformed into an artist's studio. Around me were canvases, paints, brushes, easels, and everything I would need, including all my stuff that had been sent ahead from Westhorne. It was perfect.

I walked around the room, touching the supplies and fighting the growing tightness in my chest. I didn't deserve all this generosity and kindness.

Leaving the studio, I opened the door to the attic to peer inside. It was empty except for a narrow flight of stairs to the roof. I closed the door, making a note to check out the roof later. Right now, it was time to settle in and start my new life.

A sense of anticipation filled me as I descended the stairs to the main floor. The bed in the master bedroom was stripped, so I took a few minutes to make it up with fresh sheets and a quilt from the hall linen closet. The next hour was spent unpacking my suitcases and putting away my things in the closet and adjoining bathroom. As I worked, I made a mental list of things I needed to buy.

I planned to get a job once I found my way around here, even though Tristan had told me it wasn't necessary. He'd wanted me to stay at Westhorne, but I couldn't hide among the Mohiri forever. When I'd insisted on leaving, he'd set me up with a bank account and some "getting started" money. I had no idea how much was there, but knowing him it was a generous amount.

It took me a while to realize my stomach was rumbling. After all these months, I still wasn't used to listening to the demands of my body, and I had to remind myself to eat regularly. Not that I didn't like to eat. I'd discovered so many wonderful foods since I'd been healed. It was hard sometimes to remember my body needed a different kind of sustenance now, and more frequent feedings.

I went into the kitchen to check the fridge, and a laugh bubbled from me at the sight of the full shelves. How on earth did Sara think I was going to eat all of this food?

Shaking my head, I pulled out some meats and cheese and everything else I needed to make a sandwich. In my old life, my cooking skills consisted of French toast, grilled cheese, and scrambled eggs – Marie's favorite foods. I needed to learn how to make real meals now that I was on my own. Sandwiches would serve my needs until then. I'd also rediscovered my love of pizza. Sara had told me about her favorite pizza place in town, and they delivered, which was perfect since I had no car yet. One thing at a time.

I ate my sandwich slowly, barely noticing the taste as I tried not to be overwhelmed by the fact that I was truly on my own. Tristan and Sara had done what they could to make it easier for me. I had health insurance, a new driver's license, and a social security number, compliments of the security people at Westhorne. There wasn't much those guys couldn't do.

Dax, their head of security, had even found my family for me. My parents had retired and moved to Charleston, and my sister, Marie, lived in DC. She was a children's writer now, and an activist for Child Find of America. She also lobbied the government for tougher child laws. It was all because of me, and I wished I could tell her I was alive and well. But there was no way to explain how I looked the same after all these years. As much as it killed me, I had to stay away from everyone from my past, especially my sister and parents. It was best for everyone.

That was why I'd given up my last name. I was no longer Emma Chase from Raleigh, North Carolina. I was Emma Grey from Syracuse, New York, and second cousin to Sara. When Sara had offered me her name, it only seemed right to take the last name of the person who had given me my new life. It also gave me the perfect cover story for why I was staying in her apartment.

I cleaned up after my meal and stood in the kitchen, not sure what to do next. I looked out at the sunny waterfront and thought about taking a short walk, but I quickly dismissed it. I wasn't ready to go out yet. Maybe tomorrow.

A phone rang, startling me from my thoughts, and I ran to find my cell phone, which was still in my bag. My mouth curved into a wide smile when I saw the name on the screen.

"Hey, chica! How's life in the sticks?" Jordan asked as soon as I answered.

"So far, so good. I only got here two hours ago, though."

"Are you bored out of your tree yet?" she joked. She put her hand over the phone and yelled at someone before she came back on the line. "Sorry about that. So, how do you like your new place?"

I walked into the living room and sat in the chair by the fireplace. "It's nice. Feels weird to have a whole building to myself, and it's a lot quieter than Westhorne."

"Yeah, it takes a little getting used to, but it's a nice place if you go for the small-town life. Don't forget to check out Gino's. Best pepperoni pizza you'll ever eat."

I laughed and stretched my legs across the ottoman. "Yeah, Sara already drilled that into my head."

A police siren sounded in the background. Jordan paused until it went past.

"I was only there for three days, but the people seem pretty decent. And Wolf Boy is cool. Just don't tell him I said that."

"Wolf Boy?"

She snickered. "That's Roland. You know, the werewolf."

"Oh, yes. Sara's friend."

My body tensed, and my insides recoiled. I'd spent the last two decades thinking of werewolves as my mortal enemies whose main purpose in life was to hunt and kill my kind. It was going to take a little while to get past that.

"I guess you haven't had time to meet him and Peter yet with it being your first day there." She was quiet for a moment. "Sara told me you don't want them to know about your past. I get why you feel that way. But I think they'll surprise you once you get to know them. I didn't care for them at first either, but they kind of grow on you."

"That's good to know." I cast about for a way to move the conversation to a more comfortable subject. "So, how are things in Los Angeles?"

"Awesome. I've been on the trail of a nasty incubus for the last two weeks, and I got the bastard this morning. Let me tell you, that was a very satisfying kill. Although, the team wasn't exactly thrilled about my methods. But hey, I got the job done, right?"

I could only imagine how Jordan had lured and snared a male sex demon. My warrior friend was dedicated to her work, but she definitely marched to her own drum.

"Any sign of that Egyptian warrior you were hoping to see there? What was his name?"

"Hamid." She sighed heavily. "I swear he's hiding from me. Too bad. I wouldn't mind doing a little *foreign exchange* with him, if you know what I mean."

I laughed. "Yeah, I do."

"But he's not the only hot male in California. Just going to the beach is enough to give a girl whiplash." She chuckled. "I actually think Blondie is on to something with the 'only dating humans' thing. They're nice to look at, and some of them even know how to please a woman. And the best part, no strings attached."

"You're so bad."

"I'm a woman who knows what she wants. I might have to hit the clubs tonight. A good kill always puts me in the mood to work off some energy – if you know what I mean." She opened and closed a door, and the background sounds were suddenly muted. "Maybe when you're ready for a change of scenery, you can come visit me for a few days. God knows we could use some more estrogen around here."

A male shouted something that sounded like a retort, and she said something back. "Okay, I gotta go. The guys in charge get pissy if you don't write up field reports right away. I'll let you get back to settling in."

"Thanks for calling."

"Anytime. You're my only BFF here with Sara out of the country. Get used to hearing from me. Later, chica."

The apartment seemed too quiet after talking to Jordan. I found a radio in the kitchen, and I tuned it to a station that played a mix of everything. Turning up the volume so I could hear it all over the apartment, I went upstairs to lose myself in my painting for a while.

I'd been working on a landscape of the lake back at Westhorne for the last few months, but I'd struggled with my painting since I was healed. My talent was rusty after not using it for so long, and it was taking me a while to capture the setting right. Before I'd left, I'd taken a bunch of pictures so I wouldn't have to work from memory, and I pinned them to the top of the canvas. I spent the next few hours trying to replicate the reflection of the trees on the glassy surface of the lake. I wasn't entirely satisfied with the end result, but the work left me feeling more relaxed and at home here.

It was getting dark outside when I put away my brushes and descended the stairs to shower and change into my pajamas. Outside, people laughed as they walked past the building, reminding me it was a Friday night. There'd been a time when I couldn't imagine staying in and going to bed so early. But the long day had finally caught up with me, and I was trying not to yawn as I brushed my teeth.

I almost left the lights on when I got into bed, but I made myself turn them all off except for a small lamp in the bedroom. It wasn't that the dark frightened me as much as it seemed to press down on me. Waking up in the dark made me think for a few horrible seconds that I was back in that sunless world I'd lived in for over two decades. I hadn't slept without a light on in months.

The queen-size bed was comfortable, and I felt myself slipping into sleep not long after my head hit the pillow. I snuggled beneath the quilt, thinking drowsily that my first day on my own hadn't been too bad at all. Maybe tonight would be good, too. Hopefully, for once, the dreams wouldn't come.

2

Roland

"Well, that was a total bust," I grumbled as I buckled my seat belt and rolled down my window.

Pete laughed and started the car. He was the designated driver tonight.

"You're just upset you didn't hook up with Taylor."

"Ugh. Talk about a close call." I scowled at the windshield. "Why do people get hammered like that and then end up puking in the bathroom the rest of the night? I'm all for having a beer, but that is so not attractive."

He made a face. "At least you didn't have Lisa Reid asking if you wanted to make out in the car."

"Dude, you did not make out with Justin's little sister in my car."

"Give me some credit," he retorted. "Besides, she can't be more than fifteen. No way I'm going there."

I sighed and leaned my head against the headrest. "Is it just me, or did everyone at that party seem way younger than us?"

The question sounded weird to my own ears, considering most of the people at Justin's had been in our senior class, and we'd partied with them many times. But something felt different tonight. I'd stood there drinking my beer and watching them celebrate the end of high school, and for the first time in my life, I felt like I didn't belong. It was as if I'd suddenly aged five years, and I was looking at a bunch of kids getting drunk.

"It's not them. We were just like that last year. We've changed ever since that stuff happened with Sara."

"Yeah, we have." Seeing one of your best friends get stabbed and fall off a cliff, and thinking she was dead for three weeks, that changes you. Not to mention everything else that happened last fall.

We approached the waterfront. It felt weird driving past Sara's building these days and seeing all the darkened windows and the empty parking spot. Sara had been such a big part of my life, and I missed having her around. I was happy she and Nikolas found each other, though. He was a good guy, and he'd do anything for her.

"Hey, what's that?" Pete slowed the car. "Is that a light in Sara's apartment?"

"What?" I craned my neck and saw a faint glow coming from one of the second-story windows. "That's Nate's bedroom."

Pete stopped the car, and we reached for our doors as a girl's scream came from inside the building.

I jumped out of the car and raced up the steps. When I reached the front door, I remembered Pete had my keys, and I had to wait for him to join me. He handed them over, and I unlocked the door.

Except for the soft light spilling from the bedroom, the apartment was dark when we let ourselves in. Down the hallway, we heard a girl's soft cries, and we moved toward the sound.

If I'd been in wolf form, my hackles would have been standing up straight. It was 1:00 a.m., and no one should be here. I'd seen enough awful things in my life for me to imagine what would make a girl scream in an empty building, even here in New Hastings.

I almost shifted, but I decided to see what we were dealing with first. Soundlessly, I approached the bedroom with Pete close behind me. I stepped into the room and stared at the sight before me.

"What the hell?"

In the bed, a girl lay, thrashing and crying out, the blankets twisted around her legs. A quick glance around the room told me she was alone and in no danger. She was asleep and appeared to be caught in a nightmare.

Pete crowded in behind me. "Who is that?"

The girl jerked awake with a small scream. She stared at us, wild-eyed, and scrambled back against the headboard. Her long dark hair covered half her face, but I could still see the stark terror in her brown eyes.

I held up my hands and took a step toward her. She made a small sound and jumped from the bed, grabbing the old brass lamp from the nightstand.

She was probably half my size, but she brandished the heavy lamp like she was an Amazon.

"Get away! What do you want?" she yelled, her breath coming in harsh pants. The fear in her eyes told me what she believed we wanted, and the thought of it sickened me.

"We're not going to hurt you," I said calmly.

She could be a runaway who had seen the place was empty and decided to squat here for a few days. She definitely wasn't local, and it seemed odd for a runaway from the city to come to a small place like New Hastings. Either way, I didn't want to frighten her, even if she had broken in here.

"Get out!" She took a step, swinging the lamp.

I didn't move. "Who are you? What are you doing in this apartment?"

"Who the hell are *you*?" she demanded, her voice rising. Her chest heaved, and I noticed she was wearing only a pair of shorts and a tank top. I also saw how pale she was and the damp tendrils of hair clinging to her face.

She inched toward the nightstand where a cell phone lay. "I'm calling the police if you don't leave."

I stared at her. She wouldn't call the cops if she was here illegally. But Sara had never mentioned anyone staying at the apartment. Neither had Brendan or my mother, who were taking care of the building for Sara. It made no sense.

"I'm Roland. Why are you in Sara's apartment?"

She froze, and her eyes widened. "Roland? Sara's friend?"

"Yes."

She lowered the lamp, holding it against her chest, almost like a shield. "I'm Sara's cousin, Emma. She's letting me stay here for a while."

Cousin? Disbelief and suspicion filled me. "Sara doesn't have any cousins."

She swallowed and nodded. "Yes, she does. My name is Emma Grey, and I'm from Syracuse."

She looked past me at Pete. "You must be Peter."

"Yeah."

"My wallet is on the kitchen counter. You can check my ID if you don't believe me."

Pete went to the kitchen. Emma and I stayed where we were, watching each other. I shifted from one foot to the other, and she reacted by taking a step back. Her reaction bothered me. Why was she so afraid of me? If she really knew Sara, she had to know we wouldn't hurt her.

Pete came back and held a driver's license out for me to see. "Emma Grey from Syracuse, like she said."

I took the card from him and studied it for a moment. No one smiled for their DMV photos, but there was a sadness in the face on the card that tugged at me.

I looked at Emma again. "Sara's never mentioned a cousin in all the years I've known her."

She bit her lower lip. "You can check with her if you want. Or you can call Nate."

"I believe you." Her wary expression told me she was hiding something, but she was telling the truth about who she was. "I don't know why Sara didn't tell us you were coming here."

Emma shook her head, her eyes troubled. "I...asked her not to tell anyone about me. I just want to be left alone."

Emma

Werewolves. There were two werewolves standing less than ten feet away from me. The fact that they were in their human forms did little to dispel the terror clawing at my gut. They were hunters, and for two decades, the fear of them had been ingrained in me. Friendly or not, it was impossible not to feel threatened by their presence.

I should have recognized them. Sara had pictures of them in her apartment at Westhorne, and she talked about them all the time. But I'd been too shocked, waking up to find two strange men in my room.

The red-haired one named Peter smiled at me. They were both tall and well-built like most werewolf males, but he seemed less intimidating than his friend. Roland was another matter. The way Sara talked about her best friend, I'd imagined a sweet, smiling boy. He wore a smile, but the intensity in his blue eyes unsettled me. It was as if he could see through me, right into the darkness of my past.

"You can put down the lamp. We won't hurt you," Roland said, reminding me of the heavy weight in my hands.

With trembling hands, I set the lamp down on the nightstand and straightened to face Sara's friends again. No one spoke for a moment, and I wasn't sure what to say to them. I felt exposed without the lamp between us, as small as it was.

"Are you okay?" Roland asked, startling me.

"I'm fine." Or I would be when they left.

He ran a hand through his dark hair, his gaze sweeping up my body. "You don't look okay. Are you sick?"

I must have looked pretty bad for him to ask that. I shook my head. "It was just a bad dream. I'm good now."

"That must have been some dream," Peter muttered.

"It's a little scary being alone in a new place," I lied. I was less afraid of their presence, but I wouldn't be able to relax until they were gone. I looked from Peter to Roland. "Why are you here at this hour? And how did you get in?"

"I have a key," Roland answered. "My mother and I took care of the place for Sara and Nate over the winter."

I remembered Sara mentioning the woman who watched the place for her. "Judith?"

He nodded. "That's her."

I crossed my arms over my chest. Sara trusted him with her place and he seemed like a nice enough guy, but I didn't like the idea of anyone else having a key to this apartment while I was here.

"You don't need to watch the place anymore," I told him. "You can leave the key here with me."

He opened his mouth, and for a moment, I thought he was going to argue. But then he gave a small nod and removed a key from the set in his hand. He held it out to me.

I shook my head and pointed at the dresser closest to the door. "You can put it there on top of the dresser."

Frowning, he did as I'd asked.

I swallowed hard. I hated the fear that clogged my chest, but what if Sara was wrong about her friends? They might be good people, but they were werewolves, and werewolves hated one thing above all others. They also had incredibly sensitive noses. What if they smelled me and somehow sensed what I used to be? What would they say if they knew I'd once been their mortal enemy?

I knew Nate's story, how he'd been made a vampire just to hurt Sara. Roland and Peter were okay with him and held no animosity for him. But Nate had been a vampire for a week. I'd been one for twenty-one years, and in that time, I'd done unspeakable things. Somehow, I didn't think the were-wolves would be as forgiving if they knew exactly what stood before them now.

I cleared my throat. "Thank you for coming to check on me. It's late and I-I'm very tired. I'd like to go back to bed."

Once again, Roland looked like he was going to say something, but he seemed to change his mind. "No problem. Sorry we frightened you."

I shook my head, attempting a smile. "It's my fault for asking Sara not to tell anyone I was coming here."

Peter gave me an apologetic smile and headed down the hallway to the front door. Roland looked at me for a moment longer, and then he followed his friend.

I waited until they were at the door before I walked to the bedroom doorway. The hallway was dark, but there was enough light from the bedroom to see Peter's quick wave before they let themselves out.

I let out a long breath and sagged against the doorframe. When I heard the faint sound of their feet on the steps, I ran to the door and slid the deadbolt. Leaving the door, I went to the living room to peer through the drapes at the two figures getting into a classic Ford Mustang. The car rumbled to life, and they drove off.

It wasn't until the taillights disappeared from sight that my strength deserted me. I slid down the wall and sat on the floor with my knees drawn up to my chest as I fought to stop the panic attack hovering at the edges of my frayed composure.

I'm okay. I'm safe. It was my first night on my own in a strange place, and I'd woken up to find two strange men in my room. Anyone in my shoes would have reacted the same way, especially someone with my past.

Except there was no one else with a past like mine. Nate and I had talked for many hours, and he was the only person who could even remotely understand what I was going through. As far as we knew, we were the only two people in the world to have been made human again after being a vampire. It was like being reborn and given a new lease on life.

It was also lonely and isolating to not be able to share your experience, your guilt, and your crushing fears. Nate had been a vampire for a week, and it had affected him so profoundly he couldn't even come back to the place where it had happened. What did that mean for someone like me?

I still wasn't sure why I'd agreed to come here when Sara offered it to me. She and Tristan would have set me up anywhere in the world, and I came to live in the home of a former vampire in the heart of werewolf territory. Either I was looking for some twisted form of penance, or I was trying to prove I was stronger than my demons. Perhaps both.

It grew chilly sitting there in only shorts and a tank, but I couldn't make myself get up and go back to bed. The dreams I'd been able to forget temporarily because of my unexpected visitors came back with perfect and heartless clarity. No matter how much I tried to block them out, the ghosts of my past were always there, forcing me to relive their horrors over and over.

I was raised Catholic, and I was taught there was a heaven and a hell and a place in between. A place where God sent you to suffer your sins until he decided to take you into heaven or send you to hell. I'd stopped believing in God after a week with Eli. God couldn't be real and abandon me to that kind of horror.

Now I wondered if he was real after all. I'd lived in hell, and my soul was too tattered to go to heaven.

Maybe this was my purgatory.

I grimaced and scrubbed at the skillet for what seemed like the hundredth time. How could anyone burn eggs so badly, even someone who hadn't touched a stove in twenty years? I'd thought I'd be able to make scrambled eggs, at least. Good luck there.

Letting the skillet slide back into the hot, soapy water, I looked at the two blackened slices of bread sitting in the toaster. Tears pricked my eyes. I couldn't do anything right. What was I thinking, trying to do this on my own?

Laughter reached my ears through the window I'd opened to let the smoke out. I looked down at the two teenage girls walking along the waterfront, shopping bags swinging from their arms. They were probably sixteen, and seeing them brought back a memory of going to the mall with my best friend Chelsea. Back then, my biggest worries had been what clothes to wear and how to convince my parents to let me stay out an hour later. I'd had no idea that monsters existed outside of my nightmares.

Stop this. One thing I'd learned since I'd been healed, it was that there was no use in looking back at what might have been. The past was the past, and I couldn't change it. I'd gotten a chance to start over, something no other vampire victim could do. For them, the only release from that life was death. Sara saw something in me that had made her save me, and I wouldn't repay her kindness by wallowing in self-pity.

It was a beautiful sunny day, and I was hiding out in this apartment when I should have been out there exploring and getting to know my new home. I came here to start over, and it was time to get on with it.

I dried my hands on a towel and went to my room to change into capris and a light top. There was a slight chill in the breeze coming through the window, so I grabbed a thin sweater in case I needed it. Cold was another sensation I was adjusting to. Vampires didn't like extreme cold, but they could tolerate lower temperatures than humans. This past winter in Idaho was the first time I'd been cold in a long time.

I stuffed the sweater in my messenger bag along with my wallet and phone, and headed for the door, feeling optimistic and free.

Ringing came from my bag as I opened the door, and I grabbed for my phone. Only a handful of people had my number, and I would happily talk to any one of them.

I didn't recognize the number on the screen, and I answered hesitantly. "Hello?"

"Hey stranger! How's Maine?"

"Sara!"

Lightness spread through my limbs at hearing her voice, and I realized how much I'd missed her. I'd gotten so used to seeing her every day.

"I didn't expect to hear from you today. Shouldn't you be resting after your trip?"

"I have a little jetlag, but nothing I can't handle. I slept for most of the flight. Besides, I wanted to talk to you and see how you're doing. Do you like the apartment?"

"It's wonderful. Thank you so much for everything, especially the studio." I didn't mean to get emotional, but my throat tightened anyway. "It's too much. I can't ever repay you..."

"None of that," she ordered softly. "What else should I do with my money if I don't take care of my family? And you *are* my family. You couldn't get rid of me now if you tried."

I laughed as tears spilled down my cheeks. For so long, my life had been dark, an endless cycle of violence and blood. Sara not only saved me from that, she had shown me her enormous capacity for love, and she'd refused to let me withdraw into myself. Whenever I'd felt alone, she'd told me over and over that she and Nate were my family now. She'd made me believe there was something worth living for on the days I hadn't wanted to.

"Don't you cry because then I'll start, and Nikolas will want to know what's wrong. You know how he is."

"Yes." I swiped at my wet cheeks.

"It's so weird that you're living in my place, and you'll be seeing all the people I used to know."

"Does it bother you that I'm here? Because I can go somewhere else. It's no problem –"

"No, I love having you there," she rushed to say. "I hated the idea of the place being empty, so you're actually doing me a favor."

"Okay."

"I guess it's too early to ask who you've met there. You know I'm hoping you'll change your mind about meeting Roland and Peter."

I swallowed, thinking of the two werewolves standing in my bedroom doorway. "Um, I kind of met them already."

"You did?" Excitement filled her voice. "You called them?"

"Not exactly." I took a breath and told her what had happened last night.

"Oh, Emma, I'm so sorry. Are you okay?"

"I'm good now. I was a little freaked out last night, but I think they were too when they found a strange girl in your place." A *little* freaked out. Talk about an understatement.

"What a way to start your stay there."

I smiled. "Not what I expected, but I should have known better after all your stories about this place."

"And now that you've met Roland and Peter you can see how great they are," she pressed gently. "They ran in there to save you even though they had no idea who you were."

I toyed with the strap of my bag that still hung on my shoulder. "They seemed nice..."

"But they're werewolves," she finished for me. "I understand, and I'll try not to push. It's just that they're great guys and I think you'll love them, too, once you get to know them. That's all I'm going to say about it. I promise."

"Thanks." I let out a breath. "How's Russia?"

"Amazing," she gushed. "I met Nikolas's parents, and they're great. His dad looks so much like him they could be brothers. It's a bit weird, actually. I think it'll take some getting used to."

"Two Nikolases? I can't imagine."

She laughed. "There can only be one Nikolas. And speak of the devil..."

I heard some rustling sounds on the other end of the line along with the unmistakable sounds of kissing. After a minute, Sara came back.

"Where were we?"

I chuckled. "You were telling me there can only be one Nikolas."

"So true." She sighed happily.

Nikolas spoke, and Sara said, "Give me one more minute."

"You have to go?" I asked, feeling a pang of disappointment.

"We're having dinner with Nikolas's parents. His mom is making a special dinner to celebrate our mating."

"That sounds nice." I'd forgotten they were hours ahead of me, which made it evening there now. "Have fun."

"I'll call you in a few days, okay?" She sounded happy, but there was an edge of worry in her voice. Worry for me. "And if you need anything or just want to talk, call me anytime. I'm on the house phone now, but I have my cell phone."

"I will. Don't worry about me. I was about to go out and look around when you called."

"Great! Go to Bill's Bakery and have a chocolate croissant. You'll thank me."

We hung up, and I stood in the hallway, feeling a strange mix of happiness and melancholy. Sighing, I let myself out and locked the door.

Sara's building was at the end of the row, and I stood at the corner, looking down the waterfront. A line of shops and restaurants ran down the left side of the road. To my right was the ocean. Ahead of me, the town waited to be explored.

The first thing I noticed was the small coffee shop next door to Sara's building. I could only shake my head and smile. Why on earth would she buy me that fancy espresso machine with a coffee shop next door? She was determined to spoil me.

The sun was warm on my face despite the cool ocean breeze, and I stopped to turn my face to it for a moment before I moved on. For the last two decades, I'd been a creature of the night, too young a vampire to survive daylight. I hadn't known how much I'd missed the feel of the sun on my skin until I was healed. At Westhorne, I'd spent every minute I could outside when the weather had permitted.

I started walking again, passing a bookstore, a pub, a drug store, a bakery, and a small grocery store that also sold souvenirs, based on the display in their front window. It was all so clean and quaint, the kind of place featured in one of those travel magazines. And people actually smiled and waved at me as I passed them. Where I'd grown up, I knew a lot of the people in my neighborhood, but strangers didn't greet each other on the street.

I'm living in Mayberry, I thought as I returned the smile of an older man walking a Golden Retriever. I'd been outside for ten minutes, and already I was half in love with this place. Why would anyone ever want to leave here?

I reached the end of the waterfront and stopped, debating where to go next. The intersecting street wound up a hill where a white church steeple peeked above the tops of the trees. Feeling adventurous, I started up the hill, and five minutes later, I came to a Catholic church and a high school. This must be the school Sara had gone to. She'd mentioned it more than once.

I'd never finished high school because Eli took me at the start of my senior year. I planned to enroll in school because I wanted to graduate and go to college. I could probably do online courses or do an equivalency exam, or even ask the Westhorne security guys to fake my senior year transcripts. But I wanted to have the experience that was stolen from me. I wanted to cram for an exam and hang out in the library, as lame as those things probably sounded to every other teenager. I knew school had changed a lot since I was a student, which meant I'd need to brush up over the summer. I used to be an A student, so I was confident I could get back up to speed.

I kept walking. Half a block from the school was a diner called Gail's with a sign that boasted the best seafood in town. It was a nice-looking place, and my growling stomach reminded me I still hadn't eaten yet today, so I crossed the street to check it out.

Inside, the diner was clean and bright with a mix of tables and booths and a long counter. Several of the booths were occupied, as were half the stools at the counter. A blonde waitress who looked to be in her forties was behind the counter, and a younger brunette was serving one of the tables.

I wasn't sure whether to wait to be seated or not, so I stood there until the blonde lady noticed me. She smiled and came over to me.

"Table for one?"

"Yes, please," I said and followed her to a booth.

"Haven't seen you around before. You visiting for the summer?" she asked as she handed me a large laminated menu. Normally, I'd think of the question as nosy, but from her, it sounded friendly.

"I just moved here."

"Well, welcome to our little slice of heaven." She smiled and pointed at her name tag. "I'm Brenda. I came here twenty years ago, and I never left. And you're in luck because you found the best restaurant in town."

"Amen," said a man in a checkered shirt as he left his booth and headed for the door.

"And the most understaffed," grumbled the brunette passing us. She sighed loudly and went to greet the four men coming through the door.

"Don't mind Tina," Brenda said in a lower voice. "Two of our waitresses quit last week to go to college. That's what happens when you mostly have high school students working here. Don't suppose you're looking for a job? We have a full- and a part-time position available."

My stomach fluttered with excitement. I hadn't planned to get a job right away, but I couldn't sit around the apartment all day painting. I'd go crazy in no time.

"I've never worked in a restaurant before," I said.

Brenda waved a hand. "Nothing to it, and we're used to training new girls."

I bit my lip. I wanted to get out of the apartment, but was I ready for this?

"You think about it," she said. "Now what can I get you?"

I ordered the fish and chips and a Coke, and sat back to study the place while I waited for my meal. It was a nice restaurant, and Brenda was friendly.

Tina probably was too when she wasn't overworked. And it was within walking distance of the apartment.

Brenda returned with my meal and a sheet of paper, which she laid on the table. "In case you change your mind," she said before she walked away.

I picked up the paper and saw it was a job application. Guess you didn't need a résumé for this place, which was good because I didn't have one of those.

I exhaled slowly, suddenly overwhelmed by all the things I needed to learn or catch up on. I was lucky, at least, that I knew how to use a computer. Vampires liked to keep up with technology as much as anyone else.

Laying the paper down, I started on my meal. It was as good as Brenda had boasted, and I was so famished I almost cleaned the plate. I liked food, but my appetite hadn't been good since I was healed. Looked like it was pretty healthy now. I smiled at my plate and then almost laughed at being happy over something as silly as eating.

Brenda came over to take my plate, and ask if I wanted some of their fresh apple pie. I passed on the dessert, but I asked her for a pen. I didn't know what made me decide to fill out the application, but I was only going to move forward if I kept pushing myself out of my comfort zone. Besides, if it didn't work out, I could always quit.

She smiled knowingly, handed me a pen, and then left me to fill out the form. I took my time, and I felt an odd sense of change sweep over me when I signed my name at the bottom. *This is a good thing*, I told myself as I slid out of the booth and carried the form to the cash register at the counter.

Tina was closest, and she came to take the form and my money for the meal. Her eyes glanced over the form, and she even managed a small smile as she rang up my bill.

Behind the counter, there was an open window into the kitchen, and I could see a man cooking while a dark-haired boy prepared two plates. The boy carried the plates to the window and called out the order. When he saw me, he gave me a friendly smile, and I realized he was my age or older. I gave him a tentative smile in return and took my change from Tina, leaving a nice tip on the counter.

"Gail will look at your application when she gets in on Monday," Tina said.

"Thanks."

I left the diner and headed back toward home. When I reached the bakery, I remembered what Sara had said about Bill's chocolate croissants, and I ran in to buy one. Next stop was the bookstore. I browsed for a while, and when I came across the cookbook section, I thought about my disastrous attempt to cook eggs. I found a beginner's cookbook and purchased it, along with a local tourist guidebook that had a map of the town in it. I hadn't gone far today, but my first glimpse of New Hastings made me want to see more.

My day hadn't started out well, but it had definitely taken a turn for the better. My steps were light as I walked the short distance to home.

3

Roland

"I knew you missed me," joked Paul when I pulled up to his garage on Monday. "Couldn't stay away, could you?"

I laughed and got out of the car. He wasn't wrong. The garage was on my route home from the lumberyard, and I was so used to coming here after work every day.

Paul wiped his hands on a rag and walked over to me. "How's she running?"

"Perfect. All the guys at the yard were drooling over her."

"They're not the only ones," he said. "I showed those before and after pictures I took to a guy I know in Portland, and he went nuts over them."

I laid a hand on the Mustang's roof. "Tell him my girl is not for sale."

Paul leaned against the building. "He doesn't want to buy her. He just got his hands on a nineteen seventy Chevelle. Frame's solid but the car needs a ton of work. He normally works on his own cars, but he's getting married and his fiancée doesn't like him spending all his free time in the garage. He asked me if I could restore her for him."

"You have time for that?"

Paul only had himself and another guy working here full-time, and they were pretty busy. He'd been talking for a while about expanding and hiring another mechanic, but he didn't have enough saved yet to do it.

"Actually, I was thinking you might want to take on the Chevelle."

I stared at him. "You serious? I'm not a mechanic."

"Yeah. Evan knows that, but he loves the work you did on the Mustang. I told him that was all you, and that I just helped out." Paul waved me over. "I'll supply the space and tools and help wherever you need it, and you do most of the work. We'll split the profits. I haven't worked out the numbers with him yet, because I wanted to talk to you first. But it'll be good money."

It was a tempting offer; more than tempting. I made good pay at the lumberyard, but it was just a job and not nearly as satisfying as working on the Mustang. While I'd enjoyed my hours here at the garage, I'd never thought it could be more than a hobby. The idea that I could make money doing something I actually liked sparked excitement inside me.

Working on the Mustang had gotten me thinking about taking some auto classes, and now I wondered if that might not be a bad idea. I hadn't applied for college because I wasn't sure at first if I would even graduate from high school this year. Maybe it wasn't too late to sign up for a few classes at the community college in Portland. If I could go to school part-time and keep a part-time job, I might be able to make it work.

"Can I have a few days to think about it? I'll have to cut back on my hours at the yard in order to work here, too."

Paul grinned. "I can already see it on your face that you're going to do it. I'll talk to Evan and figure out the details."

A red Jeep pulled in behind my car, and two blonde girls got out. Faith Perry had been in my senior class, and I'd never liked her, mainly because she'd always been a bitch to Sara. Sara had never let Faith bully her, but that didn't soften my feelings for the other girl.

Faith's cousin Angela was a different story. Tall and curvy with legs a mile long, Angela was a year older than us and a freshman at USM. We'd never hung out, but I'd seen her at plenty of parties in town before she started college. She'd had a boyfriend the last few years, which put her off-limits. Didn't mean a guy couldn't look, though.

Paul straightened away from the building. "Great timing, Angela. I just finished your oil change."

"Wonderful." She beamed at him and looked in my direction. "Roland Greene, I almost didn't recognize you."

"I recognized you right away."

She walked over to me, boldly eyeing me from head to toe. "You've been working out a lot since the last time I saw you. Whatever you're doing, keep it up."

Faith made a small huffing sound, which her cousin and I ignored. Male werewolves usually filled out when we hit maturity, and I had been working out hard since I got home in January. Between Maxwell's training and working at the lumberyard, I knew I'd built up some extra muscle. But my male ego still liked being stroked by a beautiful girl.

I smiled to let her know I liked what I saw, too. "Looking pretty good, yourself. I bet Aaron spends all his time chasing away the other guys on campus."

She made a face. "Aaron and I broke up in March."

"Sorry to hear that."

"I'm not." She toyed with her hair, which was pulled back in a ponytail.

"So, you home for the summer?" I asked her.

"Yes." She gave me a meaningful smile. "I thought it was going to be dull, but now I think I might have been wrong."

I leaned against the door of the Mustang. "Lots of fun to be had in New Hastings if you know where to look."

Her lashes lowered. "Is that an offer to show me where the fun is?"

"Yeah." *Hell, yeah.* As if I'd turn down a chance to go out with her. Half the guys in town, myself included, had lusted after Angela until she graduated. She was hot and she knew it, but she'd never been uppity like Faith and some of the other girls.

She smiled suggestively. "How about tonight?"

Damn, she didn't waste any time. There was nothing I'd like better than to go out with her tonight, but Brendan had ordered me to his place this evening. Probably Beta business. And tomorrow night I was on patrol.

"Can't tonight. How about Wednesday?"

"Wednesday is perfect." She pulled out her phone. "What's your number? I'll send you mine so you can call me."

I gave her my number, and she texted me to give me hers. Then she went to pay Paul and get her yellow Volkswagen Beetle.

"See you Wednesday," she called as she drove away, followed by Faith in the Jeep.

"I guess your dry spell is over," Paul joked when he came out of the garage. "I think she's gotten even hotter since she went to college."

I grinned at him, feeling pretty happy with myself. "You noticed that too, huh?"

"Hard not to. Too bad she's human. Wouldn't mind imprinting on her."

Paul was twenty-five and still single. Lucky bastard. Most males imprinted before that age because their wolves were driven to mate. Paul wanted a mate, but he hadn't found the right one yet. Unlike me, he was looking forward to the gathering.

"Her being human is exactly what makes her so attractive," I said, earning a knowing laugh from my cousin. My feelings on the subject of mating weren't exactly a secret.

I knew it would happen eventually, but the last thing I wanted now was a mate. I'd just finished high school, and I wanted to have some freedom for a few years. It was the reason I only dated human girls and I avoided unmated female wolves like the plague. Thank God wolves didn't imprint on humans or I'd be a bloody monk.

I got into the Mustang. "I'll let you know about the Chevelle job. I want to do it, but you know how Maxwell has been riding my ass about responsibility since I came home. I'll need to talk to him about cutting back my hours at the yard."

As much as I wanted to work on the car, I needed a job, too. The Chevelle job would give me a nice little profit, but it couldn't replace a full-time income. I needed the lumberyard job until I could get a job that paid enough to live off. My mother had been saving for years for my college fund, so at least I didn't need to worry about tuition and books if I did go to college. And I'd be staying here instead of Portland, so that would save on rent. I'd have to ask for one of the new houses since Sara's apartment was out of the question with Emma there.

I thought about Sara's cousin, who had occupied my mind more than once this weekend. Why had Sara never told me she had a cousin or that Emma was coming to stay at the apartment? Why had Emma not wanted anyone to know she was there? And what kind of nightmares made her scream like that?

Emma had been terrified of us, and even after she knew who we were, she'd clearly been afraid. No one had ever been afraid of me before, at least no human, and it bothered me. It was instinct for me to want to protect a human, especially Sara's family, and I'd been reluctant to leave Emma alone at the apartment Friday night. Hopefully, she was okay now that she'd had a few days to get used to the place.

I had to be at Brendan's by six-thirty, so I went there directly. The driveway close to the house was full of cars when I got there, and I recognized Pete's white Escort. I parked and got out, walking to the backyard where a bunch of men stood around talking. Pete, Francis, Kyle, and Shawn were there, along with Cody Mays, Tim Church, and Richard and Mark Bender. Except for Pete and me, everyone was in their twenties.

Francis scoffed when I walked up to them. His attitude annoyed me as usual, but I didn't totally disagree with him in this case. I didn't know why Maxwell wanted Pete and me in the Beta selection when there were only so many slots and a lot more experienced members who wanted them. The only reason I could think of was it was another one of his lessons in responsibility. Not that I hadn't had enough of those to last me a lifetime. I hoped this one wasn't as humiliating as some of them had been. One thing about Maxwell, when he made a point, you never forgot it.

The back door of the farmhouse opened, and Brendan emerged. He was two years younger than Maxwell, but they had the same reddish-brown hair and similar facial features. They were the same height, but Brendan was stockier. Brendan was also the least severe of the two.

He stopped in front of us, and everyone turned to face him. His gaze swept over us, meeting each of ours, before he spoke.

"Max and I will be observing you and the other candidates who'll be here for the gathering. And don't be surprised if one of us pulls you aside to talk. Stay on your toes because you won't know when we'll be watching."

Francis smiled as if to say, "Bring it on." I had no doubt he was already planning the changes he would make when he became a Beta. The Alpha had final say in all major decisions that affected the pack, but the Betas would make suggestions to him. I was sure my cousin had lots of ideas for how things should be done.

"Shift," Brendan barked.

No one questioned him, and we all began to strip off our clothes where we stood. Nudity was nothing to us. Werewolves had to disrobe around each other all the time unless we wanted to shift and destroy our clothes.

I let my wolf out the moment my last piece of clothing hit the ground. A surge of joy filled my chest as my body grew and reformed. When I was younger, the change was painful because my wolf was slower to emerge. Now, he came out so fast I barely felt a twinge.

Shawn's brown wolf circled me. *Damn, Roland, what the hell have you been eating? When did you get so bloody big?*

I looked down at my chest, but it didn't seem bigger to me. I'd always been larger than my friends; my mother said I got it from the males on both sides of my family.

Pete's eyes met mine, and he gave me a wolfish grin. *Guess all those drills paid off.*

A growl drew our attention to Brendan who had also shifted. He and Maxwell were the biggest wolves in the pack, and their size and power had always made me feel small in comparison. Even as an adult, I was in awe of them.

According to my mother, both of her brothers were strong enough to be Alpha, but when the time came, Brendan had said Maxwell was the true leader. I'd asked her how he knew that, and she said Maxwell's Alpha blood was too strong to follow another wolf, even his brother, and he had all the traits that gave an Alpha power to lead a pack. I felt that power when I was around Maxwell, and it made me respect him and submit to him as my leader, even when I didn't agree with him. It was a power that could be abused in the wrong hands, another reason we were lucky to have Maxwell as our Alpha.

Betas also had power, although nowhere as strong as the Alpha's. I didn't know if a Beta got his power once he was made a Beta, or if it was the power that made him a Beta. That stuff was never explained to us. I wondered if I would find out at the end of all of this.

Brendan didn't speak. He walked up to Cody and locked his gaze with the other wolf's. Cody shifted uncomfortably, and I felt a knot of unease in my stomach. Staring another wolf down was an act of dominance, and not something adult wolves did lightly. Younger wolves did it all the time for fun, and it didn't mean anything. But it took on a whole new meaning when you reached maturity, especially when it was the Alpha or Beta staring you down.

After ten seconds, Cody lowered his head and tilted it to the side, baring his throat. Without a word, Brendan moved to Mark and began to stare him down. At first, I'd thought Brendan might have some beef with Cody. Now I realized he was going to do this with all of us, and the knot in my stomach grew. What was Brendan trying to prove? We all knew he was the dominant male here.

Mark lasted a few seconds longer, probably not wanting to be the fastest one to give in. I didn't blame him, even though I had a suspicion Pete or I would have that distinction, being the youngest.

Pete was next. His head dropped after five seconds, which wasn't bad when you considered he was staring down a Beta wolf more than twice his age. I'd be glad to last that long.

After Pete was Francis, who managed to keep eye contact for at least twenty seconds. Damn, even I had to admit that was impressive. I watched him shudder and take a step back when he finally lowered his head. If Maxwell and Brendan were looking for aggression in a Beta, then Francis was definitely their man.

And then it was my turn. I steeled myself, but there was no way to prepare for a contest of wills with a wolf as strong as Brendan. Lifting my eyes to his, I was shocked to see we were at the same height, and unlike the others, my gaze was even with Brendan's. I quickly discovered my height gave me no advantage. As soon as my gaze locked with his, I felt the weight of his power pressing down on me, making my legs shake and filling me with the urge to lie down.

My knees bent, and I knew I wasn't going to last long. I told myself there was no shame in submitting to a wolf who could have been Alpha if he'd wanted it bad enough. But my wolf stubbornly fought for dominance until I was a quivering mass of fur and my eyes felt like they were burning from the heat in Brendan's yellow stare.

I dropped my head, struggling to stay on my feet. I might not have lasted as long as the others, but I'd be damned if I would lie down like a whipped dog. I did have my pride.

I opened my eyes and saw Brendan's legs moving away from me to the next wolf. My breath came in heavy pants, and I couldn't raise my head for a long moment. Man, how the hell had Francis managed to hold out so long? I felt like I'd just gone through one of Maxwell's training sessions.

When I finally looked up, I found Pete and the others staring at me. My body stiffened in annoyance, and I felt my hackles rise a little. Okay, so I'd folded like a bad poker hand. Did they have to make it worse by reminding me of it? It wasn't like some of them had lasted much longer.

Brendan's voice filled my head. *That will be all for today. You can go.*

I turned away from the others' stares to look at him. That was it? We'd come here just to be shown we couldn't stand up to him in a staring contest. I could have told him that and saved myself the embarrassment.

I shifted and dressed, wanting to be anywhere else but here. Without looking at the others, I started around the house to the driveway. Why the hell had Maxwell made me sign up for this? I didn't want it, and I obviously wasn't good enough for it. Brendan's little demonstration had proven that quickly enough. Maybe it was their way of narrowing down the candidates, and they'd tell me tomorrow I was out of the selection.

"How did you do that?"

I spun to see Pete following me to my car. "Do what?" I growled, still angry at myself.

He held up his hands. "Whoa. Chill."

I shook off the anger. None of this was Pete's fault. "Sorry."

He stared at me for a moment as if he was making sure it was safe to talk to me. I sighed and ran a hand through my hair. "You want to go for pizza with me? I missed dinner."

"Yeah, sure, but first I want to know how you did that...without you snapping my head off."

"How I did what?"

His eyes widened. "How the hell did you last that long?"

I scowled at him. I expected taunts from Francis but not my best friend.

"Go ahead and have your laugh with the other guys. And then you can pay for my pizza."

"What are you talking about?" He frowned, looking confused. "No one is laughing at what you did; trust me."

"Jesus, was I that bad?" I must have looked pretty pathetic if even Francis was taking pity on me.

"Bad? Roland, you almost stared down Brendan."

"What?" I could not have heard him right. "I didn't even last as long as you."

Pete snorted. "Funny guy. You lasted longer than anyone, almost forty seconds."

My mouth dropped. "No way! You're messing with me."

He shook his head. "I wouldn't joke about something like that. Brendan looked like he was going to drop right before you did."

I stared at him, but he didn't blink. Pete was the worst liar I'd ever met, and I could tell he was being completely honest now.

Movement behind him drew my eyes to the group of men standing at the top of the driveway, watching us with expressions ranging from curiosity to anger. I wasn't surprised to see Francis's lips curled in resentment. Some of the others didn't look happy either, but it wasn't as if I'd done that deliberately. I didn't even want to be a damn Beta.

"You in for pizza or what?" I asked more harshly than I'd meant to.

"Yeah. I'll drop my car at home and you can drive," Pete said, his voice still holding a little note of wonder.

I opened my car door, wanting to get the hell away from here and all the stares. "I'll see you there."

Emma

"How are you doing? Hanging in there?" Brenda asked when she came to the counter to ring up a table.

I removed the plates from the last two customers. "So far, so good."

"She's doing great," said Mrs. Foley, the owner and manager of Gail's Diner.

I smiled, even though I felt she was a little overgenerous with her praise. I'd worked the counter with her for lunch, and it wasn't hard to pour coffee and soda or transfer plates from the window to the counter. When she'd asked me after my interview on Monday if I could start on Wednesday, I'd been so surprised I almost said no. But she and Brenda had been so nice I couldn't refuse. So, I had my first part-time job as a waitress.

"Thanks, Mrs. Foley." I looked at the dining room, which was nearly empty of the lunch crowd. "What should I do now?"

"It's Gail," she admonished kindly. "Steve could probably use some help getting things ready for the dinner rush. Can you cut up vegetables?"

"I think I can manage that." As long as it didn't involve actual cooking, I should be okay.

I went to the kitchen where Steve, the cook, handed me an apron and a hairnet, and put me to work chopping an assortment of vegetables. He didn't talk much, but I didn't mind. It was kind of nice to be off by myself working after the busy lunch hour.

I was almost done with the vegetables when someone opened the back door and entered the kitchen. I looked over my shoulder at the dark-haired boy who'd been here when I came for lunch on Saturday.

He walked over to me. "Hi, I heard you were starting today."

"Hi. I'm Emma." I waved at the work laid out before me on the metal table. "Sorry, I can't shake your hand."

He smiled. "No problem. I'm Scott, by the way."

"You're also late," rumbled Steve from over by the stove where he was stirring something in a pot.

"Sorry," Scott called to him. "Dad's car broke down, and he took mine. You know how he is when he's late for a meeting."

"Tell that to your mother," Steve replied.

I must have looked confused because Scott made a face. "My mother owns this place. I'm working here for the summer until I go to college in the fall."

"Oh. Are you going to school in Portland?"

"Columbia, actually, to study law. That's where my dad went to law school, too." He grabbed a large apron and a pair of rubber gloves, and went to the two large sinks that were piled with pots and pans. He grimaced before he started filling one of the sinks with hot, soapy water.

"So what brings you to New Hastings?" he called over the running water. "Your family move here, or are you just here for the summer?"

I chewed my lip, not sure what to tell him. I still wasn't comfortable talking about myself to strangers, but it would seem weird if I didn't answer. I gave him the condensed version.

"I just moved here. I'm enrolling in school in August."

"St. Patrick's?"

I nodded.

"I just graduated from there. You a senior?"

"Yes."

"Ah, too bad. We just missed each other." He started scrubbing a pot. "It's a nice school. You'll like it there."

I finished cutting the vegetables and carried them over to Steve's worktable. Then I went to help Scott with the dishwashing since there seemed to be nothing else for me to do that didn't involve cooking.

"You're a lifesaver," he whispered as he handed me a baking sheet to dry.

"No problem," I whispered back.

We worked side by side for an hour until all the dishes were done. Scott spent the time telling me about New Hastings and trying to find out more about me. I evaded most of his questions, and he didn't push.

He was excited about Columbia, so we talked about that for a while. His best friend Ryan was going to NYU, and the two of them were sharing a little apartment with Scott's cousin. Ryan was already there, working an internship in his uncle's ad agency for the summer. Scott couldn't wait to join him.

I'd spent a few years in New York, but they weren't happy ones. It wasn't long after Eli changed me, so he'd kept me pretty close. We'd lived in a nice place in Manhattan, but I didn't exactly get to go out and explore. The only people I saw were other vampires and the humans Eli brought back.

I closed my eyes to block out the memories of the things I'd seen and done in that apartment, things that nightmares were made of.

"Hey, you okay?"

Scott's worried voice pulled me from the ugly place my mind had gone to. I gave him a reassuring smile and went back to drying.

"Just a slight headache. I'm fine."

"You sure? Mom will let you go home if you're not feeling well. She's cool like that."

"No, I'm good, really." The last thing I wanted was to go home sick on my first day of work. "Tell me more about St. Patrick's."

We talked until Gail came to tell me the dinner hour would be starting in ten minutes. She looked around the kitchen and nodded approvingly. "Impressive, Emma. You even got my son to finish the dishes on time."

Scott smiled at his mother. "I think she's a keeper."

Flustered by their warm praise, I turned away to remove the apron and hairnet. When I moved to follow Gail to the front of the restaurant, Scott called me back.

"Hey, Emma, since you're new in town, why don't I show you around when we both have a day off?"

"I..." I floundered, not knowing how to respond. He was a great guy, but I was so not ready to date.

"As friends," he added when I didn't answer right away.

"Okay." I could handle just hanging out. "That would be nice. Thanks."

The rest of the day flew by. Gail and Brenda told me dinner was their busiest time, and they weren't kidding. I only worked the counter, but I didn't seem to stop moving for the next two hours.

At seven o'clock, Gail handed me twenty-five dollars from the tip box. "You did well for your first day, and the customers like you."

"Thanks." I took the money and stuck it in my messenger bag, which I'd tucked under the counter. I lifted the strap of the bag over my head. "When do you want me to come in again?"

"You can come back tomorrow at the same time. I'll get you on the schedule in a few days."

"Okay." I picked up a takeout bag containing my dinner. I was already tired of eating sandwiches and pizza, and my cooking skills left a lot to be desired.

"Looks like rain," called Scott, who was taking garbage out the back door. "You have a ride?"

"No, but I don't have a long walk." I turned to the main door. "See you tomorrow."

The air outside was cool and fresh after standing next to the kitchen surrounded by the smells of food all day. Not that working in the restaurant was unpleasant. The people I worked with were patient, and the customers were friendly. My body felt a little tired from being on my feet all day, but it was a good kind of tired.

A blue car passed me and slowed to a stop a few yards ahead of me. Alarm made my fingers clench the handle of the plastic bag, and it took me a moment to recognize the Mustang Sara's friends had been driving the night they came to the apartment. I let out a breath and kept walking.

"Emma," called a voice from inside the car.

I slowed and looked over to see Roland sitting behind the wheel of the Mustang with a pretty blonde girl in the passenger seat. Her window was down, and Roland was waving me over.

I stayed where I was. "Hi."

"Hey, you need a lift home?"

I gave him a polite smile. "No, thanks. I like to walk."

His brows drew together. "You sure? It's going to rain any minute."

I glanced up at the heavy clouds that looked ready to burst open. The idea of getting drenched didn't appeal to me, but neither did being in an enclosed space with a werewolf, no matter how nice he seemed.

"I'm good. Thanks for stopping."

He didn't leave, and his girlfriend was starting to look annoyed. I waved at them and continued on my way. The car passed me a moment later and turned right at the next intersection.

I let out the breath I was holding. Sara believed her friends wouldn't care that I used to be a vampire. But her heart was so big she sometimes forgot not everyone was as kind and forgiving as she was. I didn't want to take the chance of proving her wrong.

I almost made it to the waterfront before the first raindrops hit me. A few seconds later, the sky opened up and dumped its contents on my head. I ran for home, but within a minute, my waitress uniform was drenched and my shoes were sloshing through large puddles. I knew I must have looked like a drowned rat when I scurried past the people sitting in the coffee shop.

Even though I couldn't possibly get any wetter, I raced up the stairs to the apartment and let myself in. Standing in the hallway with water running off me to pool on the floor, I felt a sudden urge to laugh. There was a long mirror near the door, and I stepped in front of it to survey the damage. Half my hair had come loose from my ponytail and was stuck to my cheeks. My light blue uniform was so wet I could see my bra through it, and the hem was splattered with dirt. I shook my head at the image in the mirror. Definitely not my best look.

The laughter that had threatened a minute ago spilled from my lips. I felt strangely buoyant as I stripped off my wet clothes and carried them to the laundry room. I toweled my hair dry, changed into clean clothes, and went to reheat my food in the microwave.

Sitting at the small table, eating my dinner and watching rain run down the kitchen window, I had a glimpse of the normalcy I'd come here looking for. This was what regular people did. They came home from work, did laundry, and ate their dinner. Some people might call that boring, but after the things I'd seen and done, it was bliss.

4

Roland

"Roland," someone yelled over the noisy forklift working nearby.

I put down the two-by-four I was stacking and looked over my shoulder at Pete, who pointed at his wrist to let me know it was time for lunch.

I stretched my back muscles, which ached from a morning of sorting and stacking lumber. Working at the yard might pay good money, but it was monotonous physical labor. I didn't mind hard work. I just wanted something to occupy my mind more.

Pulling off my work gloves, I walked to the employee building next to the main office. After stuffing my gloves and my hard hat in the little cubby I used for my things, I grabbed my car keys and phone.

Pete put his stuff away and turned to me with a questioning look.

"What?" I asked gruffly.

"That's what I'd like to know. You've been grumpy all morning. I expected you to be all smiles after your date with Angela last night. Didn't go well?"

I went to the restroom and splashed water on my face to remove the sawdust and grime of the lumberyard. "It went fine."

Pete chuckled. "That well, huh?"

"Yeah." I was not in the mood to talk about Angela, or how I'd totally messed up a date with the hot college freshman because I couldn't stop thinking about Emma and the wariness in her eyes when I'd stopped to offer her a ride. She must have gotten drenched in that downpour on the way home. Why would she prefer to walk and get wet instead of accepting a ride? She knew I was Sara's friend and I wouldn't harm her, especially with another girl in the car. But she wouldn't even come close to the car. None of it made sense.

I had to admit, it was a different experience for me, meeting a girl who wanted nothing to do with me. It wasn't that I wanted Emma that way. She was pretty, but... Okay, maybe I was a little attracted to her, and she was human, which was a big plus. But I didn't do relationships, and Sara would likely kick my ass if I messed around with her cousin.

My phone rang, and I looked at the screen. Well, what do you know? Just the person I'd been waiting to hear from all week.

"You've got some explaining to do, missy," I said.

"Hello to you, too," Sara retorted.

"Hi, Sara," Pete called over my shoulder. "How's Miroslav? Still standing?"

"Ha-ha. How is life back home?"

I pressed the speaker button so we could both talk to her as we left the building and walked to my car. "Same old thing. Did you get the pictures I sent you of the Mustang?"

"Yes. It's beautiful. I love that color blue. I can't believe that's the same old car you bought in January. I guess that means Peter is driving Jordan's old car now."

Pete jiggled his keys. "Yep! Not as pretty as the Mustang, but she gets me where I want to go."

Sara was quiet for a moment. "So, I hear you've met Emma."

"If you mean your cousin Emma who we didn't know existed and is living in your place, then yes," I said wryly. "Why didn't you ever tell us you had a cousin?"

"Emma and I didn't get to know each other until recently."

"What's her story?" I asked.

"I can't really go into it. All I can say is she's been through a lot, and the last few months have been really hard on her. She needed a quiet place to live, so I invited her to stay at the apartment."

"Why didn't you tell us she was coming?" Pete asked. "I think we scared the hell out of her Friday night."

Sara sighed. "That was probably a mistake, but Emma asked me not to tell anyone. She's a little nervous around people. If you knew what she'd been through... Well anyway, I thought she'd like New Hastings. I hope you all can be friends when she settles in there."

Her explanation only made me more curious about Emma. Why was she so secretive? What gave a person nightmares that made them scream out in terror?

"So, you fluent in Russian yet?" Pete asked Sara.

She laughed. "Most everyone at Miroslav speaks English, thank God."

A door opened in the background, and I heard Nikolas say something. I was about to call out a hello when Sara huffed softly.

"It was an accident, Nikolas. I didn't do it on purpose."

His deep laugh filled the phone, and I wished I could hear what he was saying.

"No one told me that area was off-limits," she said. "There should be signs. And all I did was pet them. How was I supposed to know?"

"Uh-oh," I said. "What did you do?"

Sara came back on the phone. "It's nothing. Well, maybe not." She let out a heavy sigh. "I took a walk earlier, and I saw a pen with some strange creatures I'd never seen before. The gate must have been unlocked because they got out and surrounded me. Someone started yelling and the weerlaks got freaked out. I was only trying to calm them down."

Pete and I looked at each other and burst out laughing.

Weerlaks looked like honey badgers with really big fangs and a temper to match. They were always born four to a litter, and they stayed together, communicating telepathically. They were deadly creatures. I'd rather face a pack of crocotta.

I found my voice. "You used your faerie magic on a pack of weerlaks?"

"Yes," Nikolas called from the background, telling me Sara had put us on speaker. Nikolas sounded amused and a little aggravated at the same time.

"I didn't mean to," Sara said defensively. "They looked upset. How was I to know you're not allowed to touch them?"

I grinned at Pete. "So, Nikolas, how's it feel to be home?"

"Not as quiet as I remember," he answered dryly.

Sara muttered something, and Nikolas spoke in a soothing voice. "My mother is not angry with you. She's just glad they didn't hurt you."

And that was our cue to go.

"We're heading out to lunch. We'll talk to you guys in a few days," I said.

"Bye," Sara and Nikolas said together.

I hung up, and Pete and I laughed again as we got into the Mustang.

"Poor Nikolas," Pete said.

I snorted. "Poor Russia, you mean. Nikolas knew what he was getting into."

"Man, it's quiet here without her." Pete buckled his seat belt. "Gino's?"

I started the car. "We had that yesterday. Let's go to Gail's. They have the chicken pot pie special on Thursdays."

"Sound's good."

Emma

"Here you go. A BLT and a Caesar salad." I laid the plates in front of the two customers at the table and straightened. "Can I get you anything else?"

"We're good, thanks," said the middle-aged woman.

I smiled and returned to the counter where Brenda gave me a thumbs-up. "You're a pro," she whispered.

I resisted the urge to roll my eyes. It was my second day at the diner, and Gail had given me two tables in the back to start me out. If I couldn't keep up with two tables, I'd fire myself.

The door opened behind me, and Brenda smiled. "And here are your next customers."

I turned as she walked out from behind the counter to greet the guests. My stomach dropped at the sight of Roland and Peter standing by the hostess stand. They smiled at Brenda, and she led them to my open table.

I passed Brenda on my way to their table. She winked and whispered, "You'll like these two, especially Roland. He's a charmer, that one."

Peter was facing me and his eyes widened when he saw me approach them. "Emma? I didn't know you were working here."

Roland's head whipped around, looking even more surprised than his friend. "Hey. Didn't expect to see you here."

I summoned a smile. "I started yesterday."

"Nice," Peter said. "The food here is great and it's not too far from the waterfront."

"Especially if you enjoy walking," Roland added with an expression I couldn't decipher. "Did you get caught in that rain last night?"

"Yes, but it wasn't too bad," I lied. "Can I get you something to drink while you look at the menu?"

"Coke and the chicken pot pie," Roland said.

Peter handed me their menus. "Same for me."

"Great. That'll be out in a few minutes." I went to put in the orders and pour their drinks. When I carried the glasses of Coke back to the table, Roland spoke before I could walk away.

"So, how are things at the apartment? You getting settled in okay?"

"It's great, thanks." I relaxed a little. This was the closest I'd gotten to the werewolves, and so far, they didn't seem to be smelling anything off of me.

Steve called their order, and I went to get it. Peter dug in as soon as I set his plate in front of him.

"Have you seen much of town yet?" Roland asked.

My smile was real this time. "No, but I love what I've seen so far. Now I know why Sara talks about this place so much."

He smiled back. "Yeah, it's a great place. If you want, we'll give you the grand tour, show you all the best spots."

I felt a moment of panic. "Thanks, but a friend has offered to show me around."

"Oh." His smile faltered. "You made a friend already? That's great."

"Yes. His name is Scott, and he works here."

Roland's eyes darkened a shade. "Scott Foley?"

Peter coughed on a mouthful of food.

"You know him?" I wasn't sure what to make of their reactions. Did they not like Scott? He was so friendly.

"Yeah. We all go way back," Roland said evenly.

I realized I was spending too much time talking to them when I should have been watching my other table. "Excuse me. I need to get back to work. Enjoy your lunch."

Brenda nudged me with her hip when I went back behind the counter. "Looks like Roland's not the only charmer in the room."

"What do you mean?"

"I mean you might have made a conquest already."

A conquest? "No, you misunderstand. Roland and Peter are my cousin's friends. They were being nice. That's all."

"If you say so," she murmured.

Two tables cleared at the same time in her section, and she went to clean them. "Can you give me a hand?" she asked me.

"Sure."

I went to the closest table and stacked the plates. As I was picking up the glasses, a man bumped into me on his way out. A glass slipped through my fingers and shattered on the tile floor.

"Oh, shoot." I grabbed the stack of unused napkins on the table to blot the spilled soda before it went everywhere.

Brenda came over with a broom and dustpan. "Careful. Don't cut yourself."

No sooner had the warning left her mouth when I felt a sharp pain in my thumb. I jerked my hand back with a small cry.

Brenda crouched beside me. "Let me see."

She bent over my hand, and I felt her pluck out the shard of glass. "You'll live," she announced. "Let's go bandage this. I'll get Scott to clean up the glass."

We stood, and I looked down at the large red drop welling from the pad of my thumb. The coppery smell of blood hit me, and my stomach lurched. A second later, dizziness slammed into me, and I swayed on my feet.

A pair of hands grabbed my arms gently from behind, holding me against a hard body. "Steady there," Roland said in a low voice.

My body stiffened. I tried to pull away, and my legs almost gave out.

"Easy," Roland murmured.

"Maybe she needs some air," Brenda suggested.

In the next instant, I was swept up into Roland's arms and carried outside. It was a cool day, and the fresh air felt good against my skin. He set me down on a bench and sat on his haunches in front of me. A hand cupped my chin and tilted my face up to his. I sucked in a breath at the worried blue eyes inches from mine, and my stomach did a weird little flip.

"You okay?"

For a moment, I forgot to answer. "Y-yes."

Brenda sat beside me on the bench. "Are you alright?"

Embarrassment pushed aside my anxiety. What must they think of me, nearly fainting because of a tiny cut on my finger?

I nodded mutely, angry at my weakness. The irony of an ex-vampire who gets sick at the sight of blood was not lost on me. Ever since I'd been healed, I couldn't stomach the smell or sight of it. If there was a God, he had a messed-up sense of humor.

"Let me see," Gail said, and Roland stood to let her in.

Having all these people fuss over me only intensified my discomfort, but I sat quietly and let her look at my finger. She cleaned the blood off with a damp cloth and applied a bandage.

"It'll be okay in a day or two," she said. "But you should go home for the rest of the day."

"I don't need to go home," I protested, sounding weak even to my own ears.

"You're white as a sheet, honey," she said kindly. "We can manage here without you for the rest of the day."

Scott handed me my bag. "Here, Emma. I'll give you a lift home."

"I'll take her." Roland reached down to help me to my feet. "No need for both of you to leave work."

Gail nodded. "Thank you, Roland."

44

There was nothing for me to do but let him lead me to his car in the small parking lot. He opened the passenger door for me, and I got in. Then he went around to the driver's side.

"What about your lunch?" I asked him as he pulled out onto the street.

He kept his eyes on the road. "It'll wait."

An awkward silence filled the car. I didn't know what to say, and he was oddly quiet. I was glad I lived close by and the ride took only a few minutes.

He parked in front of the apartment steps, and I was out of the car before he could come around to open my door. He stood on the other side of the car, looking a little bewildered. I didn't blame him because my behavior probably seemed strange.

I twisted the strap of my bag. "Thanks for bringing me home."

"No problem. You feeling better?"

"Yes. I feel silly getting sick over a little blood. And for taking you from your lunch."

He tapped the roof of the car. "Don't worry about that."

The longer we stood there, the more I felt the weight of his stare. I swallowed. "Anyway, Peter's waiting for you. You should probably go."

"Yeah." He opened his door. "I'll see you around."

He got into the car and backed out. I waited for him to leave before I went up the stairs and entered the apartment. I tossed my bag on the kitchen table with a loud groan.

"Way to go, girl. Next time, faint and the humiliation will be complete."

I sighed and went to change my clothes. At least I no longer had to worry about the werewolves somehow sensing what I used to be when they got close enough to smell me. And I'd managed not to panic about being held by one of them. Granted, I'd been occupied by other things, but it was definitely a big step for me.

I had to admit Roland had surprised me. When I thought of werewolves, gentle wasn't a word that came to mind, but he'd handled me with so much tenderness and concern. Maybe I wasn't being fair to him because of my fear of werewolves in general. As long as he didn't discover my horrible secret, I should be safe around him.

Not that I was going to spend that much time with him. I'd left Westhorne because I wanted a normal life among other humans, and there was definitely nothing normal about Roland Greene.

Roland

"You going to eat that?"

Pete's voice jerked me from my thoughts, and I looked down at the half-eaten chicken pot pie in front of me. He and I were never ones to waste good food, so I slid it across the table to him. "Go ahead."

"You're quiet," he observed as he dug into the pie.

I thought about how tense Emma had been on the drive to her place and the way she'd practically jumped from the car when we got there. "Is it just me, or does she seem uncomfortable with us?"

"Emma?"

"Yes."

He nodded. "Yes, but remember that Sara said Emma's nervous around new people."

"She seemed fine with the people here," I pointed out.

"Maybe it's just guys."

"Can't be. She said she and Scott were friends."

"Must be you then," he said with a grin.

I clenched my jaw. Of all the people Emma could have made friends with, it had to be Scott Foley. He'd been a total jerk and a bully in high school, but he changed after Sara disappeared last fall. Since then, he was like a different person. But it was hard for me to forget the way he'd treated Sara all those years.

I wondered if Scott knew Emma was Sara's cousin. The idea of him around Emma didn't sit well with me, but it wasn't like I could tell him to stay away from her. Emma worked in his family's restaurant, so they'd see each other all the time. And it was her choice who she wanted to be friends with.

Sara said Emma had been through a lot. Remembering how weak she'd been earlier, I wondered if maybe she'd recently recovered from an illness. She'd been light as a feather when I picked her up, although her body hadn't felt too thin or frail.

Pete pushed away the empty plate and leaned back in his chair with a contented sigh. "What time are you heading over to Brendan's tonight?"

"Mom told me to be there by six."

It was tradition to have a cookout at Brendan's farm to welcome the first wolves arriving for the pack gathering. The official gathering didn't start until next week, but some people liked to come ahead of time and make sure they had their choice of housing. Unfortunately, some also came early to check out potential mates. It was easy to spot those wolves – both male and female – because of the hungry look in their eyes. They were the females I wanted to stay as far away from as possible.

I'd given up on trying to find a way out of attending the party. Now I was thinking of how early I could duck out of there without pissing off Maxwell or my mother.

Pete smiled as if he'd read my mind. "Might as well suck it up. No getting out of it."

"I know." I stood and threw cash on the table to cover my lunch. "But I have to say it's days like this I wish I'd stayed in California."

I looked around Brendan's backyard that was quickly filling up with people. The smell of cooking meat made my mouth water because I'd only eaten half my lunch at the diner and I'd missed dinner to come here. But I would have gladly traded Brendan's barbecued ribs for a plain ham sandwich if it meant I didn't have to be here tonight.

"How long do I have to stay here?" I asked my mother, who was arranging bowls of potato salad on a picnic table.

She laughed. "You just got here."

"Yeah, and I'm ready to leave."

Straightening, she gave me a knowing look. She took my arm and led me away from the crowd. "Meeting unmated females doesn't mean you'll have to mate one of them. And very few wolves imprint immediately."

"Dad knew as soon as he met you." My father died in a trucking accident when I was four, but I still remembered his stories about how he and Mom met.

"Yes, but that doesn't happen often," she said with a faraway look in her eyes. Some wolves mate for life and never take another if their mate dies. When I was a kid, I'd wished she and Nate would fall in love and get married so he and Sara could live with us out here in the Knolls. But my mother never wanted another mate after my dad.

"But it can happen."

"Your wolf won't imprint when you're in human form, you know that. Your father and I met in wolf form. And even then, it took three days for him to imprint." She smiled in remembrance. "He always did like to take his time with things."

Pete split from the crowd and walked over to us. "Hiding?"

"Just trying to talk some sense into my son," my mother said. "Maybe you'll have better luck."

"Not a chance," I muttered as she walked back to the picnic table.

"Come on, man. It's not that bad," Pete said. "You don't have to hook up with anyone, and some of the girls here are pretty cool."

"Says the guy who wouldn't mind being mated," I grumbled.

He shrugged. "I didn't say I wanted to be mated yet. I'm just not against it like you are. If it happens, it happens."

I watched the people milling about, talking and laughing, a lot of them catching up with friends and family they hadn't seen in a while. Paul was there, engaged in conversation with two blonde girls I knew from Bangor. I saw them whenever I went to visit my grandmother. Allison was my age, and her cousin Patty was two years older. They were nice girls, but they were also unmated.

Paul looked in our direction. I shook my head at him, but he'd already started toward us with Allison and Patty in tow. I swore softly, earning a chuckle from Pete.

Allison giggled. "So this is where the hot single guys are hanging out."

Patty was less obvious than her cousin. "Haven't seen you two since Thanksgiving. You didn't stay in Bangor long."

"Something came up," I said.

That something had been Nate arriving at Westhorne as a vampire. Nikolas had sent the Mohiri jet for Pete and me so we could be with Sara.

Allison stood so close our arms touched. She nudged me with her shoulder. "Hopefully, you won't have to take off this time."

"We'll be here," Pete told her.

"I saw your Mustang in the driveway," Allison said to me. "Paul told us you restored her yourself. Maybe you could take me for a ride in it while I'm here."

Before I could come up with a polite excuse not to let her in my car, we were joined by two more girls. They didn't look familiar, so this was probably their first pack gathering. Some wolves didn't attend unless they had business to take care of or were in the market for a mate. I had a sinking feeling I knew which category these two fell into.

My suspicions were confirmed when the taller one, a curvaceous brunette who looked to be my age, came right for me. She wore tight jeans and a small top, and if she'd been human, she would have snagged my interest right away.

"Hi," she said huskily, sidling up to me and nudging Allison out of her way. "Alexandria Waters. You can call me Lex."

"Roland," I replied, glancing at Pete for help. But he'd been set upon by Lex's friend, a pretty raven-haired girl.

Lex smiled. "I know who you are. We heard about your little cross country adventure from our friend Dell. Julie and I have been looking forward to meeting you and Peter."

"Great," was all I could say.

She leaned closer, and her breast brushed my arm. "Dell told us about a small lake just past the Knolls that's great for swimming. Why don't we all go there later during the pack run? I bet you look as good in your fur as you do in your skin."

I swallowed. Aggressive girls were usually a turn-on, but not when they were looking for a lot more than a hookup. The gleam in Lex's eyes told me she was mate hunting, and she had me in her sights.

"Sorry, I can't," I said. "Paul and I have some business to take care of at the garage tonight."

Paul frowned at me. "We do?"

"Yeah." I gave him a meaningful stare. "You know, that Chevelle job we were talking about." Right now seemed like the perfect time to tell him I was going to work on the car.

Lex pouted. "Work? That can wait until tomorrow."

"I have to work at the yard tomorrow." I'd never been so grateful to work for Maxwell. "This is a big job Paul asked me to help him with. Unless he doesn't need me for it anymore." I shot my cousin a hard look, and he shook his head.

"No, I still need you. What time are we supposed to meet?"

"Eight." That would give us plenty of time to eat and be seen here. Maxwell wouldn't say anything about us leaving for work.

"But that's so early," complained Julie, who was practically hanging on Pete's arm. "You don't have to go too, do you, Peter?"

"I'm sure Pete would love to go for a swim with you," I said slyly. Panic flashed in his eyes, and I tossed him a lifeline. "Though we really could use his help at the garage. If he's not too busy, that is."

"Yeah, sure," he said quickly.

My mother waved and called us over to eat. The four girls started over, and I hung back with Pete and Paul.

"Damn, those two are something else," Pete said in a low voice.

I grinned. "You can always stay and go for that swim with them."

He made a face. "No, thanks."

"Didn't you just say if it happens, it happens?"

"Don't remind me." He stuck his hands in his pockets. "Is this what we have to look forward to for the next month?"

Paul chuckled. "Better get used to it, boys, because it's only going to get worse."

I stared at him. "Worse?"

"Pete is Maxwell's son and you're his nephew, which means you both have

Alpha blood. You could be butt-ugly – which you're not – and the females would want you." He nodded at the girls standing in a group with several others. "You've also built up a bit of a reputation over the last year, not good if you want to stay off their radar. I think you're both going to be very popular at the gathering this year."

"Shit." I rubbed my jaw. "You really know how to ruin a guy's appetite."

Paul smiled. "Look on the bright side."

I scoffed. "There's a bright side to all of this?"

It was easy for him to joke about it. He and I were cousins on my dad's side, which meant he wasn't directly related to Maxwell. His lack of Alpha blood made him less of a catch to some females. Not that he cared.

"Yeah. You'll spend so much time hiding out at the garage, you'll get the Chevelle done in half the time. And make some good money to boot."

I wasn't sure if hanging around a garage was enough to dissuade a bunch of unmated female wolves, but it was all I had.

"You still have that cot in the back room?" I asked him glumly. "I might need that, too."

Emma

"I've shown you the marina, the Hub, the mall, and my house. That pretty much covers the most exciting places to go here," Scott said as we pulled away from the mall. "Where to now?"

"Are you sure you don't have anything better to do with your Saturday than chauffeur me around town?" We'd spent the morning driving around New Hastings, and Scott had proven to be an entertaining guide. But I didn't want to hog all of his day off.

He shrugged one shoulder. "I could call up some of my old school buddies, but you have a much prettier face."

I didn't respond, unsure if he was flirting with me or just being sweet. I liked hanging out with him as friends, but I didn't want anything more than that.

He tapped the steering wheel. "I could show you the lighthouse if you want to see it."

"I'd love to."

The Signal Point lighthouse was one of the places Sara had told me I *had* to visit. She thought it would appeal to the painter in me. I'd been in town two weeks, and I still hadn't seen it.

My stomach chose that moment to growl loudly, and I let out a small laugh. "Sorry, I forgot to eat breakfast this morning."

"I have just the thing for that." He drove for a minute and then pulled up beside a small deli. "The sandwiches here are pretty good. Why don't we get some to take with us?"

Five minutes later, we set off for the lighthouse with our food. Signal Point was on the north end of town, and there were no houses or businesses close to it. Scott told me it was a great spot for parties in the summer and fall because they didn't bother anyone with the noise.

"It's beautiful," I said when we pulled up to the white tower surrounded by a low white picket fence. Tall grass waved in the wind, and the air was filled with the sounds of seagulls and crashing waves.

I grabbed my messenger bag, and Scott took the food. We walked through the grass to the edge of the bluff where I could see nothing but blue sky and ocean for miles.

It was no wonder Sara had insisted I come here. She was right; it was an artist's dream. To my right was a line of small cliffs and bluffs, much like this one. On my left, it was heavily wooded and a rocky beach led into what looked like a small cove a quarter of a mile away.

The old lighthouse itself inspired me. Its paint was peeling and the signal light no longer worked, but that only added to its beauty. Framed against the blue sky and ocean with waist-high grass around its base, it had a wildness that called to me. I could stay here for hours.

I turned to Scott. "I love it. Thanks for bringing me here."

He smiled. "My friends and I used to ride our bikes up here when we were kids. We wanted to bring tents and camp here, but our parents wouldn't let us."

I pulled my Nikon camera from my bag and snapped a picture of the lighthouse. "I can see why you'd want to camp here."

Walking around the building, I took shots of it from every angle. I liked to paint at night and the pictures would fill in all the details I wouldn't remember. I couldn't wait to get started on this one when I got home.

Scott followed me, and I took a few pictures of him, too. Then we sat near the edge of the bluff to eat our lunch.

"So, you're Sara's cousin," he said after a few minutes of light conversation. I gave him a questioning look, and he smiled. "My mother told me."

"Were you and Sara friends?" Sara hadn't mentioned Scott to me, but I assumed she'd had other friends besides Roland and Peter.

Scott looked away, but not before I caught a glimpse of regret in his eyes.

"A long time ago we were friends, back when she first moved here. I did something stupid and mean, and we argued. She was right and I was wrong, but I was too proud to admit it. Instead of saying I was sorry, I became a total jerk toward her."

He stared at the waves, and his voice quivered as if he was struggling to get the words out. "I never understood how things went so wrong or why I acted that way. I never stopped liking her, but she couldn't stand me after that. Not that I blame her. I wasn't a nice person for a long time."

"You're nice now." The person he described didn't sound like the one who had been so kind to me since we met. "What changed?"

He took a deep breath. "When she left town last October, it made me realize how stupid I'd been. All those years I wasted when we could have been friends."

Sara had told me everything that happened here last year and how the whole town thought she'd drowned after she fell off the cliff. For months, everyone thought she was dead, until her faerie friend Eldeorin glamoured the town to think she'd moved away instead.

"Do you talk to her much?" Scott asked quietly. "How is she?"

"She went to live with her – our grandfather out west. She's very happy."

"I'm glad." He gave me a warm smile. "You know, I've never told anyone that stuff, not even Ryan. You're really easy to talk to."

"Thanks, so are you."

Something more than casual friendship sparked in his eyes, and I looked away, pretending not to see it. He was a great guy and good-looking, too. The old me would have been thrilled to have a boy like him show interest in her. The new me didn't see him as anything but a friend. I wasn't sure I could even be attracted to someone at this point in my life.

Not true, said a voice in my head. My stomach fluttered at the memory of sapphire eyes peering into mine and a warm hand touching my face. I quickly brushed it aside. He wasn't even human, so it didn't count.

"Argh." Scott put a hand to his forehead. "I completely forgot I'm supposed to take Nan to her hairdresser at two. Mom usually does it, but she and Dad are in Portland, so that leaves me. I'm sorry."

I swallowed my disappointment. "No, I understand. I can come back here another time and look around."

"Hey, if you don't mind hanging out with my grandmother for an hour, you can come with me, and we can come back here after." He grinned as he stood. "I don't think I showed you the salon."

"No, you forgot that part of the tour." I laughed and let him help me to my feet. "Would it be okay if I waited for you here? I really want to get some pictures while the light is good."

"You don't mind being here by yourself?"

I waved an arm around me. "Are you kidding? This place is amazing. And you won't be gone that long, right?"

He shook his head. "No more than an hour."

"Good. It's settled then," I said. "You take your grandmother to the salon, and then come back for me."

It took another few minutes to convince him I'd be alright here alone for an hour. Finally, he left, and I looked around, trying to decide what to explore first. I took a few more pictures of the lighthouse and then climbed down to the beach to get some shots of the waves.

I loved the ocean, but for some reason, I could never quite capture its power when I painted. My attempts always felt like they were missing something. For two weeks every year growing up, I'd sit on the dunes at Virginia Beach and try to put what I saw on my canvases. Maybe living by the ocean year-round would help. This place was definitely beautiful enough to inspire me.

I stuck my camera back in my bag and began making my way along the beach toward the cove I thought I'd seen from the bluff. It felt isolated here and far from people, even though I was only a few minutes' drive from town. I was used to being alone, but this was different. It was kind of nice. I felt...free.

It was hard to believe I'd been in New Hastings for two weeks. I was living on my own, I had my first real job, a new friend, and I was slowly learning to be a normal human girl again. Or as normal as anyone could be in my situation.

The walk to the cove took ten minutes, and it was worth the effort. Surrounded on three sides by tall trees, it had a narrow strip of sandy beach and a flat grassy area where you could sit. I left my bag on the grass and walked from one end of the small beach to the other, taking more pictures and picking up a few shells and an interesting piece of driftwood.

It didn't take long to explore the cove, and I decided to sit for a few minutes before I headed back to the lighthouse. Pulling out my water bottle, I sipped and watched the small waves that were nothing like the powerful surf at the point. I set down my bottle and leaned back on my hands, feeling more at peace than I had in a long time. I wished I could carry this tranquility with me at all times, especially at night when I needed it the most.

A branch cracked in the woods behind me. I jerked upright and twisted my upper body to peer into the trees. I saw no one, but the feeling I was being watched made the hair stand up on the back of my neck.

You're just being paranoid. Not that I could blame myself after some of the things I'd seen. All the same, I should probably get back to the lighthouse.

I started to stand when a low growl came from the woods.

My head whipped around again, and my lungs seized up at the sight of the two shapes emerging from the trees. One was covered in light brown fur, and the other was snow white. They were twice the size of an Irish Wolfhound, with yellow eyes and short pointed ears, and their bared fangs told me they weren't happy to see me.

5

Emma

Terror gripped me. Sara had assured me the werewolves here would never harm a human, but the snarling faces on these two wolves said otherwise. I was alone here with no way to protect myself and no one to hear me if I screamed. Running would do no good. These two could chase me down in seconds. I was completely at their mercy.

The werewolves slowly stalked me, their hackles up and their heads lowered aggressively. When they were a few feet away, the white wolf let out a low, threatening growl.

A whimper escaped my lips, but I couldn't look away from the werewolves. The brown one moved to my left, and the white one advanced from the front. Their intent was clear.

From the trees came another growl, louder and deeper. The two wolves froze, and I looked past the white one at the massive black creature standing at the edge of the woods. The new werewolf was as big as a bear, and he stood on his hind legs, making him at least eight feet tall and one of the most frightening things I'd ever seen.

He took a step and growled again, turning my veins to ice.

It took me several seconds to realize his attention was not on me, but on the two smaller wolves. They didn't respond, and his growl deepened.

The wolves turned to face him, and the white one made a whining sound. The newcomer snarled and took several more steps, towering over all of us.

I struggled to drag air into my lungs.

The smaller wolves whined and lowered their heads in submission. The black wolf made another frightening sound, and the two of them ran into the woods without a backward glance at me.

All I could do was stare at the giant wolf who watched me through yellow eyes that were impossible to read. Had he driven the other two off so he could kill me himself?

He moved, and I sucked in a sharp breath. Falling to all fours, he walked toward me. I froze as he closed the distance between us and leaned down to me. His hot breath washed over my face, and I closed my eyes, waiting for him to strike.

The wolf sniffed my hair and then...nothing.

My eyes shot open to see the huge body sink down to the grass a few feet away. His head lowered to rest on his paws, and his amber eyes fixed on me.

I stared at him for a long moment before it hit me he was not going to attack. If I didn't know better, I'd think he was guarding me. But then, maybe he was. Sara said the local pack was safe, and werewolves were known to protect humans, not kill them. That didn't explain why the first two had been so aggressive, but as long as they were gone, I wasn't going to question it.

The fact that he'd sniffed me and hadn't gotten aggressive filled me with enormous relief. It meant there really was no trace of the vampire left in me. Deep inside, I'd feared it was still a part of me, but now I knew I was truly free of the demon. If it wasn't for the werewolf lying five feet away, I would have laughed or cried, or both.

We stayed like that for the next twenty minutes. He didn't seem to be in a hurry to leave, and I was afraid to move and test out my theory that he was only watching over me. His size and the way the other wolves had submitted to him made me think he must be someone with authority in the pack. Not the Alpha or the smaller wolves would not have challenged him in the first place, but definitely someone dominant.

"Emma."

Scott called to me from the direction of the lighthouse. He must be wondering where I'd gotten to. He hadn't reached the cove yet, and he was in for a hell of a shock when he did.

He called my name again, a little closer this time.

The wolf growled, and I turned back to him, my heart pounding. But he was looking down the beach and not at me. I didn't know if he was being protective of me or aggressive at the sound of Scott's voice, and I didn't want to find out.

I stood slowly, keeping my eyes on him. He lifted his head, and his gaze shifted to me.

"Um, that's my friend. He's looking for me." I picked up my bag and hooked the strap over my shoulder. "You should go before he gets here."

For a long moment, he stared at me without moving. Then he stood on four legs, and I swallowed when I saw his eyes were level with mine. Power seemed to emanate from him, and I couldn't help but see the wild beauty in his fierce features.

He blinked and made a chuffing sound, almost like he was trying to tell me something. Turning away from me, he walked into the woods. His steps were so quiet I wouldn't have known he was there if I wasn't looking at him. How could such an enormous creature walk with that kind of stealth?

He stopped walking once he reached the cover of the trees. His black fur blended into the shadows, but his eyes glowed in the darkness. I should have felt afraid knowing a werewolf was watching me from the trees, but he hadn't given me any reason to fear him.

Scott shouted my name again, and I called back to let him know where I was. A minute later, he appeared around the bend in the shore that marked the end of the cove.

"Emma, thank God. I didn't know what to think when I couldn't find you."

"I'm so sorry. I wanted to explore, and I lost track of time. I didn't mean to worry you."

"I'm just glad you're okay." He smiled when he reached me. "So you found Wolf Cove? What do you think of it?"

"Wolf Cove?" The name startled me after what I'd encountered.

He laughed. "Don't worry; we have no wolves here. When my dad was a kid, someone claimed they saw a wolf, and it's been called Wolf Cove ever since."

We started walking back to the lighthouse. I stumbled on a rock, and Scott grabbed my arm to steady me. Something that sounded like a growl came from the woods, but I ignored it and kept walking. If Scott heard anything, he didn't mention it.

I felt the wolf's eyes on me as we made our way along the beach. When we reached the end of the cove, I looked back at the spot where he'd been. I could no longer see him, but I could almost feel his presence there. A small shiver went through me, and I turned to follow Scott out of the cove.

Roland

I watched Emma and Scott until they disappeared around the bend in the shore, and then I set off after the two wolves who had frightened her. It wasn't difficult to follow their trail and to know exactly where they were headed. My longer stride covered the ground fast, and within ten minutes, I caught up to them at the edge of the woods behind Brendan's farm.

I shifted immediately, not wanting to stay in wolf form with these two any longer than necessary. I would have stayed away from them altogether, but I couldn't let them think what they'd done at the cove was acceptable.

Striding over to one of the run boxes, I grabbed the clothes I'd left there when I went out on patrol. I noticed the two wolves staring at me as I unrolled my jeans, and I presented them with my back. I'd never been shy of my nudity, but the gleam in their eyes made me feel like a steak about to be devoured.

I stiffened when a hand stroked my bare back, and I looked over my shoulder at Lex, who smiled suggestively at me.

"Your wolf is magnificent," she almost purred. "I bet he'd like to come back out and play."

I stepped away from her and pulled my T-shirt over my head. "Not today."

She pouted and put her hands on her hips, drawing my eyes downward. Man, the girl had a killer body, and she knew how to flaunt it.

"Like what you see?" she asked boldly.

The last thing I wanted was to encourage her. She was gorgeous, but I didn't really like her that much. And there was the matter of her breaking a pack law that had to be dealt with.

"Get dressed, Lex. You too, Julie," I said to the other girl. "Then you're going to tell me what the hell you were thinking back there."

Julie scurried to pull on a sundress. Lex rolled her eyes before she sauntered over to don shorts and a tank top.

I waited until they were fully clothed to speak again.

"Either of you want to tell me whose idea it was to frighten that girl?" I asked harshly, remembering the terror on Emma's face and the scent of it on her skin.

Lex scoffed. "She was trespassing on pack land."

"This whole town is in pack territory, and it's our job to protect the people who live here," I barked at her. "You two exposed our kind to a human. That's against pack law."

Julie gasped. "But at home –"

"I don't know how you do things up north, but I'm pretty sure you're not allowed to terrorize humans. Maxwell wouldn't stand for it." I crossed my arms. "What if she tells someone about you?"

Lex waved a hand dismissively. "Who would believe her?"

Her lack of concern heightened my anger. "How do you know no one would believe her? How do you know word won't travel and werewolf hunters won't come sniffing around? Or one of those crazy paranormal investigators?"

Julie paled and Lex looked guilty. It wasn't enough. I didn't want to think about what might have happened if I hadn't been out by the lighthouse on patrol.

"What are you going to do?" Julie asked shakily.

"You two are very lucky because I know that girl, and I'm going to make sure she doesn't tell anyone about this."

Lex's eyebrow shot up.

I shook my head. "I don't know if she knows what we are, but her cousin's one of my best friends. Sara knows all about us."

"You're lecturing us about exposing ourselves to humans, but you have human friends who know about us?" Lex asked angrily.

"Sara's not human. She's Mohiri," I said, and their expressions told me they'd heard about her. "But her cousin Emma is human and under *my* protection."

I didn't know where that last part had come from, but as soon as I said it, I meant it. Emma was Sara's cousin, and I'd protect her just as I would Sara. I was going to have to call Sara and tell her what happened. I didn't know if she'd told Emma about us, but there was no way Emma could have mistaken us for normal wolves. The way she'd spoken to me was not the way one would talk to an animal.

"You're not going to tell Maxwell what we did?" Julie asked in a hopeful voice.

"I don't know. It depends on whether or not I can do damage control. But if either of you pull a stunt like that again, he'll hear about it, and you can bet he won't be happy."

I understood now why we needed multiple Betas. Maxwell and Brendan couldn't be everywhere, and someone had to make sure the wolves who lived away from the main pack followed our laws.

With the threat of facing the Alpha gone, Lex's air of confidence returned. She crossed her arms under her breasts, pushing them up for my benefit. "That was kind of hot. Feel free to scold me whenever you want."

I almost growled in frustration. Paul was right. I had Alpha blood, so these females weren't going to give up no matter what I did. If I made it through this gathering with my sanity intact, it would be a damn miracle.

I patted my pockets, looking for my phone. "If you'll excuse me, I need to call my friend and try to clean up your mess."

Julie took the hint even if her friend didn't. "Come on, Lex. Let's go to the mall and find new outfits for the party tonight."

"Sure." Lex smiled as she passed me. "See you tonight."

Not if I can help it.

Maxwell hadn't ordered me to go to this one, so I was staying far away from it and all the unmated females. It wasn't just Lex and Julie I had to worry about. Pack members were arriving every day, so there'd be more of them to fend off tonight. No thanks.

Scowling, I turned to look for my phone, which must have fallen out of my jeans, and came up short when I saw Brendan standing there in wolf form. He had to have heard everything. Why hadn't he confronted Lex and Julie for breaking a pack law, or me for letting them off with it?

I waited for him to say something, but he only watched me silently for a minute then loped off into the woods.

"Weird," I muttered.

Must be that observing thing Brendan and Maxwell had mentioned. I hadn't talked to Brendan since the little staring contest last Monday, but I had noticed him watching me at some of the cookouts. It would have bothered me if he hadn't also been looking at Pete and the other Beta candidates. I wished I knew what he and Maxwell were hoping to find in us.

This week, I'd talked to Maxwell about cutting back my hours at the lumberyard so I could work on the Chevelle. At first, I was sure he was going to refuse, and I was surprised when he agreed. I think the fact the Chevelle restoration was a paying job and not a hobby was the main reason he said I could cut back to three days a week for now.

Laughter drew my attention to Lex and Julie, who were standing by the barn talking to my cousin Lydia, who was home from college for the summer, and two other girls I didn't know. The newcomers looked to be in their early twenties, and my hope they were mated was dashed when they looked at me with unabashed interest.

I was starting to feel like an unwilling participant in a werewolf version of that bachelor reality show my mother liked to watch. But humans could give the ring back and go their separate ways if things didn't work out. There was no *out* once your wolf imprinted on another.

You keep it in your pants, I warned my wolf. *Those females are nothing but trouble, and we have plenty of time to get tied down.*

I spotted my phone in the grass and picked it up. Brushing it off, I hit Sara's number and listened to it ring. It was night in Russia, but not too late to call her. And I needed to find out what, if anything, Emma knew about the pack before I went to see her. I had planned to wait until tomorrow, but tonight might be better. I glanced at the group of girls who would all be at the party here this evening. Yeah, tonight was definitely better.

My phone rang as I drove to the waterfront at eight o'clock that night, and I grinned when I saw Pete's name on the screen. I hadn't told him about my plans to ditch the party, and he was most likely calling to see where I was.

"Hey, where are you?" he asked when I answered.

"Almost downtown. Going to see Emma."

"Emma?"

I hadn't seen him all day, so I filled him in on what had happened at the cove and my call with Sara that had left me with more questions than answers.

"Emma knows what we are? Why didn't she say anything?"

"I don't know. All Sara would say was that Emma already knew about werewolves before Sara told her about us. I asked how Emma knew, but Sara wouldn't tell me." I let out a loud breath. "You know how good Sara is at keeping secrets. You couldn't pry it out of her with a jackhammer."

"Sara told us Emma's been through a lot. Do you think that has anything to do with how she knows about us?"

"Could be." I'd wondered the same thing, and if that was why she was uneasy around us. If so, being frightened by Lex and Julie today wasn't going to help.

Sara had been happy when I told her I was going to go by and make sure Emma was okay. She said she worried about Emma being there alone and hoped the three of us would hit it off. Whatever had happened in Emma's past, Sara seemed convinced that Pete and I being werewolves would not stop us from being friends.

"When will you be back here?" Pete asked.

"That depends. What time is the party over?"

An edge of panic crept into his voice. "You're not going to the party?"

I barked a laugh. "Lex almost jumped me a few hours ago. If I'd let her, we would have done it right there in front of Julie and whoever else walked by. And then I saw two more who looked at me like I was something to eat. No way I'm going near that if I don't have to."

"Are you serious about Lex?"

"Yeah. That girl doesn't take a hint, and she made it pretty clear what she wants. She even tried to get me to shift so our wolves could *play*." I laughed without humor. "Word of advice: skip the party."

"I can't," he said almost desperately. "I told Mom I'd help out with the music. I wouldn't have if I'd known you were blowing off the party."

"Sorry, man. I figured you knew I wouldn't go unless I had to." I turned onto the waterfront. "Listen, I'm almost at Sara's place. I have to go."

"Okay," he grumbled. "But next time, I'm leaving you here with these girls."

Fat chance.

"Later," I said as I pulled up to Sara's building.

Emma had no vehicle, but the light was on in the kitchen so I figured she was home. I was half expecting to find Scott's red Mustang sitting in her parking spot, and I was glad to see she was alone. Not that I wanted her to be alone. I just didn't want her hanging around with Scott. Seeing her with him today had angered my wolf, who loved Sara as much as I did. We were both feeling protective of her cousin.

At the door, I stopped myself as I reached for the doorknob and pressed the doorbell instead. It felt strange not walking in as I'd always done, as strange as it was to have someone else living in Sara's place. It was another reminder of how much our lives had changed in the last year, and it made sadness prick my chest. Funny how we can't wait to be adults, and then when we are, we miss the days of just hanging with our friends.

"Coming," called a voice from inside the apartment. The door opened, and I stared at the girl standing there. Her hair was piled on top of her head in a loose bun with strands curling around her face. Her T-shirt and shorts had splotches of paint on them, and there was a small streak of blue on her chin. She was also covered in dark spots of what looked like mud, and she seemed a bit frazzled.

Emma's expression turned to one of surprise. "Oh, hi, Roland."

"Hi. I...um...are you okay?"

Her brow furrowed, and she looked down at herself as if seeing the mess on her clothes for the first time. "Yeah, ugh. Had a little mishap in the kitchen."

My lips twitched. "Are you making mud pies?"

"Not exactly." Pink tinged her cheeks, and she opened the door wider to let me in. "Sorry about the mess."

I followed her inside and shut the door. She led me into the kitchen where I stopped to gawk at the dark splotches on the cabinets, wall, floor, and even the window. It looked like a mini mud bomb had gone off on one side of the kitchen.

"What happened?"

Emma huffed and pointed to the metal contraption at the center of the mess. "I was trying to make a latte with this espresso machine Sara bought me. The manual makes it sound easy, but they don't tell you what happens when you forget to put the little metal basket in the filter before you turn it on."

A laugh slipped out before I could stop it, and she shot me a dirty look, which made me laugh even more.

I put up a hand. "Sorry. Come on. I'll help you clean up."

"You don't have to do that."

"I know."

I tossed my keys on the table and grabbed some paper towels to wipe down the cabinets, window, and wall.

Emma cleaned the floor and counter, stopping when she got to the espresso machine. With a sigh, she rinsed the removable parts and set them in the draining tray to dry. When she finished, she turned to me with a grateful smile. "Thanks."

She tucked some loose strands of hair behind her ears, and I couldn't help but notice how pretty she was tonight. Maybe it was because for the first time, her brown eyes were warm instead of guarded when they looked at me. I found myself wondering what it would take to make her smile at me that way more often.

"No problem," I blurted when I realized she was waiting for me to respond. *No way, man, not going there. Sara's cousin, remember?*

"You know there's a coffee shop next door," I said.

She smiled sheepishly. "I thought I could make one without having to get cleaned up."

"You renovating or something?" I waved at her paint-splattered clothes. "I could help."

"Thanks, but it's not that kind of painting. I paint on canvas."

"Sara draws and you paint. You really are a Grey." I grinned at her. "Let me guess; you're working on a painting of the sky."

Her eyes widened. "How did you know that?"

I tapped my chin. "You have blue paint right here."

"Oh." She rubbed at the dried paint to no avail. "Excuse me. I'll get cleaned up."

"While you're doing that, I'll run next door and get us a couple of lattes," I said.

She opened her mouth to say something, but I waved it off and headed to the door. "Be back in a few minutes."

What are you doing, Roland? I thought as I jogged down the steps. Why was I getting coffee? I didn't even like coffee for Christ's sake.

I ordered a latte for Emma and a small iced coffee for me. By the time I got back to the apartment, she had changed into jeans and a fresh top and cleaned the paint off her face. I refused to let her pay for her drink, and we went into the living room to talk.

I could tell by her expression she was wondering why I was there. It wasn't exactly as if we'd hit it off on our first few encounters. I decided to get right to the point.

"I came by tonight to see if you were okay after what happened at the cove today."

Her face paled a little. "The cove?"

I nodded and set my drink down on the coffee table. "I called Sara, and she told me you know what we are. I wanted to apologize for today and to let you know you have nothing to fear from us."

"But those wolves..."

"Those two wolves are visiting from up north, and they were out of line." I pressed my lips together when I remembered Lex and Julie standing over Emma. "They broke pack law when they showed themselves to you, and they know better than to frighten a human. They've been warned not to do it again."

She relaxed a little and took a sip of her coffee. "What about the other wolf, the black one who drove them away?"

"What about him?" I asked, curious about what she thought of my wolf.

"Didn't he break the law, too, when he showed himself to me?" She bit her lip. "I hope he's not in trouble for helping me."

I wasn't sure why I didn't tell her I was the black wolf, but something held me back.

"No, he's not in any trouble. He didn't frighten you, did he?"

She toyed with the lid on her cup. "At first, he did because he looked fierce when he showed up. And after I... I didn't know what to expect. But then I realized he wasn't going to hurt me."

After what? I wanted to know what she'd started to say, but I didn't want to press her. It did make me wonder again what had happened in her past, and if that was why she'd wanted to stay away from us. I hated the thought that a werewolf might have hurt her and given her reason to fear us.

"I'm sorry he frightened you. He was just angry at those other wolves." I set my coffee down on a coaster. "Whatever happened to you before you moved here, I want you to know you're safe with us. We have a lot of out-of-town wolves here for a pack gathering, and they'll mostly stick close to the Knolls. Some will come into town, but they know to behave themselves. If you ever feel afraid for any reason, you can call me, and I'll come."

"Thank you," she said quietly. She gave me a wisp of a smile. "I like it here, and I just want to start over and not bother anyone."

Her eyes were sad despite her smile, and I wished I knew what had happened to her. She was eighteen and looking to start over? It had to be something bad.

I steered the conversation to a more pleasant topic. "It's a great place to live if you don't mind how quiet it is. Have you seen much of town yet?"

She nodded. "Some. Scott showed me around today. He was with me at the lighthouse."

I hid my displeasure. I hadn't been happy to see Scott with her earlier, but the thought of her spending the whole day with him bugged me. I almost said something but stopped myself. I might not like Scott for some of the things he did in his past, but he really did seem to have changed. It wouldn't be fair for me to try to come between their friendship just because of my dislike of him.

"Where did he take you?" I asked.

"The lighthouse, the mall, and a coffee shop," she said. "Oh, and the marina, although we just drove past it. We mostly drove around. New Hastings is bigger than I thought."

"Yeah, it's spread out. In the Knolls where we live, it's mostly farmland."

Her smile returned. "Sara talked about the Knolls. She said she used to love playing at the farm with you and Peter when she was little."

I laughed, remembering those days. "We had some great times."

"You miss her."

"Yes. It's hard not to."

"I know what you mean," she said softly. "I miss her, too."

For a brief moment, she let her defenses down and I saw loneliness in her eyes and a sadness that made my chest ache. I didn't like to see her hurting, but I didn't know what to do to make her feel better.

"So, you're a painter," I said, hoping to make her smile again. "What do you paint?"

Her face lit up. "I do landscapes, mostly."

"Cool." I glanced around the living room. "Can I see some of them?"

She blinked in surprise. "Are you sure? They're really not that good."

"I'm sure they are if you're anything like Sara."

"Okay." She set her coffee down and stood almost shyly. "They're upstairs."

She led the way even though I could find Sara's old room with my eyes closed. I'd spent countless hours at the apartment, and I'd slept on her old couch up there more than once.

I stopped in surprise when I reached the top of the stairs. The loft barely resembled the room I remembered. All of Sara's things were gone, except for the comfortable old couch I liked. The walls had been painted a light neutral color, and the wood floor had been refinished. Instead of the bookshelves, there were worktables and shelves of art supplies. And there were canvases everywhere, some blank and some finished. In the center of the room stood a large easel with a canvas on it. I walked over to look at the painting she must have been working on before I arrived.

"Hey, this is really good. It's the view from the kitchen window."

"You like it?" she asked from behind me. "I've been working on it for days, and I can never get the water right."

"Are you kidding?" I looked over my shoulder at her. "It's great."

Her face flushed at the praise, and she came over to stand beside me. "You don't think the light looks wrong on the water?"

"I won't pretend to know a lot about art, but it looks right to me. This is early morning, isn't it?"

"You can tell that?"

I nodded slowly. "Yeah. At least, that's what it reminds me of."

She stared at the painting for a long moment. "I wanted to do some paintings for Sara because she's been so good to me. I was starting to think I wouldn't get it right."

"She's going to love it," I said sincerely. "Although, you forgot one thing."

Her brows furrowed. "I did? What?"

I couldn't hold back a grin. "The window's too clean. It needs some wet coffee grounds."

"Oh..." She scowled at me, but it quickly turned into a smile that made my stomach do a little flip.

"So, um...can I see your other paintings?" I asked, looking away from her.

"Sure." She went to a stack leaning against a wall and selected one. It took me a few seconds to place the large stone building in the picture.

"Hey, that's Westhorne." I walked over for a closer look. It was a great likeness of the original. "I didn't know you'd been there."

She looked startled that I recognized the Mohiri stronghold. "I-I spent some time there with Sara. I forgot you've been there, too."

"Pete and I were there for almost a week last fall. Nice place."

She pressed her lips together as if she was pondering something. "I heard that Mohiri and werewolves don't like each other. Didn't you find it uncomfortable there?"

It was strange talking to her about us and the Mohiri. Except for Nate and

Greg, I didn't know another human who knew about our world. Well, not until now.

"I wouldn't say we don't like each other. It's more like we keep to ourselves. We're all on the same side though, killing vampires."

Fear flashed in her eyes, and some of the color left her cheeks.

I put up a hand. "Hey, I didn't mean to scare you. You don't have to worry about any of that around here." At least, not anymore.

She nodded and put the painting down. When she looked at me again, she appeared less frightened, though her color wasn't any better. I felt like kicking myself for upsetting her, and I wished again that I knew what had happened to her to make her so jittery around me.

"You okay?" I asked her.

She gave me a wan smile. "Yes. You just took me by surprise, talking about...them."

"I'm sorry. I won't mention them again if it bothers you."

"Thanks."

"What other paintings have you done?" I asked in an attempt to return to our easy conversation of a few minutes ago.

"Not a lot." She showed me half a dozen canvases, all landscapes, and it was clear she was talented. I didn't have to be an art expert to see that.

I looked at a painting of the river that bordered Westhorne. "You're really good. Do you plan to study art in college?"

"I'm not sure. I have to finish high school first."

"You're still in school?" The revelation surprised me, especially with her being on her own.

She pursed her lips, and I sensed we were back in that area she didn't like to talk about.

"I didn't finish my senior year, and I have to go back for that," she explained.

I nodded in understanding. "Pete and I just graduated. We missed a month of our year and we'd be going to school with you if his dad hadn't talked to the school board."

Her eyes widened a fraction. "You just graduated? Oh, that's right, you and Sara went to school together."

I laughed. "Why? Do I look that young?"

"For some reason, I thought you were a few years older. Are you going to college this fall?"

"No. I waited too long to apply. I'm going to try to do some auto classes in Portland."

She set down the canvas she was holding and walked to the stairs. "You want to be a mechanic?"

I followed her back to the living room. "Yes. My cousin Paul has a garage, and I'm going to work there a few days a week restoring a classic car."

"A car like yours?"

"No, a Chevelle. But I did restore the Mustang."

Her eyebrow rose. "You did that? It's beautiful."

I felt an absurd rush of pleasure at her praise. "Took me almost six months but she was worth it. Paul showed pictures of the restoration to a friend of his, and that's where the Chevelle job came from. We're hoping it leads to more jobs like that."

"That's great."

I sipped my coffee. If any of my friends could see me drinking iced coffee instead of a beer on a Saturday night, they'd get a good laugh out of it. For some reason, the thought didn't bother me at all.

"So, you've been here a few weeks and you already have a job and you've met the local wolves." I smiled and I was glad when she returned it. "Sounds like you're settling in."

"Yes. I love it here. I still need to pick up a few things, but for the most part, I'm good."

"Anything I can help you with?"

She shook her head. "It's mostly paint supplies. Sara stocked the loft for me, but I think I'm going to go through canvases pretty quickly. There's so much to paint here."

"There are some good art supply stores in Portland," I said. "I took Sara there a few times. If you want, I can take you there."

I expected her to decline my offer, based on her previous reactions, and I was surprised when she didn't outright say no.

"Thanks." She picked up her coffee. "I'm probably going to need a car living here, aren't I? Sara said I would."

"You'll be okay for the summer if you're not in any hurry to get one. But you'll want one before the winter." I leaned forward and rested my elbows on my knees. "You have one in mind?"

"Something practical that's good in the winter."

I grinned at her. "Well, I can definitely help you there. If there's one thing I like, it's looking at cars."

"I can tell." She smiled, and I liked seeing this lighter side of her.

I realized I'd stayed longer than I'd intended, but I found myself reluctant to leave. I enjoyed talking to her more than I'd expected to. The girls I usually talked to weren't as interesting as Emma. Probably because those were the only girls I chose to date and I didn't want anything deeper with them. Not that I wanted something more with Emma.

I stood and wiped my suddenly damp hands on my jeans. "I guess I should let you get back to your painting."

She stood as well. "Thanks for coming by and for the latte."

"You're welcome."

She followed me to the door where I turned to face her.

"Let me know if you want a ride to Portland. You can call me anytime."

"Thanks," she said softly. She smiled, and I was struck again by how beautiful her eyes were. How had I not noticed that about her the night we met?

"See you around," I said as I opened the door. I shut it behind me and stood on the landing, listening to her slide the bolt. Part of me wished I was still on the other side of that door with her, while another part of me said I should run far and fast.

"Oh, man, this is not good."

6

Emma

"Where are we going?"

I pushed open the gymnasium door. "Not far, just to the parking lot. The booze is in my mom's car."

"Oh, cool." Tess looked behind her for a moment then followed me down the corridor to the main entrance. "We can't be gone too long, or Chrissy will get mad at me for leaving her."

I didn't answer, leading her down the steps and across the parking lot to the silver minivan in the darkest corner. The side door slid open as we reached it, and Eli got out, his dark eyes running hungrily over my new friend.

"Hello, sweet thing," he drawled.

"Wh-who are you?" Tess asked fearfully.

"I'm your future," Eli said as I hooked my arm around Tess's throat and felt her go limp.

I knelt on the bed and leaned over the unconscious girl. "Wakey, wakey."

Tess's lids flickered, and she stared up at me, her eyes round with terror. "Please, don't hurt me. Please, let me go home."

"Sorry, can't do that. Eli's taken quite a fancy to you."

Eli entered the room and came over to sit on the bed on Tess's other side. "You did *well, my pet," he said to me as he smiled down at Tess. He reached across her to snag my shirt and pull me to him. His kiss was hard and punishing, the only way he liked them. Excitement flared in my chest at the raw lust in his eyes.*

He released me to give the girl his full attention. "You're a pretty thing, aren't you?"

Tess whimpered. "Please..."

He laughed and leaned over her. "I love it when they beg."

Tess's eyes widened, and she bucked against him, her lips parting in a scream as Eli showed her his fangs. I could smell her terror, and it only fed my own hunger.

I grabbed her arm and latched on to her wrist as screams filled the room. Sweet, warm blood flooded my mouth and hit the back of my throat...

I choked and sat up, gasping for air. My stomach rolled violently, and I gagged on the bile rising in my throat. I almost fell out of bed in my rush to the bathroom, barely making it to the toilet before I started to vomit.

Tears ran down my face as the retching turned to sobs. I flushed the toilet and wiped my face, but the tears continued to flow. In my head, I could hear the girl's screams, and I clapped my hands over my ears, trying to block them out.

"It wasn't me. It wasn't me," I chanted over and over as I was forced to relive the girl's horrifying last hours. I sank down on the toilet, rocking, with my arms wrapped tightly around me. But nothing could make the images go away, not until my soul had been flayed open for the evil in my past.

It was the same after every dream, each one about a different victim. The vamhir demon was dead, but I was still a prisoner, forced to bear the weight of all those murders, all those lives taken in such a gruesome manner.

When the shaking stopped, I stood weakly and splashed cold water on my face, not caring that my hair got wet in the process. I leaned against the vanity and brushed my teeth. Then I went to the dresser and pulled a thick leather-bound journal from the bottom drawer. I sat on the bed with the journal and a pen and opened it to a new page.

My fingers trembled as I began to write.

Tess Andrews, 16
Henry Ford High School
Detroit, Michigan 2002

...

I didn't stop until I had recorded every memory of Tess's last night alive. I wrote about singling her out in the school gym because she was exactly Eli's type, and how I'd easily befriended her and lured her outside. We'd taken her to the house Eli had procured for us, and the two of us killed her after Eli had played with her for hours. Before the sun came up, he'd made me bury her deep in a corner of the backyard. Eli had been fastidious about covering his tracks, which meant I'd buried hundreds of bodies over the years. Tess could still be there, alone in that hole, with her family always wondering what had happened to their little girl.

The page was wet in places by the time I finished writing, and I laid down the pen to wipe my eyes. The screaming in my head had faded away, and I lay back wearily against the pillows, feeling drained.

I'd started the journal a month ago, and it served two purposes. After each dream, I wrote down everything I could remember about the victim and how they'd died. I couldn't talk to anyone about these things, but writing them down helped me come to terms with what I – what the vampire had done.

My second reason for the journal was not for me. Someday, when it was full and there were no more victims to remember, I planned to type out the names, places, and dates and send them anonymously to the authorities, along with the locations of the bodies we'd buried. I couldn't change what had happened to those people, but maybe I could give their families some closure. It was more than I could do for my own family.

Thinking about Marie and my parents brought on a fresh wave of misery, and my chest felt like it was gripped in a vise.

"God, I miss them so much," I whispered past the lump in my throat.

Loneliness threatened to swallow me, and I wished there was someone I could talk to. My first thought was of Sara, but I would not burden my friend with this. Sara had been through her own nightmares, and she'd spent the last few months taking care of me. She needed this trip with Nikolas, but she'd be on the next plane home if she knew how unhappy I was.

"Call me anytime."

It surprised me that I would think of Roland – a werewolf – at a time like this, and I thought about his visit a week ago. I was dismayed when I'd opened the door to see him, but I'd ended up enjoying his company, and I'd even felt a little disappointed when he left. Maybe it was because I was alone here too much, or maybe Roland was easy to talk to and his smile made me forget the differences between us. I could see now why Sara spoke so fondly about him.

He'd dropped into the diner for lunch twice this week, and both times, Brenda had seated him in my section. I suspected she was trying to do a little matchmaking, and I didn't bother to tell her it was a wasted effort. I could see why she liked him, though. He was funny, outgoing, and gorgeous, without a hint of arrogance. A lethal combination.

I felt the sting of regret and sighed. There was no sense going there. He was what he was, and that would never change. It didn't matter that I liked him despite him being a werewolf. If he ever discovered the truth about me, he'd look at me with disgust and contempt. He certainly wouldn't be bringing me coffee again.

I reached for my cell phone on the night table and scrolled through my short contact list. Jordan's name was at the top, and I thought about calling her before I realized how early it was in Los Angeles. She'd told me to call her anytime, but it would be selfish to wake her, considering the late nights she put in for her job. Instead, I texted her, knowing it would be a few hours before she replied.

Hey, how's it going? Kill any demons lately?

I laid the phone down, and I was startled when it vibrated less than a minute later.

Hey. U ok?

I texted back. **Bad dreams. The usual. Why are you up?**

Stakeout, she replied. **I'd call, but I have to keep quiet.**

Understand, I said.

Must have been a bad one. Hate that UR alone.

I smiled sadly. **Just nice to know you're there.**

U sure UR ok?

Yes, I wrote back. **Just feeling a little needy. Sorry.**

Never be sorry for needing a friend, she said. **I'll call U later. Ok?**

Sounds good.

I lay back on the bed and stared at the ceiling until the silence of the apartment pressed down on me. Rolling out of bed, I put the journal away and went to shower. It was too early to go anywhere, but I couldn't lie there wallowing in misery a moment longer.

Roland

I padded through the trees, moving quickly over the uneven ground. Ahead of me, a fox darted across my path, and above me, the birds were silent in the branches. A large predator was in their midst, and they would hide until I moved on.

The faint tang of the ocean tickled my nose, and I veered off in a new direction, away from the cliffs. I didn't particularly like being in this area after what had happened to Sara here last year, but I wanted to be as far as possible from the Knolls after my mother told me a dozen more wolves had arrived yesterday, half of them unmated. The Knolls were getting far too crowded and it was only going to get worse.

It wasn't that I had anything against the visiting females. I was sure they were nice people, and some of them were probably in no hurry to mate either. But like Pete, most wolves were resigned to their fate. Mating ensured the survival of our species since only mated pairs could have children. I understood that and I wanted to have a kid someday, but not at eighteen.

My chest rumbled when I sighed heavily. Was it too much to ask to finish college and have a little freedom before I settled down? Or even to get to know a girl and feel something more than mild attraction before my wolf bound me to her for life?

Emma's face swam before my mind, and I found myself, once again, thinking about my visit with her last Saturday. What was it about her that made me unable to get her out of my head? She was pretty, sure, but I'd known a lot of pretty girls. None of them had occupied my thoughts so much that I'd sought them out just to talk to them for a few minutes. Twice this week, I'd gone to Gail's for lunch, telling myself it had nothing to do with Emma working there. Absolutely nothing to do with her cute smile when she took my order or the mesmerizing sway of her hips as she walked away.

I remembered the times during our conversation at the apartment when her eyes had turned sad and she'd withdrawn from me. I wished I could help her with whatever troubled her, but she obviously didn't want to talk about her past, and I wouldn't push her. I had a feeling it would send her running away, and that did not make me happy.

My new route took me near the old silver mine. It had been abandoned a long time ago, and it was boarded up now because it wasn't safe inside. Not that many people came down here anymore, which was exactly why it was the perfect place to get away from everyone.

The sound of movement up ahead followed by a series of clicking noises, alerted me that I was not alone here as I'd believed. I slowed and crept silently to the edge of the clearing at the front of the mine, curious about who or what was making that strange noise.

I don't know what I was expecting to see, but it definitely wasn't the girl I'd spent the morning thinking about. Emma was facing away from me, but I easily recognized her petite form. What on earth was she doing down here?

The answer came when she lifted her hands and I saw the camera she held. It looked expensive, and she seemed comfortable using it. She peered through the lens and took a few steps backward, snapping pictures of the mine's entrance as she went. She stopped and moved to her left and then to her right, taking shots of the mine from different angles.

I remembered the photographs I'd seen in her studio and realized she was taking pictures so she could paint the mine later at home. To me, it was just a black hole in the rock with cobwebs and rotting boards nailed to it, but it must look like more to her artist eye. Sara was the same way, always seeing the beauty in ugly things.

Emma spun suddenly in my direction and peered into the woods. "Hello?" she called warily, taking a step back.

I cursed my carelessness. I'd been so distracted by her that I must have made a noise. After her bad experience with Lex and Julie, I didn't blame her for being jumpy.

I stepped from the woods into the clearing, hoping she'd recognize my wolf and know she was in no danger. Sitting on my haunches, I watched her, waiting to see what she would do.

Her eyes widened before she let out a relieved breath. "Oh, it's you. At least, I hope it's you."

I nodded once and was rewarded with a nervous smile.

Her fingers twisted the camera strap. "I-I wanted to thank you for what you did last Saturday. I know you were just doing your job, but thanks."

My head tilted to one side as my wolf listened to her soft voice. Before Emma, he'd never been around a human in his true form, and he was fascinated by her. He adored Sara because we grew up with her, but something about Emma intrigued him. I think he sensed my preoccupation with her and he was trying to figure out what was so special about this particular human. He wasn't the only one.

"Anyway..." She bit her lower lip. "Roland said I'm safe here, so I'm going to trust that you're not here to hurt me."

The scent of Emma's fear reached me, and I realized I was still staring at her. I lowered myself to the ground and rested my head on my paws, hoping I'd look less threatening. She'd probably feel better if I left, but my wolf hadn't satisfied his curiosity yet. To be honest, I wasn't in any hurry to go either.

Her fear abated, and she turned back to the mine. After a few minutes, she was so engrossed in her work I might as well have not been there. I was content to lie there and watch her, but my wolf eventually got restless. He didn't like being ignored, and he wanted the human to talk to him again.

Not much I can do about that, I told him.

Emma stopped taking pictures and walked to where Sara's old blue bicycle leaned against a large rock. I thought she was leaving, and disappointment filled me, making my wolf chuff unhappily.

He quieted when she picked up her messenger bag and carried it to a flat rock in the middle of the clearing. Sitting on the rock, she stuffed her camera in the bag and pulled out a bottle of water and a Tupperware container. When she pulled off the lid, the smell of roasted chicken reached me. My mouth watered because I'd skipped out on breakfast in my hurry to get away before people woke up. I could go hunt a rabbit or squirrel to tide me over, but I was reluctant to leave Emma out here alone.

She took a few bites of her sandwich, lost in thought. When she reached for her water bottle, her eyes moved to me as if remembering she was not alone. Her brows drew together slightly, and she sighed.

"If you're going to hang around, you might as well eat with me." She took half a sandwich from her container and held it out to me.

When I didn't move, she waved it at me. "Listen, I feel weird eating with you there. I have more than enough to share."

I walked over to her, and she had to tip her head back to look up at me when I stood beside her. This close, I could see shadows under her tired eyes that made me wonder if she was getting enough sleep.

"Wow, you really are huge," she said with a mixture of awe and unease as she laid the food offering on the rock. "I hope you like chicken."

I sniffed the sandwich and ate it in one bite. When I started to walk away, Emma set out another half sandwich for me. I looked at it, and she shrugged.

"I made two in case I stayed longer than I expected."

I accepted the food. My wolf didn't want to return to the edge of the clearing, so I lay down a few feet from Emma and waited to see how she'd react to my nearness. After all the stress of the pack gathering, it was nice being around a female who wasn't looking at me as a potential mate. There was no pressure, no anxiety, and my wolf and I both enjoyed her company.

She ate quietly for a few minutes then looked over at me. "You're probably wondering why I'm out here in the woods, taking pictures of this old mine. My cousin Sara used to live in town, and I'm painting some of her favorite places for her. Maybe you know her. Sara Grey."

I lifted my head and nodded, earning a small smile from her. My tail wagged.

Emma stared at the woods. "So, that's why I'm down here."

The note of sadness in her voice told me there was more to it than that. My wolf heard it, too, and he wanted to crawl over and comfort her. I knew she was still nervous around me, though she did her best to hide it, and I wouldn't do anything to make it worse.

She ate the rest of her lunch in silence then took out her camera and clicked through the pictures she'd taken. Looking satisfied with them, she put the camera back into her bag along with her other things, and stood.

"It was nice seeing you again."

She looked like she was going to say something else but changed her mind. Walking over to the bike, she donned the helmet and pushed the bike out to the gravel road.

I waited until she was out of sight before I got up and followed her to the road where she climbed on the bike and pedaled leisurely along one of the ruts. I stayed behind her until she reached the main stretch into town. I couldn't go any farther without the risk of being seen by someone.

My wolf wasn't happy to watch her go, and I chided him as I headed deeper into the woods to resume my patrol. *You only like her because she fed you.* It wasn't entirely true. He was curious about the human girl, even a little taken with her. If I was honest, I was a little taken, too.

I sighed noisily. It didn't matter how much I liked Emma because nothing could come of it. Say she was interested in me and we had a few dates. Then what? Like with every other girl I'd dated, I'd have to end it before it got serious. I couldn't have a relationship with a human and watch her get hurt when my wolf eventually imprinted on someone else. And it would happen; there was no getting around it. I couldn't do that to other girls, and I definitely couldn't hurt Emma that way. If she'd let me, we'd be friends, but that was as far as it could go between us.

Emma

I unlocked the back door and rolled the bike inside, almost forgetting to close the door behind me in my distraction. I hadn't planned to go to the mine today, but after that particularly brutal nightmare, I'd needed to get out of here for a few hours. Sara had told me the mine was a special place for her and Remy, so I'd decided to paint it for her. Riding her bike, I could almost imagine what her life had been like before Eli and the Mohiri found her. By the time I'd reached the mine, I almost expected to see a troll waiting for me.

What I hadn't expected was the werewolf. All the way home, the only thing I could think of was my time with him and the way he'd seemed to be watching over me. Roland had said the pack protected the people in their territory. Maybe this wolf felt responsible for me after what had happened at the cove.

Whatever his reasons for staying with me, I'd felt safe with him. The realization that I could be comfortable around a werewolf floored me, especially one that towered over me on four legs. He'd scared me when he'd stepped out of the woods, and I was nervous at first, even after I'd recognized him. But he'd turned out to be good company, and it had been surprisingly easy to forget what a powerful and deadly creature he was. I wondered if this was how Sara felt when she looked at her hellhounds. Everyone else saw them as monsters, but to her they were big dogs.

Did I really just compare a werewolf to a dog?

I shook my head and climbed the stairs to the apartment, a smile tugging at my mouth. I was pretty sure he wouldn't be flattered by the comparison. Better keep that thought to myself.

An hour later, I sat at my easel, brush in hand, staring at a blank canvas. Pinned to the top of the canvas were several pictures I'd taken of the old mine that morning, and the details were fresh in my mind. But for some reason, I couldn't figure out where to start. I shifted on my stool, not sure what was causing my creative block. Normally, it was easy to lose myself in my painting, but today I felt restless for some reason.

I looked around the loft, and my gaze fell on the door to the attic, reminding me I had been planning to check out the roof. Not exactly an exciting venture, but it was better than sitting here doing anything else.

Laying down my brush, I walked over to open the small attic door. There was no light fixture inside, but plenty of light came from the loft. I tested the narrow stairs before I climbed them to the door that led to the roof. It was bolted, and I had to jiggle the lock a bit to get it to slide over. Then, I opened the door and stepped out into the sun.

I found myself near the ventilation system, facing the back of the building. Skirting the unit, my breath caught at the unobstructed view of the ocean. Colorful sailboats dotted the bay and two fishing boats, low in the water, headed to shore with their catches.

Someone, most likely Sara, had created a small terrace on the roof with loose patio tiles. Large planters marked the corners of the terrace, and it was furnished with a wicker couch and two wooden Adirondack chairs. There was even a small metal fire pit in the center. The warm sun beckoned me, and I had a feeling I was going to be spending a lot of time up here this summer.

I ran down to the main floor to grab my laptop and cell phone. Settling in one of the chairs, I started searching for art supply stores in Portland, making note of two I wanted to check out. After that, I entertained myself by researching cars and trying to decide what I liked. Roland was right. I'd need one eventually. I couldn't rely on others to cart me wherever I needed to go. And it wasn't like I couldn't afford my own vehicle.

I'd been blown away when I finally logged into the bank account Tristan and Sara had set up for me and saw the balance. I knew the Mohiri were wealthy and generous, but I had not expected all those zeros in my account. I had more than enough to pay for a car, living expenses, college, and anything else I needed. I could quit my job at the diner if I wanted to, but it gave me a reason to get out of the apartment when I would have holed up here. Maybe when I started school in the fall, I'd give it up, but for now, I was keeping it.

An ad on the website I was browsing caught my eye, and I stared at the logo for the National Center for Missing and Exploited Children. Swallowing dryly, I clicked the link before I could convince myself it was a bad idea. I'd been on this website before and knew exactly what I'd find when I searched for my name. But I did it anyway.

The picture was my school photo, taken a month before I disappeared. I remembered that day as if it had been yesterday. My friend Chelsea had stood behind the photographer, making faces at me, and I'd done everything not to laugh. The result was a picture of me with my lips pressed together and my eyes sparkling with laughter.

If I looked in a mirror now, I'd see the same face, but my eyes were no longer the same. They were the right color and shape, but the innocent joy of the girl in the picture had been extinguished a long time ago.

A lump formed in my throat, and I closed the browser. Why did I keep doing this to myself? That life was gone. I could never go back, and dwelling on it would only stop me from moving forward and making a new life for myself.

I closed the laptop and gazed out over the water, taking stock of my blessings. I was alive and free and starting over. I already loved this place, despite the nightmares and loneliness that dogged me. I didn't have to worry about money, and I was making friends. I could be happy here. The only thing standing in my way was me.

Movement in the corner of my eye startled me, and I looked up as a large black bird flew down to perch on the low roof ledge. The crow stared at me with an almost eerie intelligence. As I watched it, it hopped down from the ledge and walked over to a small plastic pet dish. It poked at the empty dish a few times then swung its black gaze to me as if expecting me to know what it was looking for.

I stared at it for a minute before I remembered Sara talking about a pet crow of hers. I wracked my brain for his name, but it wouldn't come to me. This had to be him, though. She'd been worried something had happened to him because he hadn't shown up the few times she was here. She was going to be ecstatic.

I picked up my phone and snapped a picture of the crow, which I immediately texted to Sara along with the message, **I think a friend of yours dropped by for lunch.**

A minute later, she replied. **OMG!**

Ten seconds after that, my phone rang, and I grinned when I saw it was a video call from Sara.

"Hi. Thought I might hear from you."

"Hey," she said breathlessly. "Is Harper still there?"

Harper, that was it. Sara liked to name her pets after famous authors.

"He's just sitting there by the food dish. Hold on." I turned the phone so the camera was pointed at the crow. "Can you see him?"

"Yes!" she cried. "Harper, where have you been hiding? You had me worried."

The crow cocked its head and took a step toward me, its attention fixed on the phone in my hand.

"Hey, boy. I missed you so much," Sara crooned.

Harper cawed softly and moved until he was three feet from me. He shuffled from one foot to the other and wouldn't come any closer.

"This is Emma. She's really nice, and she's going to give you treats," Sara said as if expecting the crow to understand. But then, maybe he did. Sara was half Fae, and she had a way of connecting with animals that I'd never understand.

"What does he eat?" I'd never had a pet because my mother had been allergic. What did you feed a wild crow?

Sara laughed. "Pretty much anything – fresh fruit, nuts, bread, meat. I'll send you a list of his favorites." Her voice shook with emotion. "I'm so happy you're okay, Harper."

I propped up the phone with my laptop so Sara and Harper could see each other. "You two catch up. I'll run downstairs and see what I have to feed him."

The crow backed off when I stood, but he didn't fly away. I was pretty sure he was as happy to hear Sara's voice as she was to see him. I left them and went down to the kitchen where I filled a plastic container with fresh raspberries and melon, mixed nuts, and a slice of the crusty bread I'd gotten at the bakery yesterday. I smiled wryly as I carried the food up to the roof. He was going to be spoiled if he hung around here.

I stopped when the terrace came into view and I saw Harper standing with his face inches from the phone screen. Sara's voice didn't carry to me over here, but whatever she was saying had the crow captivated.

He cawed and backed away when I walked toward him. Moving around the terrace, I dumped the contents of my container into his dish. That got his attention, and as soon as I walked away, he strutted over to see what I'd brought him. I left him to his meal and went to pick up the phone again.

"That should keep him happy for a while," I said. "How often should I feed him?"

Sara still wore a big smile. "I usually left him a treat every other day. He eats on his own, so you don't have to feed him a lot or he'll get lazy."

"Okay, I'll do that." I settled back in my chair. "You look good. Still liking Russia?"

"I love it, but these walls take some getting used to. The people are great here, though, and I'm already learning some Russian words. And Irina is going to show me how to make some of Nikolas's favorite meals."

I felt a pang of envy, which immediately filled me with guilt. I loved seeing my best friend so happy; she'd earned every second of it. Was it wrong to want that for me, to feel like I belonged somewhere and to not feel so alone all the time?

"Hey, what's wrong?"

I smiled at her. "Nothing. Just jealous of your globe-trotting."

"That's not it." Her brows drew together. "Something's upset you. Is it the wolves? Roland told me what happened last weekend. I was going to call you, but he said he'd talk to you."

"He came by that night to see if I was okay, and he promised me it wouldn't happen again."

She relaxed visibly. "Oh, I'm glad, and I hope you see now that he's a really great guy."

"Yes," I admitted. "He even went next door for lattes."

Her eyebrow shot up. "Roland drank a latte?"

"Actually, I think he had iced coffee."

"Ah." A little smile played around the corners of her mouth, and I wondered what she found amusing about coffee.

"Did he stay long?" she asked.

"About an hour. I can see why you like him. He's easy to talk to."

Her smile grew. "I can't tell you how happy I am to hear you guys are hitting it off. Not that I'm surprised. And now you know you have nothing to fear from the werewolves."

"Not the local wolves anyway." I thought about the black wolf. "The big one who came to my rescue takes his job seriously. It feels like he's watching over me."

"You saw him again?"

I told her about my visit to the old mine and my encounter with the huge wolf. "I asked him if he knew you, and he said yes. Can you tell me his name?"

She shook her head slowly, looking pensive. "I know everyone in the Knolls, so it could be any of them. Are you sure it was the same wolf you saw at the cove?"

I laughed. "I've never seen a wolf that big. He's kind of hard to forget."

"And you weren't afraid of him?"

Considering my past and my reluctance to go near her friends, I could understand her surprise. I couldn't explain what it was about the wolf, but he no longer frightened me. I didn't know if I'd feel safe around other were-wolves, but I did with him.

"At first, I was nervous, but he seemed nice. He even ate one of my sandwiches."

That pulled another chuckle from her. "Werewolves are *always* hungry. You keep feeding him and you'll have a friend for life. Like Harper, only way bigger."

"A bird I can manage." I glanced at the crow, who had finished eating and sat on the ledge, preening his feathers. "I doubt I'll see much of the wolf anyway. It's not as if he can hang out on the waterfront, and I'm done with the woods for a while."

"And what about Roland?"

I rolled my eyes at her because she didn't bother to hide how much she wanted Roland and me to be friends.

"He offered to take me to Portland for art supplies and to look at cars when I'm ready to buy one."

Her face lit up. "That's great! When are you going?"

"I don't know. I haven't taken him up on his offer yet."

"Why not?"

I shrugged. "I'm still getting to know him."

She smiled as if it was only a matter of time. "Fair enough. As long as you're making friends and you're happy, that's all I care about."

"I have made another friend. Someone you know but aren't exactly friends with."

She leaned closer to the phone. "Who?"

"Scott Foley."

"Scott?" Her mouth went slack. "How did that happen?"

"I told you I got a job at Gail's. Scott's working there for the summer." I rubbed my chin. "He told me how you two fell out and that he was a jerk to you."

"He told you that?"

"Yes. He feels pretty awful about it. He said he always liked you and he didn't know why he treated you badly."

Sara's eyes filled with regret. "I always thought he hated me because of the fight we had when we were little. Now, I'm pretty sure it was my Fae side that made him act that way. If anyone should feel bad, it's me. After I left, he was like a different person, according to Roland."

"He's nice. He showed me around town, and he asked about you. I told him you were happy, and he said he was glad."

Her smile returned. "I'm glad he's happy now, too. But you and Scott. Wow. Small world."

"Small town."

"True." She tilted her head to one side. "So, are you two more than friends, maybe?"

I shook my head. "I don't think I'm ready for any kind of relationship yet."

"Or he's just not the one." Her eyes grew dreamy. "When you meet the right one, you'll know."

"You mean like how you knew Nikolas was the one and you fell in love at first sight?"

She laughed. "Point taken. Oh, and speaking of my wonderful mate, he bought you something."

I stared at her. "Like a housewarming gift?"

"Definitely not a housewarming gift, but it's really nice."

I made a face. "I don't know if I'm ready to handle a sword."

"Not a weapon either, I promise." Her eyes sparkled with laughter. "And he picked it out himself."

I tried to think of what I didn't have that Nikolas would buy me. "It's not a car, is it? Because that's too much."

"Nope. And that's all I'm saying except that it should arrive next week."

"Fine," I conceded, although I was dying of curiosity. Nikolas had been kind to me at Westhorne, but I never got to know him as well as Sara and Jordan. It touched me to know he'd thought to buy me a gift.

Sara and I talked for another thirty minutes about all the things she'd seen and done so far in Russia. Then Nikolas came in, and she said she had to go, promising to call again in a few days.

I laid the phone on my lap and stared out at the bay. I always felt better after I talked to Sara. Smiling, I closed my eyes and relished the warm rays soaking into my skin. I never slept well at night so it was easy for the sun to lull me into a pleasant doze. I fell asleep thinking about a huge black wolf with watchful amber eyes. And for once, the nightmares stayed away.

7

Roland

"I didn't expect this many," Pete whispered to me as we stood at the back of the meeting hall Tuesday evening and watched Brendan call out the names of the Beta candidates.

"Me either."

The building was packed for the meeting to officially start the gathering, and now I could see why. I'd counted twenty-four men and five women standing at the front of the room, and Brendan didn't appear to be finished with the introductions.

"Peter Kelly," Brendan said over the murmurings of the crowd. "And Roland Greene."

I pushed away from the wall and followed Pete up the center of the room to the front, ignoring the raised whispers from a group of girls to my right.

Pete and I stood with the other candidates, facing the room. I knew only the local guys and two from Bangor. Most of them were in their mid to late twenties, but there were three just a few years older than Pete and I.

"They don't look old enough to patrol, let alone be Betas," scoffed a guy behind me.

"Guess that doesn't matter when you're the Alpha's son and nephew," someone else replied in a voice just loud enough to carry to my ears.

It was no worse than some of the cracks I'd heard from Francis and the others, but it still annoyed me. I gritted my teeth, wanting to get through the meeting and the festivities afterward.

Brendan lowered the paper he was reading from, and Maxwell stepped forward.

"We have a good turnout this year for the gathering, and I'm pleased to see so many stepping up to be Beta candidates. Brendan and I will make time to talk to each of you over the next few weeks." Maxwell's gaze swept over us, and I felt it linger on me for a few seconds. Maybe now that he saw the other candidates, he'd change his mind about me being one of them.

He moved on and addressed the whole room. "Tomorrow, we'll start meetings to discuss pack business. I want you all to have an enjoyable visit, but with so many of us here, we have to be extra careful not to draw attention. We've already had one close call, and we were fortunate the situation could be contained. I will not tolerate that happening again."

He had to be referring to the incident with Lex and Julie. I'd assumed Brendan wasn't going to tell Maxwell about it after he'd walked away without saying anything to me. I should have known better. A Beta wouldn't hold back something like that from his Alpha. What I didn't understand was why neither of them had called me out for not reporting the breaking of a pack law. Was this another one of their tests?

Maxwell ended the meeting, and people began moving toward the door. A dark-haired man behind me bumped me hard with his shoulder as he moved around me, and his smirk told me it hadn't been an accident.

I scowled at him but didn't shove back. Training under Maxwell had done more than build up my muscles and hone my fighting skills. It had also taught me not to be provoked easily because that was the surest way to let your guard down.

Kyle stopped beside me. "That's Trevor Gosse from Bethel. He's been spoiling for a fight since he got here on Saturday. No way he'll make Beta."

"Why?" Pete asked as we watched Trevor join up with two other guys. The three of them laughed as they left the building.

"Maxwell doesn't like hotheads," Kyle said.

I almost snorted because if that was the case, Francis was out of luck.

"Steer clear of Trevor unless you want trouble." Kyle started toward the exit. "You guys coming?"

"In a minute," I called, in no hurry to join the festivities.

I looked at Pete. "You think we could get away with staying in here until this thing is over?"

He chuckled. "What do you think?"

"I think it's going to be a long night." I exhaled slowly as we followed Kyle.

As soon as I walked outside, I wished I hadn't. Standing a few feet from the door was a group of eight females who surrounded us immediately. Lex pushed her way to my side and wrapped her arm possessively around one of mine.

"Roland, where have you been hiding? I haven't seen you since Saturday."

I forced a smile. "Been busy. Work doesn't stop because of the gathering."

"You have to work weekends, too?" asked Julie, who had already latched on to Pete's arm, earning dark looks from some of the other girls. I might have Alpha blood, but Pete was Maxwell's son, which ranked him slightly higher on the most eligible bachelor list. I was perfectly fine with that.

I shrugged. "I work two jobs, and I have my pack duties. Not much free time left over."

It wasn't a lie. Between the garage, the lumberyard, training, and patrols, I was keeping busy these days. I did have some down time, but I could think of more pleasant ways to spend it that didn't include being chased by a bunch of females who only wanted me because of my Alpha blood.

Lex smiled. "But you're not working tonight, right?"

"No."

"Good." She tugged on my arm. "I'm famished. Why don't we go eat and you can tell me what you normally do for fun around here?"

Seeing no way to escape from her hold without being rude, I let her lead me over to the long tables covered in bowls and platters of food. Pete followed with Julie and the rest of the girls, and we all ate together. The girls were pleasant enough, and I would have enjoyed their company more if not for the whole mating thing hanging over my head.

I looked around as I finished my meal, and what I saw was not encouraging. At last count, there were fourteen unmated males here and twenty-one unmated females. And at least half those females were openly interested in Pete and me. The odds of both of us coming out of this unmated were shrinking every day.

A hand lightly squeezed my upper thigh under the picnic table, jerking my attention back to my companions. Lex leaned into me, wearing a suggestive smile and holding a piece of steak on a fork.

"Try some of this steak. It's amazing, and I can't possibly eat it all."

I politely pushed away the hand holding the fork. "I'm full, thanks, and I think I see my mom waving at me. I'd better go see what she wants."

Ignoring Lex's pout, I stood and walked over to where my mother sat eating with my grandmother, who had arrived that afternoon. At seventy-three, Grandma was an older version of my mother, and she could be as formidable as Maxwell when she wanted to be.

86

"Roland!" Grandma held out her arms, and I leaned down dutifully for a hug. She held me away to look at me. "I think you've grown at least a foot since I last saw you."

"Maybe half a foot." I grinned at her. "How was the drive?"

She tugged me down to sit beside her. "Good. You'd know that if you came to visit me more often."

"Sorry, Grandma, but Maxwell's been working me hard since I came home in January."

Her brows drew together sternly. "*Uncle* Maxwell."

I laughed. "I'm almost nineteen, and adults don't call their Alpha *uncle*."

"Well, you'll always be my little Roland no matter how big you get." She patted my arm. "Your mother tells me you are terrified of imprinting on one of these pretty young ladies."

"Mom!" I glowered at my mother, and she smiled.

"What? It's true. I was hoping Grandma could help me make you see that mating is not the end of the world."

I rubbed the back of my neck as my ears grew warm. "I don't think it's the end of the world. I just don't want to be bound to someone I barely know. And I have things I want to do first."

"What things?" Grandma asked.

"College for one. I'm working part-time in Paul's garage, restoring a classic car, and I want to take automotive classes so I can do that kind of work full-time."

My mother's eyes widened. "You didn't tell me you wanted to become a mechanic."

"We've barely seen each other lately with everyone getting ready for the gathering," I said. "It's something I've been thinking about since I did the Mustang."

Her smile grew. "That's wonderful, honey."

Grandma nodded. "It sounds like a very sensible plan, Roland. But you can still do all of that with a mate."

I groaned silently. I should have known she wouldn't let that topic go.

"I know, but I just finished high school. I'm not ready for a mate and kids. I don't understand why everyone is in such a hurry to get tied down."

She patted my arm affectionately. "It's nature, my boy. I was seventeen when your grandpa imprinted on me, and we were together for forty-three years. When your wolf finds your mate, she will be exactly who you were meant to be with, and you'll be as happy as your grandpa and I were."

"And like your father and I were," added my mother, a sheen of tears in her eyes. "You're afraid your wolf will choose one of these females just because they're available, but have faith in him. He knows your heart even if you aren't sure of his."

I wanted to believe that so much. "I've heard of guys imprinting on someone they didn't even like. What about them?"

Grandma tutted. "I've only known of two couples who've imprinted and didn't get along. It can happen, but rarely. Trust your wolf. You're too young to be worrying so much."

"I'll try," I said even though I knew it wasn't going to be as easy as that.

"Good." She looked at something behind me. "Who is that girl with Peter?"

I looked over my shoulder at Pete, who had managed to escape Julie and who now stood over by the house talking to a tall, dark-haired girl who looked to be our age. They were smiling and appeared to know each other.

"That's Earl and Mary Waters' daughter, Shannon," my mother said. "From out in Buxton. Shannon's going to USM in the fall to study education."

Grandma nodded approvingly. "Good family. She'd make a fine match for Peter."

I didn't comment. I thought Pete was nuts for putting himself out there and possibly imprinting. But if that was what he wanted, I hoped he found someone he would be happy with.

I stayed with my grandmother when my mother went to help with the food, and she wanted to hear all about what I'd been up to since the winter. When I showed her pictures of the Mustang, she tried to get me to let her take it for a spin.

I laughed softly. "No offense, Grandma, but I've seen you drive."

Instead of being insulted, she smiled. "Then you'll have to take me for a ride."

"Let's go."

She chuckled and shook her head. "Nice try, my boy. Why don't you go talk to Peter and his friend? You don't have to sit with me."

"I like hanging with you." I nudged her arm with mine. "And all the girls are too scared of the Alpha's mother to come over here."

Her eyebrow shot up before she let out a guffaw that drew the attention of half the people there. "You rascal. Go on with you before I call those girls over here and make you sit with them for the next hour."

Laughing, I leaned over to kiss her cheek before I stood. "I'm glad you're here, Grandma."

Pete smiled when I joined him and his new friend. "You look like you're in a better mood."

"Grandma has that effect on me, but don't expect it to last."

He snickered and turned to Shannon. "Shannon, this is my cousin Roland. The one who *abandoned* me last Saturday night."

She smiled and held out her hand to me. "It's nice to finally meet you. My cousin has been talking nonstop about you since I arrived, and I was starting to wonder if you were real."

"Your cousin?"

"Lexie Waters."

A small groan slipped out. "You're Lex's cousin?"

"Yes, but please don't hold that against me." Her eyes sparkled with amusement. "Don't look now, but I think she's about to come this way."

The last thing I wanted was to have Lex groping me in front of half the pack. I turned to the house. "I could use a cold beer. How about you two?"

"Sounds good," Shannon said, and I could hear the laughter in her voice.

We grabbed beers from the kitchen and hid out in the rec room for an hour. Shannon was nice and quick to smile, and I could see why Pete liked her. His expression whenever he looked at her told me he liked her very much. It was clear that she shared the sentiment. Even if they didn't imprint, I had a feeling they'd be hooking up before the night was out.

It was dark when we went back upstairs, and we could hear the party going strong outside. It would go until ten, and then the adults would shift and take part in the pack run. When I was younger, I couldn't wait to be old enough to go on the run. Now, I'd rather be anywhere else.

It was no secret that unmated wolves sometimes stole away from the main group to have sex, and more than one couple had imprinted that way. I fully expected Lex or one of the other females to try that with me, and I shuddered at the thought of being stuck with someone for life because of a moment of stupidity.

Instead of going out back where the main party was, we left by the front door. People had spilled out onto the front lawn, and I saw my cousin Lydia and her best friend Josie talking to a couple of men I didn't know. Lydia was twenty and unmated, and from the set of her jaw, she wasn't too happy about her current admirers.

One of the males shoved at the other. "I told you to stay away from her. Go find your own mate."

Lydia glared at the aggressor. "I am *not* your mate, Gary. How many times do I have to tell you that?"

The blond male, who looked to be in his mid-twenties, ignored her outburst. "My wolf wants you. I know it'll imprint on you at the run tonight."

The red-haired man he'd shoved moved to stand between Gary and

Lydia. "Stop this, Gary. You're only upsetting her. She and I are dating, and my wolf has begun the imprint."

I started toward them when I saw Gary's fists clench in preparation of a fight. This happened every time there were too many unmated wolves in one place. Inevitably, two males would want the same female and tensions escalated until one of the males imprinted. Normally, the other would bow out then, but it looked like Gary wasn't going to play by the rules. And my cousin would be caught in the crossfire.

"Everything okay here?" I asked Lydia, who looked more angry than distressed.

Gary sneered at me. "Stay out of this, pup."

I ignored the insult. "You know how this works. If his wolf is already imprinting on my cousin, yours won't."

"He's just saying he's imprinting to get me to back off and let him have time with her," Gary accused.

"I don't care what you believe," Lydia burst out angrily. "Seth's my boyfriend, and he's the one I want. There are lots of other girls here. Maybe one of them will be your mate."

Gary gritted his teeth. "I don't want them."

Lydia huffed in frustration and anger. Her eyes met mine, and we shared a knowing look. As Brendan's daughter and Maxwell's niece, she was a very eligible mate, something I could commiserate with. This mating business was making everyone nuts.

"Lydia's made her choice. You need to let it go, man," Seth said to Gary in a conciliatory tone.

Gary's response was a sucker punch to the other man's face. I heard the cartilage in Seth's nose crunch as he staggered backward under the force of the blow. Before he could recover, Gary lunged at him again, throwing another punch to his gut. Seth groaned, and Lydia tried to shove Gary away before he could do more damage.

I grabbed Gary from behind and dragged him back until he could no longer reach Seth or Lydia. He was a strong fighter, and he tried to break my hold, even head butting me in the chin once, but he was still no match for me. I might be a pup compared to him, but as everyone liked to point out, I had strong blood in my veins.

"Let me go," Gary demanded when he realized he couldn't free himself.

"I will if you promise to behave–"

I choked off the last word as someone tackled me from behind, a muscled arm wrapping tightly around my throat and cutting off my air. I released

Gary to grip the arm of my attacker. Bending down, I pulled him over my shoulder and sent him crashing into the ground at my feet.

He rolled away and bounced to his feet to stand beside Gary. Somehow, it didn't surprise me to see Trevor Gosse, the same man who'd bumped me in the meeting hall. That was when I recognized Gary as one of Trevor's friends from the meeting.

I looked from one to the other. "Two against one. That doesn't seem fair."

Trevor barked a laugh. "If you want to hang with the big boys, pup, you need to learn that nothing is fair."

I smiled as I studied them. They were both lean and muscled and had the look of seasoned fighters. But they were also hot-tempered and full of themselves.

"You good?" Pete called.

"Yeah." I gave Trevor a cocky smirk that was sure to piss him off. "I'll try to take it easy on you."

He snarled and swung at me. I blocked his punch and landed my own against his chin. He recovered fast and kicked me in the side as I was deflecting a blow from Gary. Pain lanced up my side, but there was no time to worry about it. Spinning, I ducked one fist as I kicked out and connected with the back of Gary's knee.

Gary went down, howling in pain. With him out of the fight, I focused on Trevor, who looked less cocky without his buddy. He would not give up, though. I knew his type. His pride wouldn't let him back down from a pup, especially since he was a Beta candidate.

Trevor feinted left, but his eyes gave him away, and I blocked the strike aimed for my throat. It was a dirty move, one that could have crushed my windpipe, and it made blood roar in my ears. We were taught that nothing was off-limits when fighting vampires, but pack members didn't fight like that amongst themselves.

I struck the center of his chest hard with the heel of my hand, and he wheezed. Not waiting for him to recover, I grabbed his arm and wrenched it behind his back, forcing him to his knees.

"Yield," I commanded, anger making my voice deep.

"Fuck you," Trevor spat.

"Roland, behind you," Pete shouted.

I pushed Trevor to the ground and held him with my foot as I faced the other man I'd seen laughing with Trevor and Gary in the meeting hall. He curled his lip and took a step toward me.

Enough of this shit.

I locked eyes with the man, and a low growl rumbled from my throat. He froze and tried to back away, but the only way to end a stare down was for one of us to submit.

A feral power filled my chest as my wolf reared up inside me, demanding the other wolf's submission. My wolf had fought against Brendan, but that was nothing compared to the fierceness in him now. It was all I could do not to shift and let him take over.

The man gasped and broke eye contact with me, sinking to his knees. With him no longer a threat, I looked down at Trevor and Gary. Now what to do with these two?

"What is going on here?" boomed the commanding voice of the Alpha.

Everyone went still as his power surrounded us. Maxwell's eyes were on me, and I had a feeling I was in for another one of his lectures, the kind that were usually followed by a brutal training session.

Lydia pointed at the two men at my feet. "They started it. Gary hit Seth, and when Roland stepped in, Gary, Trevor, and Rob ganged up on him." She related everything as it had happened, and Maxwell's expression grew darker.

Maxwell gave the three men a look that would have made them curl up with their tails between their legs if they'd been in wolf form. "You three, go back to wherever you're staying. I'll deal with you tomorrow."

Trevor stood and helped Gary to his feet. They kept their eyes averted from Maxwell, but Trevor gave me a look that promised retribution as the pair of them limped past me, followed by Rob. I didn't bother to tell Trevor I was the least of his concerns. I knew what Maxwell's punishments were like, and once Maxwell was done with Trevor, the man would forget all about me.

Maxwell looked at Seth, who was holding his bloody nose. "Is your nose broken?"

"Yes, sir," Seth said in a nasal voice.

"Lydia, take him to your place so he can heal," Maxwell told her.

Lydia nodded, and Maxwell turned to me. "Are you hurt?"

I ran a hand over my aching side. "A bit bruised, but nothing a shift can't fix."

"Good." He stared at me for a few seconds, and I waited for him to tell me he'd see me tomorrow, too. But he walked past me and entered the house without another word.

Pete and Shannon came over to me as soon as the door closed behind Maxwell. Pete's grin told me what he thought of the whole incident.

"You kicked ass," he said. "I don't think those guys knew what hit them."

I shrugged. "Guess all that training with Maxwell paid off."

"You'll definitely make Beta after this."

That didn't make me feel any better. I still wasn't sure I wanted to become a Beta with everything else I had going on.

Shannon gave me a sympathetic look. "Um, Roland, don't look now but..."

"Roland, we just heard what happened!" Lex ran over to hug me.

I winced when she pressed against my bruised ribs, and she pulled away.

"Oh, you poor thing. Let's go inside, and I'll take care of that for you."

I had little doubt how she wanted to take care of me. I gave Pete a helpless look and found him trying not to laugh.

"I'm okay, Lex," I said. "Thanks."

"Did you really take on four guys at once?" asked a blonde girl whose name I couldn't remember.

"No, only two." I wondered how the story could have already changed in the five minutes since it had happened.

"Three if you count the one you stared down," said my traitorous cousin with a barely concealed smirk.

"Three? That's amazing," the blonde gushed.

I sighed inwardly. I'd come here tonight hoping to keep a low profile, and all I'd managed to do was draw more attention to me. I used to love parties and girls, but the last few weeks had left a bad taste in my mouth. I longed for a quieter place, somewhere I could be myself without all the complications.

"Roland?"

Lex's voice dragged me from my thoughts, and I found her and the others giving me questioning looks.

"Sorry. What were you saying?"

"It's almost time for the pack run, and we thought it would be nice to get started early," she said. "You'll heal faster."

It was normal for younger or unmated wolves to start the run ahead of the rest of the pack, and I could see some people already walking to the woods. But the last thing I wanted was to let my wolf out around all these females before I had to. Unfortunately, I could think of no excuse to wait.

"Yeah, sure."

The group of us, including Pete and Shannon, walked to the edge of the trees where everyone began to remove their clothes. For the first time in my life, I felt uncomfortable getting naked around other wolves, even though it was as natural as breathing to us. It might have had something to do with the heated gazes I felt on me as I stripped.

I really hope Mom and Grandma are right about you knowing my heart, I told my wolf as I let the change take me.

We decided to head to the lake. I stayed at the back of the group, and I soon found out that was a bad idea. If I thought being surrounded by eager females in human form was bad, it was nothing compared to their boldness as wolves. They took every opportunity to rub against me or nip at me playfully or, in Lex's case, suggest we go off alone and have some real fun.

By the time the lake came into view, my mood was as dark as the sky, and I was having trouble not snapping at the girls. It wasn't their fault I wasn't into this like they were, but it was hard not to be annoyed when one of them was constantly touching me.

I finally got a reprieve when Lex suggested we all go for a swim. The girls shifted and dove in while Pete and I stayed in wolf form, watching them.

This is insane, I grumbled. *Did I really go for girls like this in school?*

Pete shook his head. *None of the human girls were as bad as this. Female wolves are not afraid to go after what they want.*

If I could have laughed, I would have. *That's an understatement. Lex tried to get me to go have sex with her on the way here.*

Lex is a bit much, but they're not all like that. Some of them are pretty nice.

I followed his eyes to where Shannon floated on the water, talking to another girl. *You like Shannon, don't you?*

Yeah. We met at the party last Saturday. She saved me from an ambush after you deserted me.

I sat on my haunches. *I think she likes you, too. Maybe she's the one.*

He let out a low sigh. *With my luck, I'll imprint on someone like Allison. She's nice and all, but way too giggly for me.*

Watching his wolf stare at Shannon, I had little doubt who he'd choose.

It would be *my* luck to imprint on one of the others. The thought sent a shiver through me. Even my wolf seemed repulsed by the idea, which was a little comforting. Like me, he didn't want to be here.

The sound of running feet drew our attention to the woods behind us as Maxwell loped out of the trees in wolf form, followed by Brendan and dozens of pack members. I'd never been so glad to see Maxwell because his presence meant the girls' playtime was over for tonight. The pack run was about unity and being led by our Alpha. We'd run hard over pack land and return home tired but content.

I spotted my mother and grandmother and went to join them. I hadn't been kidding when I told Grandma the girls were afraid of her because she was the Alpha's mother. I wanted to run and enjoy myself without the hassle.

You hiding again? she asked when I drew near.

Yes.

She snorted softly. *At least you're honest about it. Okay, my boy. Let's run.*

8

Emma

"What on earth is this?"

I slowed on my walk home from work on Wednesday afternoon when I saw a large white truck parked in front of my building. I wasn't expecting a delivery, so they had to be there by mistake.

A young man in a blue polo shirt was carrying a handheld device and came around the corner of the building as if he'd just been to my door. He spotted me walking toward him and stopped to wait for me.

"Are you Emma Grey?"

"Yes."

"Great. I have a delivery for you." He held out the handheld and a stylus. "If you'll sign here, I'll get it off the truck for you."

I didn't take the device. "There must be some mistake. I haven't ordered anything."

He frowned and looked at the screen on his handheld. "Says here the order was placed by a Nikolas Danshov."

"Oh! Then I guess it is for me." I took the stylus and signed where he told me to. I'd forgotten all about the gift Nikolas had ordered for me. "What is it?" I asked eagerly.

The man smiled. "Come see for yourself."

We walked to the back of the truck, and he opened the doors. A laugh burst from me when I saw what was inside.

"A motorcycle? He got me a motorcycle?" What on earth was Nikolas thinking? I had no idea how to ride one of these.

The man smiled. "Not a motorcycle. It's a scooter."

I walked to the side to get a better look at the silver scooter. Now that I saw it from a different angle, I felt silly for thinking it was a motorcycle.

"What kind is it?" I asked him as he swung up into the truck and started unhooking the cables keeping the scooter in place.

"It's a Vespa GTV 300. Real nice one. Vintage look."

"I've heard of Vespa, but I'm afraid I don't know anything about scooters," I said, wondering what I was going to do with it.

He rolled the scooter to the lift and lowered himself and the bike to the ground. Then he rolled it up to the steps and put down the stand.

"Hold on. I think there's a helmet, too." He ran back to the truck and returned, carrying a silver helmet and a larger silver dome-shaped object. He handed the helmet to me.

"This here is a topbox," he explained, holding up the other object. "You can mount it on the back of the scooter and use it for carrying stuff. It's handy if you don't have a car and need to get groceries."

"That's perfect." My chest warmed at Nikolas's thoughtfulness.

I heard a car approaching, and I looked up as a blue Mustang came around the truck and pulled in beside the Vespa. Roland got out and joined us.

"A Vespa." He walked around the scooter, looking it over. "This is a great scooter, but I thought you were thinking about buying a car."

"I am. This is a gift from Nikolas."

"Ah." He nodded, smiling. "Yeah, this is exactly the kind of gift he'd give you."

The delivery man stepped forward. "The keys, manuals, and paperwork are all in the storage compartment beneath the seat." He pressed a button under the ignition, lifted the seat, and pulled out a set of keys, explaining the difference between the blue one and the brown one. I was still a bit overwhelmed by the Vespa, so I wasn't sure how much I'd remember after he left.

"Thank you." I reached into my bag for my wallet. I wasn't sure how much you tipped someone delivering a scooter, but I had to give him something.

He put up a hand. "That's already been taken care of by Mr. Danshov. Enjoy your Vespa."

I gave Roland a helpless look as the truck pulled away. "I don't suppose you know how to drive one of these things."

He chuckled. "I've ridden motorcycles, so I'm sure I can figure it out."

I handed him the keys, and he demonstrated how to start the scooter.

"It's pretty easy to operate. You turn the key, then lightly hold the brake and press the starter."

The Vespa purred to life. Roland put up the stand, and I pretended not to notice how his jeans stretched tight across his backside when he straddled the seat.

"Here, let me show you how easy this is to handle." Waving off the helmet I offered him, he pulled out into the street and drove to the end of the row of buildings and back again. I had to admit he made it look easy, even though the scooter didn't exactly suit him. Now that I knew him, I definitely saw him more as a classic muscle car kind of person.

He stopped beside me. "You want to give it a go?"

I hesitated. I wasn't afraid of motorcycles, but I'd never driven one. The scooter was smaller and less powerful, but it was still a motorbike.

He hopped off the scooter and waved me over. I donned the helmet and took his place on the seat, bracing my feet on the pavement. The Vespa teetered a little because I wasn't used to the weight, but I kept it upright. The scooter was small enough to fit me, and I felt comfortable reaching the handlebars. Nikolas had chosen well. Now, I just needed to learn to drive it.

"What do I do now?" I asked.

Roland showed me the gas and brakes and explained the basic operation. Once I thought I had it, I turned the throttle and the scooter shot forward a few feet, startling me.

"Start slow," he said coming up to me. "Ease off the brake and very lightly give it some gas."

"I'm afraid I'll tip over."

"Don't worry about that. You can keep your feet down and go really slow to get a feel for it."

"Okay." I did as he said, and I managed to go ten feet without falling over. I pulled up one foot, but when I lifted the other, the scooter tipped and I panicked and hit the brake. How had he made this look so easy?

Roland caught up to me and put his hand on the front of the scooter to steady it. "You're doing great."

I made a face. "I'm terrible; admit it."

"No, you're just nervous. You'll be a pro at this in no time." He pursed his lips for a few seconds and moved behind me. "Scoot up a little."

I stared at him over my shoulder. "Why?"

"I'm going to sit behind you and be your training wheels. You focus on driving, and I'll catch the scooter if it starts to tip."

"You're too big. It won't fit both of us." My stomach did a little flip, and I didn't know if it was the thought of being so close to a werewolf or the thought of being close to this one in particular.

He shook his head. "It might be a tight squeeze, but we'll fit. And it's not like we're going that far."

"But..."

He cocked an eyebrow. "You're not afraid of being that close to me, are you?"

"No," I blurted, feeling my ears grow warm. "I mean, not really."

His smile faded. "Is it because of what I am? You don't ever have to be afraid around me."

"It's not that," I rushed to reassure him. "I'm not afraid of you."

"Good. Then let's do this."

"Fine."

I shifted forward a few inches, and he mounted the scooter behind me. There was no air between us, and the feel of his warm body pressed snugly against my back made my stomach do weird things. When he placed his hands on my hips, my mouth went dry and I forgot what I was supposed to do. He'd worried I was afraid of him, but it definitely wasn't fear I was feeling now.

"You comfortable?"

"Yes," I managed to say, praying he passed off my racing heart as nervousness.

He gave my hips a light squeeze of encouragement. "Okay, go slow to the end of the street. You can put your feet up and pretend I'm not here."

Yeah, like that's going to happen. I nodded and gave the scooter some gas. When nothing bad happened, I picked up the speed a little, and we reached the end of the street without incident. I turned the scooter carefully and started back toward my building.

"See? Nothing to it," Roland said. "You want to keep going down as far as the marina?"

"Okay." I was having fun now that I was comfortable with the Vespa. It really was easy to operate once you got the hang of it. I couldn't wait to call Nikolas and tell him how much I loved his gift.

I turned at the marina and headed back home. When I pulled in beside the Mustang and shut the scooter off, Roland waited for me to put down the stand before he climbed off.

"Well, what do you think?" he asked.

I got off the scooter, removing my helmet. "I love it."

"I knew you would. They're a lot of fun."

I smoothed down my hair. "Your timing was perfect. Thanks so much for teaching me to drive it."

"Anytime."

"Were you coming here or just driving by?"

"I was coming to see you." He went to the passenger side of the car and opened the door. Reaching in, he picked up a covered casserole dish and turned to me.

"My mother made it for you. She would have come herself, but she's been busy with all the visitors and the gathering."

"Your mother made me a casserole?" I asked, touched. "She didn't have to do that."

"She loves to cook, and I think she misses making food for Sara and Nate." He held the dish out to me. "I hope you like shepherd's pie."

I took the casserole, which was still warm. "I haven't had that in a long time. I'm sure I'll love it."

"Oh, and the best part." He went back to the car and returned with a wrapped pie plate. "My grandmother's been baking nonstop since she got here. Not that you'll hear any complaints from me. When she heard I was bringing you a casserole, she sent along one of her apple pies." He grinned. "It's your lucky day. Grandma's pies are the best."

The kindness from these people whom I hadn't even met made tears prick my eyes.

"That's so sweet of her. Apple is my favorite."

"Mine, too." He gave me a lopsided smile. "She always puts away a few for me."

"A few?" I couldn't help but notice there wasn't an ounce of fat on him. He didn't look like someone who ate a lot of desserts.

His smile grew. "We have big appetites, and we burn off calories fast."

I looked down at the large casserole in my hands. Without stopping to think about it, I said, "I can't possibly eat all this food. Would you like to stay for dinner?"

Roland looked as surprised by my invitation as I was. But as soon as I said the words, I realized I really did want him to stay. And it wasn't because I was lonely or I was feeling grateful to him for teaching me to ride the Vespa. I liked talking to him.

He shook his head regretfully. "I wish I could, but I'm meeting my cousin Paul. We're starting that Chevelle job I told you about."

"I understand." I lifted the heavy dish, hiding my disappointment. "Why don't you take some with you? I'd hate to see any of this food go to waste."

His blue eyes sparkled. "I never could turn down a good meal."

I turned to the stairs. "Great. Give me a minute, and I'll put some in containers for you."

He followed me up to the apartment and held both dishes while I unlocked the door. Setting them down on the kitchen table, he said, "While you're cutting out some food, I can mount that cargo box on the scooter if you'd like."

"That'd be great. I'm not sure what tools I have here, though."

"No problem. I have some in my trunk," he said as he left the kitchen. "Should only take a few minutes."

I walked outside, five minutes later, carrying two containers of casserole and apple pie, and I found Roland finishing up with the scooter. The storage compartment would be great for groceries and other small items. And the scooter was perfect for going to work and getting around town, at least until the winter.

Roland straightened and looked at me. "What do you think?"

"I love it. Thanks for all your help today."

He eyed the containers in my hands. "If that top one is full of apple pie, that's thanks enough."

I laughed and handed the food to him. "You earned it."

"If you're going to use food as a payment, you can consider me your personal handyman." He put the containers on the passenger seat. "And if you tell me you can bake, I might have to marry you."

I choked out a laugh. "Sorry. I can barely cook yet. The stove is not my friend."

He wore a smile when he turned back to me. "Don't worry. We'll figure that out, too. Now, where do you want to put the Vespa?"

"I don't have a garage." I frowned at the scooter. "You don't think it's safe here?"

"We get a lot of tourists in town in the summer. A couple of strong guys could easily put that in the back of a truck." He thought for a moment then walked around to the back of the building. "You can keep it in the storage area when you're not using it."

"It won't fit through the door."

"But it will." He pointed at the heavy steel door. "It's actually a double door they used for deliveries back when this was a store. You just have to unbolt the top and bottom of the second one, and it'll open."

"How did I miss that? I'll be right back." I ran up to the apartment and used the stairs to get down to the first floor. It took me a minute to wriggle open the bolts that had become stuck from disuse. When I opened the two doors, Roland was waiting with the Vespa. He easily rolled it inside and turned it so it was facing the door.

"There you go." He removed the keys and handed them to me. "I better get going. Paul's waiting for me."

I walked him to his car. "Thanks again. And thank your mother and grandmother for me, too."

"I will. Enjoy your new scooter." He got behind the wheel and rolled down the window. "Hey, I meant to tell you that I might have to go to Portland on Saturday to pick up a part for the Chevelle. You want to tag along, maybe check out those stores you wanted to go to?"

"You don't mind hanging out in art stores?" I teased him, happy he'd asked. I did need new supplies, and it would be nice to do something different for a change.

"Sara dragged me to every art store and bookstore in Portland. I think I can manage a few for you."

"Okay, sounds like fun."

"Great." He started the car and put it in reverse. "I'll call you."

"See you on Saturday," I called, ignoring the little voice in my head that said it sounded like we were making a date.

It's not a date, and we're just friends. I'd be just as happy if it was Scott or Brenda who had asked me. It had nothing to do with Roland Greene. Nothing at all.

———

"Hey, you ready for our trip to the big city?"

I laughed as I sank into the passenger seat of the Mustang. "I guess Portland is big compared to New Hastings."

Roland grinned. "True. And the farther I can get from the Knolls right now, the better."

"Aren't you guys having a big family gathering? I'd think you'd want to be there for that."

He huffed softly as he pulled out onto the street. "We have three quarters of the pack here now, and you can't turn around without bumping into an un —a wolf. I love my family, but it's just too much. You know?"

"I think so." There had always been someone around at Westhorne too, only it was never crowded and there were places to go when I wanted to be alone. I liked being on my own, but I also missed having other people around. Guess I couldn't have it both ways.

Hearing Roland talk about his family made my chest constrict. I'd give anything to be able to spend an hour with mine, let alone days or months or years. I didn't begrudge him his family, but I'd be lying if I said I wasn't envious. To belong to so many people, to always know you were loved and there were people who had your back no matter what. I could imagine no better life.

"You okay? You went quiet on me."

"Just trying to imagine what it's like living in a big pack like that. Do you all get together for holidays, too?"

"No, thank God." He gave me a sideways glance. "Just once a year. This is my first time being there for the whole thing since I was fifteen. I never realized how crazy it is."

"Where did you go if you weren't at the gathering?" He seemed to almost dread the idea of being with the other wolves, and I couldn't help but wonder why.

He cleared his throat. "I...stayed with Sara whenever I could. I've slept on that old couch in the loft more times than I can remember."

"Oh."

"I didn't mean to put you on the spot," he said. "Even if I could stay at the apartment, it wouldn't matter. My Alpha is making me attend a lot of the meetings this year. All adults have to be there."

I relaxed my body. "What do you do when you're not in meetings?"

"We have cookouts and parties, lots of them."

The note of distaste in his voice told me he didn't enjoy them, which was at odds with the Roland Sara had described. She'd told me he and Peter were always trying to get her to go to parties.

"When I don't have to be there, I'm usually at the garage or patrolling," he added. "Then there's training and my job at the lumberyard."

"Wow. It doesn't sound like you have much free time."

He shrugged and gave me a playful smile. "I manage to squeeze in some fun time – like teaching pretty girls to ride scooters."

My stomach fluttered. *He thinks I'm pretty?*

Roland chuckled. "Are you blushing?"

"No."

"Yes, you are. You Grey women are all alike. Sara turned red every time I flirted with her."

"I..."

He laughed again. "I'm teasing you."

"I know," I lied.

"So, what do you do when you're not working at the diner?" he asked as he took the exit to the highway. "Other than painting and exploring old mines."

"How did you know I was at the mine?" I stared at him. "The black wolf told you."

He gave me an indecipherable look. "You didn't mind hanging out with a werewolf?"

"I'm hanging with you now."

"I mean a werewolf in his fur. I know you have some kind of history with my kind and it made you afraid of us."

I opened my mouth to say I didn't want to discuss it, but he beat me to it.

"I'm not trying to pry into your past. I get that you're private about some things, and I'm cool with that. I'm just trying to get a feel for what you think of us now. I want you to be happy here, and I'd like us to be friends."

"I'd like that, too," I said, warmed by the sincerity of his words. "And to answer your question, I am still a bit nervous around werewolves in general, like those two at the cove. But I'm not afraid to be with you. And your friend hasn't given me any reason to fear him either. He's actually pretty nice."

"You like him?" Roland asked. He didn't look at me, but he sounded pleased.

"Yes," I said, surprising myself. I liked a werewolf – well, two werewolves. How about that?

He concentrated on the road for a minute. "Did you go to the cliffs while you were down that way?"

"No. Sara told me what happened there."

A shiver went through me. Sara had almost died at the cliffs. If she hadn't killed Eli, he would have come after me, and his punishment would have been merciless. Sometimes, the nightmares felt so real, I awoke thinking he was still alive and looking for me.

"I don't like to go there either," he said gruffly.

"I don't blame you. Can we talk about something less depressing?"

"Yeah." He smiled at me. "How are you liking the Vespa?"

"I love it."

We spent the rest of the drive talking about scooters and cars I should look at when I was ready to buy one. He told me to bring the Vespa to his cousin's garage and he'd give it free tune-ups.

Our first stop in Portland was at the home of the Chevelle owner who had the part Roland needed in his garage. I stayed in the car while Roland went in to get the part. Five minutes later, he was back with a cardboard box he stored in the trunk.

"Alright, let's hit some stores," he said as we drove away. "You have any in particular you want to go to, or should I take you to the ones Sara liked?"

I pulled a small notepad from my bag and gave him the names of two art supply stores. Fortunately, he knew where they were. He took me to both, where I loaded up the back seat with canvases, paints, and a new set of brushes I didn't need but couldn't resist. Roland patiently followed me around the stores, pushing a cart and carrying my purchases to the car.

"Where to now?" he asked when we left the second store.

"Are you hungry? I wouldn't mind some lunch."

He laughed. "I'm always hungry. What are you in the mood for?"

I shrugged. "I'm not picky. Where do you like to eat here?"

"I usually go for burgers," he said.

"Burgers sound good."

"I knew I liked you." He tapped the steering wheel as he thought. "There are some nice places downtown with outdoor seating."

"Okay."

Roland found a parking spot near a busy shopping area full of restaurants, stores, and art galleries. We walked a few minutes before we found a small restaurant with open tables outside, and within minutes, we were sipping sodas and waiting for our food.

"Portland is great," I said, watching people walk past us.

"It is. It's small compared to other cities, but there's plenty to see and do here."

I returned my attention to him. "How do you like it compared to all the other places you've been to?"

He gave me a questioning look, and I smiled.

"Sara told me all about your adventures in December."

He stopped toying with his straw to stare at me. "She told you all of it? You two *must* be close."

"She's my best friend."

"Mine, too." His boyish smile sent warmth through me. "See, we already have so much in common. We'll be besties before you know it."

"Besties?" I grinned. "Isn't Peter already your *bestie*?"

He scrunched his nose. "Okay, when you say it like that it doesn't sound manly."

I laughed at his goofy expression. "If it helps, I think you are very manly, except when..."

"Except what?" he challenged.

My lips twitched. "When you ride on the back of a scooter."

He opened his mouth to say something, but he was interrupted by the waitress bringing our food. My eyes bulged at the two double burgers and fries she set before Roland. My single cheeseburger was tiny in comparison.

"Can you really eat all of that in one sitting?"

"Easily." His blue eyes sparkled. "And have room for an ice cream float for dessert."

I shook my head. "How did your mother ever keep you fed?"

"She and my aunt took turns feeding Pete and me." He ate a fry. "We all have big appetites, so they're used to cooking a lot."

"I hope you know how to cook when you get your own place, or you'll go hungry," I teased. "Or marry someone who can cook like your mother."

I paused in lifting my cheeseburger to my mouth when I saw the pained expression that crossed his face.

I lowered my voice. "I guess I said that wrong. You mate, right?"

"Yes," he said in a strained voice.

His reaction told me this wasn't a subject he liked, so I let it go. I took a bite of my burger, chewing slowly as I wondered why talking about mating made him uncomfortable. It was natural for werewolves to take a mate.

I felt a little dejected at the thought of him with a mate, but I quickly brushed it off. Roland had a way of slipping past my guard and making me forget we could only be friends.

"Will you move to Portland when you finish college?" I asked in an attempt to get back to our light conversation.

He shook his head. "I used to think I'd move away after school, but all that stuff with Sara gave me a whole new appreciation for home. I'll get my own place, and I'm hoping to eventually work full-time with Paul and save enough to buy half the garage. He and I work well together."

"Sounds like you have it all planned out."

"In my head, anyway." He smiled. "Not the most exciting life, but I'm going to give it a go."

"I think it sounds great, living near your family and doing something you love. I'd take simple small town life over the city any day."

He gave me an appraising look. "I guess you can paint anywhere, if that's what you plan to do for a living."

"I hope to." I didn't mention that I had enough funds in my bank account to live off for many years as long as I didn't live too extravagantly.

"Do you plan to stay in New Hastings then?" he asked as he picked up his second burger.

"At least until I finish high school. Sara said I can use her apartment as long as I want, so I don't have to decide right away. She tells me I might feel differently about this place after I've survived my first winter."

He let out a laugh. "I admit, New Hastings doesn't have a lot to do in winter, unless you like the outdoors and don't mind snow."

"I love snow. I'll need to buy some really thick coats, though."

"And a good car that handles well in winter."

I sipped my drink. "You just want to go car shopping with me."

"Guilty." He didn't try to hide his grin.

By the time I finished my burger and half my fries, he'd cleaned his plate. I think I got full just watching how much he put away. When he eyed my plate, I chuckled and pushed it toward him.

"Now, how about one of those ice cream floats?" he asked when he was done eating the rest of my fries.

I gaped at him. "You can seriously eat something else after all that?"

"Yes, and technically, it's a drink."

"Smartass," I retorted, surprised by how much I was enjoying our day together. "I'll try one, but you'll probably have to finish it for me."

"Deal." He looked around for our waitress, who was nowhere in sight.

His phone vibrated, and he looked down at the screen. Chuckling, he held up the phone so I could see the text from his cousin Paul.

I'm up to my elbows in grease while you're spending the day with a pretty girl. We need to rethink this business arrangement.

I toyed with my napkin. "I hope I'm not keeping you away from your work."

"No. Paul always jokes around like that." He typed a reply and laid the phone down. It immediately rang, and this time his brow furrowed when he saw the caller.

"One sec," he said apologetically. "It's Maxwell. I need to take this."

"Go ahead. I'll order our floats. What flavor do you want?"

"Chocolate."

He answered the phone as he stood and walked a short distance away. It must be pack business if the Alpha was calling him.

I flagged down our waitress and ordered two chocolate floats to go. As soon as she walked away, my own phone let me know I had a text message. It was from Scott.

Hey. Feel like hanging out tonight?

Scott and I hadn't seen each other outside of the diner since our outing, but we'd become good friends at work. I helped him in the kitchen whenever the restaurant got slow, and I enjoyed talking to him.

Doing what? I texted back.

Party at the lighthouse. Nothing crazy. Bonfire and music.

I bit my lip because I wasn't exactly a party animal. But I had fun with

Scott, and it might be nice to do something on a Saturday night other than painting. Besides, I didn't have to stay if I didn't like it.

Sure. What time?

Great! Pick you up around 8?

I almost said yes, but I decided it might be better if I took the scooter. That way it would be less like a date and I could leave whenever I wanted.

I'll meet you there, I said.

LOL. You love that Vespa, don't you?

Yep.

Ok. See you there.

I laid my phone on the table, amazed at how far I'd come in the weeks since I'd moved here. My first day in New Hastings, I'd been afraid to leave the apartment and terrified of werewolves. Now I was spending the day with a werewolf and planning to go to a party tonight.

I looked for Roland, who had strolled away from the table, and I spotted him standing a dozen yards away, still talking on his phone. His muscled form looked good in the shirt and jeans he wore, and the sun added warm highlights to his short, black hair. He made a striking figure, and yet he seemed oblivious to the women and teenage girls checking him out as they passed by.

My gaze wandered over the surrounding stores and landed on a small coffee shop across the street with a few tables out front. At one of the tables, the lone occupant drew my eye. There was nothing special about the thirtysomething bald man sipping his coffee, except for the object of his attention. Me.

9

Emma

The hair on the back of my neck stood up at the intensity of the man's stare, and I looked away from him. He wasn't familiar, but there was a hint of recognition in his expression that unnerved me.

A cold lump formed in my stomach. I'd betrayed a lot of vampires in Vegas and some who worked for Eli, and I had a deep-seated fear that one of them would find me and make me pay. Or worse, make me one of them again. I would die before I went through that hell again.

My heart began to race and sweat broke out on my brow as the edges of my vision blurred. I gripped the edge of the table and forced myself to calm down. *Look at him. He's sitting in the sun. He's just a man.*

I picked up my phone with trembling hands and pretended to play with it while I peeked at the man, who was now writing something in a small note-book. I took the opportunity to study him and found nothing out of the ordinary. He wore dark-blue pants, brown loafers, and a lighter blue button-up shirt – not exactly the attire of a criminal. He probably worked at one of these stores and was having his coffee break.

I let out a puff of air, feeling ridiculous for overreacting. Maybe I hadn't come as far in my recovery as I'd thought.

The waitress brought our ice cream floats and the bill. I handed her some cash and told her to keep the change. I figured the least I could do was pay for Roland's lunch after he'd driven me around Portland and lugged my purchases to the car.

I shivered when I felt eyes on me again, and I looked up, my gaze once again meeting that of the strange man. This time, there was no doubt he was interested in me. He wasn't a vampire, but they weren't the only predators who would single out a teenage girl.

He stood, and fear shot through me, even though I was in the middle of a busy shopping district and surrounded by people. For a moment, I forgot to breathe as I watched him to see what he would do.

"Sorry about that." Roland sat across from me, blocking my view of the man. He pulled his chocolate float toward him. "Just in time. Have you tried yours yet?"

I blinked, surprised by his sudden return. "I..."

He frowned and leaned forward. "Are you okay? You look pale."

Behind him, the coffee shop table was empty and the man was nowhere in sight. I forced my gaze back to Roland's and attempted a smile.

"It's nothing. I...drank too fast and got brain freeze." It was a lame excuse, but the only one I could come up with. I hoped he didn't notice that I hadn't touched my float yet.

He smiled. "That'll do it."

I took a sip of my drink. It was delicious, but my stomach had too many knots in it to handle something so rich. I had no idea what the man would have done if Roland hadn't been here, and my imagination conjured all kinds of horrible scenarios.

For so many years, I'd been the hunter and humans were the prey. Now I felt weak and vulnerable, and it terrified me.

Roland

"You don't like it?" I asked Emma, who'd barely touched her drink. She'd gone quiet all of a sudden, making me wonder what could have happened in the five minutes I was away.

"It's delicious. I'm just full." She smiled, but it seemed forced.

"So, what do you want to do now?" I asked. Maybe I could show her the sights and cheer her up again.

She pushed her drink away. "Would you be upset if I asked to go home? I feel a headache coming on."

"No, of course not." I studied her face, noting that she really did look ill. "Let me find our waitress and pay the bill, and then we'll go."

"I took care of it already." She picked up her phone and bag that lay on the table beside her.

"You didn't have to do that." I'd wanted to pay for her meal, and it bothered me that I couldn't.

"I wanted to. You've been so nice, taking me to those art stores. It's the least I could do."

I followed her out into the street. "Okay, but you don't have to pay me back for stuff like that. Besides, I had a good time."

She looked at me over her shoulder. "I did, too."

Emma was quieter on the drive back to New Hastings, and I couldn't stop wondering what had happened to her. I didn't believe her story about getting brain freeze. Something had upset her while I was on the phone. I'd seen her using her phone. Had she gotten a distressing call or message? There was so much I didn't know about her, and I doubted she'd tell me what was really wrong if I asked.

The closer we got to home, the more she seemed at ease. We talked about school and our jobs and laughed over a funny text from Jordan. It surprised me to discover she and Jordan were so close because Jordan was a bit prickly with people. I shared some of my Jordan stories with Emma, who got a kick out of hearing about our adventures.

"She gave you her car?"

I nodded. "Of course, she made a point to tell me not to get dog hair all over the seats."

Emma burst out laughing. "That sounds exactly like something she'd say."

I hadn't realized how much her withdrawal had bothered me until I heard her laugh again. I felt my wolf's relief, too. Neither of us liked seeing her upset.

"You look better. How's your head?" I asked as we pulled up to her place. Her face was flushed from laughing, and her eyes were warm and happy.

She unhooked her seat belt. "I'm much better. No more headache."

"Good." I reached for my door. "You go unlock the door, and I'll get your stuff out of the back."

"You can't carry all that by yourself."

I gave her a playful glare. "Are you questioning my manly ability to carry a girl's shopping bags?"

She shook her head dramatically. "Never!"

"I didn't think so."

I grinned and got out of the car, lifting my seat forward to reach her purchases. My arms loaded up with canvases and bags, I carried the lot up to the apartment and set it down in the hallway. Emma started taking it up to the studio while I went back to the car for the second load.

My phone buzzed when I reached the car. It was a text from Pete.

You going to the party tonight?

I groaned. Another party? There was no end to it. **Not if I can help it.**

He sent a smiley face. **Not a pack party. Lighthouse party.**

I used to know where all the good parties were. Lately, I'd been so caught up in pack business I had no idea what was going on in the social scene anymore. I hadn't been to a party at the lighthouse since the night Sara, Pete, and I were attacked by a pack of crocotta on the way home. Not one of my fondest memories. Still, it would be nice to see some of my old friends away from all the craziness.

Sounds good. Shannon coming, too?

He and Shannon had been seeing each other since the last party. I was just waiting for him to tell me he'd imprinted. He looked happy and willing, so I hoped he got the girl he wanted, though I was going to miss hanging with him. We'd still see each other, but male wolves settled down when they mated. Another reason I was in no hurry for a mate.

Yes.

We driving together? I asked.

No. Doing dinner first. Meet you there?

Ok.

I grabbed the rest of the bags and took them inside. I heard Emma moving around upstairs, so I carried the bags up to the loft.

"Thanks." She hurried over to take one from me. "I think I went a little crazy with the shopping."

I followed her and set the bags on the floor. "You have enough supplies here to paint all of New Hastings."

She laughed. "I think you're right. Thanks again for everything. I had a great time today."

"I did, too," I said, not wanting our day to be over yet. "Since you're feeling better, would you like to go to a party tonight?"

Her eyes widened. "The lighthouse party?"

It was my turn to be surprised. "You know about that?"

"Scott texted me about it when we were in Portland. I didn't know you were going, too."

"Pete just told me about it."

"I'm meeting Scott there at eight," she said. "What time are you planning to go?"

"He's not picking you up?" My gut hardened at the thought of her with

Scott Foley, of all people. He might be a different person now, but I found it hard to forget the old Scott.

"He offered, but I wanted to drive myself. It's not a date, and I wanted to be able to leave without pulling him away from the party. I'm not really a party person." She toyed with one of the new brushes she'd laid on her worktable. "I'm glad you're going."

I wasn't sure what pleased me more: her not going on a date with Scott or her saying she was glad I'd be there.

"I should be there around eight. I can pick you up if you'd like. I'll bring you home if you want to leave."

She smiled. "Thanks, but I like riding the Vespa."

"I guess I'll see you there." I chuckled as a thought occurred to me. "You know, Sara doesn't like parties either. Are you sure you two aren't really sisters?"

The sadness that flashed in her eyes took me aback, and I wondered what I'd said to cause it.

"No, but I love her like one," she said softly. She set the brush aside. "Would you like something to drink?"

I almost said yes, but I needed to get to the garage if I wanted to go to the party tonight. I'd planned to work on the Chevelle this evening before I'd heard about the party.

"Thanks, but I should get going. Have to get a few hours in on the Chevelle before tonight."

"Let me get your mother's dishes for you before you go."

I followed her to the kitchen. "Did you like the shepherd's pie?"

"It was delicious, and so was the apple pie." She picked up the casserole dish and pie plate from the counter and gave them to me. "Please, tell your mother and grandmother I really enjoyed them. I don't get to eat much home-cooked food."

I snickered. "As soon as I tell them that, they'll be on the phone asking you to dinner."

"I'm...not sure I'm ready for that." She swallowed then rushed to say, "I don't mean meeting your family. I mean being around so many..."

"Werewolves?" I asked gently, seeing her discomfort. She nodded, and I gave her a reassuring smile. "It's nothing for you to feel bad about. You and I are good though, right?"

Her face brightened. "Yes."

"Good." My chest warmed with pleasure, and I had a sudden urge to hug her – and not as a friend. My breath quickened when I remembered her soft body pressed against mine on the scooter a few days ago.

I left before I did something that ruined our new friendship. I liked Emma too much to get involved with her, knowing it couldn't go anywhere. It wouldn't be fair to either of us. Not that she'd want a werewolf anyway.

I sighed bitterly as I walked down the steps to my car. It figured that I'd finally start to fall for someone and I could never have her.

————————

It was close to nine when I pulled into the parking lot by the lighthouse, and I sat in the car for a minute before I turned it off and got out. I wasn't sure I should be around Emma so soon after admitting to myself that I wanted her as more than a friend. But she was expecting me to be here, and I wouldn't let her down.

Pocketing my keys and phone, I scanned the crowd for Emma as I walked toward Dylan's white van, which was blaring music through two large speakers. I didn't spot Emma, but I'd seen her Vespa in the parking lot so I knew she was here somewhere.

"Roland! Wasn't sure if you'd be here." Dylan waved me over. "Haven't seen you around much lately."

I joined him near the van. There was no sign of his bandmates in the group of people with him, but I saw a lot of familiar faces.

"Been busy. Working at the lumberyard and Paul's garage now."

"I heard. Pete told me you finished the Mustang. You driving it tonight?"

I pulled out my keys and dangled them from my finger. "What do you think?"

His eyes lit with interest. "Let's go. I want to see it."

He and a few of the other guys followed me to the parking lot, where they spent a few minutes oohing and aahing over the Mustang. I answered all their questions and laughingly turned them down when some of them asked to take her for a spin.

"You want a beer?" Dylan asked when we went back to the van.

"Can't. Driving." I looked at the glow from a fire down on the beach. "I'm going to walk around and see who's here."

I spotted Pete as soon as I walked away from the van. He and Shannon were leaning against the lighthouse, making out. A year ago, that would have been me with one of the many girls I'd dated. I had a two-date rule when it came to girls, and I'd certainly made the most of my time with them. Just because I couldn't get attached to them didn't mean we both couldn't have fun.

Leaving Pete and Shannon to their business, I continued to the edge of the bluff overlooking the beach. Below, a large fire blazed, surrounded by about a dozen people. I found Emma, sitting on a log with Scott, and my jaw clenched at seeing them together. I couldn't have her, but I didn't want her with him either. The fact that it was none of my business who she dated didn't even enter into it.

I took the path to the beach and walked over to the fire. People I knew called out to me, and Emma smiled when she saw me.

"You made it." She shifted closer to Scott and patted the log on her other side. "You want to sit with us?"

"Sure." I took the offered seat and immediately regretted it when my arm brushed hers, sending heat through me. It probably wasn't a good idea to sit so close to her, feeling as I did, but I stayed.

I looked at the guy on her other side. "Scott."

"Roland." He eyed me warily, no surprise considering our history.

Emma looked at me, and I smiled to let her know we were good.

"Did you get your work done on the Chevelle?" she asked me.

"Most of it. I'll probably spend tomorrow at the garage."

Scott's eyes widened with interest. "You're working on a Chevelle? Didn't you just finish the Mustang?"

I nodded. "The Chevelle isn't mine. It's for a guy Paul knows in Portland. He's paying us to restore it for him."

"Sweet. What year?"

"Seventy."

He let out a low whistle. "Bet she'll be something when you're done. That's one job I'd take over working in the diner. No offense, Emma."

"None taken."

I don't know if he or I was more shocked when I said, "Drop by the garage sometime to see what we're doing with her."

His smile was probably the first real one he'd ever given me. "I might do that. Thanks."

Pete and Shannon chose that moment to join us. He gave me a questioning look when he saw me sitting with Scott, and then he introduced Shannon to Emma and Scott.

"Nice to meet you." Shannon held out a hand, and I was glad to see Emma take it without hesitation. Did she think Shannon was human, or was she becoming more comfortable around us?

I stood. "Shannon, have a seat."

She flashed me a grateful smile and sat beside Emma, who didn't even flinch.

"Are you from here?" Emma asked her.

"My parents and I are visiting for a few weeks," Shannon replied. "We're staying out in the Knolls."

Emma's eyes met mine, and I saw the realization dawn in hers. I gave her a small nod, hoping she wouldn't be spooked by being in the company of three werewolves. She looked a little tense for a moment before she relaxed again.

"Emma moved here a few weeks ago," Pete told Shannon.

"Don't you just love it here?" Shannon asked Emma. "I'm from Buxton, and I love coming to the ocean."

A strong breeze off the water made the fire dance crazily and tossed the girls' hair around.

Emma rubbed her arms. "I do love it, but I need to remember to bring a sweater with me next time."

"I think I have one in my car," Scott said. "I'll get it for you."

Before he could stand, I pulled off my light sweater and handed it to Emma. "Here."

She took the sweater. "Won't you be cold in just a T-shirt?"

"I'm pretty warm-blooded." I gave her a secret smile.

She stood to put on the sweater, and it was impossible not to stare when she raised her arms over her head and her shirt rode up, flashing her bare stomach. Luckily, Pete poked me with his elbow to snap me out of it before she caught me ogling her.

"Better?" I asked her when she sat again.

"Much better." She laughed softly. "Although, this is probably long enough for me to sleep in."

The image of her in bed, wearing nothing but my sweater, flashed in my mind and sent heat straight to my belly.

Fuck. Don't think about that. All I needed was to give her a full salute in front of everyone. Emma would probably never look at me again.

"I think I'll go grab a Coke," I said, deciding distance was the answer to my problem. "Emma, Shannon, you want one?"

Shannon held up a bottle of water. "I'm good, thanks."

"I'll have one," Emma said. "Would you like me to go with you?"

"You stay here by the fire where it's warm. I'll be back soon."

I fled before she could decide to come with me after all. It wasn't until I was almost to Dylan's van that Pete caught up with me.

"What's up with you and Emma?"

"Nothing."

He snorted. "You were staring at her like she's something to eat. If I didn't know better, I'd say you had the hots for her."

I scowled at him. "She's beautiful. Any guy would stare at her."

"Yeah, but she's also Sara's cousin. You can't mess around with her like you do with other human girls."

"I know that," I shot back. "Why do you think I left just now?"

He held up his hands. "Whoa. Don't chew my head off."

"Sorry, man." I raked a hand through my hair. "I know Emma's off-limits, and I'm not going to do anything to hurt her. We're friends."

"Hate to break it to you, but you don't look at her like a friend."

I groaned. "Shit. Do you think she noticed?"

"I don't think so, but I don't know her well enough to say for sure." His eyes narrowed. "I know you've been to see Emma a few times since she moved here, but I didn't think you were interested in her. I've never seen you get worked up over a girl like this. Did something happen today?"

I rubbed my face. "I'm not sure when it started. I think it was that first night I went to her place after Lex and Julie scared her. All we did was talk. Nothing happened today either. I always thought she was pretty, but the more I get to know her, the more I like her."

"Ah, man. That's..."

"That's life. She's human and not for me. Unless you know a way to stop my wolf from imprinting, I'm out of luck." I stared at the sparks flying from the fire that was out of my sight. "She probably wouldn't want a werewolf anyway, so it's a moot point."

"I don't know. She looks happy around you."

"Not helping, Pete."

"Sorry." He waved at the van. "You should get her Coke and go back before she thinks you ran off."

We started toward the van when a group of people walked up from the parking lot. I swore softly when I recognized Lex, Julie, and a redhead named April with Paul and Dell. What the hell were they doing here? My night had just gone from bad to worse.

Pete put a hand on my shoulder. "You know, maybe this is a good thing. You haven't tried to get to know any of them. You might like them if you gave them a chance like I did with Shannon."

I stared at him. "Did you miss the part where I said I didn't want a mate yet?"

He shrugged. "Listen, your wolf will choose, whether it's now or in five years, and chances are, it'll be one of the females you meet this summer. Who knows, you might even hit it off with one of them."

I shook my head. "They're too clingy, and they'd rather feel me up than have a real conversation."

Pete barked a laugh. "Did I just hear you complain about girls wanting to make out instead of talking to you? Hold on; let me get out my phone so you can say that again. Sara won't want to miss this."

"You know what I mean, smartass. Half of them only want me because I'm the Alpha's nephew. They think having sex will make my wolf choose them."

"Then talk to the other half. They're not all like that."

"Roland!"

I hid my grimace as Lex locked on us like a heat-seeking missile. The other girls trailed her, followed by Paul and Dell. Paul gave me an apologetic look from behind their backs, telling me that coming here hadn't been his idea.

"We wondered where you two had gotten to tonight," said Lex, who was stunning in a short, flared, blue dress that showed off her long legs. Dell was practically drooling over her, and I saw more than one guy following her with their eyes. The other girls were dressed similarly, all looking like they were dressed for a night club instead of a beach party.

"We were going to Portland, but the girls heard about the party and wanted to check it out," Paul explained.

Lex pouted at me. "I thought you were working tonight."

"I was supposed to, but I thought I'd catch up with some of my old friends."

I stuck my hands in my pockets, annoyed that I had to explain myself to them. This was yet another reason I didn't want a mate. I liked my freedom and not having to check in with someone all the time.

"Where's Shannon tonight, Peter?" Julie asked, a note of jealousy in her voice.

"She's down by the fire. We were just about to go back to them."

Lex's eyes narrowed. "Them?"

"Our human friends," I said in a low voice, suddenly worried about Emma. She was still nervous about werewolves, and Lex and Julie had already frightened her once. The possessive glint in Lex's eyes made me not want to let the aggressive female wolf anywhere near Emma.

Lex smiled again. "Oh, I'd love to meet some of your friends. I might be living here myself one of these days."

Not if there's a God, I thought unhappily.

I pointed at their feet. "I don't think you can walk down there in those heels."

"No problem." Lex kicked hers off and picked them up. "I like to go bare."

The other girls followed suit, and I knew there was no way to keep them away from the fire and Emma.

"Let me grab some Cokes, and we'll head down," I said reluctantly.

I led the way to the rough path to the beach, and the girls descended ahead of me. Paul and I were the last to go.

"I'm sorry, Roland. I tried to get them to go to Portland."

"No need to explain. I know how determined Lex can be."

I followed the others and caught up to them before they reached the fire. Lex and Julie's eyes widened in recognition when they saw Emma, but they didn't say anything. She didn't know them because they'd been in wolf form the last time she saw them.

I made the introductions, and the moment I said the girls were visiting for a few weeks, fear flickered in Emma's eyes. I could see she was becoming overwhelmed being surrounded by werewolves, but I couldn't go to her without drawing attention. I caught her eye and smiled to let her know she was safe.

"So, you and Roland went to school together?" Julie asked Scott. "You must have some good stories about him."

"Roland and I never hung out much in school," he said.

"How about you, Emma? How well do you know our Roland?" Lex asked Emma, placing her hand on my arm in a clear display of ownership that annoyed the hell out of me. I wanted to push it off, but I didn't want to make a scene.

"We met a month ago," Emma replied.

Lex put a finger to her lips. "You look awfully familiar. Have we run into each other before?"

Emma's brow furrowed. "I don't think so."

Julie snickered, and I growled just loud enough for her and Lex to hear. They were walking on thin ice, and this time they wouldn't get off with a mild scolding.

Lex stiffened, and Julie cast a nervous glance at me. Message delivered.

"How long will you all be in town?" Emma asked politely, though I saw she was still uneasy.

"I'm here until the end of August," said April, one of the nice ones Pete had mentioned. "Maybe we could get together sometime."

"I...sure."

"Great!" April gave Emma a friendly smile, earning her points in my book. "Do you like espresso? I can't get enough of it."

Emma returned her smile, looking more comfortable. "I love it."

Haven

Shannon piped in. "Peter took me to a place called The Hub. We should go there. The coffee was amazing."

"How about tomorrow?" April asked.

Emma shook her head. "I'm working tomorrow. Monday?"

Shannon grinned. "It's a date."

April looked down at her black dress and sighed. "I'm all dressed up to party, and we're just standing around the fire. Who wants to dance?"

"I'll dance with you." Paul stepped forward to take her hand. "Let's go."

Pete held out a hand to Shannon. "You up for a dance?"

"You bet." She took his hand, and he pulled her to her feet.

Scott nudged Emma with his arm. "You want to show them how us diner folks dance?"

She nodded, and he helped her up, sending another stab of jealousy through me because he had the freedom to do what I couldn't.

"Excuse me," Emma said to Lex as she moved around her.

Lex inhaled sharply, and her grip tightened on my arm. "Why are you wearing Roland's sweater?"

Emma recoiled at the bite in Lex's tone. "I was cold, and he loaned it to me."

"You don't look cold now," Lex stated frostily.

"No." Emma's gaze flicked to me, and she pulled the sweater off before I could say anything. She held it out to me. "Thanks."

I took it, and she left with Scott without giving me another look. Lex watched her go with a calculating gleam in her eyes.

"Don't," I warned as anger simmered in me. "You frighten her again and I'll drag you to Maxwell myself."

She pulled away to glare at me. "You are very defensive of the human. What is she to you?"

I crossed my arms. "First of all, that human is my friend. Second, I told you last time she is under my protection."

"Why?" Her eyes widened. "Are you seeing her?"

"I told you we're friends." I stepped back to pull on my sweater and got a lungful of Emma's alluring scent.

"I don't believe you."

My patience snapped. "I don't care what you believe."

I started toward the path, and she caught my sleeve, her voice soft and wheedling.

"I'm sorry. It's just that I really like you, Roland, and I think we could have something special if you gave us a chance. You have to mate one of us, so why not make sure it's someone you want?"

I almost laughed at her suggestion that I could want someone like her. I'd seen the real Lex, and she wasn't fooling me or my wolf with her false sweetness. I couldn't have Emma, but there was no way in hell this malicious female would ever have me.

"Stay away from Emma."

I jerked out of her grasp and strode away from her, regretting my decision to come here tonight. The truth was that if I hadn't known Emma would be here, I'd still be at the garage. And Emma wouldn't be sucked into this mess.

At the top of the bluff, I spotted Emma and the others dancing. Emma's face was flushed and she was laughing at Dell, who was doing his robot dance. She looked happy.

Instead of joining them, I walked toward a small utility shed at the edge of the woods. Leaning against the shed, I watched Emma and came to a decision. Being around her, feeling how I did, was not good for either of us, and it was in her best interest if I stayed away from her. She seemed to have no trouble making friends, so she wouldn't be alone.

My wolf growled unhappily, but what other choice did I have? I was feeling things for Emma that I'd never felt for anyone else, and it was already hard to stay away from her. Better I ended this before it started and saved us both the pain that would come later. At least this way, I was the only one getting hurt.

The dance ended, and Emma, Shannon, and April started dancing together. I didn't know where Lex and Julie were, and I didn't care as long as they heeded my warning to stay away from Emma.

Paul walked over to join me. "Why are you off by yourself? I thought you used to be the life of the party."

"Don't feel much like partying these days." I looked over at him. "What about you? I can't remember the last time you went to a night club."

He sighed and watched the dancing. "I'm twenty-five and unmated. If I'm going to find a mate, it won't be under a car in my garage."

I snorted. "You really want to imprint on someone like Lex?"

"No, but April is great and Julie's nice when she's not with Lex. Besides, I don't think Lex will settle for anyone but you."

"Then she'd better learn to like disappointment." I'd tolerated her attentions until tonight, but no more. If my wolf truly knew my heart, he would not choose someone I could barely stand.

The music changed again, and I watched Dell take Emma by the hand and twirl her around. Normally, his goofy antics got a good laugh out of me, but not this time. When he pulled her close and leaned down to say something to her, my jaw clenched.

Lex and Julie joined the dancers, and I saw them send a few venomous looks at Emma, who seemed oblivious. My body tensed, expecting one of them to bump into her on purpose. Even in their human form, female wolves were stronger than human females, and they could easily hurt her. If they did, I'd –

"Damn, Roland, why didn't you tell me?" Paul's voice was full of shock.

I shot him a sideways look. "Tell you what?"

He backed away, rubbing his nose. "Phew, man, you reek of it."

"What?"

"The bonding scent. I guess it's true that you can't smell your own." He looked toward the lighthouse. "Which one is it?"

"Which one –?" My stomach lurched as the meaning of his words hit me.

No. No way! This is not happening.

But it was.

My wolf had imprinted.

10

Roland

"Who is it?" Paul asked again. "I know it's not Lex after what you just said. It's April, isn't it?"

"I..." My lungs squeezed, and I had trouble drawing a breath. I heard Paul say something, but it sounded muddled.

Next thing I knew, Paul was in my face, his eyes worried. "You okay, man? You look kind of out of it."

"I-I'm fine," I rasped, my mind still reeling. Imprinted. My wolf had imprinted. How could he have chosen one of these females? Two I couldn't stand and two I barely knew. What had happened to him knowing my heart? My heart didn't want any of them.

I couldn't look at them. As soon as I saw her I'd know, and I wanted to delay the inevitable as long as possible. Mated males said that when you saw your mate for the first time after the imprint, she was more beautiful than anyone you'd ever seen, and you felt the irresistible urge to mark her. Everyone's scent was unique, and it told all other males that she was yours.

"You sure?" Paul asked.

"Yeah. I..." Paul and I had always been close, and I could tell him anything. But I was finding it extremely hard to talk. "I don't know."

"Don't know what?"

My eyes met his again. "I don't know who."

His mouth fell open, and his eyes grew round. "You mean it just happened and you have no idea who she is?"

I nodded helplessly.

"Ah, hell, man." His eyes turned sympathetic, and he looked at the partiers. "You have to find out who it is. You know there's no sense putting it off."

"I know." There were only four unmated females here. It wouldn't take long to find her.

Dread twisted my gut as a new thought occurred to me. What if it was Shannon? Pete hadn't imprinted on her yet, but he was crazy about her. It would kill him if my wolf chose the girl he wanted for his mate.

I turned slowly to face the party. Adrenaline coursed through my body, but it wasn't from excitement. Life as I knew it was over, and I felt sick. The last time I was this miserable was when I thought Sara had died. She'd come back. There was no coming back from this for me.

The first one I saw was Julie, who danced with Pete. I held my breath as my eyes moved over her face. Nothing. I felt nothing for her. I let out my breath and moved on.

I located April and Shannon next, dancing together. My chest tightened as I looked at Shannon, expecting the worst. My relief when I knew it wasn't her was so enormous that my legs felt weak. I liked Shannon, and if she wasn't Pete's girl, I'd rather it was her than any of the others. For both their sakes, I was happy it wasn't her.

My gaze shifted to April. She was pretty and she seemed sweet, so I could make that work. But I felt nothing when I looked at her.

That left...Lex.

The bottom dropped from my stomach. *God, no. You would not do that to me.*

I searched the crowd for her, trying to understand how my wolf could have imprinted on her of all people. She was beautiful and sexy, yes, but she was also manipulative, power hungry, and a bully. I couldn't see myself spending a whole day with her, let alone my whole life.

I found her near the lighthouse, talking to Dell, and I tried in vain to mentally prepare myself for what was about to happen. Taking a deep breath, I focused on her face and waited.

And waited.

And...nothing.

My heart raced as elation filled me. *Thank you, Jesus.*

The euphoria lasted all of five seconds. If it wasn't Lex, then who was it? Was there another female wolf here?

"It's none of them. Are you sure you smelled bonding scent?" I asked hopefully.

"I have half a dozen friends who've bonded." There was no mistaking the envy in his voice. "Trust me. I know a bonding scent when I smell it."

"I don't get it. I'm supposed to know who it is as soon as I look at her." I scanned the crowd again. "Did anyone else come with you guys?"

"No, it was just the five of us. Look again. It has to be one of them."

"What do you think I'm doing?" I said through gritted teeth.

I looked at Lex first this time, wanting to get it over with. I let out a deep breath when I still felt nothing for her. My gaze moved over Shannon, April, and Julie with the same result.

A couple walking toward the bluff drew my eye away from the main crowd. It was Emma and Scott. He said something, and they both laughed. A strong wind tossed her hair, and she reached up to grab it as she turned toward me.

Warmth infused my entire body, and I stared, transfixed, at her flawless skin and delicate features. How was it possible for her to grow more beautiful every time I saw her? She was perfect, and I couldn't look away from her if I tried.

Scott reached up to brush her hair from her face, and a growl rumbled from my chest. How dare he touch her? Emma was mine.

Need coursed through me. Not desire, but something fierce and bestial that almost consumed me. It was my wolf, pushing to get out, wanting to go to Emma and cover her in his scent. To let the male beside her know she was ours.

Our mate.

"That's not possible." I staggered backward and almost tripped over my own feet.

Paul reached out to steady me. "What's wrong?"

"It can't be her." I stared at Emma. Werewolves imprinted on other werewolves, not humans. I was into her, and the idea of imprinting on one of the female wolves freaked me out so much that I'd made myself believe my wolf had chosen her. I felt a sharp pang of disappointment as the hope of being with someone I actually wanted shattered.

"It's Lex, isn't it?" Paul asked sympathetically.

I looked at him, and the second my eyes left Emma, my wolf quieted and the warmth left my body, proof I'd been fooled by my own wishful thinking. If I'd really imprinted on Emma, I should still be overcome by the need to mark her with my scent.

"Roland?"

I shook my head to clear it. "This is messed up."

"You still don't know who you've imprinted on?" he asked incredulously.

"I looked at them twice, and I felt nothing. And then I looked at..."

"Looked at who?" He frowned. "You're not making any sense, Cuz."

I stepped around him and took a fortifying breath as my eyes found Shannon, April, Lex, and Julie, one more time. Again, I felt nothing and my wolf showed no interest in them.

My gaze went to Emma and Scott at the top of the path to the beach. I could only see her profile, but it was enough to send my wolf into a frenzy. My canines elongated, and my skin felt stretched too tight as heat spread through me again.

"Mate," I growled as Emma disappeared from view.

"Jesus, Roland! You're starting to shift." Paul grabbed me by the arms. "What the hell is wrong with you?"

The alarm in his voice brought me back to my senses, and I stared at him in horror when I touched my face, which was partially covered in fur. I forced my body back to its human form and tried not to think of how close I'd come to exposing us to a bunch of humans.

Paul released me and let out a loud breath. "Well, that answers your question about whether or not you've imprinted. Your timing could have been a bit better, though."

I rubbed my face with my hands, trying to process what my heart and wolf were telling me. How could my wolf have imprinted on a human? Without her own wolf, she could never be a true mate. Could she?

"Paul, this is going to sound crazy, but have you ever heard of a wolf choosing a human mate?"

He started to laugh but quieted when he realized I wasn't laughing, too.

"Is that even possible?" he asked.

"It must be." I met his confused stare. "Because I just imprinted on Emma Grey."

He gawked at me. "You're joking."

"You really think I'd joke about something like this?" I let out a shuddering breath because I was still struggling with the need to go to her.

"Roland, think about it. Even if Emma was a wolf, you couldn't imprint on her in human form. You would have had to be with her in your wolf form at least once for the imprint to take."

"I have been. Twice," I said hoarsely as it finally hit me why my wolf had been drawn to her. It wasn't because she was Sara's cousin. It was because he knew she was his mate.

Paul stared at me. "Holy fuck."

I sagged against the shed. "Yeah, that about sums it up."

Emma

"Are you sure you don't want me to get a sweater for you?" Scott asked as we sat beside the fire again. "I should have told you it can get cool up here at night."

"I'm good. It's a lot warmer in this spot."

We were sitting with our backs to the bluff and the fire in front of us. It was sheltered from the wind and quite cozy. I probably would have been too warm if I'd still been wearing Roland's sweater.

I thought about Roland and his odd behavior tonight. He'd seemed okay when he got here. As soon as he'd given me his sweater, he'd left in a hurry and come back with all those other werewolves. He hadn't looked happy to have them join us, and I could tell he'd been angry when his girlfriend asked me about his sweater.

And why had he never mentioned he had a girlfriend? It wasn't like he and I were involved or anything, but you'd think a girlfriend would come up in conversation. She didn't seem like his type, but then, what did I know about werewolf relationships?

And then, we'd all gone up to dance and Roland had disappeared again. No one else seemed to think anything of it, except Lex who'd looked angry. I caught her glaring at me a few times while we were all dancing, and I'd tried not to let her get to me. If she'd been human, I'd just ignore her. But an angry, jealous werewolf was another matter. I'd been ready to bow out and head home when Scott asked me to come back to the fire.

"You don't have to sit with me all night, you know," I said to him.

He smiled. "I like sitting with you."

I rolled my eyes. "Yes, because I'm *so* exciting."

"And pretty and mysterious. Hanging with you is good for my image."

He laughed, and I poked him in the side. "Just for that, you can wash the pots by yourself tomorrow, Mr. Foley."

"Washing pots. How the mighty have fallen," joked a newcomer.

Scott jumped to his feet. "Ryan! What are you doing here, man? I thought you were staying in New York until the end of the month."

The blond boy made a face. "The water main broke in our building, and it won't be fixed until Tuesday. Uncle Jack told me to take a few days off and come home until then."

Scott slapped his back. "Glad you're here. I want you to meet Emma Grey.

She moved here a few weeks ago, and she works with me at the diner. Emma, this is Ryan."

Ryan smiled and held out his hand. "Hi. Are you any relation to Sara Grey?"

"She's my cousin. I'm staying at her apartment."

He smirked and pointed a thumb at Scott. "And the only person you could find to hang out with is this loser?"

I shrugged. "He has some redeeming qualities."

"Some?" Scott shook his head. "Just for that, Miss Grey, I'm not letting you help me wash the pots tomorrow."

"Ah, man, you have to work tomorrow?" Ryan's smile fell away. "I was hoping we could take the boat out."

"Some of us don't have fancy nine-to-five jobs for the summer," Scott ribbed good-naturedly.

Ryan laughed. "Yeah, it's real fancy working the mailroom and getting lunch for the execs."

I felt bad that Scott couldn't spend tomorrow with his friend, and if I hadn't already been scheduled I would have offered to take his shift for him.

I stood and smiled at them. "I've been sitting down here most of the night. I'm going to walk around a bit."

"You want me to come with you?" Scott asked.

"No. You stay and catch up with Ryan. I'm going to leave soon anyway. I'll see you tomorrow." I looked at Ryan. "It was nice to meet you."

"You, too."

I left them and went to stand by the lighthouse. Away from the fire, it was a lot cooler, and I shivered in my thin top, making a mental note to keep a sweater in the storage compartment on the Vespa.

I walked around the building until I was out of the wind. The only problem was it took me to the far side, away from everyone else. It was dark on this side, and I nearly tripped over some loose bricks on the ground. I smiled wryly. After three months as a human, I still felt clumsy in my own body sometimes. Vampires were agile, and they could see in the dark. But I'd take being a clumsy, flawed human over that any day.

I closed my eyes and listened to the waves, glad I'd come tonight. I'd spent every Saturday night since I moved here cooped up in the apartment, and I needed to get out more often. Although, I hadn't been expecting all those werewolves or that I'd be agreeing to go for coffee with two of them. I smiled. I'd surprised myself with that one.

"Emma, are you alright?"

I gasped and opened my eyes to stare at Roland, who stood several feet away. I hadn't even heard him arrive. "Roland, you scared me."

"Sorry." He stepped closer. "Why are you back here alone?"

His voice had a gruffness to it I hadn't heard before, and I wondered if it had something to do with his girlfriend. They'd looked like they were about to argue the last time I saw them.

None of my business. The last thing I needed was to be meddling in a were-wolf relationship.

"Just getting out of the wind," I said.

He reached for the bottom of his sweater. "Take my sweater again."

I held up a hand to stop him. "I'm good. I'm leaving soon anyway, and I don't want to upset your girlfriend again."

"My girlfriend?" I couldn't see his face, but I heard the derision in his voice. "Lex is not my girlfriend."

"Oh," I breathed, pleased even though it changed nothing for us.

He took another step toward me. "I'm sorry for her behavior earlier. She had no right to talk to you like that."

"You don't need to apologize. You didn't do anything wrong."

"I knew what she was like, and I should have kept her away from you," he said, sounding agitated. "I had no idea all those wolves would show up tonight. I didn't mean for you to be ambushed like that."

"That wasn't your fault. And most of them were nice." I peered through the darkness, wishing I could see his face to understand his strange mood. "I had a good time tonight."

"I'm glad."

Neither of us spoke for a minute, and I started to feel a little awkward. He wasn't acting like himself, and I was at a loss for what to say to him.

"I should go. I have to work tomorrow." It was a lame excuse since my shift didn't start until 11:00 a.m., but he didn't know that.

He was quiet for a moment before he nodded. "I'll walk you to the parking lot."

"You don't have to do that."

"I'm leaving, too. I have a long day in the garage tomorrow."

He stepped back to let me walk around him. Preoccupied, I forgot about the bricks on the ground and tripped. I let out a small cry as I fell.

In the next instant, I was in Roland's arms, my heart thumping and my face pressed against his chest. It took me a few seconds to recover and to notice several things. The first was how incredibly warm he was. I felt so toasty I didn't want to move.

Then there was his scent. It wasn't cologne; I'd never smelled cologne this good. It was woodsy and warm and tantalizing, and it made heat blossom in my stomach. Of course, that could also be because of the hard, male body I was pressed against or the warm hand at the small of my back.

I lifted my head, and he loosened his arms but didn't release me. I wasn't afraid. His hold was gentle, and I knew instinctively he would never hurt me. Not just because he was Sara's friend, but because he was a good person.

"Should have brought a flashlight," I joked. "Good thing you have fast reflexes."

His hand left my back, and my breath stuck in my throat when his fingers caressed my cheek, his thumb grazing the corner of my mouth. My heart began to race again when he cupped my chin and tilted my face up to his.

"Emma, I..." he said in a husky voice that sent a delicious tingle down my spine.

I opened my mouth, but I forgot what I was going to say when his head descended and his mouth covered mine. Shock quickly turned to pleasure as he gently kissed my bottom lip before moving to the top one. His movements were tender and deliberate, and my head was already spinning by the time he coaxed my lips open and began exploring my mouth with sensual slowness.

I clung to him, drowning in sensation. His arms trembled beneath my hands, and I felt the power in them and the hunger he held back as he kissed me until I could barely think straight. I'd been alone and afraid for so long, and in his arms, I felt safe and cherished. I lost myself in him, not wanting it to end.

I murmured in protest when his mouth left mine, and I moaned softly when his hot breath touched my ear and his lips moved down the side of my throat. He pulled me closer, and his chest vibrated as he growled in pleasure.

My eyes flew open as the spell surrounding us shattered. *What am I doing?*

Roland grew still as if he'd sensed the change in me. He lifted his head and looked down at me. I couldn't see his expression in the dark, but I knew he was confused by my sudden withdrawal.

"Emma?"

The breathless way he said my name sent a thrill through me. It would be so easy to pull him down to me and give myself up to the fire he'd ignited in me.

But then what? I liked Roland and I could see us together...if he was human. But he was a werewolf, and my heart couldn't handle falling in love, knowing there could be no future for us. And after that kiss, I knew I was already falling for him.

I'd seen his face and heard the loathing in his voice when he'd talked about vampires. If we started a relationship, I'd have to tell him about my past. And I'd watch his feelings for me turn to revulsion and hate. I'd rather have him as only a friend or nothing at all than to put both of us through that.

"I'm sorry. I-I can't," I whispered hoarsely, on the verge of tears. I pushed against his chest, and he let his arms drop, releasing me.

"What is it? What's wrong?" he asked, and my chest tightened at the confusion and hurt in his voice.

"It's not you." I winced at the cliché, but it was true. It was me. It would always be me. I turned away from him. "I have to go."

He didn't say anything as I walked away. I rounded the lighthouse and veered toward the parking lot, avoiding everyone else. I was trembling when I reached the Vespa, grateful I'd parked under the only light in the parking lot. It took me several tries to unlock the compartment where I'd stored my helmet.

The click of heels on pavement told me I was not alone, and I looked up as Lex and Julie entered the circle of light. My whole body tensed when the two female werewolves walked toward me. The set of Lex's mouth told me their arrival was not a coincidence.

Lex came up to me and got right in my face, towering over me by at least five inches. Leaning down, she sniffed my hair, and there was no mistaking the growl that issued from her throat.

"You reek of him."

I didn't need to ask who he was. Roland said Lex was not his girlfriend, but I didn't think anyone had told her that.

Her finger poked me hard in the chest, and I stumbled backward into the Vespa. She snarled, but I refused to cower, although my knees were shaking. She could hurt or kill me if she wanted to, and there was nothing I could do to stop her.

"I'm only going to tell you this once, human. Stay away from him."

"Lex," Julie hissed.

Lex continued to stare at me. "She already knows about us. Don't you, little girl?"

"Yes," I said in a voice that was surprisingly steady. "Roland is my friend. That's it."

"Bullshit. You don't smell that strongly of someone's scent from wearing their sweater. You've been with him."

"I fell and he helped me up. Go ask him if you don't believe me."

Her eyes took on a faint yellow glow. "I think you're lying."

"Think what you want, but there is nothing going on between him and me. No offense, but I don't want a werewolf boyfriend." I ignored the pain that pricked my chest at the lie. It wasn't that I didn't want Roland. It was that I couldn't have him.

She looked slightly appeased. "Good, then you won't mind staying the hell away from him."

She might be stronger than I was, but she wasn't going to tell me how to live my life. I'd spent two decades at someone else's mercy, and that would never happen again.

"No."

"No what?" she asked.

"I won't stop seeing my friends just because you don't like it." That was if Roland and I were still friends. He probably wouldn't want to look at me again after the way I'd left him.

Her lip curled. "Get some new friends. Roland is mine, and when we mate, he won't have time for the likes of you."

"Then you have nothing to worry about, do you?"

She started to raise her hand, and I tensed, expecting a blow.

"There you are," called April.

The three of us looked at April, Paul, and Dell walking toward us. Lex lowered her hand and took a step back.

"We decided to ditch the party and go to Portland," April said. "You're welcome to join us, Emma."

I managed to keep the tremble from my voice. "Thanks, but I have to work tomorrow."

She smiled. "But we're still doing coffee on Monday?"

"Yes."

"Okay, I'll see you then." She looked at Lex and Julie. "You still want to go to the club?"

"Sure," Julie answered for them.

I donned my helmet and climbed on the Vespa. "Have a good time," I said before I started the engine and drove away. I didn't look back, but I could feel Lex watching me until I was out of her sight.

I let out a shaky breath when I reached the road. Tears burned at the back of my eyes, but I refused to let them come. Driving while crying was asking for disaster. And crying over a guy I couldn't have would only make me feel worse. It wouldn't solve anything.

Why did you have to kiss me like that?

I could still feel his mouth on mine and his arms around me. I'd thought my heart was too scarred to be with someone, and here I was, ready to cry over a guy – a werewolf. How had this happened? How had he snuck past my defenses and wormed his way into my affections so easily? I hadn't even seen it coming.

For a few incredible minutes, I hadn't felt alone or scared or broken. I'd been a normal girl, kissing a handsome boy who gave me butterflies and made me feel more alive than I'd been in a very long time. I should be happy knowing I could feel that way for someone after what I'd been through.

I *would* be happy, after my heart stopped hurting.

11

Roland

I stood rooted to the spot as Emma walked away from me. My wolf was upset I'd let her go, and it would have gone after her if it could. But I'd seen the sheen of tears in her eyes and heard the pain in her voice before she left. Chasing her down would only upset her, and that was the last thing I wanted. Even if she didn't accept me as her mate, I wouldn't allow anyone to hurt her, especially me.

I sighed heavily and stared unseeing at the water. I'd been fighting the need to go to her, but when I saw her come back here alone, I couldn't stay away from her. I wasn't sure what I'd planned to say to her, just that I had to be near her. When she'd tripped and I'd held her in my arms, nothing had ever felt so right.

And that kiss. Fuck. I'd kissed a lot of girls, but none of them had responded to me like that, turning me on until I could barely form a thought. She'd set my body on fire, and if she hadn't stopped us, I might have taken her right here in the grass where anyone could have found us. The thought left me ashamed and excited at the same time.

It's not you.

Her words were stuck on repeat in my head. How many times had I uttered them to the human girls I'd dated when I'd broken it off? I'd never realized how awful it felt to be on the receiving end. Karma had bitch-slapped me, and man, it stung.

I allowed myself a few minutes to recover from the rejection, and then I followed her. She didn't want anything to do with me, but I had to make sure she got home safely. The fact that she lived on her own and could probably take care of herself didn't matter. I'd felt protective of her before tonight. Imprinting on her had intensified that instinct tenfold, and I wouldn't rest until I saw she was okay.

As I started toward the parking lot, I spotted Paul, Dell, and April ahead of me. I stopped walking. If they were leaving, then Lex and Julie were most likely going with them. The last person I wanted to see now was Lex. She thought she had some claim on me, and she'd cause an ugly scene if she smelled Emma on me. I planned to set her straight very soon, but not tonight. Right now, I had more important things to do.

I waited until I saw Dell's car pull away, and then I went to mine. Emma's scooter was gone, and I knew she'd be halfway home by now. I followed her most likely route, but I didn't drive up to her building. Parking at the end of the waterfront, I walked to her place and stood across the street where I could see the apartment. The kitchen light was on, and a few minutes later, the light upstairs came on.

I let out a breath, knowing she was home. The pull of the new imprint was strong, but I stayed where I was, not wanting to upset her. She had no idea what had happened between us, and I wasn't sure she even knew about werewolf imprinting. With her reservations about my kind, it might frighten her into leaving New Hastings. That was the last thing I wanted. I had to tell her, but I needed to think of the best way to do it.

Christ, I feel like a bloody stalker, I thought after I'd stood there for thirty minutes, watching her place. She was safe inside, and I doubted she'd go out again tonight. There was no reason for me to stay here, except for my need to be close to her.

I wondered if this was where Nikolas had stood all those weeks he watched over Sara when she lived in this same apartment. He'd bonded with her the moment they met, but she hadn't felt it right away. It had been two months before she found out about the bond, and months after that before they mated. How had Nikolas endured it? If the Mohiri bond was as strong as an imprint, I had a whole new appreciation for my warrior friend.

When the lights went out in the apartment just after midnight, I went home and sought my own bed. But sleep evaded me, and I spent a restless night waiting for the sun to come up. I was tired and cranky when I arrived at the garage. When Paul got in at nine, I'd been working for two hours and my mood hadn't improved. He wisely kept the conversation to work-related things and didn't mention last night at all.

Pete strolled in at noon, looking like he'd barely slept himself, but he was a lot happier about it. As soon as I saw his smile, I knew why.

"You imprinted on Shannon?"

He smiled broadly. "Last night when I brought her home. We were at her door, and it just...happened. We went for a run and stayed out in the woods talking all night."

Despite my dark mood, I was happy he'd gotten the girl he cared for. I wiped my hands on a rag and held one out to him. "Congrats, man."

"Congratulations!" Paul came over and slapped Pete on the back. "You lucky wolf. Shannon's a great girl."

Pete laughed. "Trust me, I know. Shannon wants to tell our parents before we make it official. We're getting them all together tonight."

Making it official was the polite way to say mating, and it was the werewolf equivalent of marriage. Except we had very short engagements and no divorce. After a male imprinted, the couple usually mated within days or weeks. The pull was too strong for either of them to deny it for long.

Paul waved at Pete and me. "What are the odds of the two of you...?"

He stopped mid-sentence and shot me a guilty look.

"The two of us, what?" Pete asked, looking between us. When no one answered, he frowned. "What aren't you telling me?"

I took a deep breath and let it out. "Last night at the party, I imprinted... on Emma."

Pete's eyebrows disappeared into his hairline. And then his jaw went slack when he realized the rest of what I'd said.

"Man, you had me there for a second." He shook his head. "What's really going on?"

"It's not a joke."

"But...that's not possible." He stared at Paul. "Is it?"

Paul nodded. "I thought the same thing, but I was there and I saw it with my own eyes."

Pete's stunned gaze swung back to me. "But..."

"She's human," I finished for him. "I didn't believe it at first, either."

I told him about the moment I imprinted and how I'd expected it to be one of the female wolves. When I described how it felt when I looked at Emma, he inhaled sharply.

"That's how it felt with Shannon." He closed the distance between us and sniffed. "It's faint, but you smell a little different. How about mine?"

I sniffed the air. We had sensitive noses, and we could identify each member of the pack by smell. Pete's scent was slightly different, stronger.

"Yours changed, too."

When a male werewolf first imprinted he released his bonding scent, which was offensive to other males and irresistible to his female. The bonding scent receded, but didn't disappear completely, and it grew stronger when the male was aroused or protecting his mate.

"Shit. Do you think everyone else will notice?" I didn't want the pack to know about Emma until I explained it to her.

Pete sniffed the air again. "I did because I know your scent so well. Your mom will smell it for sure. With so many people here, it might be hard for the others to pick it up, especially if they think you haven't imprinted yet."

He sat on an overturned oil drum and smiled at me. "Paul was right. What are the chances of us imprinting on the same night?"

"Better than the odds of a werewolf imprinting on a human," I replied.

His smile faded. "You didn't tell me what happened next. Did you talk to her? What did she say?"

"I talked to her, but I didn't tell her about the imprint. I don't think she'll accept me as a mate."

I sucked it up and told him about kissing her and her running away. I'd never shared what happened between me and the other girls I'd been with. But this was different, and I needed to talk to someone about it. I voiced my fear that she wouldn't want me because of what I was.

"You don't know that. I saw how comfortable she was with you last night, and I doubt she would have let you into her apartment or spent the day with you if she didn't like you. And you said she kissed you back, which means she is attracted to you. For all we know, her taking off might have nothing to do with what you are."

Hope flared in my chest. "She did think Lex was my girlfriend because of the way she clung to me. I told her I'm not with Lex, but maybe she didn't believe me."

Pete nodded thoughtfully. "Lex *was* acting territorial, and she's pretty aggressive. She might have scared Emma off."

I leaned against the Chevelle. "So, what do I do?"

"I think you should talk to Grandma before you see Emma again. If anyone would know about werewolves mating with humans, it'd be her. Or you could talk to Dad. As Alpha, he might know something."

I grimaced. The last person I wanted to talk to about this was Maxwell.

"Grandma, it is."

As the mother of the Alpha, Grandma was staying in Maxwell's house during her visit, but she spent half her time at our place. She was there, baking with Mom, when I got home late that afternoon.

"Just in time, my boy," Grandma called when I entered the house. "I made your favorite."

I walked into the kitchen and gave her a hug. She made me sit and set a huge slice of apple pie in front of me. Mom poured me a tall glass of milk and smiled when I told her I wasn't five years old anymore.

"What are you baking for this time?" I looked around the kitchen at the pies and fresh bread on every available surface.

"The cookout at Brendan's tonight," Grandma said.

"Another party?"

My mother gave me a stern look. "I told you about it yesterday morning."

"Sorry, Mom, but I can't keep up with it all." Not to mention the life-changing event I'd had since then. It was a wonder I could remember what day it was.

Grandma looked up from the crust she was rolling out. "Why aren't you eating? Are you sick?"

"No." I met her eyes. "I need to talk to you about something. Both of you."

My mother wiped her hands on her apron. "What is it?"

I swallowed. "Did you two mean it when you said my wolf knows my heart and he'll choose someone I'm meant to be with?"

"Are you still worried about that? Oh, honey." My mother came over and hugged me. "Yes, of course we meant it. Your wolf won't –" She pulled back and placed a hand over her heart. "You smell... You've imprinted."

"Yes."

She sank down on the chair next to mine. "Who? When?"

Grandma abandoned her pie and joined us at the table. Her wrinkled hand covered mine. "Don't look so glum, my boy. It's not the end of the world."

"I know." I wasn't upset by my wolf's choice. I cared about Emma, and last night, she'd set my blood on fire with one kiss. I was worried about what happened when a wolf imprinted on a human, and I was afraid of her rejecting me because of what I was.

Grandma scowled. "Then why do you look like it is?"

"Do you not like her?" Mom asked. "Who is she?"

I exhaled slowly. "Before I get to that, I need to tell you that I've been spending time with a human girl, and I have feelings for her."

"Oh, Roland." Mom covered her mouth with her hand. "I'm sorry, honey. Why didn't you tell me?"

I shrugged. "I haven't known her that long, and we're just friends. I wasn't expecting to care about her like this."

"Is she someone you went to school with?"

"It's Emma."

She gave me an incredulous look. "Sara's cousin?"

"Yes."

Her eyes misted. "I see why you're upset. But you know it could never have gone anywhere between you. It's better this happened now before the two of you got involved and both of you ended up hurt."

"How do you know it couldn't have gone anywhere?" I asked her. "You said my wolf knows my heart. What if I wanted Emma for a mate? Could he choose a human?"

"Your wolf has imprinted," Grandma said. "Wondering about what could have been won't change that."

"Humor me. Can a werewolf have a human mate?"

Grandma clasped her hands together. "It's rare, but it can happen."

My pulse leaped. "How?"

"Well, the male would have to want the human, but that's not enough. His wolf also has to care for her enough to want her for his mate. For that to happen, he'd have to spend time with her in wolf form." She pursed her lips. "The problem there is that most humans don't know about us, and we are bound by law not to reveal ourselves to them. So very few males would ever be in the situation to imprint on a human."

"Have you ever known someone it happened to?"

She nodded. "When I was a girl, I knew a male named Andy who had a human mate. The pack wouldn't accept the girl, so Andy took her and moved away."

My stomach dropped. "They wouldn't accept her?"

"You have to understand that things were a lot different back then. Our people feared humans and being hunted if anyone found out about us. It wasn't until Maxwell became Alpha that we started living and working with the humans and we got past those old fears. If a wolf imprinted on a human now, she'd be considered one of the pack. There'll always be a few wolves who won't accept a human, but by law, she'd be pack and have all the rights and protections as one of us."

Relief filled me. Even if Emma didn't want me, she'd be protected by the pack. At least one weight was lifted from me.

"Does that answer all your questions?" she asked.

"I think so."

Mom laid her hand on my arm. "Now, are you going to tell us who you imprinted on? I didn't know you had spent enough time with any of the females for your wolf to choose one."

The knots in my stomach loosened, now that I knew it hadn't been wishful thinking or desperation that made me believe I'd imprinted on Emma.

"I didn't. It's Emma. She's the one."

Mom inhaled sharply. "Emma? Are you sure?"

"More than I've ever been sure of anything." I told them about last night, glossing over some details. "I didn't believe it, at first. But as soon as I touched her, I knew she was my mate."

She looked at Grandma then back to me. "I won't say I'm not shocked. A lot of people will be."

I folded my arms across my chest. "I don't care what anyone else thinks."

"That's my boy," Grandma said with an approving nod.

"The main thing is that you're happy," my mother said. "Are you? You don't seem as upset as I'd expected after all your talk about not wanting a mate."

"I admit I didn't want one yet, but I didn't think I'd feel this way about someone either."

Their faces softened, and my mother looked like she was going to tear up. "Do you love her?" she asked.

I sighed. "I think it's too soon to call it love. I care a lot about her and I feel protective of her, but it's more than that. There's something about her that feels different than any of the girls I've dated. I like just being with her."

"Sounds like love to me," Grandma quipped. "I can't wait to meet this young lady."

"You don't mind that she's human?"

My mother frowned. "Why on earth would we mind? I thought Sara was human, and she's like a daughter to me. I'm getting another daughter, and I'll love her, too."

"And I'll like any female who makes my grandson happy," Grandma added. "Do you plan to live in the Knolls or in town after you mate?"

"I...don't know," I said slowly, heat radiating through my chest at the thought of Emma and I mating. If only it was that simple.

"I'm not sure Emma will want me as a mate. I haven't told her about the imprint yet."

"Why wouldn't she want you?" Grandma demanded.

"I think before she moved here she had a bad experience with a werewolf.

I don't know what happened, but it made her afraid of us. It took her weeks to warm up to me." I rubbed my jaw. "And without a wolf, I'm not sure she can even feel the imprint."

Grandma nodded. "It is different for humans. They don't feel the pull like a female wolf does, not until they're mated."

"So, she could decide not to have me," I said dejectedly. I tried not to think of how wretched it would be to live my life, wanting someone who didn't want me.

She smacked my arm. "Enough of that. I know how eager imprinted males are to get on with the mating, but you're going to have to be patient. If you care for this girl and want her as your mate, you'll need to show her you're worthy of her trust and affection."

I leaned forward. "How do I do that?"

She made a tsk sound. "Be yourself, you silly pup. She saw something in you that made her like you even though she's afraid of our kind. You keep that up, and she'll be head over heels for you in no time."

I felt the tension leave my body. "I hope you're right."

"I'm always right." She shoved my plate of pie toward me. "Now finish your pie like a good boy."

I grinned at her. "Yes, ma'am."

Emma

"Emma, over here!"

I looked around the coffee shop until I spotted April and Shannon waving at me from a corner. I smiled and lifted a hand to let them know I saw them, and then I went up to the counter to order a drink.

I still couldn't believe I was having coffee with two werewolves. Shannon and April seemed nice, but I never would have imagined me doing this a month ago. I'd come a long way.

A very long way, if Saturday night was any indication. My stomach fluttered wildly when I remembered kissing Roland. Every detail of that moment was etched in my brain, and I'd replayed it over and over since then. The reckless part of me that didn't care about consequences wondered what would have happened if I hadn't left. My cautious side said I'd done the right thing no matter how much I'd wanted to stay.

I got my latte and joined the girls in the cozy little nook that was just big enough for three leather chairs and a small round table.

"So glad you could make it," Shannon said as I dropped my bag on the floor and sat.

I immediately noticed something different about her. She looked the same, but there was a glow about her like she was bursting with happiness.

"I'm glad, too." I took a sip of my latte and smiled. "This stuff is amazing."

Shannon beamed. "Told you. I might move here just for the coffee."

"Move here?" April asked slyly. "And I don't suppose a certain handsome redhead has anything to do with it."

Shannon grinned behind her cup. "If I don't tell you soon, I'm going to explode. It happened."

April squealed, and the two of them jumped up, hugging and laughing. I didn't know what *it* was, but it had to be big if they were this excited.

They sat again, and Shannon smiled at me. "Your expression tells me you have no idea what we're going on about."

"Not a clue."

She leaned toward me and lowered her voice. "Peter told me about you and your cousin and that you know about us."

I bit my lip and nodded.

"How much do you know about werewolves?" she whispered.

"Not a whole lot. Why?" I took a sip from my cup.

"I'm trying to think of the best way to explain this. I've never talked to a human about us before." She laughed shakily. "Sorry, I'm a little nervous."

My eyes widened. "Why would you be nervous around me?"

"I don't want to say anything that makes you think we're strange and scares you off."

A laugh bubbled from me. "You change into a wolf. I doubt anything you tell me will be stranger than that."

April snorted, and Shannon motioned for us to move closer. April and I shifted our chairs until we were as close as we could get to her.

"Okay," she began. "If you don't know much about us, you probably don't know how we mate."

"TMI," April teased.

Shannon blushed. "I don't mean the physical part. I mean how we find our mate. When a male's wolf is attracted to an unmated female, he will imprint on her and claim her so all other males know she's his."

I looked between them. "Claim?" It sounded like ownership, and the thought of being owned by anyone made me want to shudder.

"He puts his bonding scent on her," April explained. "If they're in wolf form, he rubs against her. Scents are unique, so other males will know he's imprinted on her."

"Oh." That wasn't as bad as I'd expected. "What happens if he imprints on someone who already has a mate?"

"Males can only imprint on a female who hasn't been imprinted or mated," Shannon said.

"Can a female imprint on a male?" I asked, fascinated. Before I met Roland and Peter, I'd only seen werewolves as killers, and I'd never given much thought to their personal lives.

April made a face. "Only males can imprint."

"What if you don't like him?"

"We don't have to accept him as a mate, but that never happens," Shannon said. "There's usually some interest between the couple first. And the imprint creates a bond that's kind of hard to resist." She cleared her throat. "The male and female are drawn to each other...physically."

April chimed in. "Think of imprinting as an engagement. Unlike you humans, our pheromones go into overdrive, making us need to mate." She grinned and nudged Shannon with her shoulder. "It's a very short engagement."

Shannon's cheeks grew pink again. "Yes."

Her excitement made sense now. "So, Peter imprinted on you? Congratulations."

"Thanks." She put a hand to her chest. "I'm so lucky. I was worried about what his father would say, but he was really nice."

"Why would they object to you?" It sounded like there wasn't much anyone could do once a male made up his mind.

"Peter's father is the Alpha," Shannon said. "That means Peter could be in line to be Alpha someday. I was afraid Maxwell would think I wasn't good enough for his son."

I smiled at her. "I'm sure the Alpha was very happy with Peter's choice for a mate."

She looked like she was trying to form her next words. "The male doesn't choose. His wolf does."

"His wolf?" My brows drew together. "But he is the wolf."

"This is harder to explain than I thought." She pressed her lips together for a moment. "I'm in my human form now and my wolf is inside me. Not physically, of course, but her essence is there. When I shift, I take on her form, but I'm still the dominant side. She's an animal and she has the instincts of a wolf." She gave me a wry smile. "Have I lost you yet?"

"No, I think I see." This had to be one of the strangest conversations I'd ever had. "You're human and a wolf sharing a body. Do you share a soul, too?"

"Yes." She looked pleased that I understood her explanation. "Because our wolves' instincts are much stronger than ours, it's the wolf that imprints, not the male."

I gawked at her. "But what if the guy doesn't like who his wolf picks? Or does it only happen when you're together, like you and Peter?"

"The male has to spend time with the female in order for his wolf to form an attachment. My mother says a wolf won't imprint on a female the male doesn't like."

I sat back to process what she'd said, and it made me think about Roland and Lex. She'd acted like his girlfriend and told me to stay away from him because he was hers. But Roland didn't seem to like her much, and if Shannon was right, his wolf wouldn't choose someone he disliked. Lex was not a nice person, and it made me feel a little better knowing he wouldn't end up with her.

On another note, Shannon's story only reinforced what I already knew. Even if I thought Roland could get past my history, we never would have been able to be together. Someday, his wolf would choose a werewolf mate, and where would that leave me? Brokenhearted and alone again. It was good I'd ended it before it went any further.

"Are you going to move here?" April asked Shannon.

"Yes. His father is giving us one of the new houses, so I'm going to try commuting to school. Peter's hoping to get accepted for classes in January so we can drive together. If it gets too hard in the winter, we might get an apartment there."

"I'm so jealous of you right now." April sighed. "I hope someone imprints on me this year."

"Can males only imprint once a year?" I asked, earning smiles from them.

"It can happen anytime, but we don't have many unmated males at home," April said. "Most of the unmated wolves come to the annual gathering, so if I'm going to find a mate, it's here."

"I'm sure you will," I told her sincerely.

April reached over to squeeze my hand. "I'm so glad we met. I have to tell you, though, that I'm dying of curiosity. You're human and your cousin is Mohiri? Is that true?"

"Yes."

"Wow." She tugged on my sleeve. "Have you met any of them besides her? We heard stories about them being here last fall. It's hard to know what's true."

I hesitated before saying, "I've met some of them."

April gave me a knowing look. "You're not supposed to talk about them."

"Not really. Sorry."

"Hey, I get it. We're not allowed to tell humans about us either." She smiled. "You're an exception because you already knew about us."

Shannon shook her empty cup. "Who's up for another one?"

"Me," April and I said at the same time.

We stayed there for another hour, and by the time we left, we'd already agreed to get together again that weekend. I waved goodbye to them and walked to the Vespa, feeling lighthearted.

I was putting on my helmet when I got the feeling I was being watched. I scanned the small parking lot, but Shannon and April had already left and there was no one else nearby.

Movement drew my eyes to a man walking away up the street. I could only see his profile, but his build and bald head were eerily similar to those of the man I'd seen in Portland on Saturday. My mouth went dry as a bolt of fear shot through me. What were the odds of seeing the same man twice in three days and in two different towns?

My fingers shook when I inserted the key into the ignition. I had to make myself drive at the speed limit and not race home, and I kept checking my mirrors to make sure I wasn't being followed.

At home, I quickly stowed away the Vespa and ran upstairs, checking that the doors were bolted. I still didn't feel safe, and my first instinct was to call Roland. But I didn't know how to face him so soon after what had happened between us. I sat at the kitchen table, willing my heart to slow down and telling myself I was just being paranoid.

I jumped when my cell phone rang, and I grabbed for it, half hoping it was Roland. I let out a shaky breath when I saw it was Sara.

"Hey. I wasn't expecting to hear from you today." I glanced at the clock on the wall. It was close to midnight where she was.

"Why do you sound like that?" she asked.

"Like what?"

"I don't know, like you're a little out of breath. Is everything okay there?"

"Everything's great," I lied. "I was running."

"You don't like to run." Her voice rose. "Emma, what's wrong? And don't you dare lie because I'll know."

I bit my lip. "It's nothing. I saw this man and thought he was watching me. You know I still get nervous around strangers. I feel silly telling you about it."

"What man? Where did you see him?" Worry flooded her voice.

"Sara, it's nothing."

"It's not nothing," she chided. "I can hear in your voice that you're scared. Tell me exactly what happened."

I sighed because there was no putting her off when she got like this. I told her about seeing the bald man in Portland and then seeing someone who resembled him today.

"I didn't even see his face today, so I'm not sure it was the same man."

"And you've never seen this man before? Could he be someone you knew when you were a vampire?"

One of the things I liked about Sara was that she never tried to gloss over my old life. She called it like it was. Other people at Westhorne used to tiptoe around the fact that I had been a vampire. I guess they wanted to protect my feelings. Sara said I'd been a victim and I should never feel guilt or shame for that. I wished it was that easy.

"He's definitely not a vampire because he was out in the sun. And Eli didn't deal with too many humans, so I would have remembered him."

"Okay, that's good. But I still don't like it." There was a short pause. "Why didn't you tell Roland when it happened in Portland?"

"I was a little shaken up, and then the man disappeared. And I was afraid of Roland asking questions about my past."

She sighed. "You should call him. He'll want to help and you don't have to mention your past."

I rubbed the back of my neck. "If I see the man again, I'll call him. I promise."

"If you see him again, you call Chris," she said firmly. "Or let Dax know. He'll send someone to check it out. You still have their numbers?"

"Yes."

"Good." She let out a breath. "I'm glad to know you and Roland are hitting it off. He must really like you if he hung out in two art stores. He used to grumble the whole time he was with me."

"His eyes did glaze over a few times."

She laughed. "I remember that look. You have to admit, I was right about you two clicking once you got to know him."

"You were right."

If she only knew how much he and I had clicked. Thank God she couldn't see my face because it felt like it was on fire. There was no way I was telling her what had happened between Roland and me at the lighthouse. That kiss would not be repeated, and it was better to forget about it.

"So, what else has been going on since I last talked to you?" she asked.

I smiled. "Let's see. I went to a party Saturday night at the lighthouse, and

I met Peter's girlfriend, Shannon. Well, I guess she'll be his mate soon. And I had coffee with her and her friend April today."

"You had coffee with two werewolves?" she asked. "Wait. Peter has a mate?"

I chuckled. "Yes and yes."

She made a noise like she was moving around. "Okay, I just got comfortable. Now, I want to hear *everything*."

12

Roland

"Last order of business for today," Maxwell said from the front of the meeting hall. "I've had word that ranc demons were spotted in Portland last week. Normally, we wouldn't bother with demons unless they posed a serious threat, but we learned last year that ranc demons are known to follow vampires. I will not have vampires in my city again."

"How do you know about the ranc demons?" Francis asked.

"The Mohiri gave me a heads-up. They've been keeping closer tabs on Maine since October."

Murmurs spread through the room. Most werewolves didn't like the Mohiri because of old grudges against the warrior race. There'd been a time when our kind wasn't that civilized and some of them had been hunted and killed by the Mohiri for hurting humans. I used to dislike the Mohiri until I got to know Nikolas and Chris. Now, I considered them my friends.

Maxwell held up his hand for silence. "I'm sending extra patrols to Portland until we are sure we don't have another vampire problem. You'll go in teams of four, and we'll rotate the patrols twice daily. Brendan and I have divided the people who will patrol into twelve teams with a leader for each one."

Brendan stood with a notepad in his hand and began reading off names. I quickly noticed the team leaders were Beta candidates. In fact, most of the people in the teams were on the Beta list. I wasn't surprised Francis was the leader of the first team, and I was relieved not to be in that one. My cousin and I still couldn't spend ten minutes together without butting heads.

One of the female candidates looked surprised and pleased to be named leader of her team. Traditionally, females couldn't become Betas, but Maxwell had declared that any pack member of age was eligible.

"In team eight, we have Roland Greene, Peter Kelly, Shawn Walsh, and Trevor Gosse," Brendan announced, and I grimaced at hearing I'd have to work with Trevor. He'd kept his distance from me since our fight last week, but I'd caught him glaring at me a few times. The guy was itching for payback. I wasn't sure what Maxwell was thinking, putting the two of us on the same team, but the Alpha never did anything without a reason.

"Leader for team eight is Roland Greene," Brendan said. "Your first patrol is Wednesday night."

"No fucking way," Trevor growled in a low voice. "He's a goddamned kid."

"A kid who kicked your ass," retorted Shawn, who sat behind me. A few people tittered. At least Shawn didn't sound upset to have me as his team leader.

"You have something to say, Mr. Gosse?" Maxwell stepped forward, his arms crossed over his chest.

Trevor stood. "No offense, Alpha, but the kid is barely out of school and I have years of experience. I should be team leader, not him."

Maxwell nodded. "You're right, he's young. How many vampire kills have you had?"

Trevor lifted his chin proudly. "Two."

"Roland?" Maxwell looked at me.

I stood slowly, trying to remember the number, but there were too many to count. "I don't know. Two crocotta and about thirty vampires, maybe more."

"Bullshit," Trevor spat as the room erupted in whispers again.

Maxwell's hard gaze swept the room, and everyone fell silent. The tic in his jaw told me Trevor was walking a dangerous line.

"Mr. Gosse, are you questioning me or my judgement?"

"N-no, sir."

"Then we're good." Maxwell looked at Brendan. "Continue."

The rest of the teams were announced without interruption. I don't think anyone dared speak up after Trevor's little outburst. Maxwell could be one scary son of a bitch when you pissed him off. I knew that firsthand.

The meeting ended once all the groups were called out. I glanced at my watch as I waited for the crowd to file out. It was still early, so Paul and I were going to try to get in a few more hours at the garage today. The Chevelle was coming along better than I'd expected, and we'd be finished ahead of schedule at this rate.

"Did you really kill that many vampires?"

I looked up at the blonde female candidate who'd been made team leader. "Yes."

Her expression changed from curious to admiring. "Are you one of the guys who took off across the country with the Mohiri girl?"

"Yes." I smiled and held out my hand. "Roland."

She shook my hand. "Sheila. I'd love to hear about all those vampires sometime. I hunted two up near the Canadian border, but my brothers made the kills."

"Sure." I couldn't smell a male on her, which meant she was unmated. But she made no move to flirt with me. Either she wasn't attracted to me, or she didn't want a mate. It was nice to talk to a female wolf who wanted nothing beyond friendly conversation.

We started toward the door, and I groaned when I spotted Lex standing at the back of the room. She waved, and I managed a weak smile.

"Word of advice," Sheila said in a low voice. "Watch out for that one."

"You know her?"

"Yes." Sheila made a face. "Lex knows Maxwell's son or one of his nephews will be the next Alpha, and she's determined to have one of you. She wouldn't let any male from home get close to her, afraid one of them would imprint on her before she met you."

I'd known from the beginning she was after me because of my connection to Maxwell. And I'd seen how possessive she was of me and how aggressive she was with other females.

"Any advice for getting her to back off?"

Sheila snorted. "Yeah. Find a mate."

"Hey, Roland. Sheila." Lex smiled, but I saw that it didn't reach her eyes when she looked at my companion.

"Lex." Sheila continued to the door. "See you around, Roland."

As soon as we were alone, Lex moved in. I evaded her touch by pretending not to see her reach for my arm as I turned on my phone and waited for the display to come up. Maxwell had a strict "no phones" policy in meetings, and you had to leave your phone outside or turn it off.

The first thing I saw was a new voicemail from Sara. I looked at the time of her call and frowned. It was 2:00 a.m. in Russia. Why would she call me at this hour? I hoped she and Nikolas were okay.

"Excuse me, Lex. I need to make a call." Leaving her, I walked a short distance from the building before I listened to the voicemail.

"Hey, Roland. It's me. Everything's good here, but I need a favor. I'm worried about Emma, and I wanted to ask if you'd check on her for me. It's probably nothing, but I'd rather be safe than sorry. I talked to her tonight, and she told me she saw a strange man watching her. He was in Portland when you guys were having lunch, and she thinks she saw him again today outside The Hub. She said she was just being paranoid, but she sounded shaken up. I told her to let the Westhorne security guys know if she sees him again, but I'm still worried. She'll probably be upset that I called you, but at least I'll know she's safe. Talk to you soon. Love you."

The cell phone made a squeaking sound, and I realized I was about to crush it with my hand. I eased my hold on it and replayed Sara's message. A man had been watching Emma when we were in Portland? How had I not seen him, and why hadn't she mentioned it? Then I remembered how different she'd been when I came back from my phone call. She'd claimed she was sick, but I'd suspected it was more than that.

I wanted to kick myself for not keeping her safe. Someone had frightened her while I stood a few feet away, talking on the damn phone. And now he was here? A growl threatened to escape me. Even if she never accepted me as her mate, she was mine to protect. Any male, human or not, who harmed her would have to deal with me.

After the talk with my mother and grandmother, I'd planned to wait a few days before I went to see Emma. But there was no way I could stay away from her now. I wouldn't rest until I saw for myself that she was okay.

"Roland," Lex called when I started walking away.

I took a calming breath and stopped to let her catch up.

"Sorry, Lex, I have to go."

"You can take a few hours off from the garage," she wheedled in what she probably thought was a sexy voice. "A bunch of us are going out to eat and play pool. Doesn't that sound like more fun than working under a car?"

"I'm not going to the garage."

I knew I'd said the wrong thing when her eyes narrowed and her lip curled. "You're going to see that *human*, aren't you?"

The way she said *human*, like it was something stuck to the bottom of her shoe, killed the last of my patience with her.

"It's none of your business where I'm going," I bit out. "Enjoy your dinner."

I fumed as I strode to my car, glad I'd parked on the road so I didn't get blocked in. All I could think about now was seeing Emma.

I forced myself to calm down as I drove to her place, because it wouldn't help if I showed up like this. I wanted to reassure her, not freak her out.

Emma opened the door on my second knock. She sighed, not looking surprised by my visit. I couldn't tell if she was happy to see me or not.

"Sara called you." It wasn't a question.

"She left me a voicemail. Can I come in?"

For a second, I thought she was going to say no. She stepped back, opening the door wider. I entered, closed it behind me, and followed her into the living room.

"I should have known she'd call you," Emma said, sitting on the couch. "She worries about me too much."

I took the chair by the window and tried not to stare at her. The pull of the imprint was strong, and it hadn't been easy to stay away from her the last two days.

"I'm glad she called me," I said gruffly. "Tell me about the man."

She folded her hands in her lap. "He was sitting at the coffee shop across the street from us. I caught him looking at me while you were on the phone. When you came back to the table, he disappeared."

"What did he look like?"

"He was bald, probably in his thirties, average height, and he had no mustache or beard. He looked like a normal guy." She shook her head. "Like I told Sara, I'm probably making something out of nothing."

"It is something if he frightened you." I leaned forward, resting my elbows on my knees. "Why didn't you tell me about him? I hate that someone scared you with me standing right there."

Her face softened. "It's not your fault. And he didn't do anything but look at me."

"And what about today? You saw him here?" The thought that a strange man might be stalking her made my stomach knot.

She picked up a decorative pillow and hugged it to her chest. "I don't know if it was the same man. I was at The Hub with Shannon and April, and when I left, I saw a bald man walking away. He reminded me of the man in Portland because he was bald and had the same build, but I didn't see much of his face."

The slight quiver in her voice told me she believed he was the man from Portland, and it had spooked her more than she wanted to admit. It gnawed at me, too. She lived here alone, and the waterfront was practically deserted after the shops closed. If that man was following her, it wouldn't take him long to realize how vulnerable she was, if he didn't already know it.

"Did Shannon or April see him?" I asked.

"I don't know. Their car was at the other end of the parking lot."

I clasped my hands together, trying to frame my next question so I didn't frighten her. "Do you feel safe here in the apartment?"

"I think so," she replied. Her eyes said something else.

"You don't sound so sure." I took a breath. "If you want, I can stay here with you for a few days. On the couch," I quickly added.

Her arms tightened around the pillow. "Thanks, but I'm fine, really."

I could sense her withdrawing, and I knew what it was really about. "Emma…"

She got up quickly, dropping the pillow to the couch. "I'm thirsty. Would you like something to drink?"

"I'm good," I said, but she was already out of the room. I sighed. "Water or juice is f–"

Her scream made my blood go cold. I felt my teeth lengthen as I tore through the doorway and skidded to a stop in the hallway. Emma was pressed back against the wall, her face frozen in terror as she stared at the slender, gray creature standing by the front door. He clutched a cloth sack in his hand, and his large violet eyes darted between Emma and me.

I put a hand to the wall. "Jesus, Remy! You gotta stop doing that, man."

His eyes lit with recognition, and he gave a small nod. "Werewolf."

I pushed away from the wall and went to Emma, who jumped when I laid a hand on her shoulder.

"Emma, it's okay," I said gently. "This is Sara's friend, Remy. He has a habit of popping in like that, but he won't hurt you."

She turned her head until her eyes met mine. "R-Remy?"

"Did Sara tell you about Remy?" I hoped so because it was not going to be easy to explain trolls to her.

She gave a jerky nod, and her voice was a hoarse whisper. "Yes, but it's not the same as…"

"Trust me, I know." I smiled, very aware that she'd moved closer to me. Warmth filled my chest at the knowledge she felt safe with me.

I rubbed her arm comfortingly. "You okay?"

"Just give me a minute," she said shakily.

"Take your time."

I looked at Remy, who hadn't moved. His shaggy gray-brown hair and round eyes made him look like some weird life-size Muppet, a very deadly one. Trolls were some of the scariest creatures on earth, and even vampires feared them.

"What are you doing here, Remy? Were you looking for Sara?"

He held up the sack. "Sara ask me to ward home. Keep bad people out." He looked at Emma. "I not mean to make you afraid."

"What does he mean?" she asked me.

"Troll magic is strong. He came to put magic wards on the building to keep you safe. Remy showed Sara how to do it when she lived here, but I guess they wear off after a while."

Remy nodded. "Sara's ward last while this her home."

"Oh." Emma relaxed a little but didn't move away from me. "What does it do?"

"It keep out bad people. Only good people come in."

"How does it know if they are good or bad?" she asked less fearfully.

He tapped his chest. "It know what in here."

"What happens if a bad person tries to come in?"

The troll smiled, showing his teeth. "Big hurt."

Emma sucked in a sharp breath and pressed closer to me. I didn't blame her. Remy might be friendly, but that grin would make a vampire wet himself.

"You safe now," Remy told her. "Mate protect you, too."

"Your mate?" Emma looked around. "Is she here?"

Remy's confused gaze met mine, and I saw a disaster about to happen. I had no idea how he knew I'd imprinted on Emma, but she was not ready to learn that. Especially not like this.

"Thanks, Remy," I said. "It was great of you to help out like this."

"Yes, thank you," Emma told him.

"I happy to help Sara's friends," he replied. And just like that, he was gone.

Emma

My knees nearly gave out, and I sagged against the wall. A troll. I'd just met a real live troll. I'd heard about them; there weren't many things that scared vampires more than sunlight and the Mohiri. Trolls were one of them. But I never in my life expected to stand in the same room with one of them.

"I know how you feel," said Roland as he led me to the couch. "I met Remy the same way, right here in this apartment, and I nearly stroked out. I think Nikolas almost did, too."

I stared at the hall through the archway. "I can't believe I screamed like that. Sara talked about him all the time, and I should have known who he was."

Roland chuckled. "I think he has that effect on everyone."

"How do you contact a troll?" I asked, still slightly dazed from the encounter.

"I have no idea. Must be a Fae thing."

I opened my mouth to say something when it registered that he was sitting beside me with his arm around me, and I was leaning into his warmth like it was the most natural thing in the world. I smiled sadly. How could something so wrong feel so right?

I pulled away from him and moved over on the couch until my back pressed against the armrest and my feet were tucked under me. An awkward silence descended upon the room, and I had no idea how to fix it. But staying near him wasn't an option. I didn't know what he was thinking, but if he tried to kiss me again, I didn't trust myself to refuse him. And I had to because there was nothing down that road for me but heartbreak.

"So, you had coffee with Shannon and April today."

I looked at him and found him watching me with a neutral expression that told me nothing of what he was feeling. Maybe I'd imagined the closeness between us because I'd wanted to feel something. Maybe the kiss had just been a heat of the moment thing for him after all.

"Yes. We had a great time. I really like them."

He smiled and settled back against the couch. "I hope now you see for yourself that we're not so bad."

"I already knew that about you."

His eyes warmed. "I'm glad to hear that."

My stomach did a little flip, and I rushed to find safer ground. "How is the Chevelle coming along?"

I knew I'd asked the right question when his mouth curved into a wide smile.

"Great. We're ahead of schedule, and Paul's already talking to another guy about restoring a seventy-one Dodge Challenger. If we get that job, he thinks he can line up two more."

"That's fantastic."

He nodded happily. "Yeah. If we can get five or six big jobs, I might be able to bank enough to buy into the garage with Paul."

I thought about all the money sitting in my account, money I hadn't done a thing to earn, and guilt pressed down on me. I had more than I needed, and Roland was working two jobs to make enough money to realize his dream. It didn't seem fair, and I wished I could give him some of mine.

"I never expected all of this when I was working on the Mustang," he said with a note of wonder in his voice.

"The Mustang is beautiful. Did you always want to do that?"

"Thanks." His chest swelled at my compliment. "I never thought about restoring a car until Paul suggested it when I found the Mustang. But I've always been into classic cars."

I made a face. "I have to confess I don't know much about muscle cars. I know a Mustang when I see one, but I don't know the difference between a Chevelle and a Challenger."

"Are you serious?" His look of disbelief was almost comical. He pulled out his phone and played with it for a minute before he handed it to me. "This is a Chevelle. The one I'm working on will look like that when I'm done."

I studied the sleek red car on the screen. "It's pretty."

He shook his head at my choice of words. I grinned and gave the phone back to him. He searched again and showed me a blue car this time. "And this is like the Dodge Challenger we might be doing. I can't wait to get my hands on this one."

I loved how excited he was about his work. It was the same way I felt when I started a new painting.

"I can't wait to see them when you're done," I said.

He laid the phone on his lap. "You don't have to wait. You're welcome to come by the garage anytime."

"Paul won't mind?" I felt both relieved and sad that we were back in the friend zone again.

"Not at all. He's pretty easygoing."

"Steve, the cook at the diner, said he'd teach me how to make cookies. If they're edible, I'll bring you guys some."

He let out a laugh. "They'd have to be pretty awful for us not to eat them."

It was my turn to snort. "You obviously don't realize how bad I am in the kitchen."

"I don't know," he said with a sly smile. "You make a mean espresso."

I grabbed the pillow beside me and hit him in the chest with it. He caught it, laughing, and tossed it back at me. I retaliated automatically by nudging his ribs with my foot, like I used to do with Chelsea when we horsed around.

Roland's hand captured my bare foot, and my breath caught as a tingle shot up my leg. His playful grin faded, and heat blazed in his eyes, turning my insides to warm goo. His heady scent seemed to fill the room, reminding me of our scorching kiss and making me want to climb into his lap and pick up where we'd left off.

He swallowed, his gaze lowering to my mouth. "Emma, I –"

His voice broke the spell over us, and I released the breath I was holding as reality came crashing in. I fought the insane urge to cry as I eased my foot away from him and tucked it safely under me. Where had I thought this was going anyway? I didn't want a casual hookup, and there could be nothing beyond that for Roland and me.

I managed a smile. "Thanks for being here. It's nice to know I have so many friends watching out for me."

"Friends...yeah." His brow furrowed slightly, and he tapped his thigh. "I guess I should get going. I was supposed to meet Paul at the garage half an hour ago."

"Oh."

I stood, and after a short hesitation, he did the same. It wasn't that I wanted him to leave. I was afraid of what would happen if he stayed.

"Are you okay here alone?" he asked when we reached the front door.

"Yes."

It wasn't a total lie. Remy's magic might keep out the bad guys, but it couldn't keep the loneliness at bay.

He opened the door. "If you don't mind, I'll come by to check on the place until we know that man isn't a problem."

"You don't have to –"

"I want to." He stepped outside and turned to smile at me. "And I'll be waiting for those cookies."

The tension inside me lifted. "Don't expect much. I wasn't joking about my awful cooking skills."

He chuckled and headed down the steps. "I have a lot of faith in Steve's teaching abilities. And in you."

The next evening after the dinner rush was over, Steve took me into the kitchen for my first baking lesson. We were making chocolate chip cookies, and he had all the ingredients laid out on the metal worktable. He explained the basics before he had me help him measure and mix the ingredients, and drop the cookie dough on the baking sheets. Then he opened the door to the big convection oven so I could slide the two sheets onto the rack.

"Delicious," he said fifteen minutes later, nibbling on one of the cookies, fresh from the oven. "You're a natural."

I laughed and broke my own cookie in two. "You did most of the work." I took my first bite. "Oh my God, this is amazing!"

"It's the sea salt. Makes all the difference."

"Mmmm," I said through a mouthful of cookie. "Beft cookie efer."

Steve set the racks of cookies on another table to cool, and then he started getting stuff to make apple pies for tomorrow. I wasn't ready to tackle pastry, so I only watched as he went about his work. After he'd put four pies in the oven, I helped him clean up, and then he sent me home with two cookies and a promise of another lesson on Thursday.

It was dusk when I left the diner, but I was nervous being out alone after my little scare yesterday. I was glad for the scooter because it meant I didn't have to walk alone, but it bothered me that I was afraid here now. I'd seen no sign of the bald man, and I hoped it had been my paranoia and overactive imagination at work.

At home, I drove around to the back door to put the scooter up for the night. I kept the outside light on back here when I knew I'd be late getting home. The light didn't do much to help my jitters, though. I dropped my keys and let out a cry when I heard a noise farther down the long alley behind the buildings. My breath came out in a whoosh when a small shape darted out from between two buildings.

Just a cat. I picked up my keys with a shaking hand and reached for the door.

It took me several seconds to realize I wasn't alone. My heart slammed into my ribs, and I whirled to face the corner I'd just come around. I made a choked sound at the sight of the large dark shape standing just outside the circle of light.

13

Emma

The thing took several steps until it entered the light, and my knees almost gave out when I recognized the black werewolf.

"Oh, my God, you scared me half to death," I scolded him as I tried to calm my racing heart. "You really need to stop sneaking up on me like that."

His only answer was to sit on his haunches.

I pulled off my helmet and brushed hair from my face. "What are you doing here anyway? Aren't you worried you'll be seen?"

He shook his head once.

"You should be. People will freak if they see a monstrous wolf walking around the waterfront."

He snorted and cocked his head at me.

"What?" I rolled my eyes. "Have you seen yourself? You're not exactly inconspicuous."

Nothing.

I sighed. "Roland sent you, didn't he? You're here because of what happened yesterday."

This time I got a nod.

"I'm okay, thanks. I really appreciate you guys watching out for me, but you don't have to hang around here."

I hung the helmet on the handle bar and inserted my key into the door lock. The werewolf didn't move as I opened the double doors and rolled the

Vespa inside. I started to close the doors when I saw the werewolf was where I'd left him.

"Are you planning to stay out here all night?"

He gave another shake of his head.

"Good. I'd feel terrible if someone saw you and you got in trouble because of me." I pulled the door toward me. "Night."

Upstairs, I showered and changed into a T-shirt and a pair of cotton capris, the whole time thinking about the werewolf. What was he thinking, coming downtown in his fur? I hadn't been kidding when I said people would freak. Even a normal wolf in town would cause a commotion. And there was nothing normal about him.

I went to the kitchen to heat up leftover pizza from last night. Gino's had a two-for-one sale going on this week, so I'd ended up with two large meat pizzas. I was going to be eating this stuff until I was sick of it.

Pouring a glass of soda, I sat at the table with my dinner. As I took my first bite, my thoughts went back to the wolf. It had been half an hour since I came upstairs. Was he still out there? My eyes fell on the pizza box on the counter. Maybe he was hungry. If he was going to hang around here for me, the least I could do was feed him.

I went to the counter and lifted the lid of the box, debating whether or not to heat the pizza. Deciding against it, I pulled on a pair of sandals and carried the pizza downstairs. I opened the back door and looked out, but there was no sign of the wolf. He must have left already. I felt a tiny prick of disappointment as I pulled back inside. As much as I didn't want him to get caught, I'd felt better knowing he was nearby.

Movement drew my eye, and I smiled when I saw him walk around the corner of the building.

"Hey," I called softly, beckoning him over. I held up the box. "I thought you might like some pizza in case you get hungry."

His amber eyes looked at the box and back at me, but he made no move to take it from me.

"Do you like pizza?" I asked, and he nodded.

"Don't worry. I have plenty. I'll never be able to eat it all." I lifted the box again. "Please, take it. I want you to have it."

He closed the distance between us and took the box in his powerful jaws. Even on four legs, his eyes were level with mine, and his chest was almost twice as wide as me. I should have been terrified, standing before such a fearsome creature. Instead, I wondered if his fur was as coarse as it looked, and I had the sudden urge to reach out and touch it.

"Enjoy your pizza," I said and retreated inside before I could act on my crazy impulse. What the hell had gotten into me, wanting to touch a were-wolf? I doubted he'd appreciate me petting him like a big dog.

I went back upstairs and ate my own pizza, my thoughts once again occupied by the wolf. As I rinsed my plate, it occurred to me this was the third time I'd seen him, and I still didn't know his name. It wasn't like he could tell me while he was in wolf form, but it would be nice to have something to call him if I saw him again.

Roland

"This is stupid. We've been here for hours and we haven't seen a single demon," Trevor complained loudly from the back seat of Shawn's Cherokee. "What a fucking waste of a night."

I gritted my teeth and bit back an angry reply. The guy hadn't stopped bitching since we left home four hours ago, and I was starting to think Maxwell was punishing me for something. Not just me. The way Shawn's hands gripped the wheel told me I wasn't the only one fed up with Trevor's attitude.

I could think of a lot of things I'd rather be doing than driving around all night, listening to Trevor griping. Emma's face filled my mind, and I thought about her standing before me, last night, offering me some of her pizza. For a few seconds, I'd thought she was going to touch me, and I'd been disappointed when she hadn't. But the way she'd spoken to me made it clear she was comfortable with my wolf, which made him and me happy. I'd hated leaving her tonight, but pack business called. Paul had promised to drive by and keep an eye on her place since Pete and I were working.

Trevor huffed. "If the Mohiri know the ranc demons are in Portland, you'd think they'd be able to tell us where the bloody demons are holed up."

"They gave us a list of places to check." I glanced down at the paper Maxwell had given me.

"I bet they gave Maxwell those just to watch us make fools of ourselves."

"The Mohiri have better things to do than toy with us," I said evenly. "They take their job very seriously."

"And I suppose you're the expert on them," he shot back. He'd been trying to provoke me all night, but I wasn't falling for it.

"I know enough."

Shawn pulled into a small motel that looked like it had been closed down for at least a year. He parked in front of the glass front door, the headlights shining into the dark, deserted lobby.

"This is the last place on the list." He turned off the engine and looked over at me. "What do you think, oh mighty leader?"

I scowled at him, and he smirked.

Shaking my head, I studied the two-story building and eyed the thick chain and padlock on the front door. "If anyone is using this place, they didn't go in through that door. Let's check the back."

Shawn drove us around the motel and stopped near the rear exit that didn't have a padlock.

I unbuckled my seat belt. "I'll check the door."

Trevor muttered something, but I ignored him and got out of the SUV. I gave the door handle a small tug, expecting it to be locked, so I was surprised when the door opened. Easing it shut, I waved at the others to join me.

"Looks like someone's been here," I told them. "It's not that big, so it shouldn't take long to search the place."

"We going in pairs again?" Shawn asked.

"Yeah. You and Pete take the second floor. Trevor and I will search down here."

Shawn's eyebrows shot up. I'd paired him with Trevor at the last three places, and he'd clearly expected that again. But Trevor was becoming more belligerent by the hour, and it wasn't fair to keep pawning him off on Shawn.

I opened the door, and we entered the building. Pete and Shawn went to the door to the stairs, and Trevor and I continued silently down the dark hall. Our eyesight was best in wolf form, but even in this form it was better than a human's and enough to help us easily find our way.

At the first door, I motioned for Trevor to stand guard while I checked the room. He huffed but didn't argue, which was a first.

I opened the door and walked into the small room. To my left was the bathroom, and ahead of me was the bare room that had been stripped of all its furniture and drapes. A quick sweep of the room told me no one had been in here. I left, and we moved to the next one.

It didn't take long to work our way to the lobby. Neither of us spoke as we searched the rooms on the other side of the building and arrived back at the lobby empty-handed.

"Empty," Trevor scoffed, breaking his silence. "Another waste of time."

Instead of replying, I opened the employee door that led to the service and housekeeping area. I doubted I'd find anything, but I wanted to be able to tell Maxwell I did a thorough search of the places we'd been to.

My nose picked up a foreign scent as soon as I walked through the door. It took me a minute to figure out where it was coming from, and then I walked quietly toward the employee lounge. The smell got strong enough for me to know it was demon in origin, but I couldn't tell what species of demon. I definitely knew it wasn't a vampire. I'd been around enough of them to recognize their stench anywhere.

A muffled sound up ahead let me know I wasn't alone. My muscles tensed for an attack, and I slowed my approach to the lounge. The only window provided enough light to make out the shapes inside: two couches and a small round table with two chairs. But no demons.

I stood still, straining my ears, and I picked up a faint rustle from the small kitchenette at the other end of the room. Someone was in here, and they were trying very hard to stay hidden. If I was human, they might have succeeded, but my hearing and smell were even better than my eyesight.

"I know you're back there, so you might as well come out," I called in my most nonthreatening voice.

No one moved.

"I won't hurt you. I just want to ask you a few questions."

Still nothing.

I folded my arms. "I'm blocking the only way out of this room, and I'm not leaving until we talk."

It was another minute before a head of brown, curly hair peeked above the counter, followed by a pale, chubby face. My brows drew together. It was a demon, all right, but definitely not the one I was after. Ranc demons were thin and dark with large horns and catlike eyes. This one was a vrell demon, one of the few who could pass for human if they hid their tiny horns and fangs. They were a timid race, and harmless.

"Please. I know we are not supposed to be here, but we meant no harm," he said in a pleading voice.

We? "How many of you are back there?"

"M-my mate...and our young," he stammered.

Ah hell. I'd busted a family. I sighed and let my arms fall to my sides. "It's okay. You can come out. No one will hurt you."

A second demon appeared beside him, this one obviously female. She bent and came back holding a little male who couldn't be more than three years old. The adults came out from behind the counter, followed by a young female who looked to be about ten. The girl clung to her mother's shirt and stared at me with wide, frightened eyes.

I smiled at the girl, but she shrank away from me. Great, now I was scaring children.

"We will leave," the mother said softly. "Please, don't call the human authorities."

I waved a hand. "Don't worry about them. I don't care about you being in here. I came here looking for –"

"What the hell are those?"

Trevor came through the door, growling, and I put an arm up to keep him away from the demons. He tried to push past me, but I was too strong for him.

"These are not the demons we're looking for," I said.

"Who gives a shit?" he snarled, struggling against me. "They're demons, and the only good demon is a dead demon."

"What's going on?" Pete asked as he and Shawn filled the doorway.

The little girl whimpered and the male shoved his family behind him. Seeing them so frightened after I'd promised they were safe angered me.

"Stand down, Trevor," I ordered.

He ignored me and tried to duck under my arm.

That's it. I grabbed him and slammed him into the wall, holding him there with an arm against his throat. He made a choked sound and clawed at my arm. I applied more pressure until his eyes bulged and he stopped struggling. As soon as he did, I eased off to give him air.

"I told you to stand down," I ground out, staring into his furious eyes until he dropped his gaze. "Do I have to tell you again?"

"No," he sputtered.

"Good." I released him and walked to the center of the room so I was between him and the vrell family. "We have orders to find and question ranc demons. These are vrell demons."

"How do you know what they are?" Shawn asked. We didn't get many demons in Maine, and I doubted he'd ever seen one in person.

"We met one out west. Nice guy."

Pete nodded. "Yeah, Kelvan is cool. He's like a super hacker or something."

Trevor sneered. "You two ran off last year to hang out with demons? You don't deserve to be Betas."

"And you do?" I barked a laugh. "At least I can tell one demon from another."

I turned to the vrell family. "We're looking for some ranc demons. You see any in town?"

The female's lip curled, telling me exactly what she thought of the other demons.

Her mate shook his head. "We haven't seen them, but we were told to stay away from the wharves to avoid them."

"Told by who?" I asked him.

"Another of our kind who we met when we arrived in town," he said.

I rubbed my jaw. "Did your friend say anything about vampires?"

"Vampires?" the female squeaked. She grabbed her mate's arm. "Markas, you said this city would be safe for our young. We gave up everything to come here."

Markas hugged her with one arm. "We are safe here, Risa."

I looked from him to her. "You guys in some kind of trouble?"

"No," Markas replied. "We lived in Miami until I had a run-in with a vampire. We decided to move to Maine because everyone knows it's werewolf territory and there are no vampires here."

"Why are you staying in this place?" Pete asked. "No money?"

Markas shook his head. "I was supposed to have a job waiting for me, but when we got here, the job was gone. We have enough saved to get an apartment, but no one will rent to us since I am unemployed."

Trevor scoffed. "Nice sob story. Next thing you know, we'll be overrun by these things."

"Trevor," I snapped without looking at him. "Wait for us outside."

He stomped off without a word, and the demons visibly relaxed.

"I'm sorry about that." Looking at the little boy clinging to his mother's neck, I knew I couldn't leave them here like this. Demons or not, kids shouldn't be living in an abandoned motel.

"I need to call someone," I told the couple. "Can you tell my friends here what you know about the ranc demons?"

"Yes," Markas said.

I walked out into the hall and checked the time on my phone. It was just after 8:00 a.m. for Sara, so I figured she was awake. I texted her, and sure enough, she replied within a minute. I quickly filled her in on the vrell demons' dilemma and asked her to contact Kelvan and give him my number. She and Kelvan had become good friends after she'd healed his dying cat, and they chatted all the time. The two of them had been working together for months, helping demons in need. If anyone could help this family, it was them.

Sara and I were still texting when my phone rang a few minutes later. Kelvan didn't waste time on pleasantries, asking to speak to Markas as soon as I'd explained the situation to him. I handed my phone to the vrell demon, who looked at it warily for a few seconds before accepting it.

I walked over to Pete and Shawn while the demons were talking. Pete looked like he was holding back a grin, and Shawn was giving me an odd look like he was trying to figure me out.

"What did you find out?" I asked them.

"Not much," Pete said. "They met another vrell demon down by the waterfront on Monday. He told them he'd run across three ranc demons down there the night before. Said they looked like trouble."

"Ranc demons are always trouble." The big question was whether or not they were here on their own or following vampires. I didn't want to think about what had happened the last time vampires had entered our territory.

"Excuse me, sir," Markas called.

I turned to find him holding out my phone. "It's Roland," I said as I took the phone. "Was Kelvan able to help you?"

His head bobbed. "Yes. He's going to help us find an apartment, and he knows of a place I can get a good job."

"That's great."

Risa's dark eyes welled. "We can't thank you enough for what you've done for us. We never dreamed we'd meet friends of *talael esledur.*"

I frowned. "I'm sorry. I don't know what that means."

"The kind warrior," she explained. "The Mohiri female who comes to us in need."

"Ah, Sara." I smiled. "Yeah, that's a good name for her."

Markas returned my smile, showing off his tiny fangs. "We are in your debt."

"Glad we could help." I pocketed my phone. "We need to get going. You guys okay here for tonight?"

"Yes," Risa said.

"You might want to lock the door behind us," Pete suggested.

Markas followed us to the back door, thanking us again before we left. Outside, we found Trevor leaning against the front of the Jeep, his arms crossed and his face sullen. He wisely kept his mouth shut as I pulled out my phone again and called Maxwell.

"Good job," he praised gruffly after I'd related the story to him. "Check out the waterfront, and see what you can find."

"Yes, sir."

I hid my surprise. I'd expected him to say he was sending in more experienced wolves to round up the ranc demons. That he was giving me the job spoke loudly of his confidence in my team. I wondered if he'd feel the same way if I told him about my problems with Trevor, but this wasn't the time or place to go into that with him.

"So, we done for the night?" Shawn asked after I hung up.

"Not quite. Maxwell wants us to follow up on the waterfront lead."

He gave me a disbelieving look. "You're serious?"

"Yep." I walked over and opened the front passenger door. "Let's go find some ranc demons."

Shawn's face split in a wide grin. "Lead on, boss."

It was 7:00 a.m. when I walked into Pete's kitchen where Maxwell and Brendan sat having coffee. Suppressing a yawn, I poured a coffee and added just enough cream and sugar to take the bitterness away. I wasn't a coffee person, but I needed some caffeine or I was going to fall asleep on my feet.

Setting my mug on the table, I rubbed my face wearily as I sat and told my Alpha what he was waiting to hear.

"We found the ranc demons breaking into a butcher shop in South Portland around 4:00 a.m. There were three of them, and it took a while to get anything out of them." I scowled at the memory. "They weren't that scared of us until I shifted. That got them talking."

"What did they tell you?" Maxwell asked.

"They're bounty hunters, looking for a taag demon who used to work for a gulak named Draegan in LA. Nikolas killed Draegan in December, and the taag demon apparently made off with a ton of money. Some of Draegan's pals hired the ranc demons to track him down. They swore the job had nothing to do with vampires."

Brendan tapped a finger on the table. "You believe them?"

I shrugged. "I don't think you can ever trust those guys completely, but their story sounded real. Nikolas did kill Draegan, and we met the taag demon when we went to the gulak's place."

Maxwell leaned back in his chair. "How did you track them down at the butcher shop?"

"We drove around the waterfront for a few hours first," I admitted. "Then I remembered that ranc demons live off animal blood. Best place to find that is a butcher shop, and they couldn't exactly go into one during the day and buy a bucket of pig's blood. We got lucky and found them at the third place we went to."

"I wouldn't call that luck," Brendan said.

Maxwell nodded. "Nor would I. Your team did well."

"Thanks." I covered my mouth to stifle another yawn. "I'm beat. Do you mind if I get in a few hours' sleep before I head over to the yard?"

"Take the day. You've earned it."

I felt my eyebrows shoot up. Maxwell had never given me a day off. Unless you were half dead, you had to be there for your shift.

Instead of answering my unspoken question, he said, "I take it your team worked well together last night."

"Good enough to get the job done."

"And Gosse?"

I met his stare. "We had a difference of opinion, but we worked it out."

He took a drink of coffee. "Tell me."

I knew that tone. It was the one he used when he already knew the answer to his question. But how could he possibly know about last night?

"Trevor went after the vrell demons. I ordered him to back off, but he wouldn't listen, so I had to use force."

"According to him, you strangled him and you would have killed him if Peter and Shawn hadn't shown up."

I choked on my coffee and ended up wheezing for a minute before I could respond. That lying weasel. He must have called Maxwell as soon as we dropped him off this morning. I should have kicked his ass at that motel. It wasn't like he hadn't been spoiling for it all night.

"I restrained him with my arm against his throat until he stopped fighting me." I let out an angry breath. "It was either that or punch his lights out, and I'm starting to wish I'd done that instead."

"Why didn't you?" Brendan asked, surprising me.

"I didn't have to. I'm bigger, stronger, and a better fighter. There was no reason to hit him when I could subdue him."

Maxwell looked thoughtful. "If I were to assign you four to the same team again with Gosse as leader, would you follow him?"

I took a deep breath. "Honestly? I'd do it if you ordered it, but if he got out of line like he did last night, I'd have to stop him. I won't stand back and allow him to hurt an innocent."

I wasn't sure what Maxwell was looking for, but he didn't seem displeased by my statement. Even if I'd angered him, I wouldn't change my answer.

He got up and went to refill his coffee cup. "That'll be all for now. Go get some sleep."

"Okay." I carried my mug to the sink and rinsed it. Then I got out of there before they changed their minds and asked me more questions.

I tumbled into my bed when I got home, but as tired as I was, I didn't fall asleep immediately. I lay there, staring at the ceiling and thinking about Emma. It had only been a day and a half since I saw her last, but it felt like a week. I could feel the pull of the imprint growing, but I didn't want to come on too strong with her. To be honest, I wasn't sure what to do.

Emma and I had chemistry, and it wasn't just on my side. I'd felt it in the way she'd kissed me, and it was there again when we were playing around on her couch. And she liked being with me; I wasn't imagining that. So, why had she run from me after the kiss? Why had she pulled away the other night at her apartment?

"Argh." I threw an arm across my eyes. A week ago, I dreaded imprinting and I'd done all I could to stay away from the females. Now, I couldn't stop thinking about a girl who seemed determined to keep me at arm's length. It was enough to drive a guy crazy.

14

Emma

The bell above the door chimed, and I peered over the top of the cash register as Brenda grabbed a menu and led a blonde woman to one of my booths.

I suppressed a groan and finished ringing up the bill for my other occupied table. I was fifteen minutes away from finishing a double shift after covering for Tina, who was out with the flu. My feet hurt, and my stomach was going to cave in if I didn't put something in it soon. Hoping the woman was a light eater, I put on a smile and went to her booth.

"Hi. What can I get for you this evening?"

She glanced at the menu then smiled up at me. "I'll have a coffee and a piece of cherry pie."

"Sure thing." I took her menu and went to get her food.

"This looks delicious," she said when I laid the pie in front of her. "I probably shouldn't eat it, but calories don't count when you're on vacation, right?"

I laughed. "Right."

"This is my first visit to this area. Such a pretty place and the people are so friendly."

"They are."

She poured creamer into her coffee. "Maybe you can suggest the best things to see and do in town. I'm only here for a few days, and I want to make the most of it."

"I'm new here, too," I said apologetically. "But Brenda would know."

"Oh. Your family just moved here? Lucky girl. I love the ocean." She took a sip of her coffee. "Where did you move from?"

"New York."

"Wow. This must feel pretty different for you then. I'm from Minnesota, born and raised, but I may have to move to Maine after this vacation." She chuckled and tucked her shoulder-length hair behind her ear. "I wonder what the job market is like here. You don't look that old. Are you still in school?"

"Yes," I answered vaguely, starting to get uncomfortable. The woman was friendly enough and she looked normal – late twenties, nicely dressed – but something about her niggled at me.

"Excuse me. I need to check on my other customers. Enjoy your pie."

I walked over to my only other occupied table and asked if they needed anything else. Collecting their plates, I carried them to the kitchen then went back to the counter to see if anyone there needed a refill on their drinks. Every now and then, I glanced over at the woman's table to see if she had finished eating. I hoped she didn't order anything else because I was so ready for this shift to be over.

She waved to get my attention, and I hurried over to her, relieved to see her pulling cash from her wallet to pay her bill.

"That pie was amazing." She handed me a ten-dollar bill. "Keep the change."

"Thanks." A four-dollar tip for pie and coffee. Not bad.

She shimmied out of the booth and picked up her small purse. "I need to go walk off the pie, but it was worth it. Maybe I'll see you again tomorrow."

"Have a good night."

As I watched her leave, I suddenly realized what was off about her. I'd been all over the US and I'd spent time in Minnesota, where they had a very distinct accent, one that had been missing from the woman's voice. If I had to guess, I'd say she was from the East Coast. Why would she lie about that?

My other customers had left, so I cleaned both tables and went to clock out. Steve was waiting for me at the window with a takeout bag when I grabbed my bag from beneath the counter.

I took the heavy bag from him. "What's this?"

"Dinner."

He waved me off when I reached for my wallet. "It's on the house. You earned it."

"Thanks." I gave him a grateful smile. The last thing I wanted to do was go home and try to cook. I'd gotten the hang of the basics like grilled cheese and hamburgers, and I'd been wanting to try my hand at actual recipes from the cookbook I'd bought. Not tonight, though. I was too tired to go anywhere near a stove now.

Outside, it was darker than normal for this time of day, and I looked up at the overcast sky, hoping it didn't rain until I got home. Hurrying to the Vespa, I stowed my messenger bag and dinner in the compartment and pulled on my helmet. My stomach growled angrily at the wonderful smell of fried food coming from the bag, and I hopped on the scooter, eager to get home.

I was pulling out of my spot when I noticed the woman I'd served, sitting in a silver Hyundai a few parking spaces away. The car was running, and she appeared to be typing something on her phone. Before I could look away, her head lifted and she stared straight at me. A smile curved her lips and she waved, but not before I saw the shrewd way she'd looked at me.

A chill skittered down my spine as I left the parking lot, and I found myself checking my mirrors all the way home. There was no sign of the Hyundai, and I wondered if I was imagining danger everywhere now because of the bald man in Portland.

Once I put the scooter away, I double-checked that all the doors were bolted before I went to shower and change. Sara's troll friend had promised no one bad could get inside the building, but I still didn't feel completely safe. I told myself I was being silly, but the fear lingered as I walked into the kitchen to eat, my hair still damp from the shower.

I opened the Styrofoam container and laughed at the amount of food Steve had stuffed into the box. I loved his fish and chips, but he'd put in enough to feed a small family. What the heck was I going to do with all this food?

I thought about the black wolf. Werewolves had huge appetites, and I bet he wouldn't turn down some of this.

Shaking off the idea, I got a plate and dished up a large piece of fish and a generous heap of fries for myself. I hadn't seen the wolf last night so I doubted he'd be here tonight. Most likely he'd been here as a favor for Roland and that was the last I'd see of him.

I carried my food and a glass of soda to the living room and flicked on the television. I didn't care much for TV shows, but it was too quiet here and I wanted a distraction. I flipped through the channels, but it seemed like every one of them was playing one of those reality shows. Whatever happened to shows with real actors? I mean, seriously, who wants to watch a bunch of guys cleaning out storage units? TV had changed a lot in the last two decades and not for the better, in my opinion.

I settled on a rerun of *The Fresh Prince*, but halfway through, my nostalgia turned to depression when I remembered watching the episode at Chelsea's house. It was one of the reasons I didn't watch TV anymore. There were too many memories, and I needed to move forward, not look back. Someday, I hoped I'd be able to look at things from my past without feeling all the sadness. I just wasn't there yet.

Turning off the television, I went to rinse my plate. I picked up the takeout box to put it in the fridge and paused with my hand on the door. I hated day old fries, so I wasn't going to eat this tomorrow. Maybe I should check to see if the wolf was there. If he wasn't, another of Roland's friends could be there, and I was sure they'd appreciate Steve's cooking.

I went downstairs and opened the back door gingerly. "Hello?" I called softly. "Are you there?"

It surprised me how disappointed I felt when he didn't appear. It wasn't as if I'd really believed he'd be here, and the guy had to have a life besides hanging around at my place.

A sound drew my attention to the corner, and I stared, breathlessly, as he walked toward me, as big and fierce as ever. He stopped two feet away, and I was a little shocked at how happy I was to see him. Or was I relieved? Either way, I was glad he'd come.

I cleared my throat. "Hi. I wasn't sure if you'd be here. I...um...wondered if you wanted something to eat. I brought home fish and chips from work, and it's enough for three people...or one werewolf."

He cocked his head, his amber eyes staring into mine, and it hit me I might have insulted him by offering him leftovers like he was a stray dog. How thoughtless of me. Under that fur was an intelligent person who had feelings, too.

"I'm sorry. I thought you might be hungry. I won't bother you again."

He moved so fast he was beside me before I could blink. His hot breath washed over my face and hands as he gently took the box in his mouth. I should have felt fear, having those long canines so close to my throat. Instead, warmth filled my chest, and I smiled like a fool as I let go of the box.

"Oh, good." I watched him lay the box on the ground. "I didn't think to bring you something to drink. I hope that's okay."

He lifted his head and nodded. If I didn't know better, I'd say he was smiling at me. Could wolves smile?

"Enjoy your food." I pulled the door toward me. "Night."

I heard a soft chuffing sound as the door closed, and I felt much lighter as I made my way upstairs again. No longer tired, I changed and went up to the studio to work on the painting of the mine. It was coming along slower than I liked, but the picture was gradually coming to life. I really hoped Sara liked it when I gave it to her. She and Nikolas were going to visit when they got back from Russia, and I wanted to have her paintings done by then.

Knowing the wolf was close by put me strangely at ease, and I happily lost myself in my art as I hadn't been able to do for a long time. I would have stayed there painting for hours if I hadn't been distracted by the sound of rain suddenly pelting the windows and drumming on the roof. I walked to one of the windows and looked out at the waterfront, but the streetlights were nothing but a watery blur. A woman ran from the coffee shop next door to a waiting car, and I heard a faint squeal as she got drenched.

Better you than me.

I started back to my easel and stopped as I pictured the wolf out there in this downpour. He was here because of me when he could be somewhere warm and dry.

He's a werewolf, I reminded myself. In their fur, they were more than equipped to handle the elements. For all I knew, he liked the rain. And if he didn't, he'd probably take cover under the front steps. I had a suspicion that was where he was staying out of sight anyway. I walked over and picked up my brush. *He's fine.*

It took me several minutes to realize I'd been staring at the canvas without making a single brush stroke. All I could see was the wolf huddled under the steps, soaking wet. I sighed, knowing it was silly to worry about a huge werewolf getting wet, but I couldn't help it. The least I could do was check on him and make sure he was comfortable out there.

Laying down the brush, I headed downstairs. The rain was muted on the second floor, but I could still hear it battering the windows. Grabbing some shoes and a large umbrella from the coat closet, I went down to the first floor for the third time tonight.

I unbolted the door and pushed it open, unprepared for the cold spray that doused me before I could open my umbrella. I let out a small shriek as water ran into my bra and down my back.

A black shape charged around the corner and came to a stop three feet from me. The wolf's eyes were narrowed, and his mouth was open in a snarl as he looked around, searching for the threat. My lungs squeezed at the feral power emanating from him, and it took me a minute to find my voice.

"There's nothing wrong." I put up my umbrella to keep the spray off my face. "I'm sorry I startled you."

He swung his head toward me and water flew off him. If he had been dry under the step, he certainly wasn't now. *Great job, Emma.*

"I wanted to make sure you were okay down here. I mean...I know you can take care of yourself, but it's raining pretty hard, and I hate getting wet, so I thought..."

I stopped rambling like an idiot and swallowed. "Listen, if you're going to hang around here tonight, you can stay in here if you want. It's dry, at least, and there's less chance of someone seeing you."

He stared at me and I thought he was going to decline my offer, so I was surprised when he walked toward me. I backed up through the door, holding it open until he wedged his body into the doorway. At first. I thought he wouldn't fit and I'd have to open the second door, but he squeezed through.

Once he was inside, the storage area seemed a lot smaller. God, he was massive. Forget the troll's magic. I wouldn't want to be the person who came through that door and found themselves face-to-face with this guy.

Water ran off him to pool on the concrete floor, and I looked around for something he could use to dry himself.

"Hold on while I run up and get some towels for –"

"Hey!" I sputtered when a spray of water hit me in the face. I glared at the wolf as he shook his fur out vigorously. "You did that on purpose."

If I'd thought he was smiling earlier, he was positively grinning now. It was hard to keep a stern face when he stood there with his tongue hanging out and his fur sticking up in every direction. He didn't look so fierce now.

I rolled my eyes and turned to the stairs. "Men."

The wolf snorted.

"Keep it up," I called over my shoulder as I climbed the stairs, "and you won't be getting any more pizza here."

He huffed and sank to the floor.

I was smiling so hard my face hurt when I closed the door behind me.

"Please?" I whimpered, straining against the ropes that held my arms above my head. "Please, let me go."

Eli's hungry eyes moved over me. "But the fun is just beginning."

My stomach clenched in fear, and I began to sob. "I won't tell anyone. I promise. I just want to go h-home."

"Ah, sweet thing, you are home. And you and I are going to get to know each other real well."

He crossed the room toward me. Terror clawed at my chest when his hand reached out to cup my chin, forcing me to look at him. His lips parted in a smile, and two glistening fangs sprouted from his mouth.

I screamed.

. . .

A crash ripped me from the nightmare, and I jolted upright in bed as an enormous black shape filled the bedroom doorway. I scrabbled backward until my back hit the headboard, and opened my mouth to scream.

The thing dropped to all fours, and it took several heart-pounding seconds for my brain to register that it was the wolf. I gulped in air and slumped against the pillows, my muscles weak.

"I'm okay. It was just a bad dream. I-I get them sometimes," I babbled, hugging the blanket to my chest.

He stepped cautiously into the room and sat, as if trying not to frighten me. His presence filled the bedroom, and my fear abated. In its wake, I was overcome by the knowledge that I wasn't alone anymore.

My eyes welled, and to my mortification, I began to cry.

"I'm sorry." I buried my face in my hands. "I'm just..." *So glad you're here.*

I didn't care that he was a werewolf, or that I'd be the last person he'd protect if he knew what I'd done. All that mattered was that, for the first time in months, I felt truly safe. I didn't even know his name, but I knew that as long as he was near, nothing would harm me.

The wolf whined softly.

I lifted my head to see him in the same spot, watching me with worried eyes. Sniffling, I wiped my face on the bedsheet, wishing I had a tissue. I must look a mess with my crazy bed hair and puffy eyes.

"I'm fine," I said hoarsely. I looked at the window and saw it was still dark outside. I was surprised he'd stayed all night, but happy he was here. Though, after this, he might not want to do Roland any more favors.

"Sorry for the trouble. I feel bad that I woke you up for a nightmare."

I got out of bed and went into the bathroom to splash water on my face and brush the tangles from my hair. When I came out, the wolf was where I'd left him.

I glanced at my clock radio and saw it was only 5:00 a.m. Sighing, I grabbed some clothes and looked at the wolf.

"Would you mind leaving so I can get dressed?"

He backed out into the hallway. I shut the door and changed out of the T-shirt and shorts I'd worn to bed. I was still tired, but too wound up from the dream to go back to sleep. It was a good thing I had the afternoon shift at the diner today. I'd try to take a nap before then.

The wolf had moved to the other end of the hallway, looking like a monstrous dog guarding the front door. He made even Sara's hellhounds look small, though I didn't think any werewolf could beat Hugo or Woolf in a fight, no matter how big he was.

I went to the kitchen and flicked on the light. Might as well make us breakfast now that I was up.

"You hungry?" I asked over my shoulder as I peered into the fridge. What would a werewolf eat for breakfast? Meat, of course. Lots of it.

I pulled out a pack of bacon and a carton of eggs. There wasn't a lot I could cook, but bacon and eggs I could handle. Soon the kitchen filled with the delicious smell of bacon frying. I cooked the whole pack, placing three slices on my plate and the rest on his. Then I added a modest portion of scrambled eggs to mine and a mountain to his. I almost laughed at the ridiculous pile of food on his plate, but he could probably eat twice that amount.

I picked up his heavy plate and hesitated. It seemed like an insult to put it on the floor for him. He was a person, after all, even with the fur. I set it on the table instead.

"Breakfast is ready," I called to him, carrying my own plate to the table as if having breakfast with a werewolf was an everyday occurrence.

I was sitting at the table when he appeared in the doorway, looking uncertain for the first time since I'd met him. I'd placed a fork beside his plate because werewolves could use their front paws like hands, but maybe he preferred to forego cutlery in wolf form.

"I wasn't sure how you like to eat. Should I put it on the floor for you?"

He nodded, and I brought his plate to him, laying it at his feet. I noticed he waited until I started eating my food before he dug into his. He finished it in half the time it took me to eat mine, and I suspected he was eating slower than normal.

I washed my breakfast down with orange juice, and it made me realize I hadn't offered him anything to drink.

"Would you be offended if I put a bowl of water down for you?"

He snorted and shook his head. I filled a large glass bowl and put it on the floor by the door. I could hear him lapping the water as I washed up our plates and the frying pan. My reflection in the window caught my eye, and it surprised me to see the smile on my face. I looked...happy.

I'd never recovered from one of my dreams this quickly. I certainly never looked this happy when I saw myself in a mirror. I didn't know if it was the wolf or just having someone here that made me feel lighter than I had in ages. Whatever the reason, I was reluctant for it to end.

I hung up the dish towel and faced the wolf, who lay on the floor, half in the kitchen and half in the hallway, watching me. He looked comfortable and in no hurry to leave, although he'd probably have to go before it got light out.

I wondered if he'd go all the way home as a wolf or if he had clothes stashed nearby. For that matter, why didn't he come here in his human form? I'd grown used to the wolf, but it would have been nice to have someone to talk to. And I still didn't know his name or what he looked like as a human. I could pass him on the street or serve him at the diner and never know he was my new friend.

Friend? Were we friends now? I'd fed him a few times and he'd stayed in my apartment tonight, but was I just a job to him, a favor for Roland? It wasn't like the wolf and I could carry on a real conversation, not like Roland and I did, but I felt comfortable with him. My friendship with Roland was complicated because I'd started to develop feelings for him. It was a lot easier to be around a wolf, where attraction wasn't an issue.

I thought about what to do now. If I was alone, I'd probably read or go upstairs to paint, but it seemed rude to do those things with him in the apartment.

"I have a bunch of movie channels. You want to watch a movie with me?" I'd told Sara I didn't need all those channels, but I was glad for them now.

He lifted his head and looked at me for a moment before he stood and padded into the living room, his long claws clicking on the hardwood floor. There wasn't a space big enough for him to lie down so I pushed the coffee table over to make room beside the couch. It was more than a little surreal to be sitting a foot from a massive werewolf, watching a movie together. Surreal, but oddly not uncomfortable.

I flipped through the movie channels. "What do you want to watch? I'm not picky as long as it's not horror. Let me know when I find something you like."

I hit a dozen channels before he snorted. I tossed the remote on the couch and lay back, resting my head on a pillow.

"*Gone in 60 Seconds*. What is it with you guys and cars?"

He didn't answer, not that I expected him to, and we sat in companionable silence, watching the movie.

Despite the loud action scenes, I soon felt my eyes growing heavy, until I could no longer keep them open. The wolf was engrossed in the movie, so he wouldn't mind me taking a quick nap. Just to rest my eyes for a few minutes...

I awoke to the sound of my alarm clock going off in the bedroom, and it took me several seconds to remember why I was on the couch instead of in my bed. I looked down at the floor, but the wolf was gone. He must have left before daylight.

I tossed aside the soft throw that covered me. Funny, I didn't remember getting it from the chair. Yawning, I stood and went to shut off the alarm.

Most mornings, my dreams woke me before it went off, and it was strange and nice waking from an untroubled sleep for once.

My good mood dampened a little at the knowledge it was the wolf's presence that had helped me sleep better. I hadn't seen the bald man since Monday – if that had, in fact, been him – so there was no reason for Roland or his friends to continue watching my place. I was relieved not to be in danger, but I'd miss the wolf.

Probably for the best.

I'd come to like the werewolves, but I had to learn to take care of myself. Roland had enough to handle with two jobs and the pack. He didn't have time to be worrying about me. And for all I knew, my wolf friend could have a mate and kids he had to take care of. It was selfish of me to want to keep him away from his life.

I thought about how nice it had been to cook for someone, to hang out with them and watch a movie. To sleep peacefully without fear.

Heaving a sigh, I went to my lonely kitchen for a coffee to start my day.

15

Roland

"How's it coming?"

I pulled my head out from under the hood of the Chevelle on Saturday afternoon and gave Paul a greasy thumbs-up.

"Almost there. We'll be able to paint her next week."

He tossed a cleaning rag at me. "That's great because we got the Challenger."

"No way." I wiped my hands on the rag, but it only removed the top layer of grease. "I thought that guy was waiting to see how the Chevelle turned out."

Paul smiled widely. "He was going to, until Evan showed him the pictures I've been sending him of the Chevelle work. Evan's been sharing them with some of his buddies who are into classic muscle cars. We could get enough work from this group alone to keep us busy until Christmas."

"That's great, man." I tried to do the math in my head, but that had never been my strong suit. I did know it added up to a number with at least four zeroes on the end. More money than I'd ever seen. At this rate, Paul and I could be partners before the year was out.

"You haven't heard the best part." His eyes sparkled with anticipation. "Evan's friend, Dean, bought a sixty-five Shelby GT at auction, and it needs a ton of work. He's seen the pictures of your Mustang, and he wants to come by next week to look at her."

I stared at him. "You're shitting me, right?"

"Nope."

"Damn." I'd expected it to take months and a bunch of jobs for us to start building a name for ourselves. I certainly never thought I'd have the opportunity to work on a Mustang Shelby this soon.

Paul chuckled. "I think the name *Greene's Classic Restoration* has a nice ring to it."

"I like that."

He had already worked out how much it would cost to expand the garage and hire another mechanic. It wasn't cheap, but together we could do it if we pooled the money we made for the next six months. That was providing we got the jobs we were hoping for.

The sound of an engine drew our attention to the open bay door, and I smiled when a silver Vespa pulled up outside. I hadn't seen Emma since yesterday morning, and it surprised me how much I missed her already.

I hadn't expected her today, and I'd planned to go see her after work – as me, not my wolf, this time. Both times I'd been to her place this week, I'd gone in my fur because she seemed more comfortable with me in that form. But as much as I liked being with her in any form, I couldn't talk to her in my fur. My wolf loved being with her, but I wanted her to be as comfortable with me as she was with him.

When she'd brought me food and invited me in from the rain the other night, I'd figured it was out of kindness more than any affection she had for my wolf. But when she woke up screaming from that nightmare, she'd relaxed when she saw me there. I hadn't imagined that. She felt safe with me. And when she'd cried, it tore me up inside not to be able to hold her.

After she dressed and came out of the bedroom, I'd been about to go back downstairs when she surprised me with her offer of breakfast. And then she'd asked me to stay and watch a movie. I figured it was because she was afraid of being alone, but it filled me with pleasure to know she took comfort in my presence.

I'd pretended to watch the movie, but I was more attuned to her, which was why I'd known the moment she'd fallen asleep. She'd looked so peaceful and beautiful in her sleep, and it hadn't been easy to leave her, especially after seeing the terror on her face when she'd woken from the nightmare. If I ever found the person who caused her to scream like that, they'd wish they'd never been born.

I walked out to meet her as she shut off the Vespa. She pulled off her helmet, revealing glowing cheeks and a smile that made my heart squeeze.

"This is a nice surprise," I said.

"I thought I'd come by and see where you work. And..." She went to the compartment at the back and pulled out a large plastic container. "Cookies, as promised."

"You made cookies?"

She nodded proudly. "Last night after my shift. Steve supervised, but I did all the work. I hope you like chocolate chip."

I grinned. "Who doesn't like chocolate chip? Come on in. I need to wash my hands."

She walked into the garage with me, her gaze taking everything in. The cleanest area was the office, so I took her there.

"You remember my cousin Paul?" I said when he followed us in, no doubt lured by the smell of homemade cookies.

She smiled at him. "It's nice to see you again."

I left them to run to the bathroom to try to wash most of the gunk off my hands. When I returned, I found Paul with two cookies in his hand and another in his mouth.

"Hey!" I shouldered him aside playfully. "She brought those for me."

"Don't see your name on them," he retorted.

Emma laughed. "I made a whole batch for you to share."

Paul shot me a triumphant look. "See." He beamed at Emma as he snagged two more cookies from the container. "You are my new favorite person."

She smiled prettily, and I shot him a look that said, "Stop flirting with my mate." He smirked and went back into the garage.

"Would you like to try one?" She held up the container.

"Just one?" I gave her a wounded look, and she smacked my arm lightly. The brief touch of her skin on mine sent heat straight to my belly. Man, I was a goner.

She looked away quickly, her teeth tugging at her bottom lip, definitely not the reaction of someone unaffected by me. I could work with that. She might be keeping me at arm's length now, but I had no intention of giving up.

"Take all you want." She pushed the container into my hands. "I hope you like them."

I bit into one. "Mmmm. This is as good as Grandma's."

"Liar. You're just being sweet."

"I'm always sweet," I said with mock chagrin. "And I never, ever lie about food."

Her face lit up. "I'm glad you like them. They're my first cookies."

"I'm honored." I finished my first one and picked up a second. "Come on. I want to show you the car I've been working on."

We went into the garage, and I walked her around the Chevelle, pointing out the work I'd done. She nodded and asked questions, even though I could tell she didn't understand half of what I said. I didn't care, I just liked having her there.

I patted the roof. "She still doesn't look like much yet, but wait until we put on the new tires and get her painted next week. You won't recognize her."

"What color are you painting it?"

"Maroon. The owner wants her restored to her original state."

Emma ran a hand along the side. "Does it run?"

"Does it run?" I slapped a hand to my chest. "I can't believe you asked me that."

Her laughter filled the garage, drawing me closer to her. My eyes met Paul's over her shoulder, and he smiled knowingly.

Handing Emma the cookie container, I sat behind the wheel and fired up the engine. The Chevelle rumbled to life, filling me with pride. It had arrived here on a flatbed, barely able to start. When it left, it would look and drive like new. Better than new – classic.

I shut off the car and got out. I reached for the container and saw Emma rub one of her arms. She wore a light sweater, but Paul and I usually kept it cooler than normal in the garage.

"Let's go outside," I said.

We sat on the bench, soaking up the sun, and I devoured another cookie. "These really are amazing."

"Thanks." She smiled demurely. "You're good for my ego."

"You keep bringing me cookies and I'll write songs about you."

Her eyes widened. "You write songs, too?"

"No. That's how good these are."

I was pouring it on thick, but it worked. She laughed again and relaxed against the back of the bench. I wished it could always be this easy between us.

"I had another reason for coming today," she said, looking a little more serious. "I wanted to thank you for all you've done for me this week. It's nice to know I have friends like you here."

Friends? Yeah. "You're welcome."

"I haven't seen that man since Monday. I'm still not sure it was the same man from Portland. Anyway, I think you and your friend can stop watching my place."

"If you don't mind, I think we'll keep an eye on it for a little while longer." Maybe I was being overprotective, but I'd learned to be cautious.

"I don't mind. Will you send someone else this time?"

Her question took me off guard because I'd gotten the feeling she liked my wolf. Had I misread her?

"You don't want my...friend there?"

She gave me a bright smile. "Oh, no, he's great – even if he doesn't talk. I just feel bad about taking him away from his own life. Hanging around my place isn't the most exciting thing to do."

"Don't worry about that. He wants to do it."

"Oh...good." She watched a car drive past then looked at me again. "Can you at least tell me his –"

"Roland, can you give me a hand with this?" Paul yelled.

"Excuse me a minute." I set the cookie container down on the bench and ran to help him with the Camry he was working on.

When I returned five minutes later, Emma was busy texting someone. My first thought was that it was Scott, and jealousy burned in my gut.

"Shannon," she said, laying the phone on her lap. "She asked me to go to a thing with her and April tonight."

"A thing?" I hid my disappointment. I'd planned to ask Emma if she wanted to do something tonight. But I was also glad to see her and Shannon becoming friends. Pete was my best friend, and I wanted our mates to be close, too. I just needed to convince mine to accept me.

"She said it's like a battle of the bands. It's in Portland at a place called..." She looked down at her phone. "It's called the Attic. You know it?"

"Yeah."

My stomach dipped, and not in a good way, as bad memories surfaced. I still felt guilty for convincing Sara to go to the Attic with Pete and me, and for not keeping her safe from Eli. If it hadn't been for Nikolas, we would have lost her that night.

But that was last fall. There hadn't been a vampire sighting in Portland since then, and Shannon and April were perfectly capable of protecting Emma if they had to.

Emma took a cookie and nibbled on it. "I'm not into clubs, but Shannon said it's more of a place people go to listen to local bands. She knows a girl who sings in one of the bands."

"Sounds like fun. Maybe I should see if Paul wants to go," I said casually. I didn't need to call Pete. He and Shannon were newly mated, so there was no way they were spending the night apart.

Paul walked out of the garage, wiping his hands on a rag. "Go where?"

"To the Attic tonight," I said. "Bunch of bands playing."

"I haven't been there in ages. Who else is going?"

"Shannon, April, and me, for sure," Emma told him. "I don't know if she asked anyone else."

Paul's eyes lit with interest when he heard April's name. I'd suspected he liked her, although he hadn't said anything.

He tucked the rag in the pocket of his coveralls. "I could use a night away from here. Count me in."

I looked at Emma. "You mind us inviting ourselves along?"

"The more the merrier."

"Cool." Paul snagged another cookie. "These things are addictive."

"I'm glad you like them." She took a small bite of hers and chewed it. "I might attempt real food next."

Paul laughed. "This is real food."

"I mean a meal."

I picked up the container. "I could make a meal out of these. And I volunteer as official taster for all your cooking."

"Me too," Paul mumbled through a mouthful of cookie.

"You guys might regret that once you see how bad I am in the kitchen." She got up, brushed crumbs from her top, and donned her helmet. "I'll let you get back to work."

I stood and waved a cookie as she started the Vespa. "See you tonight, Cookie Girl."

The helmet didn't hide her grin. "Later, Wolf Boy."

"Where did you...?" I huffed. "Jordan."

Emma's laughter floated behind her as she drove away. I watched her go, unable to keep the smile from my face.

Paul chuckled and slapped me on the back. "Oh, man, you've got it bad. She's a keeper."

"Yes, she is."

"When are you going to tell her she's your mate?"

I let out a deep breath. "Soon. It's complicated with her being human. She doesn't feel the imprint like our females do, and she might not want to be my mate. Humans don't usually marry that young."

My chest ached every time I thought of Emma not wanting me. It was too soon to say I was in love with her, but I cared about her deeply. I'd wanted her before my wolf chose her, so I knew the imprint wasn't the only reason I felt this strongly for her.

Paul looked unconvinced. "She might not feel the imprint, but that girl definitely likes you."

"As a friend," I muttered, remembering her evasion when I'd tried to talk about us.

Paul chuckled. "If that's friendship, then I want a friend like her."

"Bringing someone cookies doesn't mean anything. When I try to get close to her, she pushes me away."

He shrugged. "I don't know about that, but I can tell you she doesn't look at you like a friend. Like you said, she's young. Maybe she's shy when it comes to dating."

Shy? I hadn't even considered that because there had been nothing timid about the way she'd kissed me. My body warmed every time I relived that smoldering kiss. But then she'd run away, and I'd been too confused to think straight.

Paul's words gave me hope, and I was more determined than ever to spend time with her. And if she needed me to take it slow, I would, even if it killed me.

Emma

I shouldn't have come here. I gulped some water to moisten my dry throat and tried to pay attention to the conversation between April and one of Shannon's friends. Shannon was dancing with Peter, who had come with us tonight.

I'd thought I was ready to go to a club, but as soon as we'd walked in the door of the Attic, the bad memories began to flood my mind. It was at a place much like this one that I met Eli and entered the nightmare that would become my life. I'd gone with Chelsea and some other friends to hear a band. This was a different place and a different group of friends, but I still looked like I had that night so many years ago. It felt like the world had sped up around me, but I was stuck in that night, waiting to lose everything all over again. I couldn't help but wonder if every male I looked at was human or another Eli searching for his next victim.

A hand touched my shoulder, and I jumped, my heart racing.

"Didn't mean to scare you," said the red-haired boy Peter had introduced us to when we got there. His name was Dylan, and he played in one of the bands. "You want to dance?"

I nodded, and he led me to the edge of the crowded dance floor. Shannon grinned when we joined her and Peter, and the four of us danced together for the next two songs. By the time we went back to our table, I was feeling a little more relaxed but still wary of the people around us. Despite being here with four werewolves, I still didn't feel safe. I wasn't sure I ever would in a place like this.

"What time are you guys on?" Peter asked Dylan.

"We're up last. Hope you guys stick around for it." He waved at us and went to join his bandmates at another table.

Peter slipped an arm around Shannon's waist. "What do you say?"

She leaned into him. "I think I can be persuaded."

I smiled. It was impossible not to like Shannon and Peter, and to see how crazy they were about each other. They'd barely taken their hands off each other since we got here.

Shannon had confided that the imprint made werewolves all touchy feely and made the male possessive of his female. It couldn't be too bad. She didn't seem to mind Pete's possessiveness one bit.

Would Roland be like this when he imprinted? The thought of him looking at another girl with such devotion made my chest ache. I kept telling myself we were just friends, but my heart stubbornly refused to listen.

I'd even gone to visit him at the garage today to show myself I could be around him without him affecting me. I'd failed miserably. Every time he'd smiled at me, butterflies had taken flight in my stomach. And when he'd gotten close, I could smell his mouthwatering scent that made me want things I couldn't have. Even now, just thinking about him, I imagined I could smell it.

"About time you guys got here." Peter smiled at someone behind me, and I didn't need to turn around to know who it was.

My stomach quivered as Roland squeezed into the space beside me, his warm body pressed against one half of my back. If it had been anyone else, I would have felt crowded and anxious. His nearness felt familiar and comforting, and he did what none of the other werewolves here could do. He made me feel safe.

He also made me feel breathless and hyperaware of every inch of him that touched me. I needed to move away from him, but my body refused to cooperate.

"What did we miss?" Roland set a glass of soda on the table and smiled down at me. "Hey, Cookie Girl."

"Hi," I squeaked.

Shannon laughed. "Cookie Girl?"

"Emma baked us the best chocolate chip cookies," Paul said from behind me.

Roland reached back to shove Paul lightly. "She brought them for me. You're just lucky to work with me."

"They were for both of us, loser," Paul retorted. "Tell him, Emma."

"I like cookies." Peter gave Shannon a mournful look. "Why don't you make me cookies?"

She poked him in the side. "I made you a blueberry pie yesterday, you ungrateful wretch."

He pulled her closer and whispered in her ear. She giggled and looked at him adoringly.

"Okay, if you're really good, I'll make cookies. Maybe Emma and I can make some together."

It was my turn to laugh. "I made mine at the diner under the supervision of the cook. That's the only reason they were edible."

She gave me a bright smile. "Then you are in luck because I learned to bake from my granny. If you want, I can come over next week and teach you some recipes."

"That would be great."

"Now you're talking," Paul said.

Peter feigned a scowl. "My female bakes for me, buddy."

"Fine. I'm sure Emma will make me –"

Paul grunted. I looked back at him to see him rubbing his side.

A new song began to play, and Shannon perked up. "I love this song. Come on, girls. Let's dance."

She took my hand and tugged me out onto the floor. April followed us, and we all danced together to the upbeat rock song. We stayed out for the next song, and then the boys joined us. I tried not to notice whenever Roland brushed up against me on the crowded floor, but it was impossible to ignore his presence.

The song ended, and the singer's warm soulful voice began a ballad. I turned toward the table, and a hand caught my wrist in a loose grip. I looked up into Roland's dark blue eyes.

"Dance with me?"

I nodded mutely. It was a bad idea to get so close to him, but I was unable to say no when he looked at me like that. I justified it by telling myself I was only doing it so he wouldn't think it odd that I didn't want to dance with him. Apparently, I could lie to myself as convincingly as I could to everyone else.

Roland pulled me into his arms, and I rested my cheek against his chest, content to let him lead us. I was having trouble concentrating on anything but the feel of his body pressed against mine and the warm hands on my back. In his arms, the club, the people around us, and the bad memories all disappeared.

"Having a good time tonight?" he asked against my ear.

"Yes." It wasn't a total lie. The night had gotten better since he'd arrived.

"I'm glad you and Shannon are hitting it off. And April, too."

I smiled. "Me, too. And Shannon said she'll be around a lot now that she and Peter are mating."

His steps slowed. "You know about that?"

"Yes." I bit my lip, hoping I hadn't gotten the girls in trouble for telling me stuff I wasn't supposed to know. "Is it okay that I know?"

"Yeah." He started moving again. "What else did Shannon tell you?"

I thought about how much to say and settled for the bare minimum. "She and April told me you guys choose your mates by imprinting. They tried to explain it, and I think I got the gist of it."

"You must think it's strange to choose a mate that way."

"It's different," I admitted. "But Shannon and Peter certainly look happy together."

"I've never seen Pete this happy," he said almost wistfully. Was he hoping to find his mate, too? My throat tightened a little at the thought.

"Have you...? Do you ever wonder who your mate will be?" I asked, determined to torture myself.

"No," he replied gruffly. "I just hope she accepts me as a mate."

I leaned back to look up at him. "What girl wouldn't want you as her mate?"

He smiled and pulled me to him again. I hadn't realized he'd grown tense until I felt his back muscles relax under my hands.

We danced without speaking for the rest of the song, and he seemed as reluctant as I was to end it. I stifled a sigh as he escorted me back to the table.

Shannon gave me a curious look when I reclaimed my stool. Her eyes flicked to Roland, who stood beside me, and I gave a small shake of my head. People in love always try to pair up their single friends, but a human and a werewolf could never be a match, no matter how one or both of them felt about the other.

Dylan came over to our table again. "Roland, you think you could help us carry our gear from the van. Two of our buddies who were supposed to come couldn't make it."

"Sure." Roland touched my arm. "Back soon."

"Okay."

He and Peter left with Dylan. Paul was dancing with April, leaving Shannon and me at the table. As soon as the others were out of earshot, she leaned across the small table to me.

"Are you and Roland –?"

"No."

She gave me a dubious look. "You guys looked pretty cozy out there."

I summoned a smile. "Just friends. Sorry to mess up your plans for a double wedding."

"Damn, and I thought I was being so sneaky," she said, laughing. "You like him, though, don't you?"

"How can anyone not like him? He's a great guy."

"And gorgeous and totally ripped," she said slyly.

"Who's ripped?" asked a girl with a cute platinum bob as she slid onto an empty stool at our table. I recognized her as Shannon's friend, Lizzy.

"My boyfriend, of course," Shannon said.

A group of people descended on our table, and I figured they must be Lizzy's band. They all had the same hip rocker look, except for the boy who came to stand beside me. Tall and clean-shaven with short black hair, he looked more like an honors student than a musician.

"Are you in the band, too?" I asked him above the noisy conversation at the table.

"God, no. Just a groupie. I'm a student at USM. How about you?"

"Senior."

"College?"

I smiled. "High school."

"Oh. You seem older." He held up a hand. "I don't mean that in a bad way."

"No offense taken. What are you studying at USM?"

"Economics, second year." He made a face. "I know, I know, not as exciting as these guys."

"More exciting than high school." I assumed it was anyway. It had been a long time since I'd been in a school.

"True." He glanced around the club. "Place is full tonight. You come here often? I usually go to a place closer to campus."

I shook my head. "First time for me. I'm not much of a club person."

"Me either, although this place is nice." He held out a hand. "I'm Keith, by the way."

I took his hand. "Emma."

Paul appeared at my other side, slightly out of breath. "I think it's my turn to have a dance, Cookie Girl."

I glowered playfully at him. "Only if you stop calling me that."

"Deal."

I smiled at Keith and followed Paul to the dance floor. He was a bit of a goofball, and the more I got to know him, the more I liked him.

It still amazed me how quickly I'd gone from seeing the werewolves as something to fear to thinking of them as friends. Now I understood why it had been so hard for Sara to leave them.

"You thirsty?" Paul asked when the song ended.

I nodded, and he led me over to the bar where he bought a bottle of water for me and a beer for himself. When someone bumped into me at the bar, Paul put his body between me and the jostling crowd. It was sweet how protective he was, like I was one of his pack members.

We met up with the others on our way back to the table, and my stomach did a little flutter when Roland's gaze met mine and he smiled.

"Getting kind of stuffy in here," Shannon said. "We're going to the deck for some fresh air."

The handful of tables on the wide deck were occupied, so we stood near the rail. Once again, I found myself between Roland and Paul, and I was glad for their warmth. The night had cooled, and goose bumps covered my arms. None of the werewolves seemed to mind the slight chill in the air. I really needed to start carrying a sweater.

"You cold?" Roland asked.

"Just a little. I'm soaking up the heat you guys are putting off."

He moved closer until he stood behind me like my own personal heater. "Better?"

"Yes," I managed to say.

Having him that close felt more intimate than friendship, even though he didn't put his hands on me. No one else in our group seemed to think anything of it, and I wondered if werewolves were less reserved that way. They were used to going naked around each other when they shifted, so casual touching must be nothing for them.

I sipped my water and listened to the others compare the bands we'd heard so far. Shannon argued that Lizzy's band was the best, and Peter said Dylan's band would blow everyone else out of the water. It was cute how the two of them argued passionately, holding hands the entire time. That was the kind of relationship I wanted to have someday. One where you could be yourself and disagree with each other sometimes, and always know you were loved, no matter what.

"You're pretty quiet."

I craned my neck to look up at Roland. "You're not saying much either."

"Not much to say."

He rubbed his lips together, and all I could think about was how they'd felt against mine. Heat suffused my body, and I suddenly felt too warm. Needing a little distance from him, I moved to the rail and looked down at the people walking along the street. The soft breeze felt nice against my heated skin, and I was able to think clearly again.

I had to stop letting him affect me like this. The way I felt for him was not how you were supposed to feel for a friend, and I was going to end up hurt when he found his mate and looked at her the way Peter looked at Shannon.

"That's a great idea," Shannon gushed. "And Emma will come too, won't you?"

I turned to face her. "Where?"

"Camping." She bounced from one foot to the other. "What do you say?"

I'd gone camping once when I was ten, with Chelsea and her family in their RV. I wasn't even sure that classified as camping.

"Ah...I've never been in a tent," I told her. "I'm not sure I'm cut out for sleeping in the woods."

Her eyes sparkled with laughter. "We won't be going into the woods. Peter said there's a nice isolated cove five miles from town. You can get to it by boat."

Camping near the beach didn't sound too bad. "How long would we be gone? I have my job at the diner."

"We were thinking we'd go up next Saturday and come back Sunday afternoon. What do you say?"

I thought about it. "I usually work one day on the weekend. I'll ask Gail if I can switch a shift."

"Yay! We're going to have a blast; I promise." Her enthusiasm was infectious.

"What should I bring? I don't have any camping gear."

Peter waved a hand. "Don't worry about that. We have everything, including sleeping bags."

"Okay, thanks."

Shannon looked at Roland and Paul. "You're coming too, right?"

Roland nodded. "We should be finished with the Chevelle next week, so I can take a weekend off."

"I think I'm on patrol Saturday night. I'll let you know," Paul said.

For some reason, I'd thought she'd meant it would be only the girls. Thinking about spending two days with Roland, and sleeping in a tent with him, made my stomach do funny things. Maybe this wasn't such a good idea after all.

I looked down at the street again to hide my heated cheeks. A white Lexus SUV pulled up and stopped across the street, and Keith, the guy I met earlier, walked toward it.

The driver's side door opened, and a man got out. My hand flew to my mouth as the bald man from the coffee shop greeted Keith, and the two of them smiled as if they knew each other. Why would Keith be meeting up with that man of all people? Unless...

16

Emma

P anic twisted my gut. I gripped the railing, and my water bottle slipped from my fingers to splatter on the sidewalk below. The sound drew the attention of the two men, and they looked up. As soon as they saw me, they got into the SUV and drove off.

"Emma?"

Roland's voice sounded far away as I fought off the first panic attack I'd had in weeks. Then his face was next to mine, his eyes narrowed in concern.

"What is it? What's wrong?" he asked.

"I-I saw him," I stammered.

"Who?" Roland's eyes widened, and then his expression grew thunderous. "The man from last Saturday? He's here?"

I pointed a trembling finger at the street. "He w-was there, talking to Keith. They left."

Roland swore loudly, and I flinched.

"Sorry." He drew me close to his side with an arm wrapped protectively around me. I was too upset to care that I shouldn't be taking comfort in his touch.

"What's going on?" Shannon asked.

I looked up to see them all gathered around Roland and me.

"Some guy's been following Emma," Roland said harshly. "She saw him watching her when we were here in Portland last week and again on Monday outside the Hub. And he was just here."

"What?" Shannon's voice rose. "Why didn't you say anything?"

"You were already gone, and I wasn't even sure it was the same man." I took a shaky breath. "Now, I'm pretty sure it was him."

April's lips thinned. "You should call the police."

"No," I blurted. The last thing I needed was the police poking around in my life. Dax had assured me the identity and background he'd invented for me were solid, but I couldn't take any chances.

"What am I supposed to tell them, that I saw the same guy a few times?" I asked when she gave me a puzzled look. "He's never approached me or spoken to me."

"But he's obviously scaring the hell out of you," Shannon fumed. "What are we going to do about this?"

Paul gave me a reassuring smile. "Don't worry, Emma. He'll have to go through us to get to you."

"Yeah." Peter nodded. "No one messes with one of ours."

Tears pricked my eyes. "Thank you."

Roland's hand squeezed my shoulder, and I looked up at him. The angry set of his jaw belied his gentle touch.

"You mentioned someone named Keith. Who is that?" he asked in a hard voice.

"I met him tonight. He's Lizzy's friend."

Shannon's brow furrowed. "I don't remember a Keith. What does he look like?"

I described Keith for her. "He came to our table with Lizzy and the others. I thought he said he was a friend of the band."

Her frown deepened. "Lizzy and her friends are total rockers. I can't see her hanging out with an economics major."

"Son of a bitch," Roland growled. "Is Lizzy still here? We need to be sure."

"I'll find her." Shannon said, heading inside.

April came over and rubbed the arm that wasn't pressed against Roland. "You still look pale. You doing okay?"

"Maybe she needs to sit down," Peter suggested.

"No, I'm fine," I lied, even as I leaned against Roland for support.

"We'll leave after we talk to Lizzy." Roland's tone told me he didn't believe for one second that I was fine.

I didn't argue with him. Seeing that man again had freaked me out a lot more than I wanted to admit. I'd been afraid for a long time, but this was different. A strange man was stalking me, and he might have sent that guy

Keith to lure me outside, something I'd done many times for Eli. The man wasn't a vampire, but predators came in all forms.

Shannon came through the door with the blonde singer. I described Keith, and Lizzy nodded.

"I saw you talking to him, but I thought he was one of your friends. Was he a creep?"

"Something like that," I replied.

Lizzy scowled. "I hate guys like that. I hope he didn't ruin your night."

"He didn't."

We talked to her for a few more minutes, and then she went back to her friends. As soon as she left, Shannon turned to Peter.

"I think we're ready to leave. Can you get the car and pick us up out front?"

"Sure."

"You guys don't have to leave because of me," I protested.

Shannon shook her head. "I wouldn't enjoy myself after what happened."

"Me either," April said. "Let's all go together."

We went outside, and Paul stayed with the girls while Roland and Peter went to get their cars from the parking garage. Before they left, the two of them had a quiet word with Paul, who stayed glued to my side until they returned. I don't know what they thought might happen, but I felt pretty safe surrounded by werewolves.

The cars pulled up, and everyone decided who would ride with whom. I'd come in Peter's car, but I found myself shuffled to the front seat of the Mustang with Paul taking my place in the other car. I'd be lying if I said I wasn't glad to be with Roland, even if neither of us spoke much during the drive home.

When we got to my place, Roland parked in my spot and looked over at me. "You want me to come in?"

"Yes." The last thing I wanted was to be alone.

We entered the apartment, and I grabbed two sodas from the fridge before we headed into the living room. I sat on one end of the couch, and Roland took the other end, looking like he was worried I'd fall apart any second.

"I'm alright now," I assured him. "It just freaked me out a bit."

His brows pulled down. "You had every right to be upset. I wish I'd gotten my hands on those two bastards before they took off. They wouldn't be bothering you again."

My fingers began to shred the label on my bottle. "What does he want from me?"

"It doesn't matter because he's never getting near you again," he said with a ferocity I'd never heard in his voice. "You're safe with me, with us."

"I know, but you and your friend can't protect me around the clock."

He started to say something, and I cut him off.

"You know I'm right. You have jobs and lives of your own, and you can't keep dropping everything to babysit me. I don't want to live that way."

Silence fell between us for a moment. When he spoke, his voice was tight.

"You won't call the police, and you won't let us protect you. Are you planning to leave New Hastings?"

I shook my head fervently. "I love it here, and I'm not letting someone scare me away. I'm going to do what Sara told me to do if I saw the man again. I'm calling Dax."

"Dax?"

"He's head of Westhorne security."

His eyes widened. "You know their security guys? How long did you visit?"

"A while." I floundered, searching for an answer that wouldn't arouse his suspicions. "I met Dax, but I don't really know him."

He nodded approvingly. "If there's one thing I know about the Mohiri, it's that they are really good at detective work. Give them a few days, and they'll know everything about this guy, right down to his favorite toothpaste."

I rested my head against the back cushion and sighed heavily. "I know. I should have called them on Monday. I guess I was hoping it wasn't the same guy."

Roland pulled out his phone and checked the time. "It's not too late in Idaho. You should call them now. Do you need the number?"

"You have the number for Westhorne?" I laughed. "Oh, wait, of course you do."

"Don't tell the others. I have a reputation to protect." He smiled for the first time since we got home, and my heart squeezed.

"Your secret's safe with me."

He found the number in his contacts and handed the phone to me. The number took me to a directory where I chose Dax's name. A few seconds later, he answered.

"Dax here."

"Hi, Dax. It's Emma. Emma Grey," I added because Roland was listening.

"Emma! How's Maine?"

I smiled. "I love it here. How are things with you?"

He let out a laugh. "Quiet without you girls around. Now, what can I do for you tonight?"

I glanced at Roland, and he gave a little nod of encouragement.

"I have a problem, and Sara said I should contact you."

"Must be big if she told you to call me," he said with more seriousness. "Tell me."

I related the whole story to him about first seeing the man in Portland and the times since. He asked questions about the man's description, the SUV he was driving, and the other man, Keith. I knew it wasn't a lot to go on, but Dax didn't seem fazed by it.

"I've worked with less," he said, his fingers tapping on his keyboard. The man was never without a computer. "I'll probably have to send someone to Portland to check it out, so don't be surprised if a warrior knocks on your door tomorrow or the next day. Are you okay there alone until then?"

"I'm not alone. Sara's friend Roland is here with me."

"Ah, the werewolf. You can't do much better than one of them for protection. Well, except for one of us," he added with a chuckle. "You're in good hands. And we'll get this other guy; don't you worry."

My shoulders slumped, and it felt like a weight had been lifted off me. "Thanks, Dax."

"Anytime. Now, get some rest. We'll take it from here."

I hung up and held the phone out to Roland. "They're sending someone to check it out. Dax said not to worry."

Roland looked as relieved as I was. "I've seen those guys in action. This will be over before you know it."

"Dax said not to worry." I pulled my legs up under me and sighed. "I don't know how to thank you for –"

"You don't have to thank me. I want to be here." His gaze held mine. "I'm staying here tonight. I'll sleep in the car if you want to be alone, but I'm not leaving you here without protection."

I almost mentioned Remy's magical wards, but something stopped me. Even if I was safe from danger in here, I didn't want to be alone tonight. More than that, I wanted Roland here. I blocked out the niggling voice in my head that argued it was a bad idea to spend time alone with him.

"You can have the couch. You don't snore, do you?"

"You'll have to let me know." He smiled, making my stomach flutter madly.

"You want to watch a movie? I can make popcorn."

He nodded. "Yeah. You're not too tired, are you? Because you don't have to stay up and keep me company."

I bit my lip. "I don't think I can sleep yet."

His eyes softened. "You make the popcorn and I'll find a movie. Anything except horror, right?"

"How did you know that?" I tried to remember when we'd talked about our movie preferences.

He reached for the TV remote that lay on the coffee table. "I figured you'd be in the mood for something lighter."

"You're right." I headed to the kitchen. "You like lots of butter on your popcorn?"

"Only if you do," he called over the TV.

When I returned to the living room with a giant bowl of buttery popcorn, he was stretched out with his feet on the coffee table and looking totally at home.

"Sorry." He took his feet down to let me pass. "Old habits."

I placed the bowl on the couch between us. "You spent a lot of time here with Sara, didn't you?"

"Yeah, except for the last year. I got more into partying and stuff, and Sara was off doing her thing." He gave me a lopsided smile. "I can't tell you how many movies I've watched in this living room."

"We'll have to continue that tradition, then." *As friends*, I reminded myself. I got comfortable on my side of the couch. "What are we watching?"

"*The Hangover*. Ever seen it?"

"No."

He took a handful of popcorn. "Then you're in for a good laugh. I figured you could use one."

"Thanks," I said, touched by his thoughtfulness. "I'm glad you're here."

He gave me another of those heart-melting smiles, and his wonderful scent wrapped around me.

"Wouldn't be anywhere else."

Roland

My eyes strayed from the TV to Emma, who was curled up asleep on the other end of the couch. She'd made it halfway through the movie before she'd given up trying to keep her eyes open. And I'd spent the rest of the movie trying not to watch her like a creep. It was a losing battle because she was as beautiful in sleep as she was awake.

Moving carefully so I didn't jostle her, I turned off the TV and went to her bedroom to turn down her covers.

Emma barely made a sound when I scooped her into my arms and carried her to her bed. I pulled the blankets over her and turned on the lamp. She'd slept with it on the other night, and I suspected it was because of her nightmares. I'd give anything to be able to lie beside her and hold her, to keep those bad dreams at bay.

"Goodnight, Emma," I whispered.

Back in the living room, I stretched out on the couch with my arms folded behind my head. It was getting harder to keep my feelings hidden from her and everyone else. A few times tonight, I'd seen Shannon watching us curiously as if she suspected there was more to us than friendship. When Emma had been frightened, my protective instincts had fired up, and I'd held her close, not caring how it looked to the others. It wasn't uncommon for werewolves to date humans, but I'd been acting like a mate, something Pete had pointed out to me when the two of us went to get the cars.

What girl wouldn't want you as a mate?

Emma's words to me while we were dancing had been on replay in my head all night. Had she been referring to werewolf females or herself? When she'd looked into my eyes and said that to me, I'd never wanted to kiss someone more in my life. Just thinking it now made my body ache with need, and I shifted to get more comfortable.

I was running out of time. I had to tell her soon before she found out on her own. But I also couldn't lay something this big on her while she was dealing with so much. I'd seen the strain in her eyes as she'd told the Mohiri security guy about the man stalking her. She was a lot more stressed than she let on, and I wouldn't add to that.

I had every confidence that the Mohiri would catch this guy soon. No one was better than them when it came to stuff like this, and I was grateful to them for helping Emma. Once the man was no longer a threat, I would tell Emma the truth about the imprint and my feelings for her. And hope she cared enough for me to give us a chance.

Emma insisted on going to work in the morning, saying she wasn't letting anyone mess with her life. I followed her to the diner at nine and told her I'd be back when her shift was over. I made her promise not to leave the diner alone and to call me or Pete if she saw anyone suspicious. She didn't argue with me, which told me she was more afraid than she was letting on.

I went to the garage for a few hours because I had patrol duty at noon. New Hastings had been quiet since last fall, and Maxwell was determined to keep it that way. We had twenty-four hour patrols around the town and surrounding areas, with each adult taking six-hour shifts. If anything did try to enter our territory, we'd know about it.

My mind was on Emma as I walked to the run boxes behind Brendan's farm, so I didn't see the two female wolves coming out of the woods until they shifted in front of me.

Lex stood between me and the run box, her breasts heaving slightly from her run. My eyes lifted to hers, and she smiled suggestively. Only a blind man wouldn't look at an attractive naked female standing in front of him. She was wasting her time if she thought it meant anything more than that.

Walking around her, I stopped at the box and stripped, ignoring the two pairs of eyes watching me. Lex huffed in annoyance, but I didn't bother to acknowledge her. I was done pretending to tolerate her or her scheming, and I couldn't wait to tell her and everyone else that I'd found my mate.

Shifting, I padded into the trees without a backward glance at Lex or her friend. I'd noticed she and Julie had been spending less time together the last week. With Pete out of the picture and me ignoring their advances, Julie had turned her attention to other unmated males. I'd seen her cozying up to Francis on Friday and both of them had looked happy about it. Not much made Francis smile, so he must really like her.

Today, I was patrolling the area behind the Knolls, one of my favorite spots because it was a great place for my wolf to run and stretch his legs. A normal wolf could go maybe thirty-five miles per hour. An adult werewolf could do between seventy-five and ninety. My best speed was ninety-five, though I didn't get to go that fast often. Right now, I was doing around fifty as I weaved through the trees and leaped over several small streams.

It was a constant effort to keep my mind from drifting to Emma. But I had to stay focused, especially in my fur. We didn't get hikers out here, but you never knew when a couple of humans would get adventurous, or in most cases, lost. The last thing we wanted was for one of them to stumble upon us.

I was on my second pass of my route when I scented other werewolves nearby. With so many pack members visiting, it wasn't unusual to run into some of them out on patrol, so I paid no mind to it.

Ten minutes later, the wind shifted and I caught their scent again. I lifted my head and sniffed the air, picking up three distinct scents. One of them was familiar, but not someone from the Knolls, so it was a visiting wolf. It had to be females. It wasn't the first time some of them had followed me on patrol in the last few weeks.

I groaned and picked up my pace, hoping to lose them. At least I didn't smell Lex among them. That female would run me into the ground if she thought it would help her get what she wanted.

When I was sure I'd lost them, I slowed my pace and headed for a stream I liked. The water was cold and clear, and I lapped it thirstily, taking a moment to rest before I resumed my run.

Inevitably, my mind went to Emma, and I wondered how her day was going. I'd told her this morning that I would stay at her place again tonight, and to my pleasure, she'd agreed.

Anticipation filled me at the thought of spending more time alone with her, even if we were just talking and watching movies. I wanted to touch her and make her mine so much it hurt, but I had to be patient and give her time. I'd earned her trust and her friendship, and now I had to rein in my own desires until she was ready for the next step. If it didn't kill me first.

The snap of a twig was the only warning I got before a shaggy brown werewolf stepped from the trees on the other side of the narrow stream.

My lips pulled back in a silent snarl when I recognized Trevor Gosse because I knew he wasn't here for a friendly chat. Or by chance. He also knew he couldn't take me in a fight, so he hadn't come alone.

As if they'd read my mind, two more werewolves came out of the woods behind me. I cursed myself for being so distracted that I'd allowed them to surround me. Maxwell would kick my ass if he saw me forgetting a rule he'd spent months drilling into my head.

I swung my head toward the main threat. *Go home, Trevor, if you know what's good for you.*

He bared his teeth, but kept his eyes averted from mine. *You aren't my team leader now. I don't have to follow your orders.*

Like you weren't going to follow them in Portland? I taunted. *And how'd that work out for you?*

Trevor growled loudly. *You ran crying to the Alpha and got me thrown out of the Beta program, you little bastard.*

I hadn't known about Maxwell booting him, but I wasn't surprised. Trevor Gosse was not fit to be a Beta, and Maxwell knew it.

You complained to Maxwell, and he asked me about it. If you hadn't lied about what happened, I would have let it go. But you brought this on yourself.

A sound alerted me to movement behind me, and I snarled at Trevor's two companions.

I'm only telling you this once. Leave before you get hurt.

One of them, a gray wolf, snorted. *You're just like that bitch cousin of yours. Think you're too good for the rest of us because you're the Alpha's kin.*

Gary. I should have known he was a part of this. He was still sore because Seth had imprinted on Lydia first. He wasn't too happy with me either for taking him down in front of everyone. Looked like he was after some payback. I'd bet my next paycheck that the red wolf beside him was the man I'd forced to submit that night.

So, I guess you three are here to put me in my place, huh?

We're going to teach you to respect your betters, said the red wolf, whose name evaded me.

My laugh came out as a choked growl. Had he really just said that? *When I see my "betters" I'll be sure to show them some respect.*

Cocky little pup, aren't you? Gary took a step toward me. *You'll change your tune when we're done with you.*

My chest rumbled a warning. *You three couldn't take me before. What makes you think you can do it now?*

Trevor suddenly shifted. Before I could figure out what he was up to, he picked up a small sack he must have dropped before he showed himself. He smiled maliciously as he untied the sack and pulled out a pair of leather gloves. Slipping on the gloves, he reached into the sack again, and his hand reappeared, holding a long thin silver chain with a collar fashioned at one end.

My stomach pitched when I realized he planned to use the chain on me. Silver was one of the few things that could harm us, and it burned like hell. I'd been shot with a silver bullet last year, and I'd almost died from it. The memory of that pain would stay with me the rest of my life.

I lifted my head to hide my fear. *Are you insane? The penalty for using silver on another pack member is banishment.*

Trevor dangled the chain from his hand, careful to not let it touch his bare skin. "Maybe we'll start our own pack, or find one that suits us better. Right, fellows?" He looked past me. "Guys?"

You said we'd teach him a lesson, the red wolf replied hesitantly. *You didn't say anything about using silver.*

"Don't wimp out on me, Rob," Trevor warned him. He swung the chain, and it gleamed dangerously in the sunlight. "We are going to teach him a lesson, one he'll never forget."

Gary stepped back nervously. *Trevor, what are you doing? Put that away before someone gets hurt.*

Trevor scowled at him. "What do you think we came out here for? A picnic?"

Sorry, man. I can't be part of this. Rob turned and disappeared into the trees.

"Coward," Trevor yelled after him.

I snorted. *You're the coward, Trevor. You can't even fight me like a wolf.*

His face twisted in rage, and he threw the chain and gloves on the ground. "By the time I'm done with you, pup, you'll be crying for your mommy."

He leaped at me, shifting in the air. I tried to move out of his path, but Gary hit me from behind and I stumbled from the blow. Trevor slammed into me, his teeth sinking into my shoulder.

A howl of pain bellowed from me as muscle and sinew tore under his powerful jaws, and I jerked violently, flinging both wolves off me.

Trevor landed in the stream. Snarling, he jumped out and spun back to me. *What the fuck? You reek of a human.*

A human? Gary asked from behind me.

A female. Trevor snorted. *So, that's why you're never around. Wonder if the Alpha knows his nephew is doing a human.*

He shook the water from his fur. *I bet you've never even had one of our females, have you, pup? All you can handle is a puny little human.*

Before I could respond, Gary tackled me, sending me to my knees. His teeth locked onto the back of my neck to force me to submit as Trevor rushed me again. With my injured shoulder, my legs gave out under the weight of them both, and my belly hit the ground.

What do you have to say now? Trevor gloated, as if he had me beaten. My wolf was already gathering his strength to make these bastards regret stepping into the woods today.

I grunted as one of them pressed down on my bad shoulder. *You can't even fight me without your sidekick. It's no wonder Maxwell booted you from the Beta selection.*

You arrogant son of a bitch. I can take you anytime, anywhere, Trevor snarled.

I grinned despite the pain. *No thanks. I prefer females.*

I know what you prefer. Trevor inhaled deeply. *Mmmm, she smells pretty good, actually, for a human. Maybe when I'm done here, I'll go show her a real –*

A growl ripped from my throat, and I pushed off the ground, fueled by blind rage. Gary flew backward, but I didn't care about him. My eyes were on Trevor, who scrambled to his feet and backed away.

In the next instant, he shifted again, and I realized his intent too late. Snatching up one of the gloves, he used it to grab the end of the silver chain in the grass. His face twisted into an ugly sneer as he swung the chain over his head and let the end fly at me.

Not even my thick fur could protect me from pure silver, and I howled as the chain wrapped around my neck and burned into my skin like acid. My vision darkened, and for moment, my legs threatened to give out.

He pulled on the chain, his arms bulging from the effort to strangle me into submission. Ignoring the excruciating pain, I grabbed the chain and jerked him toward me.

My teeth closed around his wrist, and he screamed as the bones snapped. The chain went slack, and I used my free hand to tear the thing from my neck. He'd pulled it so tight it had sunk into my flesh, and I could barely hold back my own scream as it came free.

I loomed over Trevor who was on his knees, cowering like the rat he was. My wolf wanted me to kill him for threatening our mate, and I was close to doing it. I'd take whatever punishment Maxwell gave me for taking the life of a pack member, even banishment, to protect Emma.

Sharp teeth sank into my hindquarter as Gary tried to drag me away from his friend.

I grunted in pain and reached back to grab him around the throat. My claws dug into his throat, and he made a choked sound as I pulled him around me and slammed him into Trevor, who had tried to crawl away. Man and wolf fell to the ground in a tangle of arms and legs.

I rose to my full height over them, mouth foaming, pain and rage sending me almost beyond rational thought. Trevor tried to disentangle himself from Gary, and I grabbed him by the foot and dragged him roughly to me. I wrapped my hand around his throat and lifted him until he was dangling and gasping for air.

"Roland, no!"

17

Roland

B rendan's deep voice rang with dominance, and my body trembled in response. But my wolf would not submit, not this time. He wanted to hurt the ones who would harm our mate.

My claws tightened around Trevor's throat, and his face turned a mottled blue as his good hand fell limply to his side.

A large body slammed into mine, taking us all to the ground. Hands pried my claws from Trevor, and someone else dragged him out of my reach. I watched in a dazed state as Francis checked the other man's pulse.

"He's alive."

Brendan's arms remained tight around me. Even in his human form, he was strong enough to hold me down. Or maybe the fight was gone out of me.

"It's over. You hear me?" he growled in my ear. "Francis and I will take it from here."

I could only pant from exertion and pain.

"Roland, you hear me?" Brendan asked.

Yes.

He released me and got to his feet. I stayed on the ground, afraid I'd do something to Trevor and Gary if I moved.

Brendan sat on his haunches and studied the bloody, raw wounds on my neck. He looked around until he saw the silver chain lying several feet away. His eyes narrowed, and his pupils grew until his irises looked black.

His gaze swung to Trevor, who was naked except for the damning leather glove on his hand. That was all it took for Brendan to know what had gone down here. No other words were necessary.

Francis came over to me, his mouth set in a grim line. "How bad are you hurt?"

I'll make it, I said in an attempt at humor. I tried to stand, and an agonized groan slipped out.

"Here." His strong arms reached around me and helped me to my feet. "You're bleeding pretty bad. Don't shift. You'll heal faster in your fur."

My shoulder stung, but it was nothing compared to the burns on my neck. Francis stepped back and looked at me, his jaw clenching at the sight of my ravaged throat.

How did you know? I asked him.

"Julie overheard Trevor and Gary talking about jumping you on patrol. She came to me, and I found Brendan. We were searching for you when we heard you howl." He stared at the silver chain that still lay in the grass. "They'll be lucky if Maxwell doesn't kill them for this."

"Francis, help me with these two," Brendan called. He looked at me. "Can you walk?"

Yeah.

Brendan and Francis hauled Gary, who had shifted to his human form, and Trevor to their feet. Francis took Trevor's gloves and used them to stuff the chain back into the sack. He carried the sack in one hand and gripped Gary's arm with the other. Then the four of them started back to the Knolls, with me taking up the rear. They could have shifted, but I had a feeling Brendan was taking his time for my sake.

Every step hurt like hell, and I was never so glad to see Brendan's house in the distance. When we reached the run box, I nudged Francis, who nodded and grabbed my clothes for me. Not that I would be wearing them again today. The bite on my shoulder would be okay in an hour or two, but a silver wound took a lot longer to heal. I'd probably have to stay in wolf form until tomorrow.

Lydia opened the back door as we neared the house, her mouth gaping at the sight of us. "What happened?"

No one answered her. We entered the kitchen where Brendan and Francis shoved Trevor and Gary down onto chairs. The two wolves who had attacked me so viciously were meek now in the face of the Beta, who was so furious he could barely speak.

Brendan stormed out of the room, most likely to call Maxwell and fill him in. The shit was about to hit the fan in a big way.

"Roland, you're dripping blood everywhere," Lydia admonished. She let out a loud gasp, and her hand flew to her mouth. "Oh, my God, what happened to your neck?"

Francis tossed the sack on the table, the chain clinking softly. "Silver."

Lydia paled, and her eyes filled with horror.

Francis glowered at my attackers who were staring at the floor. "These two are lucky we found them when we did. A few minutes later, and I think Roland would have dealt out his own justice."

Was that pride I heard in my cousin's voice? Or was I delirious from pain and blood loss?

I lay down on the tile floor with a groan to wait for Brendan's return. The last thing I wanted was to be in the same room with Trevor and Gary, but I didn't want to get blood all over Brendan's house.

Barely ten minutes passed before the front door slammed and Maxwell strode into the kitchen with Brendan. I thought I'd seen the Alpha angry before, but the look on his face now made me want to curl up into a ball and hide my head beneath my paws. And he wasn't even looking at me.

Trevor and Gary wilted under his stare, their shoulders caving in as they made themselves as small as possible. But nothing was going to save them from the wrath about to be unleashed on them.

Maxwell's thunderous gaze found me. "Tell me what happened."

I nodded and sat up. Then I told him everything except for the part about Emma being my mate. I didn't think his expression could get any darker until I got to the part about the chain.

Maxwell didn't even blink when I admitted that I might have killed Trevor if Brendan and Francis hadn't arrived. That spoke volumes for how bad I must look and the seriousness of the crime.

"Get some sleep," Maxwell said harshly. "Tomorrow, we'll talk more."

I nodded, aware that his anger wasn't directed at me. I'd like to say I felt bad for Trevor and Gary, but those two deserved what was coming to them.

Lydia followed me to the downstairs guest room where I stretched out on the floor. In my fur, I was too big for the bed.

"Here's your stuff." She laid my clothes on the bed and stood back, shaking her head. "I still can't believe they did that. Are you in a lot of pain?"

Yes, but it's already getting better.

"Let me know if you need anything."

I closed my eyes and thought about Emma. She was expecting me to meet her at the diner after her shift, but I needed to stay in my fur to heal. I'd have to ask Pete to see her home, and I would go to her apartment in my fur again.

I hated that I wouldn't be able to talk to her, but at least I'd be near her. For now, that would have to be enough.

I stood beneath the stairs to Emma's front door and pulled off my T-shirt with a grimace. My wounds had closed up, but they still hurt like a son of a bitch when I moved the wrong way. I'd had to take my human form so Pete could drive me here, but once I shifted I would feel better and the healing could continue.

Word about the attack had spread quickly, and by the time dinner had rolled around, the whole pack was in an uproar. My mother was so enraged, it had taken Maxwell and Brendan to keep her away from Trevor and Gary, who were locked in a holding cell behind the meeting house. I wasn't sure what would happen next, but it wasn't something people would stop talking about for a long time.

I removed the rest of my clothes and placed them in the small backpack I'd brought with me. Then I stuffed the bag into an opening beneath the bottom step where no one could see it if they happened to look back here.

"Hello? Are you there?"

I started and knocked my head on a step, letting out a muttered curse. Christ, this day was determined to kill me.

Footsteps came toward me.

Shit. I shifted fast, trying not to groan as my body reshaped itself and pulled at my neck wounds. I was panting when I walked out to meet Emma.

"I thought I heard you," she said softly, not a hint of fear in her voice. "Peter told me someone would be here, and I hoped it was you."

I walked up to her, wanting to scold her for leaving the building without knowing for sure if I was out here. But then I saw her smile and the relief in her eyes, and I realized what she'd said. She'd come down, hoping I'd be here. A happy glow settled somewhere beneath my breastbone, and just like that, my horrible day became nothing more than an unpleasant blur.

"Roland was supposed to be here, so I brought home dinner for the two of us. Would you like to come up and share it with me?"

I nodded, pleasantly surprised. She'd planned for us to have dinner together? I wanted to beat Trevor again for screwing this up for me.

I followed her upstairs and found dinner already laid out on the table. For her, there was a grilled chicken salad. For me, it was a thick steak and a baked potato. My mouth watered at the smell of meat. My mother had made me a large meal a few hours ago, but healing from a bad injury burned a lot of calories, and I was ravenous again.

Emma looked at me. "It didn't feel right, putting yours on the floor. Do you want –?"

She let out a gasp and rushed to my side. "What happened to you?" she demanded as she leaned in to inspect my neck. "Did someone hurt you?"

I shook my head, trying to reassure her. Her concern warmed me, but I didn't want her to be upset. I did like how close she was to me, though.

"These cuts look bad. I know you guys heal fast, but are you sure you should be here?"

My answer was to walk over to the table, push the chair away, and plunk my ass down in front of my plate.

She huffed and went to her chair. "I should have known a werewolf wouldn't pass up a nice, juicy steak."

I looked down at my plate, suddenly unsure how to do this. My hands were too big to handle the knife and fork she'd laid out for me, and chewing wouldn't exactly be pretty.

Emma paused in reaching for her own fork. "If you need to use your hands, go ahead. You won't bother me."

I tore a piece from the steak and put it in my mouth, chewing slowly. The meat was rare and seasoned just right.

I could have eaten the steak in one bite, but I took my time, keeping pace with Emma. I couldn't talk, so she filled in the silence by talking about her painting and all the things she wanted to learn to cook.

"I'll have to learn to double the recipes with you guys around," she said happily. "Roland could probably eat a whole pie himself. I've never seen anyone with an appetite like his."

I grinned, and she snorted. "Okay, you're just as bad."

We finished our meal, and she carried the plates to the sink. She stared out the window for a long moment before she turned back to me.

"I need to work on this painting I'm doing for Sara. You can come up if you want. Or you can watch a movie. Just make yourself at home."

I went upstairs while she changed into her painting clothes. The smells of oil paints and turpentine bothered my sensitive nose and made me want to sneeze, but it was a small sacrifice to spend time with Emma. I eyed the comfortable old couch and decided it wouldn't hold up under my weight. With a small sigh, I lowered my body to the floor beside it.

Emma came up a few minutes later and smiled when she saw me. She didn't say anything, but her expression told me she was happy I'd decided to join her. She went to her workbench and got her paints and brushes then sat on a tall stool in front of the canvas on the easel.

"I've been working on a painting of that mine south of town," she said as she studied the canvas. "I'm more used to doing seascapes, so it's taking longer than I expected."

She started working, and soon all I could hear in the room was the soft swish of a brush against canvas and the rustle of her clothes when she moved. From my position, I could see the look of concentration on her face and the way her teeth tugged at her bottom lip. If I had to use a word to describe her, I'd say she looked content.

After a little while, I dozed lightly, but my eyes opened whenever she shifted on her stool or went to get more paint. When she stood and stretched her back, I lifted my head and my eyes met hers.

"I think that's the best work I've done in ages." She carried her brushes to the sink in the bathroom and washed them. Yawning, she stored the clean brushes and walked to the top of the stairs. "Do you mind if I go to bed a bit early? I'm kind of pooped."

I shook my head and got up to follow her.

"Feel free to watch TV. You can sleep in the living room if you want," she said as we descended the stairs. She started toward her bedroom then stopped and turned back to me, almost shyly. "Thank you...for everything."

I watched her enter her room and shut the door, and then I went to lie down in the living room. My sharp ears picked up every move she made as she got ready for bed, and I pictured her removing each piece of clothing.

When the shower came on, I swallowed loudly and turned on the TV so I couldn't hear the water spraying her naked body. The old me wouldn't have thought twice about listening in and letting my imagination run wild. But it didn't feel right doing that with Emma.

Soon the bed creaked as she climbed into it, and the only sounds were from the TV. I wasn't really interested in watching anything, so I turned it off and settled down for some needed rest. My neck already felt much improved, and I should be fully healed after a good night's sleep.

I jerked awake, my heart pounding, and stared around me in confusion. It took me a few seconds to remember I was at Emma's. The clock on the cable box said it was just after 3:00 a.m., and I wondered what had woken me.

"No!"

I shot to my feet at Emma's terrified cry and barreled down the hallway to her closed door. Twisting the knob roughly, I pushed the door open so fast it almost slammed into the wall.

My noisy entrance didn't wake Emma, who lay tangled in the sheets, making little frightened sounds and struggling against the monsters in her dreams.

I flipped on the light, and Emma came awake with a choked cry. She sat upright and stared at me in terror for a few seconds before recognition filled her eyes. Her lower lip trembled and her face became pinched as she tried not to cry. Losing the battle, she curled up on her side and hid her face as her shoulders shook.

My heart wrenched at her pain, and I walked over to sit beside the bed. Quietly, I lay my head on the edge of the mattress, which shook from her muffled sobs. I watched her helplessly, aching to reach out but afraid of frightening her.

After a while, her tears stopped and she grew still except for an occasional sniffle. I was trying to decide if I should stay or go, when she moved her head and peered at me above the blanket. Her eyes were deep pools of sadness, and she looked so lost I wanted to hold her and shield her from whatever it was that haunted her dreams.

We stared at each other for a long moment. The blanket moved, and a slender hand emerged, reaching toward me.

My breath caught.

The hand paused. "May I...?" she asked in a hoarse voice.

I nodded, and her cool hand touched my snout then traveled up my face and between my ears. It was all I could do not to shudder with pleasure as she timidly explored the contours of my head and ran her fingers through my fur.

"You're so warm," she whispered. "Your fur is softer than I imagined."

I stayed very still, afraid of doing anything to make her stop touching me.

"Is this okay? I just needed to... I need to know I'm not alone. That sounds silly, doesn't it?"

I moved my head slightly from side to side, my eyes never leaving hers. *I'm here, Emma. You'll never be alone again.*

She sucked in a shaky breath, and her nose twitched. "You smell like Roland. I never noticed that before. Is that why I feel so safe with you?"

My heart skipped a few beats. She knew my smell.

"Can I tell you something?" She pulled her hand back and tucked it beneath her cheek. It was another moment before she spoke again. "Before I moved here, I was in a very dark place. I came to New Hastings to start over, even though I wasn't sure I deserved to be happy. I was scared all the time, and I felt so alone."

Her tormented words made my chest feel like it was in a vise. What had happened to her? Who had hurt her so badly she didn't think she deserved happiness?

She swallowed hard. "Werewolves scared me, even Roland and Peter, and I didn't want anything to do with them no matter how much Sara liked them. It wasn't them. They were really nice to me. It was me.

"And then I went to the cove that day, and you ran off those other two wolves. I was so afraid, but you just sat there with me. You made me see I didn't have to fear your kind. After that, Roland and I became friends. You and I did, too, even if you never talk. I hope, someday, you'll let me see you in your human form and tell me your name."

She smiled, and her brown eyes lost their haunted look. "Now I have friends here, and I don't feel as alone anymore. I wanted to let you know that...and to say thank you."

I chuffed softly, and her smile deepened. It turned into a yawn, which she covered with the blanket.

"I think I might be able to sleep now." She gave me a hopeful look. "Would you mind sleeping on the floor in here?"

I nodded, my heart swelling at her request. I'd rather share her bed, but I'd take the floor if it helped her sleep better.

Standing, I walked over to turn off the light. I left the bedside lamp on because Emma didn't seem to like the dark. I lay down on the rug beside the bed and closed my eyes, oddly content. Sleeping on a girl's bedroom floor had never played in any of my fantasies, but then, I'd never felt this way about any of the other girls I'd known.

"Night," Emma murmured.

A few minutes later, she was sound asleep. I followed soon after.

Emma

"I think you're supposed to put the flour in the bowl and not in your hair, Emma."

I coughed and tried to scowl at April who stood at the counter, dropping cookie dough onto a baking sheet. She snickered when more flour fell around me like a snow flurry.

"Ha-ha." I glared down at the heavy bag of flour I'd dropped on the table.

White powder covered the table, the floor, and me. Ugh. What a mess. I grabbed some paper towels and started the tedious job of cleaning it up.

"I think it makes the place look festive...like Christmas," Shannon joked as she lifted a sheet of cookies from the oven. "Oh, these look amazing."

"I have the next batch ready to go in." April carried over her baking sheet and slipped it into the oven. "Mmmm, I love the smell of butter pecan cookies."

Shannon placed the cookies on a cooling rack. "They're Peter's favorite. He put in a special request for them."

"Paul asked for oatmeal raisin," April said, grabbing a broom and dustpan to help with the cleanup. I gave her a grateful smile as I wiped flour off one of the chairs.

"Paul, huh?" Shannon said slyly. "I thought you two looked a bit cozy yesterday. Did something happen that you're not telling us about?"

April wore a secretive little smile. "We kind of hooked up Saturday night after the club."

"You *kind of* hooked up?" Shannon gawked at her. "Oh, my God! Did he...?"

"Not yet, but we spent all yesterday together, and we went for a long run last night. We're definitely compatible, if you know what I mean." She let out a lusty sigh. "I think I'm half in love with him already."

Shannon hugged her. "I'm so happy for you! If he likes you, then his wolf does, too."

"That's great, April." I tossed a wad of paper towels in the garbage. I was happy for the girls, but it was hard not to feel like I was on the outside looking in.

I turned to find them looking at me. "What?"

April pursed her lips. "So, Emma, you have something you want to share, too?"

"Maybe something about you and a certain wolf who was acting more than a little friendly Saturday night?" Shannon suggested.

I shook my head. "He's my friend; that's all."

"A friend who insisted on driving you home and who stayed here *all* night," April said.

My ears grew warm. "He was being nice, and he slept on the couch. My cousin owns this place, and Roland grew up with her. He's a little protective of me because of Sara."

"Uh-huh." Shannon crossed her arms. "And what was he protecting you from when you two did that slow dance?"

I sputtered, trying not to think of Roland's arms around me. "It was only a dance."

April quirked an eyebrow. "Methinks the girl doth protest too much."

Shannon nodded. "Methinks you are right."

My face heated, and I busied myself, washing my hands in the sink. "It's really not what you think. I do like Roland, but we're not dating. Even if he was interested, it wouldn't work."

"Why not?" April asked.

I stared out the window at the bay sparkling in the late afternoon sun. "He's a werewolf, and someday he'll have to take a werewolf mate. You said yourself that he really has no choice in the matter. I can't get involved with someone who'll only end up hurting me, even if he doesn't mean to."

That was only one of the reasons I couldn't be with Roland, but I couldn't tell them I was terrified of him finding out what I used to be and what I'd done. The thought of his eyes filled with loathing and disgust made my stomach harden painfully. I wouldn't chance it. I couldn't.

"I'm sorry, Emma. I wasn't thinking," April said quietly. "I didn't mean to upset you."

"Me either," Shannon added.

I turned to face them. "I'm not upset, and I know you didn't mean anything by it. Besides, it's not as if I'm in love with the guy. We had one dance." And one kiss that still made my breath quicken when I thought about it.

I went to the table where I had all my ingredients assembled, along with Steve's recipe. "Who wants to help me with my cookies so they don't come out like hockey pucks?"

April laughed. "I will."

By the time her batch of cookies came out of the oven, I had two sheets ready to go in. Between the three of us, we cleaned the kitchen in no time then sat around the table, talking and munching on cookies.

"You girls have plans for dinner?" I asked when I got up to take my cookies out of the oven. I didn't want our day to end yet.

Shannon shook her head. "Peter and I didn't make plans. What do you have in mind?"

"There's a Chinese restaurant not far from here that's pretty good. I was thinking we could order in. Or pizza if you prefer that."

"I'm in." April gave me a wry smile. "As much as I like being with Paul, I'm so over all the cookouts and pack parties. It'll be nice to do something else for a change. What do you say, Shannon?"

"Chinese sounds yummy. Let me text Peter so he doesn't wonder where I am."

"Great. I have a takeout menu –"

The doorbell cut me off and I got up, wondering who it could be. I peered through the peephole, and my loud gasp brought the girls running as I swung the door open.

"What on earth are you doing here?" I asked the blond Mohiri warrior.

Chris held out his arms, laughing. "Emma, is that any way to greet a friend?"

"Sorry." I smiled as my shock passed. "It's great to see you. Please, come in."

I stepped back to let him enter and collided with Shannon and April, who stood behind me, ogling Chris. Not that I blamed them. Like most Mohiri males, Chris was tall, well-built, and gorgeous. In addition to that, he had the greenest eyes I'd ever seen, and when he smiled like he was now, he had a pair of dimples that could make women swoon.

"Shannon, April, this is Chris." I looked at him. "Chris, meet Shannon and April."

"Ladies, nice to meet you." He held out a hand, and they all shook. For a moment, he wore a puzzled look, and then his eyes widened slightly. "Werewolves, huh? And pretty ones at that."

April's mouth fell open. "How...?"

I nudged her down the hallway. "Let's go inside first."

The four of us went into the living room. Chris and I sat on the couch, and the girls took the two chairs.

"How did you know what we are?" April asked Chris warily before I could explain.

"I didn't until I got close," he said with a disarming smile. "I'm Mohiri, so I was able to pick up your scent."

"Mohiri?" Shannon breathed, floored. "I've never met a Mohiri before."

Chris chuckled. "You must not be from around here."

"We're visiting," she said, still staring. "How do you know Emma?"

"My cousin Sara is Mohiri, and I met Chris through her."

Sara had told me it was common knowledge with the local pack that she was Mohiri, so I didn't see anything wrong with telling the girls about her.

Shannon's mouth formed an O. "That's right. Peter told me about Sara and what went on here last year. I don't know why I didn't put you and her together."

She looked at Chris. "Are you the same Chris who kept putting tracking devices on Peter's car?"

He gave her a cocky smile. "The one and only."

"Wasn't there another warrior? A Russian guy. Peter said he was always in a bad mood."

"Nikolas," Chris and I said together then laughed.

"Nikolas is Sara's mate," I told the girls. "They're in Russia now, visiting his family. And apparently, Chris is so bored he came to visit me."

He inhaled deeply. "I would have come sooner if I'd known you were starting a bakery. This place smells like heaven."

The girls flushed in pleasure, and April found her voice again. "We're teaching Emma to bake cookies. Would you like to try some?"

"Absolutely." He flashed his dimples again, and I could have sworn I heard both girls sigh as they went to fetch his cookies.

"You're looking good," Chris said in a low voice. "I guess this place agrees with you."

"I think so."

"And you're making friends, too." His smile was warm and genuine. "I'm happy for you."

My eyes misted. "Thanks."

His face grew serious. "I wish this was only a social call, but I hear you're having some trouble. Dax said it sounds like a stalker."

"He sent you to handle it?" I knew Chris, and I trusted him. Knowing he was here to deal with my problem sent a wave of relief through me.

"I volunteered when I heard you needed help." He gave me a chiding look. "And if you ever need help again, you call me directly, you hear?"

"I will, I promise."

"Dax gave me what you told him, but I want to hear it from you. Don't leave anything out."

Shannon and April returned with a large plate of cookies, which they set on the coffee table. Chris gave me a questioning look when they sat, and I gave him a small nod to let him know it was okay to talk in front of them.

He took one of each cookie and leaned back. "Go ahead."

I told him everything I could remember about the bald man, from the first time I'd seen him in Portland to Saturday night outside the club. My conversation with Keith – if that was his real name – hadn't been that long, so I was able to recall it pretty easily.

Chris made a face at the mention of the Attic. "Of all the places in Portland you could have gone."

"Why? What's wrong with the Attic? It seemed like a nice enough place."

He shrugged. "Did Sara tell you how she and Nikolas met?"

"Yes, she said..." I stared at Chris. "That was the club? But that's where Eli..."

My stomach pitched, and bile rose in my throat. Eli had found Sara at that club, and if it hadn't been for Nikolas, she would have died. Roland and Peter had been there that night, as well. And Chris.

I'd almost been there, too. Eli had liked to select a girl and have me lure them away from their friends. But for some reason, he and Joel had gone out without me that night. If I'd been with them, Sara might be dead now.

"Hey." Chris gave me a knowing look. "It's all in the past."

"Emma, are you okay?" Shannon asked.

I nodded and took a calming breath while Chris gave them a brief explanation.

"A vampire attacked Sara at the Attic last fall. Emma didn't know that was where it happened when she went there Saturday night."

"Peter didn't tell me any of this when I said we were going to the Attic," Shannon said with a frown. "If I'd known, I would have suggested we go somewhere else."

"It's okay," I assured her. "I was just surprised, that's all."

April leaned forward in her chair. "It *is* a weird coincidence, though, that you saw that stalker guy at the same place your cousin was attacked."

"Very weird." I shivered. "I hope it's the last time I see him."

"That's why *I'm* here." Chris reached for the plate again. "And for the cookies."

I grinned when he stuffed a whole butter pecan cookie in his mouth. "Would you like some milk to wash those down?"

"Love some," he mumbled, his mouth full.

I fetched him a tall glass of milk, and we caught up while he finished off the entire plate of cookies. Shannon and April didn't say much, probably because they were still shocked to be sitting there with a Mohiri warrior. I had a feeling Chris was going to be a hot topic in the pack tonight.

"What happens now?" I asked Chris after he'd been there an hour. "How will you find this guy without a name or anything to go on?"

"You'd be surprised what Dax can do with a computer. I'll check out the businesses near that restaurant and see if any of them have security cameras. A lot of places delete their recordings after a day or two, but some keep them for weeks."

"They'll let you walk in and view their security footage?" April asked with a skeptical look.

He gave her a rakish smile. "No, that's where my breaking and entering skills come in. I'll make a copy of the recordings and they'll never know I was there. Then we'll go through them and take stills of anyone who matches the description of Emma's stalker. We'll do the same with the businesses near the Hub and the Attic."

"Impressive." April nodded appreciatively. "What will you guys do to him when you catch him?"

"We'll do a full background check on him. If he's broken the law, we'll turn him over to the human authorities. Otherwise, we'll convince him it's in his best interest to leave Emma alone."

"What if he goes after another girl?" Shannon's mouth turned down.

Chris's smile was grim. "We'll make sure he knows we're watching. He won't be a danger to anyone else."

"That's a relief." If the man was dangerous, I didn't want him hurting someone else because he couldn't get to me. When one prey gets away, predators always seek out a new one.

Chris stood. "As much as I'm enjoying hanging out with you ladies, I need to head back to Portland and get started on this."

I walked him to the door. "It's really great to see you, Chris. Thanks for coming."

"Anytime. You'll be hearing from me soon."

"Wait!" April ran into the hallway, carrying a large baggie full of cookies. "For the road."

His green eyes lit up as he took the bag from her. "You keep feeding me like this and I might have to propose. And I really don't want a pack of werewolves chasing me out of Maine."

April actually giggled. Rolling my eyes, I pushed Chris out the door.

"Bye, Chris."

He winked at me before he started down the steps. "See you around, Emma."

18

Roland

On Tuesday night, I walked through the crowd milling around outside the meeting house, ignoring the stares and hushed voices. I'd gotten used to people talking about me in the two days since the attack. I understood why the pack was in an uproar over it – using silver against another wolf was almost unheard of – but I just wanted to get tonight over with so things could go back to normal.

At the door to the hall, Francis was admitting people, and he stepped aside to let me in. Everyone in the Knolls wanted to come to this meeting, but Maxwell had limited it to only the people he thought needed to be there. Not that anything said inside was a big secret. By this time tomorrow, every wolf in Maine would know exactly what had happened here tonight.

My mother was talking to Brendan when I entered. When she saw me, an encouraging smile softened her fierce expression. Despite my repeated assurances that I was fully healed and not emotionally scarred, she'd been fussing over me for two days. I hoped she'd calm down once this was all over.

On one side of the room, two small groups of people stood near each other. The worry and shame on their faces said they were Trevor's and Gary's families. I'd never met any of them, but Grandma said they were good people.

One of them, a boy who looked about twelve, jerked his gaze away when I met it. His chin trembled, and he looked like he was trying hard not to cry.

The resemblance to Gary told me they were brothers. Poor kid. After Gary was banished, his family would have to live with the stigma of what he'd done, and I knew how cruel other kids could be.

Maxwell's grave voice rang out across the room. "I think everyone is here. Let's get this started."

I sat in the front row, and my mother took the chair beside me. The two families sat together on the other side of the room. Once everyone was settled, Maxwell nodded to Shawn, who stood guarding the door to the holding cell. Shawn unlocked the door and ushered Trevor and Gary into the main room.

The two men had been given clothes, but their unshaven jaws and disheveled hair told me they hadn't seen a shower in a few days. They were subdued as Shawn led them to two chairs set apart for them, and neither of them met my eyes.

Maxwell didn't waste time with speeches. He turned his hard gaze on my attackers, and the two of them sank lower in their seats.

"Trevor and Gary, you attacked another pack member without provocation and with intent to do serious injury. Then you used silver as a weapon against him, a crime punishable by banishment." Maxwell's voice grew deeper and scarier with each word, and the temperature in the room seemed to drop. "This is not a trial. The attack was witnessed by Brendan and Francis, and I saw the silver burns on Roland's neck. That is all the evidence I need."

Trevor and Gary stared at the floor, unable to meet Maxwell's condemning eyes. My mother reached over and clung to my hand, and on the other side of the room, a woman began to cry softly.

Maxwell's gaze swept the room. "If anyone would like to speak before I render judgement, you may do so now."

I looked over at the families as a middle-aged couple stood, the man's arm around the shoulders of his mate. The woman's face was drawn, and the dark circles under her eyes said she hadn't seen much sleep the last few days.

"Please, Alpha," she pleaded hoarsely. "Gary's never done anything like this before. He came here hoping for a mate, and he was upset when someone else imprinted on the girl he favored. It made him a little crazy."

My mother released my hand and stood to face them. "Martha, there is no defense for what your son did. He knew what he was doing when he went after Roland, and God knows what would have happened if Brendan and Francis hadn't shown up when they did."

I knew what would have happened. I would have killed Trevor for threatening my mate and spent the rest of my life with his blood on my hands.

"And you." My mother swung toward Trevor and Gary, her voice rising.

"Two grown men attacking an eighteen-year-old just out of school because he bruised your egos. And to use silver on him..."

"Mom, it's okay." I reached for her hand, but she pulled away, stalking toward the two men until Brendan blocked her from going any farther.

"Let me tell you right now," she growled at them. "If anything had happened to my son, you would not be facing banishment tonight, because I would have put you down myself."

Martha let out a choked sob. The boy began to cry. God, this was even worse than I'd expected, and I just wanted it to be over. Trevor and Gary had earned their punishment, but their families didn't deserve this. That boy didn't deserve to lose his brother even if Gary was an asshole.

Brendan led my mother back to her seat and sat on her other side, most likely to keep her from going after Trevor and Gary again. Maxwell gave her a questioning look, and she nodded to let him know she was okay.

Maxwell turned to Trevor and Gary again, and the tension in the room grew so thick you could barely breathe. This was it.

"There hasn't been a banishment since I became Alpha of this pack. I think the last one was over seventy years ago, and it grieves me deeply to exile any member of my pack, even if the punishment fits the crime. So, before I give my judgement, I want to hear from the victim of this crime." Maxwell looked at me. "Roland, how would you punish your attackers?"

I stared at Maxwell, and I wasn't alone in my surprise. Maxwell never deferred to anyone else, and his word was law.

Maxwell watched me expectantly. Confused, I stayed in my chair until my mother pushed at my arm, urging me to stand.

"I..." I looked at the two men awaiting their fate. Gary's eyes were downcast, his posture one of resignation. Trevor met my stare belligerently, but he couldn't camouflage his fear. I couldn't pretend I didn't despise these two for what they'd done, and I would not be sorry to see the last of them.

Banishment was forever, and to a werewolf it was worse than a death sentence. We needed the social structure that came from a pack. The Alpha's power ran through all of us, connecting us, making us stronger together. I couldn't imagine going the rest of my life without that sense of belonging.

Most packs wouldn't accept a banished wolf, which meant they'd be doomed to never have a mate because lone wolves could not imprint on a female. Before Emma, I hadn't been in any hurry to take a mate, but I'd known I would someday. How would I feel if I knew I could never have that bond, never have children or a true mate?

I thought about Gary's little brother who would also be punished by the banishment. Pete was the closest I had to a brother, and I couldn't even bring myself to imagine how it would feel if he was no longer in the pack. How could I put a kid through that?

But I also couldn't let Gary's and Trevor's crime go unpunished. Using silver against another wolf was an unspeakable act, and to grant leniency for one would send the wrong message to the pack, not to mention undermine the Alpha's authority.

It was too bad we didn't have the equivalent of a human prison, because what these two really needed was to do some hard time. Or maybe a long, tough boot camp to do some serious character building. Hell, a few months with Maxwell and they'd be singing a whole different tune.

"I'd give them a choice of punishment," I said at last.

Gary's head came up, and he stared at me. Ignoring him, I looked at Maxwell.

"I would have them choose between banishment and training under you. They'd work at the lumberyard and spend their free time training or patrolling. There'd be no extracurricular activities, and they'd be on probation until you decided they had reformed enough to stay in the pack."

My mother harrumphed angrily. "You would let them off easy after what they did to you?"

I almost smiled for the first time since arriving. "You've obviously never trained under Maxwell." A Navy SEAL boot camp would feel like a spa after just a week with the Alpha.

Maxwell studied me with narrowed eyes, and I could see I'd surprised him with my answer. He rubbed at his beard as if he was actually considering my proposal.

"Is that all?" he asked.

"No. I'd order their wolves to not imprint until the probation was over."

There were gasps around me. The Alpha could command his pack to do anything he wished, including prohibiting a wolf from choosing a mate. It was extreme but necessary in this case.

"If they mated while they were under probation, you couldn't banish them if it came to that. You'd have to banish their mates as well, or make the females suffer the separation. And there could be children."

Maxwell crossed his arms thoughtfully. "You're aware that if they trained under me, they'd have to live here in the Knolls. You'd see them often."

That was the only downside to my suggestion. I'd be happy to never lay eyes on them again, but that would mean punishing their loved ones. At least, this way, their families could visit them whenever they wanted. And I planned to be too busy with the garage, school, and, hopefully, Emma to worry about anything else.

"I can live with that."

It sounded like everyone in the room had been holding their breath, and they all exhaled at the same time. I didn't need to look at Trevor's and Gary's families to know they were all watching us, hoping for a miracle. I would be, too, in their shoes.

Maxwell nodded and faced the two men again. "Stand."

They stood, but it was another long moment before Maxwell spoke again.

"I was set to banish you tonight. Instead, I'm going to offer you the choices Roland proposed: banishment or probation. Don't think for a minute that if you stay, it will be a light punishment. For your foreseeable future, you'll work, you'll train, and you'll sleep. You will not leave New Hastings, but your families will be permitted to visit you here. And you won't be able to choose a mate until you've proven to me that you're worthy to remain a member of this pack. You have two minutes to decide."

"Probation," Gary blurted. His gaze flicked to his family. "I-I'll take probation."

Trevor shot me a look of pure loathing before he glanced at his family. Gary was a follower, and Maxwell would reform him inside of six months. I wasn't so sure about Trevor. He hated authority, and he wasn't going to take well to the heavy restrictions of probation. People like him didn't bend. He'd either break under Maxwell, or he'd end up banished.

"Probation," he said right before his time was up.

Maxwell turned to the rest of us. "Everyone but Trevor and Gary may leave. Once we discuss the terms of their stay, they'll be free to go to their families."

Cries of happiness broke out on the other side of the room, and I stole a glance in that direction as I stood. My gaze landed on Gary's little brother, who was smiling and wiping his eyes with the back of his hand. If I had any doubts about what I'd done, they vanished at the joy on that kid's face.

My mother pulled me down to her height and kissed my cheek. "That was a generous thing you did. I'm proud of you."

"Even if you'll have to put up with them living here for the next few years?"

She put an arm through mine. "If you can live with it, so can I. Now, I'm pretty sure Grandma has a couple of pies waiting for you at home."

"Lead the way."

I'd hoped to see Emma tonight, since Shannon and April had slept there last night. I'd had no idea how long the pack business would last, so April had volunteered to stay at Emma's. I was happy to see the three of them bonding, and grateful to Shannon and April for helping me keep her safe. But I wished I was the one with her.

Every eye was on me when we left the building, and the grim faces told me they thought Trevor and Gary had been banished. I hurried my mother through the crowd, wanting to get out of there before word spread and the questions started.

Pete caught up to us as we walked down the lane to our house.

"Hey, where are you off to in a hurry?"

"Grandma made pie. You want some."

"Hell, yes." He fell into step beside us. "You going to tell me what happened in there?"

"Yeah, after pie."

I had a feeling I was going to need it.

Emma

Saturday afternoon found me standing on a wharf with a backpack over my shoulder, waiting to board the twenty-foot motorboat Roland and Peter had borrowed from their friend Dell. April and Shannon were beside me, checking the contents of a huge cooler before Peter stowed it on the boat. Everyone in our group was in high spirits as we prepared to set off for our little camping trip.

April shielded her eyes against the sun. "Those are some dark clouds in the distance. It's not going to rain, is it?"

Peter followed her gaze. "I checked the weather. It's supposed to stay south of us."

Roland rooted around in a storage compartment and handed out life jackets to all of us. Once I got mine on, he took my hand to help me into the boat. Ignoring the tingle that rippled through me, I sat on a cushioned seat and set my backpack at my feet. I'd been in boats many times in my old life, and I was pretty comfortable in them. I could probably drive this one if they let me.

April and Shannon climbed into the boat and sat beside me while Peter untied the mooring lines. I looked around the boat and noticed how little stuff we had with us.

"Don't we need tents and sleeping bags?" I asked no one in particular.

Peter jumped into the boat. "We thought we might rough it. You know, sleep around the fire, under the stars."

I stared at him. Was he serious?

Shannon nudged me with her shoulder. "Don't listen to him. He and Roland carried everything up to the cove this morning so we didn't load down the boat."

Peter grinned and sat as Roland eased the boat away from the wharf. It was a beautiful, calm day, which meant the harbor was busy with tourists and locals. We passed a lot of other motorboats as well as sailboats, fishing boats, tour boats, and several small white yachts. Roland easily maneuvered around them, and soon we were out of the crowded harbor, skimming northward along the rocky coast.

I watched the shore go by, enraptured by the rugged beauty of the granite cliffs and towering pines. The cliffs were alive with birds, and I recognized osprey, herons, and gulls. A movement near the water in one inlet caught my attention, and I looked just in time to see a long brown sea otter disappearing beneath the waves. I exhaled happily. I could definitely get used to this.

We passed the lighthouse, and I thought about the kiss I'd shared with Roland there. My body grew warm as I remembered every touch of his lips and hands like it had happened yesterday. I had to stop thinking about that kiss. It made me want things I couldn't have, and I was starting to wish it had never happened. Better not to know what I was missing than to long for something out of my reach.

I hadn't seen much of Roland this week. Shannon and April had ended up staying over on Monday night, and April had slept over on Tuesday. All I could get from them was that something was going on in the pack and Roland was involved.

Roland had come over on Wednesday night, and we'd had a *Lord of the Rings* marathon. When I'd told him I'd never seen the movies, he'd been appalled and insisted on us watching them. It had been a fun night, and I'd kept it totally on a friendship basis. A few times, I'd noticed him looking at me, but I pretended not to see it. Even if Shannon and April were right, and he was into me, it didn't change anything.

That was the last I'd seen of him until today. Even the black wolf had been a no-show since Sunday night, and I'd found myself missing him. My friendship with him was simple, uncomplicated by the kind of feelings I had for Roland. I wished it could be that easy with Roland.

We traveled for a few more miles before Roland turned the boat into a large sheltered cove surrounded by tall trees. The beach was littered with driftwood and large rocks, and beyond it was a wide grassy area where three tents had already been set up.

"This is perfect," I said as Roland eased the boat into the shallows. "Do you guys come here a lot?"

Roland smiled. "Not as much as we used to. There's an old trail through the woods that we used to take, but it's mostly overgrown now."

Peter hopped over the bow and grabbed a line to pull the boat in and secure it to a large rusted iron ring imbedded in a boulder. When he was done, Roland cast off the anchor and we all followed Peter onto the beach.

Roland and Peter unloaded the cooler, while Shannon, April, and I went to check out the two-man tents set in a wide semicircle around a fire pit. In each tent, we found two rolled sleeping bags and foam mats for padding, plus a battery-operated lantern and flashlight.

Shannon pointed to the tent on the right. "I'm taking this tent for Peter and me. You two are roomies unless one of you wants to share with Roland."

I pretended not to see the coy smile she aimed at me. Opening the door flap of the tent on the left, I tossed my backpack inside. April had warned me that newly mated wolves were very amorous, and I didn't want to listen to Shannon and Peter getting it on later.

I watched Roland throw an armload of dried wood down by the fire pit. "Is there anything I can help with?" I asked him.

"You know how to skin a rabbit?"

"What?" I croaked.

He burst out laughing. "You should see your face. Priceless."

I folded my arms. "Don't make me push you in the water."

His devilish smile did funny things to my insides. "Pete and I will take care of this. You girls relax and have a look around since it's your first time here."

"Come on, Emma." Shannon came up to me, carrying a blanket. "I see a patch of sand down there that looks promising."

We made our way along the cove, and sure enough, there was a small sandy section almost free of rocks. April joined us, and we lay on the blanket, soaking up the sun and being lazy. I couldn't remember the last time I'd been this relaxed.

"Has that hot Mohiri been to visit you again?" April asked drowsily.

"No, but he called a few times. Yesterday, he said he's close to finding that man. He sounded pretty confident."

Shannon rose up on her elbows. "That's great news."

"Yeah, I'll be glad when this is over."

April sighed contentedly. "Well, you don't have to worry about the creepy bald man today. You're in the middle of nowhere with a bunch of werewolves, and you are only allowed to have fun here."

"I second that." Shannon fell back to the blanket. "If I'd known how nice it was here, I would've brought my bikini."

"Bikini? Did someone say bikini?" Peter threw himself down next to Shannon, sending a spray of sand across her.

"Watch it, buddy." Her stern look was ruined by the smile playing around her mouth. She grabbed his shirt front and pulled him in for a kiss.

April turned her head toward me. "I told you. Just like rabbits."

"I heard that," Shannon murmured between kisses. I noticed she didn't try to refute it.

A shadow fell over us. "Fire's started. Who wants to help me catch some fish for dinner?"

I squinted up at Roland. "I thought we brought food with us."

"We did, but you haven't eaten until you've had trout cooked over a fire. There's a nice stream about a quarter of a mile from here that we used to fish at. Want to come?"

I sat up. "Okay. You coming, April?"

"Too comfy. You guys go without me."

Roland reached for my hand and helped me to my feet. We left the beach and entered the woods behind the tents where a narrow path wound through the trees.

"Game trail," he said, moving to walk ahead of me. "Lots of deer around here."

The trail took us straight to the wide stream. Roland led me a few hundred yards downstream to a deep pool teeming with trout. From the way the rocks were piled round the pool, I could tell it was manmade.

"A bunch of us did it when we were kids," he said when I mentioned it. "Took half the summer, but it made a great swimming hole. Now it's a fishing hole."

I noticed then that he had no gear with him. "Where is your fishing pole?"

"Don't need one." He kicked off his sneakers and reached for the hem of his T-shirt.

I spun, presenting him with my back. "What are you doing?"

Amusement laced his voice. "Going to show you how a werewolf catches fish. I can leave my clothes on if you want, but then they'd be too wet to wear tonight."

I swallowed dryly. "N-no, go ahead."

Clothes rustled behind me and landed on the ground. My stomach did a series of flips as I imagined him standing naked a few feet away.

"You can look now."

"No, thanks."

His low laugh made my toes want to curl. "It's safe. I'm wearing shorts."

I peeked over my shoulder at him, and forgot to breathe when I took in the wide muscled shoulders and chest that tapered off to a narrow waist and chiseled abs. His black shorts hung low on his hips, kept in place only by a drawstring.

It took me a second to realize I was staring at him, and I jerked my head around before my gaze could travel lower. I squeezed my eyes shut and waited for him to tease me for checking him out.

"You going to look off in the woods or watch me catch dinner?"

I turned back to him. "You did that on purpose."

He smiled shamelessly. "Yep."

"Do you even know how to fish?"

"I can't believe you just said that." He gave me a fake wounded look and stepped up to the edge of the pool. "Prepare to eat those words, woman."

He bent his legs and went still, staring down into the pool. Several minutes passed, and he didn't move. Neither did I as I waited to see what he was up to.

Without warning, he dove headfirst into the water, barely making a splash. Seconds later, he broke the surface, holding a large speckled trout. He swam to the bank and killed the trout quickly. Then he tossed it on the grass near my feet and climbed out, water sluicing off his tanned body.

"That's a nice trick," I said, impressed. "How did you learn to do that?"

His chest puffed out a little. "Lots of practice. Want to see it again?"

"Yes."

He waited a few minutes, and then he dove in. Again he resurfaced with a wriggling trout, which he killed and put with the first one. He went in three more times until he had five big trout, one for each of us. He pulled out a pocket knife and cleaned them efficiently, leaving a small pile of entrails a dozen feet from the stream for the animals to feast on.

"There's no way I'll be able to eat a whole trout," I said as he threaded them on a thin branch to carry them back to the campsite.

He washed his hands in the stream and dressed. "Don't worry. It won't go to waste."

We returned to the beach to find the others already working on dinner. Peter either didn't have faith in Roland's fishing skills, or he was really hungry, because he had half a dozen large hamburger patties ready to go in the pan. Shannon was frying onions and mushrooms, while April checked on the foil wrapped potatoes sitting in the fire.

Roland went to work, placing each trout in a foil packet with butter and seasonings. He placed them in the coals with the potatoes. Then he went to the cooler and pulled out a beer.

"Anyone want one?"

Peter took one. I declined as did the girls. I often wondered if things would have gone differently the night I met Eli if my judgement hadn't been impaired by alcohol. I couldn't change the past, but I didn't think I'd ever be able to touch the stuff again.

Roland checked on the trout a few minutes later, and the smell wafting from the foil made my mouth water. He pulled the packets from the fire and set them on a flat rock while Peter cooked the burgers.

"Who is going to eat all this food?" I asked them.

"I will," called a voice from the woods behind us.

"Paul!" April ran and tackled him. He dropped the small duffle bag he was carrying and kissed her soundly. I would be shocked if these two didn't imprint soon, based on how much they were into each other.

They broke apart, and April took his hand to lead him over to the fire. "I thought you couldn't come tonight," she said, her face glowing.

"I switched patrols with Shawn, so I figured I'd surprise you."

She kissed his cheek. "Best surprise ever."

Roland handed Paul a beer. Then he started dishing up the food. I waved off the burger, going for the trout and a baked potato. Soon, the six of us were sitting around the fire, enjoying our meal. The fish was delicious, and I ate with gusto, something I hadn't done in forever. I didn't know if it was the company or this place, but everything tasted better.

I made it through half my trout before I could eat no more. Roland reached for my plate as I laid it on the ground.

"I'll take that."

I watched him eat my leftover trout with something akin to awe. He'd already polished off a plate of food that could have fed me for days.

"Where do you put it all?"

"Our stomachs are bigger than yours, even in human form. We need it because our metabolism is twice as fast and we burn through calories quickly. And we train a lot, too."

Peter grabbed a second burger. "Gotta stay in shape. Never know when you'll need to fight."

Roland nodded. "Most suckers are young, but sometimes you'll run into an older one."

"Oh." My stomach knotted.

"Don't worry. You're safe with us." Paul grinned and waved at Roland and Peter. "They don't look like much, but these two have killed more vamps than anyone else in the pack."

"That's us, vampire killing machines." Roland lifted his beer. "Because the only good sucker..."

"...is a dead sucker," Peter finished for him. The others cheered.

I swallowed, suddenly nauseous. The werewolves were good people, and I understood their hatred of vampires. Looking at their faces, I knew in my gut they wouldn't be able to get past what I used to be. I no longer feared they would hurt me. I feared losing their friendship.

Shannon looked at Roland. "Tell us about that really old vampire you guys killed in New Mexico. Peter is terrible at telling stories."

"Hey!" Peter tickled her side, and she blew him a kiss.

Roland shook his head, laughing. "That one totally handed my ass to me. Sara is the one who killed him."

"What about that pack of crocotta you guys killed in town?" April asked. "They are still talking about that back home."

"Now that was a crazy night." Roland took a swig from his beer. "Sara, Pete, and I were driving home from a party at the lighthouse when my truck got a flat on Fell Road. Pete went to get his mother's car, and the next thing I knew, Sara and I were surrounded by crocotta. I killed two and Pete got one. Nikolas and Chris killed the other three. One of the crocotta totaled my truck, trying to get to Sara."

Shannon shuddered. "Six crocotta. Why would they come so close to the pack?"

"Someone sent them to find Sara. Luckily, she was with us and Nikolas and Chris were there."

April wrapped her arms around her knees. "Is that the same Chris we met at Emma's place this week?"

"That's him," Roland said.

She turned her face so Paul couldn't see it and smiled at me. "Is this Nikolas guy as hot as Chris?"

I thought about Nikolas and smiled. "Yes, if you like moody Russian warriors who ride motorcycles."

"Yes, please."

Paul gave her a look of disbelief that had us all laughing. She turned and gave him a peck on the lips.

We all chipped in to clean up after our meal. I took the frying pan down to the water to scour it, and I jumped when I realized April was behind me.

"Sorry." She laughed and grabbed me when I almost fell into the water.

I went back to cleaning the pan. "What's up?"

"I, um..." She lowered her voice to a whisper. "I wanted to talk to you about the sleeping arrangements."

"Okay," I said slowly, because I knew where this was going.

She rubbed her lips together. "Would you mind terribly if I shared a tent with Paul? I've barely seen him all week, and I'd really like to have tonight with him. But I'll totally understand if you're uncomfortable sharing with Roland."

Share a tent with Roland? My pulse leaped at the thought of lying close to him, in the dark, all night.

"I shouldn't have put you on the spot like that."

"It's okay. He's stayed on my couch twice, so I guess we can sleep in the same tent for one night."

"Are you sure?" she asked.

"Sure about what?"

The two of us gasped when Roland spoke behind us. How could someone his size sneak up on you without making a sound?

I studied the pan in my hands while April answered him.

"I asked her if she minded sharing with you so Paul and I could have a tent together."

Roland's voice sounded a little deeper when he spoke again. "Emma?"

I lifted my eyes to his.

He gave me a small smile. "Since it's such a nice night, I was thinking about sleeping by the fire. April and Paul can take my tent."

"You don't have to do that." It was obvious he'd said it just to make me feel more comfortable. Now I felt bad for making him sleep outside.

"I love sleeping under the stars." He took the pan from me. "Come on. It's time for dessert."

I felt myself relaxing under his easy manner. "Dessert?"

"S'mores. Official dessert of campers everywhere," he said as we started back to the fire.

"I haven't had s'mores in forever. My father used to make them for us at the beach…"

A lump formed in my throat as I remembered going to beach bonfires with my parents and little sister. Marie would have one s'more and then she'd fall asleep, and my father would carry her home. Those were some of my favorite memories of my family, and the most bittersweet.

Roland slowed. "That's the first time you've mentioned anyone in your family besides Sara. Are they still in Syracuse?"

"No, they… Do you mind if we don't talk about them?"

His eyebrows drew together, but he didn't push. "No problem."

After two s'mores, I declared I would explode if I ate another bite. The others laughed at my puny human appetite, and I told them I was glad I wasn't the one paying for their grocery bills.

When the sun went down, so did the temperature. It didn't bother the werewolves, and I envied them when I had to run to my tent and pull on the sweater I'd brought just in case. Every now and then a breeze from the ocean made me shiver until Shannon wrapped her blanket around my shoulders. After that, I was toasty warm by the fire.

April and Paul were the first two to quietly slip away to their tent as the night began to wind down. Shannon and Peter stayed by the fire with Roland and me, but I could tell by the looks they kept giving each other that they wouldn't be far behind the other couple.

The wind picked up suddenly, making the flames dance crazily. The fire hissed, and seconds later, a fat raindrop hit my cheek.

I scrambled to my feet when cold drops began to pelt me. I ran for the tents, but I barely made it five feet before a wall of rain slammed into me. I squealed as the cold rain ran down my back and into the front of my bra. By the time I got to my tent, I was soaked through.

The flap moved behind me, and Roland ducked inside, his large body making the tent feel tiny and crowded. He zipped the flap closed.

"Looks like I'll need a place to stay after all."

19

Roland

Emma looked away from me. "I guess there'll be no stargazing tonight."
I couldn't tell if her voice trembled from nervousness or cold. She picked up the battery-operated lantern and turned it on. Pale light flooded the tent, illuminating her wet clothes and dripping hair. She shivered and set the lantern down on top of a rolled sleeping bag to reach for her backpack.

"Can you turn around so I can change into dry clothes?"

"Yeah." There wasn't a lot of room to maneuver, but I managed to turn away. I tried not to think about her getting undressed behind me, but the sound of her wet clothes landing on the floor of the tent made it an impossible task.

"I'm done."

I looked to find her drying her hair with a small towel. She wore a pair of cotton capris and a T-shirt that didn't hide the fact she wasn't wearing a bra. A shiver went through her, and she hunched her shoulders to get warm.

"Here." I unrolled one of the mats and a sleeping bag. Unzipping the bag, I lifted the corner. "Get in. You'll warm up faster."

"Thanks." She flashed me a smile and scurried over to get into the bag.

"Better?" I asked as I zipped her in.

She rubbed her legs together for warmth. "Yes."

"Good. You might want to cover your eyes, though."

"Why?"

I pointed at my wet jeans. "My backpack is still in the other tent, and I have nothing to change into. Unless you want to see a strip show..."

Her eyes widened, and she hid her face in the sleeping bag. "Go ahead."

Grinning, I pulled off my wet clothes except for my underwear, using my T-shirt to get the excess water from my hair. I unrolled the second mat and sleeping bag and made myself comfortable. Rain pelted the tent, and I was glad it was a good waterproof one. I hated sleeping in a wet bag, but at least I wouldn't be cold. I was more concerned about Emma's comfort.

"You can look now."

She lowered the top of her sleeping bag. "I hope the others are okay. I can't hear anything over the rain."

Considering what was probably happening in the other two tents, not being able to hear was a good thing.

"They've been camping a lot, and they're used to rain."

She rolled onto her side, facing me, and pulled her legs up. "I'm glad you guys have thick sleeping bags."

"Apparently not thick enough. You're cold."

"A little, mostly my feet." She rubbed them. "They're getting warmer."

I rolled to face her. "I'm sorry your first camping trip got rained out. I wanted it to be fun for you."

"It *was* fun. But we should check the weather next time." She snuggled deeper into her bag. "Did Sara ever go camping with you?"

"When we were younger, we went a few times during the summers. This was her favorite camping spot. The last few years, she started doing more of her own thing. I thought she was at home drawing or reading or something. Little did I know she was hanging out with a troll."

Emma's mouth turned up. "I guess you guys all had secrets. She told me she had no idea you and Peter were werewolves until last fall."

I nodded. "It was a crazy time for all of us. She found out she was Mohiri and that we were werewolves, and she thought we'd hate her when we found out what she was. As if we could ever hate her just because she had a demon inside her. She's Sara."

She cleared her throat. "How did you feel when Nate was a...you know?"

I stared at her, surprised she knew about that. "Sara told you about Nate?"

"Yes, and I talked to him about it. It still upsets him."

I ran a hand through my damp hair. "I'm not surprised. He was a vampire for only a week, but he has to live with what he did in that week."

Her voice rose a notch. "He was the victim. The demon did those things, not him."

233

"I know. I meant he remembers a lot of it and that's hard to live with. Nate's a great guy, and he'd never hurt someone on purpose."

"Would you have felt the same way if he'd been like that for months or years?"

"I don't know," I said honestly. It was a question I'd asked myself after Nate was healed. "I like to think I would."

She grew quiet, and I figured she was done talking. I sat up and reached over to turn off the lantern. Then I lay on my back, staring at the ceiling of the tent and listening to Emma move around.

"Are you still cold?"

"A little. I think it's because my hair is damp."

I turned on my side again and stretched out my hand to touch her cold, wet hair.

"Do you want to move closer to me so I can warm you?" I smiled in the dark. "I know that sounds like a line, but I promise to behave. I won't be able to sleep knowing you're cold."

She thought about it and wriggled until she was pressed against me. She turned on her side and curled into my chest.

"Thanks," she murmured.

"Anytime," I managed to say. Having her so close was heaven and hell at the same time. Her scent teased my nose, but two sleeping bags separated us. I'd kill to feel her body pressed to mine without a barrier and to sleep with her in my arms.

It took me a while to doze off. When I woke again, the rain had lessened but the air was colder. That hadn't woken me. Emma's shivering had.

"Hey." I put an arm around her to draw her closer. "Why didn't you tell me you were still cold?"

"D-didn't want to wake you up. Remind me to bring thermal underwear next time."

Her attempt at humor would have been funny if her teeth weren't chattering. I rubbed her back vigorously through the bag, and she tried to press closer to me.

"This isn't working," I said against her still-damp hair. "We need to share a bag."

Her head came up. "Share a sleeping bag? But you're not wearing anything."

"I have underwear on."

She swallowed hard. "We won't fit in one bag."

"No, but we can zip them together. That way it won't be too crowded."

I held my breath as she thought it over. I'd be lying if I said I wanted this only for her. My body stirred at the possibility of her skin touching mine, her soft curves pressed against me.

"Okay."

We got out of the sleeping bags and I quickly connected them, making one big bag. She settled in first, and then I joined her, zipping the bag on my other side. We lay on our backs with six inches separating us. It was almost too warm for me, but I could still feel Emma shivering.

I sighed. "Don't hit me, okay?"

She sucked in a sharp breath when I reached for her and closed the distance between us. Turning us both on our sides, I fit her snugly against me, spooning her. Her body was stiff for a minute, but she didn't resist or pull away. Finally, she relaxed and a soft sigh escaped her.

"You're like a furnace," she breathed, sticking her icy feet between my calves.

I couldn't speak. I'd imagined what it would be like to hold her like this, but nothing could have prepared me for the intense need that clawed at my gut. All I could think of was turning her around and kissing her like I had at the lighthouse. Only this time, we wouldn't stop.

She breathed deeply. "Why do you smell like that sometimes? It's really nice, whatever it is."

My mouth grew moist, and I had to swallow several times. In my current state, the tent was probably full of my bonding scent. Only a male's mate liked his scent, and it was supposed to heighten her need for him. I had no idea if it had the same effect on humans, but the mere thought sent a new wave of desire through me.

Emma shifted, and her backside rubbed against me. I froze as my body responded. *Ah, hell.* There was no way she couldn't feel that. Her sharp inhale confirmed it.

"Sorry." I whispered, not daring to move. "It's impossible to be this close to you and not be turned on."

"Oh," she said breathlessly.

"You're safe with me. I'd never do anything you didn't want."

"I know."

We lay there, unmoving. I wanted her, but I wouldn't take more than she offered. If she only allowed me to hold her tonight, I'd do it gladly because it was a big step for us. The fact that she hadn't pulled away from me gave me hope.

Minutes passed. Emma stayed in my arms, but her body wasn't relaxed. Finally, I couldn't take not knowing any longer.

"You feel so tense. Do you want me to move away from you?"

"No."

My pulse sped up. Emboldened, I stroked her arm. "What can I do to help you relax?"

She sighed, and her body softened against me. "This."

I trailed my hand down her arm to her much smaller hand and threaded my fingers loosely through hers. Her thumb caressed mine, and heat shot up my arm to my chest. Impulsively, I pressed a light kiss to her shoulder through her T-shirt. She surprised me by lifting our joined hands to her mouth and kissing the back of mine. I nearly groaned at the feel of her lips against my skin.

I nuzzled the back of her neck with my nose, daring to drop a brief kiss there. A tremble went through her, and her fingers tightened around mine. My lips grazed a spot below her ear before I nipped lightly at her ear lobe and soothed it with a brush of my tongue.

Emma gasped softly and turned her face toward me. I kissed the corner of her mouth tenderly, though I was starved for the taste of her. If she didn't let me kiss her soon, I'd go mad.

As if she'd read my mind, she released my hand and shifted until she was facing me on her side. Wordlessly, I cupped the back of her head with my hand and brought her mouth to mine. I kissed her slowly, my lips relearning the soft fullness of hers. Her tongue coaxed my lips open, and it was all I could do not to groan out loud as she explored my mouth hungrily, stoking the fire blazing in my belly.

I rolled onto my back, taking her with me. Gripping her hips, I lifted her up until she straddled me, giving her full control. My hands slid inside her shirt, running over the soft skin of her back, and she made a soft, happy sound against my mouth. It was all the encouragement I needed, and I let my fingers skim over her ribs to cup one of her breasts. God, she felt amazing, and I couldn't wait to explore every inch of her.

She pressed against my hand, seeking my touch, and I growled my pleasure. I deepened the kiss as my excitement mounted. She wanted me, and I was going to make her mine. My mate.

A sliver of reason pierced the haze of desire in my brain. Emma didn't know we were imprinted or that having sex would make us mates. I wanted her so much it hurt, but I couldn't do that to her. I couldn't take away her freedom to say whether or not she wanted me as her mate. I had to tell her the truth about us.

I pulled out of the kiss as my arms went around her. My voice was rough with need when I spoke.

"Emma, I have to tell you some–"

"No."

She pushed away from me, breaking my loose hold on her, and rolled away as far as the sleeping bag would allow. I watched her curl into a ball, her heavy breaths echoing mine, and I wanted nothing more than to reach out to her.

"I can't," she whispered hoarsely. "I want to so much, but I can't."

The pain in her voice cooled my ardor. "It's okay. We don't have to do anything."

Her body shook. "I didn't mean to lead you on."

"You didn't," I said softly. "I made the first move. I should have asked if you wanted it before I started anything."

"I did. It's just..." She took a deep breath. "I care about you, but I can't be with you."

The joy of hearing she cared for me was dulled by the words that followed it. An ache started up in my chest. "Is it because of what I am?"

"No." She rolled to face me, still keeping her distance. "Do you think I'd be here with you if I cared about you being a werewolf?"

"Then why? What is it?" The pain of rejection was like a knife in my gut, and my wolf wanted to howl in despair.

"It's..." Her voice broke, and she put a hand over her mouth. "I can't talk about this. Not now. Please."

I needed answers, but I couldn't push her when she was so upset. We had to talk, though, and soon. We cared about each other, and my wolf had chosen her. In my heart, she was my mate, and I couldn't bear it if she walked away. I had to prove to her that what we had was stronger than any reservations she might have.

"We'll talk tomorrow."

She sniffed. "Yes."

"Don't cry," I pleaded. "Whatever it is, we'll work it out."

I extended my hand to cover hers, and I frowned when I felt how cold she was. We were back to where we'd started.

I tugged on her hand. "Come here. Let me keep you warm, at least."

She shook her head. "I don't..."

"I promise nothing else will happen tonight. You're never going to be able to sleep if you're shivering."

She let me pull her toward me. This time, instead of turning around so I could spoon her, she curled into my side with her head on my shoulder. I wrapped my arm around her, holding her against me.

I lay awake for a long time after she fell asleep, thinking about what I'd say to her tomorrow and wondering how she'd react to the news. It was best to wait until we went home so we could have privacy. This was not a conversation I wanted to have an audience for. First, I had to tell Emma about the imprint and that I was pretty sure I was in love with her. Then I had to convince her to give us a chance.

I heaved a sigh and hugged her closer. She snuggled against me, murmuring incoherently. At least she was warm and she wasn't having one of those awful nightmares. My gut told me they had something to do with her withdrawal from me, and I wanted to kill the person who'd made her suffer like that.

I kissed the top of her head. "They'll never hurt you again. I promise. They'll have to go through me first."

"I don't believe this!"

Shouting ripped me from the great dream I was having, and I lifted my head to meet Emma's startled brown eyes. I was lying on my side with an arm across her stomach and a leg over hers. There wasn't an inch of space between us.

Before I could say good morning, the screeching started again.

"What the fuck is this, Roland?"

I scowled at the girl framed in the doorway of the tent. "What are you doing here, Lex?"

Her mouth twisted into an ugly snarl. "What am I doing? What the hell is that human doing here? You won't give me or any of the other females in the pack a second glance. You ignore your own kind to sleep with this human bitch."

I sat up, blocking Emma from her sight. "Watch your mouth when you talk about her."

Lex sneered. "Why? Am I scaring your little plaything?"

"Get out," I growled at her.

"Oh, I get it. Poor little human thinks she's your girlfriend, and she has no idea she'll never be anything to you but a good time. Did you tell her you'll dump her as soon as you choose a proper mate? No female will tolerate her mate coming home stinking of human. I sure as hell won't."

I'd had all I was going to take from this girl. I climbed out of the sleeping bag, making sure to cover Emma before I stood. Ignoring Lex's eyes on me, I snatched up my damp jeans and pulled them on.

Lex jumped aside when I stormed barefoot from the tent to confront her.

Behind her, Pete, Shannon, Paul, and April watched, along with Julie, who didn't look happy to be here.

I narrowed my gaze on Lex. "You were not invited here, and you need to leave before I say or do something I'm going to regret. I told you once before that who I see and where I go are none of your business. They will never be your business."

She crossed her arms. "If your wolf chooses me –"

"Jesus Christ! My wolf is *never* going to imprint on you. Never. You need to get that through your head and go look for someone else to be your mate because I..."

I took a deep breath to rein in my anger. I'd almost let it slip that I'd imprinted on Emma. I needed to tell Emma that news before the rest of the pack heard it. She was too important to me to let someone like Lex come between us.

I strode to the middle tent to get dry clothes from my backpack. It was safe to say our camping trip was over, at least for Emma and me. I was going to take her home so we could talk and get things sorted out between us.

Pete stopped me before I entered the tent. "I guess we're leaving."

The sun was out, and it was going to be another nice day. It wasn't fair for the others to have to leave early because of me.

"You guys stay. I'll take Emma home in the boat, and you can take the trail." In wolf form, it was an easy run from here to the Knolls.

He lowered his voice. "Is Emma alright? Did you tell her?"

"I'm telling her today."

I went into the tent and found my backpack. As I pulled my clean jeans from the bag, a loud growl came from outside, followed by shouts and a small scream.

Emma.

I ran from the tent to see a snarling white wolf advancing on Emma, who stood frozen near the cold fire pit.

A growl tore from my throat as I shifted, shredding the jeans I was wearing. In seconds, I was on top of Lex, pinning her to the ground.

Touch her and you die.

Get off me. She struggled, but she'd never be able to move me. *You're acting insane, like she's your...*

She sniffed the air. *No fucking way! That's impossible. You did not imprint on that little bitch.*

I growled again. *I told you not to call her that.*

"Oh, my God," April squeaked.

I looked up to find the others staring at me, their noses twitching as they smelled the bonding scent that was probably coming off me in waves now. The way Shannon and April kept glancing at Emma told me they knew exactly who it was for.

"Roland?"

I lifted my head to look behind me at Emma, whose face was slowly draining of color. Her brown eyes met mine, and I saw her shock and confusion get replaced by recognition.

"You?" she choked out. "It was you all along."

20

Emma

Roland was the black wolf.

I stared at the wolf as my mind tried to accept what my eyes told me was true. I'd watched him shift – I didn't need more proof than that – but still I couldn't bring myself to believe it. Because that would mean he'd been lying to me for weeks, and Roland wouldn't deceive me that way.

Plaything. That's what Lex had called me. Was that all I was to him, someone for him to have fun with until he chose a werewolf mate? I thought of the way he'd kissed and touched me last night, and how close I'd come to giving myself to him. He'd been so gentle, so loving, and I'd let my heart believe he cared for me because I wanted it so much.

The wolf – Roland – released Lex and took a step toward me.

"No."

I backed up automatically, not out of fear, but because I couldn't bear to be close to him now. No matter his intentions last night, he had lied to me, and that hurt me more. How many times had I seen the wolf whom I'd come to think of as a friend? I'd fed him, talked to him, slept in the same apartment with him. He'd made me feel safe, and I'd started to confide in him.

His unique scent was strong in the air. I loved that scent, but now it was a reminder of what a fool I'd been. No wonder the wolf smelled like Roland – they were the same person.

My chest squeezed painfully and tears burned behind my eyes, but I would not cry in front of these people, especially Lex.

I'd recognized her, too. She was the white wolf who'd menaced me that day at the lighthouse, the same day I met the black wolf. She'd threatened me the night of the party to stay away from Roland because she wanted him for herself. She no longer had to worry about me being in her way.

I rubbed my arms against the early morning chill. The sun hadn't reached this part of the cove yet, and I was still wearing the thin T-shirt and capris I'd slept in. Everything else I had was damp.

"Here, Emma." Shannon came toward me slowly as if she feared I'd bolt. She glanced at Roland as she held out a man's windbreaker. "It's Peter's."

"Thanks." I took the coat and put it on. The material was thin, but I felt warmer immediately. It fell to my knees and I had to roll up the sleeves, but appearance was the last thing I cared about.

April was right behind Shannon, her expression a mix of shock and concern. "Why don't the three of us go down to the other end of the cove? It's sunny down there and a lot warmer."

I nodded and went with them, deliberately avoiding the amber gaze of the black wolf who watched me. For once, I was glad the wolf couldn't speak because I wasn't ready to talk to Roland yet. I needed to pull myself together a bit more to prepare for that.

We walked until we found some flat rocks in the sun. Neither girl spoke at first, and I got the impression they were surprised by all of this, too. It would hurt too much to find out they'd been in on Roland's deception, but I had to know.

"Did you know Roland was the black wolf?" I asked, looking at Shannon first then April.

April's brow furrowed. "Yes. You didn't?"

"No." I bent to pick up a pretty blue rock and rolled it around in my hands. "He never told me."

The two girls shared a look I couldn't decipher.

"Have you seen him – the wolf – a lot?" Shannon asked.

"Yes." I told them how I'd first met the wolf in the cove and how he'd been coming to my apartment since Roland heard about the bald man.

"Why would he keep that from me?" I swallowed around the lump in my throat. "Is this some kind of game to him?"

"No," Shannon said earnestly. "I don't know why he didn't tell you, but it's not a game. It's easy to see he cares a lot about you."

I tossed the rocks at the water. "I thought he cared, too. Now, I don't know what to believe."

"I take it this is your first relationship with a werewolf," April said.

"We're not in a relationship."

She smiled kindly. "For argument's sake, let's say you are. What you probably don't know is that our males don't think like human men when it comes to their females. They're a possessive lot, but not in a bad way. They're loving and affectionate, but they're also overly protective. All of that adds up to a male who can be a total bonehead sometimes and who does stupid things that make sense only to him. But his heart is in the right place."

"I get what you're saying, but I'm not a female werewolf, and I'm not Roland's anything. Like Lex said, he'll choose a proper werewolf mate."

Shannon's nostrils flared. "Lex is jealous, and she'll do anything to get Roland. Don't listen to a word that comes out of her mouth."

I shrugged despondently. "But it's true. Even if he does care for me, it won't matter in the end. It's my own fault for letting it go this far. I knew I'd get hurt if I let myself feel anything for him."

April looked ready to cry. "Oh, Emma."

Shannon's nose twitched, and she looked at something behind us. I knew it was Roland before he spoke.

"Emma, can we talk?"

I almost said no, but we'd have to do this sometime. It was best to get it over with so I could put this behind me. Last night, lying in his arms after I'd stopped us from going too far, I'd decided to tell him today that we shouldn't see each other for a while. I was too weak when it came to him, and that couldn't happen again.

I nodded without looking at him.

"We'll be up by the tents if you need us," Shannon said. She and April stood and headed up the beach.

I stared at the water as Roland sat on the rock Shannon had vacated. He was close enough to reach out and touch, but not too close that I felt crowded. I could feel him looking at me, but I couldn't meet his eyes.

"Last night, I thought I figured out how to talk to you about this, and now I don't know what to say."

"How about the truth?" I asked, unable to keep the anger and hurt out of my tone.

He let out a deep sigh. "I guess I deserve that."

I didn't respond.

"Before I go any further, I want you to know that none of what Lex said is true. I've been attracted to you almost from the moment we met, but I *never* saw you as just a good time. In fact, I tried not to think of you as anything but a friend, because you're Sara's cousin and I didn't want to hurt you."

He kicked at a small rock. "You know about werewolf imprinting, but what you don't know is how much I dreaded it happening to me. I knew it would eventually, but I wanted to go to college and do other things before I settled down. When I got old enough for my wolf to imprint, I did everything I could to stop it from happening. I avoided unmated females, and I only dated human girls. I never dated them for long because I didn't want either of us to get attached. Looking back, it was selfish of me, but I never wanted to hurt anyone."

"Why are you telling me this?" I already knew there was no future for us. Hearing him say it only twisted the knife deeper.

"I want you to know where my head was when I met you, and why I tried not to feel anything for you but friendship. But the more I got to know you, the more I fell for you."

My breath caught, and I found myself looking into his troubled blue eyes.

"After I saw you in the cove near the lighthouse, I talked to Sara and she hinted that something happened to you to make you afraid of werewolves. I figured that was why you didn't warm up to us at first, and why you pushed me away when I got close. When I found you down by the old mine, I could smell your fear, and all I wanted to do was reassure you. I should have left, but my wolf liked how you talked to him – to us. He wanted to be there with you, and so did I. I didn't realize what was happening until..."

He stood and walked to the water. When he returned, he sat on his haunches in front of me, so close I could feel his body heat against my knees. My stomach fluttered when he took my cold hands in his.

"I didn't know it was possible, and I was shocked when it happened. But it felt so right, and I was glad it was you."

"What are you talking about?" I asked hoarsely, trying to tug my hands from his.

Naked emotions filled his eyes, stealing my breath.

"Emma, I imprinted on you."

I stopped trying to pull away and stared at him. I couldn't have heard him right.

His grip on my hands tightened as if he was afraid I would run. He needn't have worried. I couldn't form words, let alone run.

"My wolf chose you for our mate. I never knew a werewolf could imprint on a human until it happened to me. My grandmother says my wolf knows my heart, and he knew I wanted you."

My heart thudded. He wanted me? He chose me?

He rubbed his thumbs gently over the back of my wrists. "Say something, please."

I said the first thing that came to mind. "When?"

"The night of the lighthouse party. At first, I thought I'd imprinted on one of the female wolves there. I didn't even consider it could be you." His eyes softened. "And then I saw you walking to the beach with Scott, and I knew."

I remembered sitting by the fire with Scott and wondering where Roland had disappeared to. Then he'd found me behind the lighthouse.

"Is that why you kissed me? Because of your wolf?" I asked quietly, not sure I wanted to hear the answer.

Something fierce and carnal blazed in his eyes, and his voice deepened. "Trust me, I wanted to kiss you before that night. After I imprinted on you, I couldn't think of anything but touching you and putting my scent all over you so every other male would know you were mine."

My breath quickened at his words, and the air around us was suddenly infused with his delicious scent. It filled me with longing and made me want to climb onto his lap and pick up where we'd left off last night.

"I wanted to go to you as soon as I imprinted, but it took me a while to get my emotions and my wolf under control. It's a good thing Paul was with me because I almost shifted in front of a bunch of humans."

I couldn't think straight with him so close. "Do you mind sitting again? I... need a little space."

Hurt flitted across his face, but he released my hands and did as I asked.

I toyed with the zipper on my borrowed coat. "The party was weeks ago. Why didn't you tell me all of this before now?"

His gaze held mine. "After you ran away from me, I didn't know what to do. I was going to give you a few days, and then Sara told me about the man following you. I tried to talk to you that night, but you wouldn't let me. It felt like you were pushing me away, and I didn't know if it was because I was a werewolf or you just didn't care for me that way."

"Is that why you lied to me about the wolf? Why didn't you tell me that was you?" My anger resurfaced when I thought of all the hours I'd spent with the wolf, never knowing it was Roland. He'd watched me cry after my nightmares, and he'd even slept in my room.

He scrubbed his face with a hand. "I shouldn't have done that. I'm sorry. I was so worried when I heard about that man, and I wanted to keep you safe. But it was more than that. A new imprint makes a male a little crazy if he doesn't see his female. I had to be near you, even if I was outside your building. You were more comfortable with my wolf, so I shifted when I got there."

I pressed my lips together and stared at the ground near my feet. "I talked to you and told you things. I feel like an idiot."

"Don't ever think that. This is my fault. I didn't expect you to start inviting me upstairs, and I should have said no, but I wanted to be with you in any way I could. I never meant to deceive you. I stopped coming to you as the wolf this week, because I wanted to be with you as me, not my wolf."

A dull throbbing started in my head. This was too much to absorb all at once. I rubbed my temples and tried to process it all.

"Were you ever going to tell me?"

He exhaled noisily. "After your scare at the Attic, I decided to wait until we knew you were safe. You were so upset, and I didn't want to add to it. After things got a little out of control last night, I knew I couldn't wait any longer to tell you. I was going to tell you everything today when we went home."

I stood and walked the dozen or so yards to the end of the beach, trying to think of what to say to him. I was ecstatic he wanted me, but I was also terrified. Shannon had said mates were for life, and it was normal for werewolves to mate at our age. I'd never been in love before, but I was pretty sure what I felt for him was love, and I wanted to be with him more than anything. But I couldn't give him that kind of commitment. Not yet. There was still so much I didn't know about him or his life in the pack. I hadn't even known what his wolf looked like until today.

And then there was my secret. When he learned about my past, he wouldn't want to look at me, let alone take me as his mate. But I had to tell him. We could have no future if our relationship was built on lies.

"Emma?"

I closed my eyes at the hope and worry lacing his voice as he came up behind me. I wanted so badly to turn around and throw myself into his strong arms. Why couldn't it be that easy? Why couldn't I fall in love without fear of my past taking everything from me? Hadn't it taken enough from me already?

Steeling myself, I faced him. The pain in his eyes told me he expected me to tell him I didn't want to be his mate. The last thing I wanted to do was hurt him, but I felt too overwhelmed to make promises I wasn't sure I could keep. I needed time to let it all sink in and figure out what to do next.

"I know we planned to stay here today, but could you take me home now?"

He nodded sadly.

I was grateful he didn't push me to stay, but I hated to see him hurting. I closed the distance between us and slipped my arms around his waist, laying my cheek against his chest. His arms came around me, and I could hear his rapid heartbeat beneath my ear.

"I just need to be alone for a while, okay? There are some things I have to work out."

"Things from your past."

"Yes." I bit my lip, hoping he didn't ask questions I couldn't answer yet.

His chest expanded and fell heavily. He tightened his embrace, and then he released me and stepped back, wearing a resigned expression. It was better than the hurt I'd seen there a few minutes ago.

"Let's get your stuff, and I'll take you home."

"Thanks."

We started back to the campsite, and I was relieved to see that Lex had gone. I expected to find a fire going for breakfast, but instead, I found the others packing up. It took me a good ten minutes to convince them they didn't have to leave just because I wanted to go. They kept sneaking looks at me like I was a fragile doll about to break, and I was relieved when Roland cast off the boat and we waved goodbye to our friends.

Roland didn't try to talk to me on the trip back to town. At the wharf, he helped me out and we walked quietly to the waterfront.

I looked at my building on the far end of the street, and I suddenly dreaded the thought of being there alone. But I couldn't ask him to come in, and there was no one else to call.

I gave him a small smile. "Thanks for bringing me home."

"You're not home yet. I'll walk you to the door."

"I think it's better if you don't." If he came to my door, he'd ask to come in, and I didn't know if I was strong enough to say no.

He took my hand before I walked away. "Can I come see you tomorrow night?"

"I... think I need a few days." My chest started to ache again at the dejection on his face. "I'll text you."

"Okay."

He let go of my hand, and I walked away from him. I didn't look back to see if he was still there because I couldn't stand to see him hurting. I didn't want to think about how much pain he'd be in when he found out his chosen mate used to be the thing he abhorred the most in this world.

The last thing I expected to find when I reached my place was a motorcycle parked in my spot and Chris sitting on the top step, playing with his phone.

He stopped whatever he was doing and gave me a stern look. "You have some explaining to do, young lady."

"What?" For a second, I thought he was referring to Roland and me, but then I realized he couldn't know about that. And why would he even care?

"I've been trying to get ahold of you since yesterday. I called you half a dozen times and you didn't answer your phone, so I drove out here to make sure you were okay.

I put a hand to my mouth. "Oh Lord, I forgot to take my phone with me."

"I know. I saw it on the kitchen counter when I broke in here last night." He stood and came down the steps toward me. "By the way, you need milk. I drank the last of yours when I ate that pie in the fridge."

I blinked, trying to keep up with him. "You broke into my place and ate my pie?"

"I skipped dinner to come here, and I got hungry." He took my backpack from me. "When I saw that nothing had been disturbed, I assumed you were out with friends. I called Roland's mother, and she told me he was on an overnight camping trip with you. I figured I was here, so I might as well wait."

I climbed the steps and opened the door. Chris followed me inside, setting my backpack down in the hallway. I caught a glimpse of myself in the hall mirror and grimaced. Sleeping with wet hair did not make for a good look the next morning.

Chris smirked at me over my shoulder. "Looks like one of us had a fun night."

"You have no idea." I turned to him. "Why were you trying to get ahold of me? Do you have news about that man?"

"Better. I have him."

I stared at him. "What do you mean? Did you...?"

"Kill him? No." He checked his phone. "In fact, he'll be here in about twenty minutes."

"H-he's coming here?" I knew Chris wouldn't let anyone hurt me, but that didn't stop a tendril of fear from coiling in my stomach.

"He and I had a long talk yesterday, and I explained to him that it's not wise to stalk a girl with friends like yours."

I fingered my messy hair. "So, you threatened the man to get him to leave me alone?"

"Not quite. Why don't you go shower and change before he gets here?" He wrinkled his nose. "No offense, but you smell like wet dog."

I crossed my arms. "You did not just say that."

His eyes sparkled, and he tapped his nose. "Just be glad you don't have demon smell. Sometimes, it can be a curse."

"I know."

For a moment, neither of us knew what to say. I usually didn't talk much about my time as a vampire, even to the people who'd been there the night I was healed.

He gave me a small smile. "Go get cleaned up. Your visitor will be here soon, and all your questions will be answered."

I hurried to do as he'd said, my mind spinning with questions and speculations about the man coming to see me. Chris would have done a thorough background search on the guy, and he wouldn't let the man near me if he was dangerous. But if he wasn't out to hurt me, why had he been following me?

I'd just finished drying my hair when the doorbell rang. Chris answered it, and my pulse jumped when I heard the murmur of male voices. Taking a deep breath, I went out to meet my visitor.

Chris and the man were in the living room, and they stood when I entered the room. I held my breath when I found myself face-to-face with the man from Portland. Up close, he didn't look threatening or scary, but maybe that was because of Chris's presence.

Chris came to stand beside me. "Emma, I'd like you to meet Mark Rowan."

"Hello," I said.

The man smiled. "It's nice to finally meet you, Emma. You have no idea how long I've been looking for you."

I glanced from him to Chris. Looking for me? He'd known where I was for weeks.

Chris led me over to the couch and sat beside me. "Mark, why don't you start by telling Emma what you do for a living."

Mark pulled a business card from his pocket and held it out to me. I took it with some trepidation and read the words on the front.

Mark Rowan Private Investigator

I looked at Mark as he sat across from us. "What would a private investigator want with me?"

He crossed his legs and rested his hands on his knee. "That depends on whether or not you are who I think you are. Your friend would neither confirm nor deny your identity for me."

I shifted uncomfortably under his sharp gaze. "Who do you think I am?"

"At first, I believed you were the daughter of a woman I've been searching for." He uncrossed his legs and leaned forward. "Now I believe, as incredible as it sounds, that you are the woman I've been looking for."

"E-excuse me?" My stomach clenched and sweat beaded my upper lip. I had the urge to run, and I might have if Chris hadn't been there.

Mark smiled. "Let me explain. I was hired five years ago, by a woman looking for answers about her sister who went missing when they were children. No trace was ever found of the sister despite an exhaustive police search. My client doesn't believe her sister is dead because of various tips they've received over the years that indicate the girl is still alive."

I swallowed dryly, unable to speak.

He reached for a brown envelope I hadn't noticed on the chair beside him. Opening the envelope, he withdrew several photographs.

"My client's name is Marie Chase. This is her sister Emma, who disappeared from Raleigh, North Carolina when she was seventeen. As you can see, Emma Chase bears an uncanny resemblance to you. You could be twins."

I took the photographs with trembling hands and was immediately sucked into the past. The first one was my school photo, the same one I'd seen on the missing children's websites. It was the last picture taken of me before I'd disappeared.

The second photo was of Marie and me at Virginia Beach that summer. It was her tenth birthday, and we were dressed up to go to dinner. My fingers traced her round smiling face as my vision blurred.

"Marie," I whispered as a tear splashed on the glossy photo.

"I'm sorry to upset you, but your reaction confirms my suspicions. You're Emma Chase."

I nodded jerkily, still staring at the photo. Marie and I had been close, despite our age difference. What she and my parents must have suffered when I went missing. I'd lived through hell, but I couldn't imagine what I would have done if Marie had gone missing instead of me. To never know if she was alive or dead or out there suffering. It would have destroyed me.

"Give her a minute," Chris said, and I looked up to see the private investigator watching me with barely-concealed excitement.

"How did you find me?"

I hadn't been in Maine that long. Before that I was at a Mohiri stronghold. I didn't use social media, and no one here knew about my past. How could an investigator track me down so quickly, no matter how good he was?

He pulled another picture from the envelope and handed it to me. It was slightly out of focus but clear enough to make out my face and the face of the person standing beside me, his hand laid possessively on my shoulder. Blood roared in my ears, and the edges of my vision darkened as the photo slipped from my fingers. I was dimly aware of Chris talking to me and his hand rubbing my back.

It took me a few minutes to recover from the panic attack. I hadn't had one in weeks, and this was a bad one. Seeing Eli again had sent me back to the place that spawned every one of my nightmares, and I had to remind myself over and over that he was dead.

"I apologize. I had no idea the picture would upset you so much."

I looked at the investigator. Nodding weakly, I forced myself to pick up the photo again and lay it on the coffee table.

"Where did you get that?" I asked him. It looked like a nightclub, but I'd been in so many with Eli they'd blurred together.

"That was taken at the Oasis night club in Portland last September by a man named Preston Bruce. Mr. Bruce is originally from Raleigh, and he went to high school with Emma Chase – you. He recognized you and took a picture with his cell phone to show his friends back home. The picture made it into Marie Chase's hands, and she forwarded it to me. I've been focusing my efforts on Portland since then."

Preston Bruce. The name didn't ring a bell, but there had been over a thousand people in my school. And that had been a lifetime ago.

I remembered the club, though. Eli had brought me to Portland with him, looking for Sara, and he'd taken me to a few clubs to be his lure if he found a girl that met his eye. After a week or so, he'd left me at home and gone out with Joel instead, a decision that had saved my life. I hadn't been at the house when the Mohiri raided it, and after that, I'd taken off for Vegas, thinking Eli was dead.

Mark shook his head. "It was sheer luck that I ran across you that day in Portland. I'd pretty much written off Portland, but your sister wanted me to give it one more try. When I saw you and your friend coming out of an art store, I was surprised, to say the least. I followed you to lunch and then here. After that, I started looking into your identity. This building is owned by a Sara Grey and you went by the name Emma Grey. I found out you moved here from Syracuse, New York, but I could find no trace of you there. It was like you didn't exist before a few months ago."

"I'm not sure I did," I said almost to myself.

No one spoke for a long moment.

I gave the investigator a hard look. "Why didn't you just ask me instead of making me think I had a crazy stalker after me? Why did you send that guy Keith to talk to me – if that really is his name?"

He pinched the bridge of his nose. "I'm sorry for that. I've honestly never dealt with a situation like this, and I wasn't sure how to handle it. I wasn't aware you'd seen me after that time in Portland, and I should have been more careful. As for Keith, I thought he'd be less conspicuous in a club full of college students. He's my nephew. I normally work with my associate Pamela."

"Is she blonde, in her thirties?" I asked.

Mark's face registered his surprise. "How do you know that?"

"She came into the diner one day. I wouldn't have noticed her except she said she was from Minnesota but she had no accent. Then I saw her in her car after my shift. It freaked me out a bit."

He nodded wryly. "Pamela usually helps me with runaway cases. She's good with teenagers, but I'm thinking she was in over her head on this one."

I gave him a small smile. "I'm not good with strangers. I don't think anyone would have done a better job."

He leaned forward again. "Emma, I have to know. How are you here, looking like you haven't aged a day in twenty years? Where have you been all this time?"

I looked to Chris for guidance because I had no idea how to answer the man's questions. My story was so incredible that I'd find it hard to believe in his shoes.

Chris smiled. "Go ahead. Mark knows about vampires and demons."

I sucked in a sharp breath at hearing Chris speak so bluntly about it. Most humans had no idea about the real world around them.

Mark nodded. "I've been a PI for fifteen years, and I've seen a lot more than I ever wanted to. When your sister hired me, and I started digging into your disappearance, I suspected it could be vampires, but I had no proof. Not that I could have told anyone that. People would have thought I was delusional, and I would have lost my license."

He rested his elbows on his knees. "You can be assured that whatever you tell me will be kept in the strictest confidence, unless you give me permission to share it."

"How do I know I can trust you?"

His eyes darted to Chris. "Your friend here has made it clear it's in my best interest to exercise discretion in this case."

I wrapped my arms around myself, but there was no way to prepare for talking about what had happened to me.

"I was at a club with my friends when I met him, and I remember being surprised that an older guy like him would be interested in me. I was drinking and stupid, and he convinced me to go outside for some air. We were in the parking lot when he...he showed me that he was a vampire. I tried to run, but he was too fast. He knocked me out, and when I woke up again, I was in a strange house."

My heart began to pound, and bile rose in my throat as I relived the horrors of that first night with Eli, thinking I was going to die. Praying for it. But Eli knew exactly how far to go without killing me, and he kept me alive so he could amuse himself night after night.

"You don't have to do this if it's too hard," Chris said gently.

"I need to." Marie would never know how much I'd suffered at Eli's hands, but my sister deserved to know how I'd disappeared and where I'd been since then. I rubbed my shaking hands together and continued my story.

"Eli held me there for a week before he changed me. The police were looking for me in North Carolina, so he took me to his place in New York where we stayed for a few years. I wasn't allowed to go out, and I never challenged him. He was old and strong, and I was a new vampire. He told me he owned me, and I believed him."

Mark paled. "Jesus."

"Eli kept me with him all these years, up until last fall. I came to Portland with him, looking for someone. We got separated and I thought he was dead, so I ran."

I could see the question burning in Mark's eyes. He ran a hand over his bald head and asked what I knew was coming next.

"How are you here now? I don't know a lot about vampires, but I've heard there's no coming back from that. Yet, you're human..." He faltered. "You *are* human, aren't you?"

"Yes, I am." My mind raced for an answer for him. I wouldn't tell him or anyone else about Sara because that might put her in danger. I had to come up with something that sounded plausible, but no one would be able to verify.

"I ran into a faerie in Vegas. She could have killed me, but she saved me instead. Somehow, she was able to make me human again."

Mark did a double take. "Faeries are real, too?"

"Very." Chris nodded slowly. "They normally keep to themselves, but this one took a liking to Emma."

He nudged me with his shoulder. When I looked up, he smiled at me.

"My people were there when Emma was healed, and we took her to live with us. She was welcome to stay as long as she wished, but she wanted to live among humans again."

Mark's eyes widened even more, and he stared at Chris. "You're...not human? You said you were a vampire hunter, so I thought..."

"I *am* a vampire hunter. I'm just not human."

"What are you?"

Chris lifted a shoulder. "I'm a warrior who is strong enough and fast enough to fight a vampire. That's all I can tell you."

The investigator rubbed his face with his hands. "This is incredible. If I wasn't looking at Emma, I'd think it a fantastic story."

"Our world is too much for most humans to accept as real," Chris said. "You can count yourself among the few who know the truth."

"I'm not sure if that's a good or a bad thing," Mark replied. He looked at me. "Why didn't you try to find your family and let them know you're alive?"

A weight settled on my chest. "How would I explain my not aging to my family and friends? You know the media would pick up a story of a missing person coming home. I'd be a freak, and they wouldn't leave me alone. And how could I tell my little sister and my parents I spent the last twenty years as a monster? Because that's what I was. I have to live with that for the rest of my life. I don't want that for them."

Silence fell over the room. There wasn't much anyone could say in response. The demon had used my body to kill countless people, many of them girls just like me. You couldn't sugarcoat that, and you couldn't pretend it never happened.

Mark spoke first. "I've met a lot of people who've been through horrendous experiences. Your situation is different, but like them, you were the victim in all this. That vampire stole you from your family and made you one of them. You are not to blame here."

"That's what we keep telling her," Chris said.

"Your sister is an amazing woman, and she's spent most of her life trying to find out what happened to you. She loves you, and I don't think she'll rest until she finds you." Mark's voice grew softer. "Don't you think it's kinder to let her know you're alive than to let her always wonder your fate?"

Tears scalded my cheeks, and I couldn't speak around the tightness in my throat. I jumped up from the couch and ran from the living room. Instead of going to my bedroom, I went upstairs and climbed the stairs to the roof. The air in the apartment felt suffocating, and I needed to be outdoors.

The cushion on the wicker couch was still wet from last night's rain, so I sat on the roof with my back to the ledge. The sun was warm on my face, but it did little to melt the lump of ice in my chest. I'd already been tired and overwhelmed when I got home. After talking to Mark Rowan, I felt brittle, like a strong wind could blow me apart and scatter me.

Marie. God, how many times I'd thought about her since I was healed. I'd been close to my mom and dad, but Marie was my little sister. I was supposed to be there for her, to give her advice and to watch out for her. I'd failed her and left her alone without a big sister. And she'd been looking for me ever since.

How could I continue to let her suffer? But how could I tell her what I'd done? Mark knew about vampires, but he hadn't said if Marie did. Most humans wouldn't be able to sleep at night if they knew what was out there.

Was it right to expose Marie to the cruelty of that world? And my parents? There was no way I could face them and tell them what had happened to me.

"I've never been up here. Nice view."

I opened my eyes to look at Chris. "Is he still here?"

"No. He left his card for you. He promised not to say anything to your sister for a few days, but he'll have to tell her eventually. The question is, where do you go from here?"

I pulled my knees up and rested my forehead on them. "I don't know what to do."

Chris sat on the ledge beside me. "Do you want to see her?"

"More than anything. But I don't know if I can face her."

He let out a quiet sigh. "I've seen a lot in my lifetime, but I can't begin to imagine what you've been through. I don't think anyone can. You've come a long way since Sara healed you, and I hope someday soon you'll accept that you don't deserve this guilt you carry around."

I hugged my knees. "I know the demon did those things, not me."

"Your mind knows it, but I don't think your heart does. Maybe seeing your family again will help with that."

"What if it doesn't? What if Marie hates me?"

He slid down to sit beside me on the roof. "Your sister went through a lot to find you. According to Mark, he's the third private investigator she's hired in the last ten years. That sounds like a person who will love her sister no matter what. Do you really want your fear to get in the way of you two being together again?"

"No." I lifted my head to look at him. "It won't be the same as it was. She's older than I am now. What if it's too weird for us?"

A corner of his mouth lifted. "You went camping with a bunch of werewolves. I already think you're weird."

I gave him a teary smile. "You like the werewolves. You're just saying that to make me feel better."

"Is it working?"

"A little."

"Good." He stood and hauled me to my feet. "Sitting up here is not going to change anything. Have you eaten?"

"No."

He tugged me toward the door to the attic. "You're in luck because I'm a great cook, and I'm going to make us a huge breakfast."

"I don't know if I can eat," I said right before my stomach growled.

"That's because you haven't had my French toast. It's practically legendary and guaranteed to make you forget all your troubles."

It would take a lot more than food to make me forget. I thought about Roland and wished he was here. Chris was good company, but Roland was the one I needed. All it would take was one phone call and he'd be here.

But that wouldn't be fair to him. We couldn't be together until I told him about my past, and I wasn't ready to do that. I needed to see where things stood with Marie before I could think about my relationship with Roland. If there was a relationship left after he knew my secret.

21

Roland

"Still no word?"

Pete joined me near the back wall of the meeting room as I checked my phone again. I'd gotten one text from Emma since I dropped her off yesterday, letting me know Chris had found the man who'd been following her and it had all been a misunderstanding. She didn't elaborate, except to say she was safe and she'd explain later. I was relieved to hear she wasn't in danger, but it worried me that she hadn't said a word about us. If there was an *us*.

I rubbed at the ache in my chest. She couldn't have found out about the imprint in a worse way. And then to discover I was the wolf she'd befriended and that I'd kept it from her. I'd waited too long to tell her, and I'd ended up making a mess of everything. I was afraid I'd lost her, and it was my own doing.

"No." I stuck my phone in my back pocket. "I really screwed up this time."

"I have to agree with you on that one."

"Thanks."

He ignored my scowl. "I get why you felt you had to wait to tell her about the imprint, with her being human and all, but why did you lie to her about your wolf?"

I groaned. "I don't know. Stupidity."

"Shannon thinks she's upset about that more than anything else."

"Shannon spoke to her?"

He shook his head. "Not since Sunday morning. April called Emma today, but Emma said she had to go to work. She said Emma sounded strange."

Alarm filled me. "Strange how?"

"She only said Emma didn't sound like herself. But can you blame her after what happened?"

My shoulders slumped. "No."

Maxwell's deep voice cut through the din in the room. "Is everyone here? Good. Let's get this thing underway."

Pete and I faced the front of the room filled with Beta candidates. Maxwell hadn't told us why we were meeting today, but I suspected he was going to announce that he and Brendan had selected the Betas. I'd seen what looked like a list of names in Brendan's hand when he'd arrived. The air of excitement in the room told me I wasn't the only one expecting an announcement.

"I want to thank you for signing up for the Beta positions. Here in this room are some of the best hunters and fighters in the country, and I'm proud to call you my pack."

Smiles broke out around the room, lightening the air of nervous excitement. There wasn't a person here who didn't want one of the coveted Beta slots. I hadn't wanted to be a candidate at first, but over the last few weeks, I'd come to appreciate the importance of strong leadership in a pack. I was younger than most of the other candidates, but I thought I'd proven myself as well as anyone else.

"After considering the pack size and the distribution throughout the state, I decided to start with twelve Betas. We'll have four here, in addition to Brendan, and the other eight will be responsible for our smaller communities around the state. If I think there is a need for more Betas down the road, I'll choose from the remaining candidates."

He held up a sheet of paper, and my stomach fluttered in anticipation. Beside me, Pete shifted from one foot to the other.

"If I call your name, come to the front and stand to my left. As soon as we're done here, Brendan and I will go over your new responsibilities with you."

He peered at the list in his hand. "Francis Kelly."

Pete and I shared a look as people clapped. Neither of us was surprised our cousin had made the list, but he was going to be even more impossible now.

"Sheila Reid."

I clapped loudly as Sheila walked proudly to stand beside Francis. She'd just become the first female Beta in the country, and that had to feel pretty damn good.

"Peter Kelly."

Pete's mouth fell open.

I slapped him on the back and gave him a little shove forward. "Congrats, man."

"Thanks," he mumbled, then left to make his way to the front of the room. He still looked dumbfounded when he took his place beside Sheila. I didn't know why he was so shocked. He was the Alpha's son and a damn good fighter. If that didn't make him fit to be a Beta, nothing would.

Maxwell continued to call out the names. As expected, Shawn Walsh made the list. I'd expected him or Kyle to be selected, if not both.

Pete's eyes met mine across the room when his father hesitated before calling out the last name on the list. Maxwell had filled three of the four local positions, which meant the last Beta was someone from the Knolls.

"Kyle Walsh."

Surprise swept through me. I hadn't realized how much I wanted to be on the list until that moment, or how disappointed I'd feel if I wasn't selected. Pete's face showed his surprise, too. He'd said more than once he expected me to make the cut before him.

I should be happy. Being a Beta meant more responsibility, and I already had two jobs. And Emma, if she'd have me. I didn't want anything to take me away from her, especially now.

The meeting came to a close, and we went to congratulate the new Betas before leaving. There were some disappointed faces, but most were in good spirits. Pete still looked a bit shocked when I stopped to tell him I'd see him later. Francis was already talking about his plans to improve patrols. Maybe not being selected as a Beta wasn't such a bad thing.

Even though I hadn't made Beta, I received stares from almost everyone in the room. The news that I'd imprinted on Emma had spread like wildfire, and it was even bigger than what Trevor and Gary had done. Most pack members were curious because, like me, they hadn't known it was possible to imprint on a human.

I'd gotten a few sympathetic looks from people who mistakenly thought I didn't want a human as a mate. And then there were the resentful stares from a few of the unmated females, as if I'd deliberately chosen Emma to keep them from finding a mate.

Looks and whispers didn't faze me, and I couldn't care less what people thought of me as long as they treated Emma with respect. If she became my mate, she'd be a part of this pack, and I wouldn't allow anyone to make her feel unwelcome.

I left the building and headed for my car. Paul was working on an engine rebuild, and I'd promised to help him so we'd be free for when the Dodge Challenger arrived next week. Maybe the work would help me think about something other than Emma for a few hours. Not being able to talk to her was killing me, and I hoped she called or texted me soon.

"Roland."

I stopped and looked back at Maxwell, who was walking toward me. He caught up to me and waved a hand at the house.

"Come inside. We need to talk."

Whenever Maxwell called me aside for a talk, it usually meant bad news or I was in trouble for something. Since I hadn't broken any pack rules lately, I could only assume he wanted to talk about Emma. My mother had assured me Maxwell would have no problem with my human mate, but my body tensed as I took a chair across from the desk in his office.

He sat in his big chair and studied me with shrewd eyes. "I hear you've imprinted on Emma Grey."

"Yes."

"How do you feel about that?"

My eyebrows shot up. "I think my wolf chose well."

He leaned back in his chair. "And she accepts you as a mate?"

"I don't know. I hope so." I couldn't think about the possibility of Emma telling me she didn't want to be with me.

"There'll be some challenges for a human in a werewolf pack. She can't shift, and she's more fragile than we are. She'll feel the pack link once you're mated, but not as strongly as you do, so she won't submit to pack laws like a wolf would. But she will be a full member of this pack with all the rights and privileges as anyone else."

The tension flowed out of me. "Thank you."

He crossed his arms and stretched out his legs. "What do you think of the new Betas?"

I blinked at the abrupt change of topic. Was he actually asking my opinion of the people he'd chosen? I felt another test coming on.

"I think they'll do a good job."

I wanted to ask how he'd narrowed down the list to the twelve selected, but Maxwell surprised me by offering up the information.

"There are certain traits we look for in a Beta. He or she must be a strong fighter and show enough dominance to be able to maintain order. They also have to demonstrate good leadership skills and be willing to put the pack's welfare above their own."

I'd proven more than once I was strong, and I'd forced wolves older than I was to submit. He must have found my leadership lacking, or the trouble with Trevor and Gary had made him think the other wolves wouldn't respect me. Or maybe he thought a wolf with a human mate wouldn't be able to put the pack first. Doubts assailed me, but I was too proud to ask him why he'd passed me over.

Maxwell nodded as if he'd read my mind. "You have all the qualities we look for in a Beta. You're one of our best fighters, and you displayed strong leadership when you took the team to Portland, despite Trevor's attempts to undermine you."

He rubbed his beard. "Tell me, why did you give Trevor and Gary the opportunity to reform themselves and stay with the pack after what they did to you? I don't know if many wolves would have been that generous, myself included."

"Their families didn't deserve to suffer for what those two did. I have no love for Trevor and Gary, but I couldn't punish someone else for their crime."

"You put the pack's needs before your own as a good leader would."

"I don't understand. If I have everything it takes to be a good Beta, why wasn't I selected? I'm not saying I'm better than the other candidates. I'd just like to know what it was."

Maxwell leaned forward and rested his elbows on the desk. "I said that a Beta has to be dominant enough to do their job, but there are some wolves who are too dominant to be a Beta. When the old Alpha stepped down, either Brendan or I could have taken his place with the other as Beta. But we both knew I had too many Alpha traits to be a Beta, and my wolf would have eventually wanted to fight Brendan for the position. Just like yours would."

A laugh burst from me. "Maxwell, I've done some stupid things, but I'm not dumb enough to fight you."

His mouth curved in a rare smile. "You're still young. In a few years, your wolf will begin to feel the strain of submitting to my authority, just as my wolf did with the old Alpha. I didn't fight him because I already knew I was going to succeed him."

I stared at him for a few seconds as the meaning of his words sank in. "What are you saying? I'll be the next Alpha?"

"Yes."

Words failed me, which was just as well because Maxwell wasn't finished.

"Until recently, I wasn't sure if your Alpha blood was strong enough because you got it from your mother, not your father. You have the size and strength of an Alpha, but you didn't display any other Alpha qualities. In the last few months, Brendan and I began to see your Alpha traits emerging. You've forced older wolves to submit, and Brendan says you're almost as dominant as he is.

"You've matured a lot since January, and you've taken on the responsibility of two jobs in addition to your pack duties. You already have more battle experience than most of the pack will see in a lifetime, and you have a good relationship with humans and the Mohiri. All of these are vital to the survival of the pack. The world is changing, making it harder for our kind to remain hidden from humans, and packs need leaders who can adapt and guide them. With the right training, you can be such a leader."

I finally found my voice. "This is not another one of your tests, is it?"

Maxwell actually chuckled. "You are smart to question it, but no, this is not a test. This is me letting you know we'll start your new training in two weeks."

"Two weeks?" I echoed dumbly.

"I'm giving you some time with your new mate before you take on the extra training. This will be hard work, and I won't go easy on you, but I know you're up to it or we wouldn't be talking now."

I frowned as a new thought struck me. "What about Pete? He has Alpha blood, too. And Francis." I had a feeling Maxwell's decision wasn't going to go over well with Francis, who had always hoped to be in line for Alpha.

"Neither of them have your dominance. Francis is aggressive and he's devoted to the pack, but he leans toward the old ways. We need progressive leaders who look forward, not backward."

"Does Pete know?"

Maxwell shook his head. "He knows he won't be Alpha, but not that I've chosen you as my successor. I'm going to announce it to the pack tomorrow."

My head spun from his news. The last thing I'd expected when he called me in here was to find out I would be the next Alpha. Of course, I'd dreamed of being Alpha someday, and I'd played the Alpha game with Pete and the other boys. But I'd never believed it would really happen to me.

"Roland, I have no plans of stepping down anytime soon. You'll have years to worry about filling my shoes. Focus on training now, and the rest will come to you."

He stood and came around the desk. "I have to go back to the Betas. From what I hear, you have your hands full with your new mate. Work things out with her so your head is clear when training starts."

"I will if I can get her to talk to me."

We walked outside, and he turned to face me. "I'm no expert on human women, but a female wolf needs to see that you're sorry for your wrongdoing. You have to prove you're worthy of their forgiveness."

I snorted. "You mean beg."

"If that's what it takes," he said, setting off toward the meeting hall.

Just checking to see how you're doing.

We don't have to talk. Just text me to let me know you're ok.

I'm here if you want to talk.

I stared at my phone for a good five minutes before I set it aside and stripped out of my clothes. Rolling them up, I stuck them in the spot under the steps, along with my phone. Then I shifted and settled down on the hard ground. I had to be close to Emma, even if it meant sleeping under her steps like a stray dog, and it was a lot more comfortable sleeping outside in my fur.

The sound of the back door opening woke me from my doze, and I lifted my head as footsteps came toward me. I blinked when a flashlight beam blinded me.

"What are you doing here?" Emma whispered. "You don't have to stand guard anymore."

I tilted my head in response.

She let out a long breath. "I can't be around you right now. I'm sorry."

She whirled and walked back to the door.

The door opened. She walked over and peered under the steps.

"I told you last night you don't have to be here anymore. Go home, Roland."

I chuffed softly.

"I can't do this now. I'm dealing with other things...family stuff. I wish..."

She ran inside.

Wish what? I wondered until sleep claimed me.

She let out a resigned sigh.

"Don't you have a comfortable bed at home? Wouldn't you rather sleep there?"

I shook my head sadly. I wanted to sleep with my mate.

She crossed her arms. "If you think those sad eyes are going to work on me just because you're all furry, you can forget it."

I let out a soft whine.

"I know I said it would be a few days, but something came up and I have to take care of it first. I-I'll talk to you soon. I promise."

I watched the flashlight beam move toward me and stop. Emma stood quietly for a moment before she spoke. Her voice was hoarse, like she'd been crying.

"I can't talk yet, but I...I don't want to be alone."

I stood and walked slowly to her until my head nudged her shoulder gently. She reached up and touched my face, and a shiver went through me.

She walked to the door and held it open. "Just for tonight."

Warmth filled my chest, and I followed her inside. She didn't say much as we ascended the stairs to the apartment. When she reached the hallway, she turned to look at me. Her face was paler than usual, and dark smudges lay under her eyes.

"I know this is hard for you, and I'm not trying to hurt you or get back at you for what happened. I need another day or two, and then I'll explain everything."

I nodded, and she gave me a small smile before she went into the bedroom and shut the door. I heard her moving about for a few minutes, and then the door opened.

"Would you mind sleeping on my floor again?"

I entered her bedroom and waited until she was under the covers to lie down beside the bed. It killed me to be so close to her and not be able to hold her, but this was a hell of a lot better than sleeping under the steps.

"Thank you, Roland."

Anytime.

Emma

I gazed around the kitchen, frowning when I realized there was nothing left to clean. Turning, I headed for the living room to find it in the same state. The whole place was spotless, the result of too much free time and a six-hour cleaning spree. It was my day off, but I should have offered to go in, because anything was better than wandering around the apartment, waiting for news.

I'd called Mark Rowan yesterday, right before he left for DC to talk to

Marie. He was going to tell her he'd found me under very *unusual* circumstances. I had no idea how much he planned to tell her, or how she'd react to the news that I was alive after all these years. Would she believe him? Want to talk to me?

I'd given him permission to give her my number, and I'd nearly jumped out of my skin the two times the phone had rung today. One was Chris, checking in, and the other was Shannon, who said she might drop by this afternoon. I hoped she did because I was slowly going out of my mind, wondering what was going on in DC.

My cell phone buzzed on the kitchen counter, and I raced to answer it. It was a text from Roland. He was gone when I woke up this morning, but the warm spot on the floor by my bed had told me he'd stayed all night. That and my first restful sleep since our night in the tent.

Pack business tonight. Will come tomorrow.

I smiled at his persistence. Night after night he'd come here, not trying to talk to me or to get me to forgive him. He seemed content just to be near me. I knew he was playing on the soft spot I had for the wolf, using that to try to earn my forgiveness, but I couldn't find it in my heart to be angry at him. I'd already forgiven him, and I missed him.

Last night, I had to bite my lip to keep from asking him to shift so he could hold me. But I'd been afraid of where it would lead. I wanted Roland, but I couldn't bind him to me without him knowing the truth about me.

The doorbell rang, and I ran to get the door. *Shannon, you have perfect timing.*

The door swung open, and I stared, confused, at the woman on the landing. She was a few inches taller than I was with shoulder-length brown hair, and familiar brown eyes that stared at me with a mixture of disbelief and hope.

The world tilted, and I gripped the doorframe for support.

"Marie," I breathed.

"Emma? Oh, God, it *is* you."

Her face crumpled, and I no longer saw the woman, but my ten-year-old sister who had caught me sneaking out of the house that fateful night. I'd begged her not to tell and promised to take her to a movie that weekend. A promise I'd never kept.

She threw her arms around me, hugging me so tightly I could barely breathe. Sobs wracked her body, and I touched her hair soothingly as my own tears came. Through all the years of suffering, I'd held on to the memories of my family, knowing I'd never see them again.

After the nightmare ended, I'd had to accept that my sister and parents were out of my reach forever. Part of me believed my mind was playing tricks on me again and I'd wake up to find this was a cruel dream. I held on to her tighter, trying to stay in the dream as long as possible.

"I knew you were alive," she said against my hair. "They said you were dead, but I never gave up."

A long moment passed before she pulled back, her face streaked with tears, and held me at arm's length. "You look exactly as I remember you."

"You don't," I said with a watery smile.

"When Mark told me you were still a teenager, I thought he was crazy. Then he showed me some pictures of you, and I knew it was you. I had to come."

"I'm glad you did."

I'd been so afraid of facing her. Seeing her now, I knew the pain of rejection would be a small price to pay for being with her again and seeing the joy in her eyes.

I stepped back to give her room to enter. "Would you like to come in? We have a lot to talk about."

We went into the living room and sat beside each other on the couch because Marie wouldn't relinquish my hand. I couldn't stop staring at her, still afraid to believe she was really here.

She wiped under her eyes with her free hand. "All the way here, I thought about what to say, and I can't remember any of it. I don't think I really believed it was you until you opened the door."

I fought back another wave of tears. "I don't think there's any way to prepare for something like this. I was waiting for you to call me. The last thing I expected was for you to be here today."

"You didn't want me to come?"

Her eyes darkened with hurt, and I rushed to reassure her.

"I'm happy you're here, just a bit shocked. I didn't think I'd ever see you again, and here you are, all grown up."

"And you're still the same," she said in wonder. "How is this possible?"

My stomach hardened. Physically, I was the same person, but inside I was nothing like the stupid, innocent girl who had met Eli in that club.

I looked down at our joined hands. Hers used to be so small. Now, it covered mine. Her fingers were long and slender with pretty manicured nails. My nails were trimmed short with no polish.

"How much did Mark tell you?" I asked her.

"More than I expected." She let out a shaky laugh. "He asked me to have an open mind, but I thought he'd lost it when he started talking about vampires and demons. He told me a vampire took you the night you disappeared and made you into one of them, and that's why you haven't aged. Mark had always seemed so professional, but the crazy stuff he was saying scared me. I grabbed my gun and told him to get out of my house before I called the police."

My eyes widened. "You have a gun?"

She nodded gravely. "I also have a black belt. The gun is only for home protection."

Sadness and regret washed over me. I knew without asking that my sister had taken these extreme measures to protect herself because of me. I wasn't the only one whose innocence had been stolen that night.

"There I was, threatening to have Mark arrested, and he pulls out his cell phone to show me pictures he took of you at a coffee shop with two other girls. I still wasn't convinced until he played a video clip. I couldn't make out what you were saying, but as soon as I heard your laugh, I knew he was telling the truth.

"I write children's fantasy, so you'd think I'd be more open to the idea of vampires. Hearing you were a vampire all these years, and now you're human again, it was almost too much. But it's all true, isn't it?"

"Yes."

She drew a trembling breath. "Did it hurt?"

I nodded, grateful Mark hadn't told her everything. It wouldn't help her or me to tell her how much I'd suffered at Eli's hands. She'd lost too much already.

"It was over quickly," I lied.

I bit the inside of my cheek, remembering the four terrifying days of my transition. On the first day, I'd woken up violently ill, disoriented, and thinking Eli had drugged me. I'd had no idea what was happening to me. And then I'd felt something moving in my chest. I'd screamed and pulled against my bonds, but I was too weak to fight. Eli took great pleasure in describing how the demon was growing inside me and would soon take over my body, making me into a monster like him.

"I'm glad for that, at least." She gave me a searching look. "Mark said he'd never heard of a vampire becoming human, until you."

"I'm very lucky."

She fell quiet for a moment. "What was it like? Did...did you ever think about us?"

I squeezed her fingers. "Every single day. I never stopped missing you."

"Why didn't you try to contact us, to let us know you were alive?"

In her voice, I heard the scared little girl I'd left behind. How did I explain why I couldn't have gone home without telling her the whole truth about the evil that had lived inside me?

"Marie, I don't know how much Mark told you about vampires, but they're nothing like what you read in books. They're evil. The demon lives inside you like a parasite, and it takes control of your body. I could think, but that was all I could do."

Her free hand flew to her mouth. "Oh, God."

"I'm here now, and the demon is dead. That's all that matters."

Marie could never know how every day of my life as a vampire had been a living hell, and that thinking of her and our parents was the only thing that had kept me sane through it all.

It took her a minute to recover. "Mark said you've been human again for a few months. Why didn't you try to find me, or Mom and Dad?"

I smiled sadly. "I wanted to, more than you know, but how could I explain where I've been and why I look like this? I can't go back to my old life."

"You weren't going to tell us, ever?"

"I thought it was the best thing for you guys if I didn't come back. It killed me to make that decision, but it was to protect you. Mom and Dad wouldn't be able to handle the truth, and there'd be a media circus. I didn't want that for any of you."

She pressed her lips together and looked around the living room. "Is that why you came to this little town? Because no one here would recognize you?"

"Yes."

"How are you able to support yourself here? The rent on this building can't be cheap. And what about school?"

I smiled. "You sound like an older sister."

She returned my smile. "I guess I am the older one now. That will take some getting used to."

"For both of us. To answer your questions, a friend of mine owns this building and she's letting me stay here as long as I want. Everyone here thinks I'm Sara's cousin from Syracuse. I'm a waitress at a diner, and I plan to finish high school before I apply to college."

Her brow creased. "You can't pay for college working as a waitress."

I placed my other hand over our joined ones. "I have money in the bank for college and anything else I need. You don't have to worry about me."

"But..."

"Why don't I show you around?" I let go of her hand and stood. "You'll love my studio."

Her face brightened. "You still paint?"

"Not until I was healed – made human again. It's taken a while to get back into it, but I'm getting better at it every day."

I led her up to the loft, and I smiled at her gasp of delight when she saw the studio Sara had created for me. She went immediately to the stack of canvases and flipped through them.

"These are beautiful, Emma." She walked around the room. "I remember how much you wanted your own studio. You hated sharing the playroom with me."

Her words brought on a tide of fresh memories, and my throat tightened.

"Only because you kept stealing my brushes and losing them."

She walked to one of the windows that overlooked the bay. Her tone grew wistful. "You always did love the ocean."

I joined her. "You did, too. I remember how excited you used to get when we packed up the car to go to Virginia Beach."

She nodded sadly. "We sold the house there after you disappeared. It reminded Mom too much of the way things used to be."

My chest squeezed. Our parents had loved that house, and Dad used to joke about retiring there. It hurt to think of all the ways my disappearance had changed their lives.

I hugged Marie. "I'm so sorry for what you went through."

"Don't ever apologize for what that monster did to you," she said fiercely. "He took you from us."

"If I hadn't snuck out that night, I might never have met him, and –"

Marie pulled back to fix me with a stern look. "One foolish mistake doesn't mean you deserve what happened to you. I hate that thing for what he did to you. I hope he's dead, too."

I nodded and looked away, unable to meet her eyes. "I was one of those monsters for a long time. I did things...awful things. I was just as evil as he was."

"Don't say that. That demon parasite was evil. It took over your body and made you do those things."

"But—"

"You are the victim here. Could you have stopped the demon from doing those things?"

"No."

She smiled tenderly. "Then how can you be to blame for what it did?"

I let out a shuddering breath. "It's hard to believe that when I remember everything the vampire did."

"What the *vampire* did, not what *you* did. Maybe we should find you someone to talk to about this. A professional."

I made a face. "That would go over well. As soon as I started talking about vampires, I'd find myself locked up in a mental ward. I have to deal with this on my own."

"Not on your own." She gave me a determined look. "I just got you back. I'm not letting you go through this alone."

My whole body felt light with happiness. "I can't believe you're actually here. I missed you so much."

"I missed you too, Em."

My eyes teared up again at her old nickname for me. "No one's called me that in a long time."

"Then I'll have to use it a lot to make up for lost time."

"I won't complain. And I should probably send your PI a bonus. If not for him, we wouldn't be here talking right now."

"Don't worry. Mark got a nice fat check from me yesterday. He was worth every cent."

We walked over to Sara's old couch and sat. My heart felt near to bursting having Marie there after all I'd been through. I had a feeling it was going to take me a little while to work through all my emotions. But I had my sister back. That was all that mattered.

"So, you're a writer now. When you were little, all you wanted to be when you grew up was an astronaut."

She chuckled. "I outgrew that by the time I was twelve. I got into creative writing in high school, and my teacher encouraged me to continue it in college. It paid off. My first book was a best seller and won the Newbery Medal. Been writing ever since."

"Wow. Congrats. To think, my little sister is a bestselling author. How'd you end up in DC?"

A shadow crossed her face. "After college, I also became a lobbyist for several children's organizations. It's easier to live there, and I can write anywhere."

"Do you see Mom and Dad often?"

"A couple of times a year. I go stay with them in Charleston for Thanksgiving and Christmas. Mom likes to come visit me in the summer."

The thought of them spending holidays together sent a pang of loneliness through me for all I'd missed. Christmas, especially, used to be fun at our house, and Mom had always made the tree decorating into a big event.

Marie tugged at her hair, her expression thoughtful. "We have to figure out the best way to tell them about you. I know you're afraid of people finding out, but we can't let them continue to believe you're dead. Don't worry. We'll work it out."

"Okay." Now that I had Marie back, I wanted all of my family together, even if we had to meet secretly.

Her eyes sparkled with excitement. "Why don't you come back to DC with me? I have plenty of room in my house, and you could go to school there. You could pretend to be my younger cousin."

"I can't."

Her face fell, and I rushed to explain. "It's not just my fear of someone finding out about me. I don't like cities. Too many bad memories. It's one of the reasons I wanted to go somewhere small. And I love it here."

And I loved Roland. The thought of leaving him caused a pit to open in my stomach. I didn't know if I'd have a future with him after I told him my secret, but I had to try. If Marie could get past what I'd been and done, maybe he could, too. He hadn't told me he loved me, but his wolf had chosen me for his mate. That had to mean something.

"Maybe I can come stay with you sometimes," she said hopefully. "I can't stand the thought of not seeing you often. You'll have to forgive me if I'm a bit clingy for the next ten years or so."

I laughed, feeling almost weightless in my joy. "I'd love that. Can you stay tonight?"

Her eyebrow rose. "You couldn't make me leave."

"We can order pizza and hang out here."

"Like when we used to have movie night?"

I grinned. "Pepperoni on my side and Hawaiian on yours. I bet we can find *The Goonies* on TV." Marie used to love that movie, and I'd always teased her because she had a crush on Sean Astin.

"You remembered."

She looked so young in that moment, and it was almost easy to forget she was nearly twice my age now. When I looked at her, I didn't see a thirty-one-year-old woman. I saw a little girl who needed her big sister's reassurance.

I took her hand again. "I remember everything about you, Sis. No matter how far away I was, my heart was with you, Mom, and Dad."

"And we were always with you." She blinked back tears. "I feel...whole again for the first time since..."

"I know."

It would take time for me to feel that way, but getting Marie back had filled one of the gaping holes in my heart. Eli had taken everything from me, but I was reclaiming my family and my life piece by piece. I would never be the girl I was back then, but I could be happy.

22

Roland

I glanced up from the tire I was changing when I heard Paul enter the garage. He was always in before me, and I'd been here an hour already.

"About time you dragged your ass in here. I was starting to think I was the only one working here –"

I stopped when a new smell hit my nose. It was musky and strong, and it made my nose wrinkle in distaste. I looked at Paul who wore a satisfied smile, and I knew exactly what the smell was.

"April?"

His smile widened. "Last night."

I stood and extended my hand. "Congrats."

I put a hand over my nose when he got within a few feet of me. "Man, I hope my bonding scent is not that bad."

He chuckled. "Yours was pretty damn awful when you imprinted. April loves mine."

Emma loved mine, too. Or she used to. I had no idea what she felt about me anymore. Seeing how happy my cousin was, I was envious that things had never been as easy between Emma and me. If I'd imprinted on a female wolf, we would have been mated by now. But she wouldn't be Emma.

Paul sat on an overturned oil drum, and I went back to removing the lug nuts from the tire. After a few minutes, he cleared his throat.

"Are we not going to talk about Maxwell's big announcement yesterday? You know, the one the whole pack is buzzing about."

I shrugged. Seemed like all the pack talked about these days was me. First, it was the thing with Trevor and Gary, then it was me imprinting on a human. Now it was because Maxwell had chosen me to be his successor. I just wanted to mind my own business, but I figured I might as well get used to the attention. As the future Alpha, I could no longer fly below the radar in the pack. I didn't like it, but I accepted it.

Reactions to Maxwell's news had been pretty much what I'd expected. My mother and grandmother were beaming with pride, and Pete was happy for me. He said he'd never wanted to fill his father's shoes, and he was content to be a Beta. Like me, he'd thought Francis would be next in line for Alpha, and he was glad it was me instead.

Francis, unsurprisingly, was furious when he heard the news. Maxwell had taken him aside for a private talk, and he'd been oddly subdued when they returned an hour later. I had no idea what Maxwell said to him, but Francis didn't say another word about it, though I'd caught him casting resentful looks at me a few times.

As for the rest of the pack, they'd always known the Alpha's son or one of his nephews would likely be his successor. That was the way it was done, and it was just a matter of him deciding who it would be. Of course, it didn't stop them from gossiping and staring at me like I was suddenly going to sprout an extra tail.

"What do you want to know?" I asked without looking up.

"How long have you known?"

I removed the last nut and laid the wrench on the floor. "He called me aside after the Beta selection and told me. And yes, I was as shocked as you are."

"Actually, I'm not all that surprised. Pete's not aggressive enough to lead a pack this big, and Francis is too temperamental. That leaves you, Cuz. I guess Maxwell figures that you survived months of training under him so you must be worthy to be Alpha."

"I guess so."

Paul laughed. "You just found out you're going to be the next Alpha. How can you be so calm about it?"

I removed the tire and set it down next to him. "Emma is all I can think about now. Once I work things out with her, I'll worry about the rest."

He took that as an end to the conversation, and we spent the rest of the day working on his engine job. I was so engrossed in the work that I almost missed the text from Emma later that afternoon. My chest warmed when I read her short message.

Can we talk tonight?

Yes, I wrote back.

I felt lighter when I resumed my work. She wanted to talk. I hoped it meant she'd forgiven me or would soon. I thought about her inviting me in the night before last and asking me to sleep in her room. The fact that she'd wanted me near told me she cared about me.

After work, I went home to shower and eat before heading to Emma's. I'd been showing up at her place around nine so she most likely meant for me to come at that time. I was so preoccupied, thinking about seeing her, that I barely tasted my mother's casserole or heard the conversation between her and Grandma at the table.

"Roland, did you hear what I said?"

I gave my mother an apologetic smile. "Sorry."

"I saw Max earlier, and he said to remind you that you haven't hunted in over a month. Peter and Francis are going tomorrow, and Max wants you to go with them."

I groaned silently. Pete and I always went on the monthly hunt together, and Francis usually went with his friends. The only reason Maxwell would want the three of us to go together was to force me to deal with Francis's resentment about not being selected for Alpha. Maxwell didn't believe in letting things fester. The sooner you cleared the air and moved on, the better for the pack.

It was exactly nine when I knocked on Emma's door, my gut fluttering in anticipation. On the drive over, I'd thought about what Maxwell had said about proving I was worthy of her forgiveness. I'd do whatever she asked of me to earn her trust again.

Emma opened the door and smiled warmly at me. "Hi. Thanks for coming."

"Thanks for inviting me."

She stepped back to let me in, and we found ourselves face-to-face in the small entranceway. Her scent and her closeness teased me, reminding me how long it had been since I'd held her. All I had to do was lower my head and claim her sweet mouth. God, I wanted to kiss her so bad, but I couldn't push her. This was too important.

I moved past her and waited in the hallway until she indicated we should go into the living room. Something in the way she kept averting her gaze from me told me she was nervous and trying to hide it. I tried not to make too much of it because she did look happy to see me.

"Will you sit with me?" she asked softly as I walked to one of the chairs.

I turned to see her sitting on the couch. My pulse skittered with surprise and pleasure as I went to join her. We sat on either end, facing each other, and I couldn't help but notice how tightly she clutched her hands in her lap.

"Are you okay? You said Chris found the guy following you."

I expected her to be relieved not to have a stalker, but she looked troubled.

"Yes. His name is Mark Rowan, and he's a private investigator who was hired by my sister to find me."

I stared at her. "Your sister?"

"Marie and I haven't seen each other in a very long time, and she thought I was..." Emma let out a trembling breath. "She was looking for me."

"You said you had family stuff to take care of before we could talk. Was this it?"

She nodded.

Her sister must be older to be able to hire a private investigator. I had a suspicion that their separation had something to do with what had happened to Emma before she came here.

"Did you and your sister work things out?"

She gave me a small smile. "Yes. She came here yesterday, and we talked all night."

"That's great."

I couldn't understand why she didn't look happier about reconciling with her sister. Or maybe she was happy about that, and something else was upsetting her. Dread twisted my stomach.

"Emma, about us," I started.

She held up a hand. "I've had all week to think about what happened. I was upset and mad at you, at first, but I think I understand why you didn't tell me about your wolf. I won't pretend to know how werewolf males think, but Shannon and April said you don't think or act like human men. It took me a few days to get what they were saying and what you said about me pushing you away. You were right. I was doing that, but not because I don't want to be with you."

Her brown gaze held mine. "What happened between us Saturday night wasn't one-sided. I wanted that as much as you did, and I don't know if I could have stopped us if you hadn't."

I swallowed at the memory of her body on top of mine. "I couldn't let us go any further. We would have been mated before you knew about the imprint. I wouldn't do that to you."

"Thank you for that. I need to tell you things too about my past, and it wouldn't have been fair to you to take our relationship further before you knew them."

I heard her say something about her past, but I was stuck on something else she'd said.

"Our relationship?"

"Yes. If you still want one with me after you hear what I have to say."

My heart thudded. "Do you even have to ask? I came here prepared to beg you to forgive me and to give us a chance."

"You don't have to beg." She looked down at her hands. When she raised her eyes to mine again, they were stark and vulnerable, like she was baring her soul to me. "I love you, Roland."

"You...?" The need to touch her drove me to the center of the couch. Taking her hand, I tugged her to me until she sat on my lap. She turned her face toward me, and I saw the sheen of tears in her eyes before I brushed my lips against hers.

"I love you, too," I said, my voice rough. "So much it'll kill me if I don't kiss you now."

She pressed herself against me, and that was all the permission I needed. My mouth covered hers, and she opened to me, kissing me back with an urgency that left me light-headed and hungry for all of her.

Her fingers threaded through my hair, sending shivers through me, and her slight weight on my lap made my body ache. If we continued much longer, I was going to carry her to the bedroom, and this time, we wouldn't stop.

It took a minute for me to register the salty taste of tears on our lips. Breaking the kiss, I looked at Emma's brimming eyes and wet cheeks.

"What is it? Am I going too fast?"

"No. I..." She pressed her lips together and looked away from me. Then she set her shoulders and got off my lap to sit on her end of the couch again. Her tears and the misery on her face confused and scared me after her declaration and the way she'd kissed me.

"What's wrong?"

I reached my hand out to her, and she shook her head as she wiped her cheeks. I tried not to let the rejection bother me. More important was why she suddenly was so upset.

She took a deep breath and let it out. "Before we can be together, I need to tell you things about me, about my past. I'm afraid..." Her breath hitched. "I'm afraid you won't feel the same about me when you hear what I have to say."

"I love you. Nothing you say will change that."

"This will."

The certainty and fear in her eyes made my gut clench. I knew something bad had happened to her before she came here, but why would she think it would change how I felt about her? Coldness spread through me as I imagined the worst.

"Emma, did someone hurt you?" I asked gruffly.

Her silent nod sent a knife through my heart. My hands curled into fists, and I wanted to hunt down the man and make sure he'd never hurt another female. I looked at her helplessly, unsure of what to do for her.

It was a few minutes before she spoke again, her voice hoarse and strained. "This is very hard for me to talk about, especially to you. All I ask is that you don't leave before I finish. Please."

"I'm not going anywhere," I vowed.

Her sad smile told me she didn't believe that even though she wanted to.

Jesus, what did they do to you?

"I'm not who you think I am," she began slowly. "My name is Emma, but my last name is Chase, not Grey. And I'm not Sara's cousin, though she and Nate are like family to me."

"What?" I croaked.

"I needed a place to live, somewhere quiet, and Sara offered her apartment. I agreed to come on the condition she didn't tell anyone the truth about me. That's why we made up the story about me being her cousin."

"Sara knew?" I asked dumbly, trying to make sense of what she was saying.

"Please, don't be angry with her. I made her promise not to tell anyone. You know Sara never breaks a promise."

"Why did you change your name? Who are you hiding from?"

"No one...everyone." She let out a ragged breath. "Sometimes, I think I'm running from myself."

"I don't understand."

"I know." She rubbed her hands along her thighs. "This is so hard to explain."

She looked ready to run from the room, so I softened my tone.

"How do you know Sara?"

I'd been with Sara up until January, and after that she'd been tucked away in a faerie mansion in California for months. Something didn't add up.

"I met Sara in Las Vegas in March. She...healed me."

"Oh."

Now it made sense. Sara *had* been in Vegas in March looking for her mother, and they'd had a run-in with a big group of vampires. Strange, she hadn't mentioned meeting a girl there, or that she could heal humans now.

I remembered how pale Emma had been when she first came here, and I wondered if that was because of her illness. The thought that she could have been so sick she needed Sara to heal her sent a chill through me.

"Were you very sick?"

"It wasn't that kind of healing." She looked away, biting her lip. "Sara healed me the way she healed Nate."

I stared at her. "Nate? But he was a..."

"Vampire," she finished for me, her voice barely a whisper.

My stomach lurched sickeningly. No. She couldn't have been a vampire. I'd know. Wouldn't I?

I thought about Nate. I hadn't seen him as a vampire, but I was there the day Sara made him human again. I'd shifted and smelled him, and there hadn't been a trace of a vampire on him.

But that was Nate. It was one thing for Sara to help her uncle who'd been a vampire less than a week. Why would she heal a strange vampire with everything that was going on back then? Every sucker in the country had been looking for her, along with a Master. It made no sense unless she'd known Emma before she was changed. That must be it.

"How long were you a vampire before Sara healed you?" I asked with surprising calm.

Silence.

"Emma?"

She breathed deep and looked at me. "Twenty-one years."

"What?" I felt my body grow cold as the implications of her words sank in. I tried to reconcile the sweet girl I knew with one of those sadistic bastards, but I couldn't do it. My mind wouldn't let me imagine the girl I loved as a brutal killer.

"Please, tell me this is some kind of joke."

She jerked her head from side to side.

My gaze dropped to her mouth and bile burned the back of my throat when I imagined her with a pair of snake-like fangs. I'd killed so many vampires, and I'd seen what they could do. They were killing machines, and they took joy in inflicting pain. Sara had seen that firsthand when her father was killed by them, and she hated bloodsuckers even more than I did. It didn't make sense for her to save one unless she was close to them, like Nate.

"Why did she heal you?"

Emma flinched. I felt bad for my harsh tone, but my emotions were all over the map. I didn't know how to cope with what I was hearing.

"It was because of Eli," she said hoarsely.

I recoiled from her. "Eli? The same Eli who was obsessed with Sara and nearly killed her?"

"Yes."

A shudder went through me. The familiar way Emma said Eli's name told me she'd known him, and not just in passing. The thought of her with him made my stomach roll violently, and I moved to get up.

"Please, let me explain," she pleaded desperately. "If you want to leave after, I understand. But I need you to know the truth. All of it."

I returned to the far end of the couch, my body stiff as I waited for her to continue.

"I grew up in Raleigh, North Carolina. It was me, my little sister Marie, and our parents. I was a normal teenage girl who liked to go to the mall and hang out with my best friend. I loved to paint, and my dream was to go to art school. I was happy."

She wrapped her arms around herself. "One night I snuck out to go to a club with my friend Chelsea. We got separated. That's when Eli found me. I didn't know what he was until he got me to go outside with him. By then, it was too late."

Her eyes took on a faraway look filled with horror. "The things he did to me... I prayed he would kill me, but he had other plans. A week after he took me, he made me into a monster just like him."

The sheer agony and despair in her voice lashed at my heart until it felt like it had been shredded. Every breath hurt, and my wolf wanted to howl out his pain.

"Eli owned me after that. He was so strong, and he loved to control me. The vampire I became didn't try to escape him. It was as twisted as he was, and it wanted to be with him. The demon possessed my body completely, and I could only watch as it did to others what Eli had done to me."

She raised her hands and looked at them as if they belonged to someone else. "The blood of so many innocent people is on these hands, and no matter what I do, they don't feel clean. I see the faces when I close my eyes. I hear them cry and beg. They come into my dreams, and every night I relive the things that I – the vampire did to them. The demon is dead, but I'm not free. I don't know if I'll ever be free."

Her eyes were desolate when she looked at me again. "I lived in hell for twenty-one years, until I went with a group of vampires to attack a Mohiri safe house in Las Vegas. I had no idea Sara was there or what she could do. I attacked her, and instead of killing me as she should have, she made me human again.

"You wanted to know why she chose me. She touched me, saw my memories, and took pity on me. She told me later that when she saw it was Eli who took me, she knew my fate would have been hers if not for Nikolas and you. That's why she saved me."

My throat was so tight I couldn't speak. I wanted to reach out to her, but I was still reeling from her story and trying to sort out my emotions. Hatred for vampires had been ingrained in me since I learned to talk, and a part of me felt revulsion when I looked at her. But I also saw the girl I loved, the person I wanted as my mate, in terrible pain. The two sides of me battled each other, and I felt like I was being torn apart inside.

Emma pulled her knees up to her chest and hugged them. "I was terrified and so confused after Sara healed me. I had no one, and I couldn't go back to my family. Sara took care of me and brought me to Westhorne to live with her. The Mohiri were kind to me, despite what I used to be, but I couldn't stay there forever. I needed to try to make a life for myself among humans again. When she couldn't convince me to stay, Sara offered to let me live here as long as I wanted.

"I was afraid of moving to werewolf territory because of my past, but Sara said there was no safer place for me outside of a Mohiri stronghold. The security guy at Westhorne got me fake IDs and a social security number, and I changed my last name to Grey. Sara and Tristan gave me enough money to live off for a long time, and she even put the studio upstairs for me. I can't ever repay her for all she's done for me."

I found my voice, at last. "I thought one of my kind hurt you before you came here, and that was why you were nervous around us. But you were afraid we'd find out the truth about you."

"Yes."

I felt betrayed, and it stung. I'd befriended her, fallen in love with her, and my wolf had chosen her for our mate. She let me get close to her, knowing how I'd feel when I learned the truth. Why else would she have kept it a secret? If I'd known, my wolf might never have imprinted on her.

The rational part of me said I was being unfair. Emma had tried to keep her distance from me when she moved here. I was the one who kept coming to her. She hadn't tried to lure me into a relationship or make me fall for her. That was all me.

And no matter what she'd done as a vampire, she was a victim just like Nate. My mind struggled with that, too, because it went against all of my conditioning to see vampires as anything but evil. Nate was different because I'd known him all my life and he'd only been a vampire for a week.

Emma's questions about Nate on Saturday night made sense now. How would I have felt about him if he'd been a vampire for as long as she had?

I rubbed my forehead. "I don't know what to say. I'm not even sure how to feel."

"Do you hate me?" she whispered.

"No." I met her eyes, and the pain in them almost gutted me. "What happened to you wasn't your fault. It's just..."

She gave a tiny nod. "You can't look at me without seeing what I used to be."

"I'm a werewolf, and I just found out that the girl I chose for my mate was a vampire a few months ago."

Her shoulders slumped. "I'm sorry. I never wanted to hurt you or deceive you. Whatever else you think of me, I hope you know that."

I stared at the fireplace, not sure what to say next. I was so confused, torn between wanting to comfort her and needing to leave and clear my head. My wolf was agitated, and he wanted to run. Maybe it was a good thing I was going on a hunt tomorrow. A few days away in my fur might be what I needed to help me come to terms with all of this.

"I think I should go," I said after minutes passed with neither of us speaking. "I need..."

"You don't have to explain," she said thickly as we stood and faced each other. "Is this goodbye?"

The thought of never seeing her again made my heart feel like it was in a vise. The pain gave me comfort because it wouldn't hurt so much if I didn't belong with her.

"No. I just need a few days."

We walked to the door. I opened it and looked to where she stood a few feet away, hugging herself. I hated leaving her like this, but I couldn't stay.

"Will you be okay here?" I asked her.

She attempted a smile. "I'll be fine. Don't worry about me."

Telling me not to worry about her was as effective as telling me not to breathe. Despite everything, she was the only person I could imagine spending my life with, and I'd always be protective of her. I wouldn't think of anything *but* her while we were apart.

"I'll see you soon."

I stepped outside and closed the door behind me.

Emma

I sat a few feet from the edge of the cliff and gazed out over the wide expanse of ocean. The wind plucked strands of hair from my loose braid and tossed them in my face, and I used both hands to tuck them behind my ears.

What a wild, beautiful place. It was no wonder Sara had spent so much time down here with Remy. I'd peered over the edge, trying to see the cave she'd told me about, but it wasn't visible from up here. The foaming water below had made me dizzy, and I'd had to back up. I obviously wasn't as brave as Sara.

So, this is it.

This was where Sara had killed Eli and freed me from him at last. She didn't know it, but she'd saved me twice – once when she ended his life, and again when she killed the demon he'd put inside me. A person who hadn't even been born when Eli took me had been the one to save me from him. I'd never been a big believer in fate, but it felt like a higher power had sent her to me.

I'd avoided coming to the cliffs because I hadn't wanted to go anywhere Eli had been. He'd controlled me so completely all those years, and I'd been afraid some part of him was still here, waiting to enslave me again. I think it was also because I was hiding from that life, and being here where my maker had died resurrected a lot of old memories of him.

Today, I'd come here to confront my past, and to put the ghost of Eli to rest forever. I'd cried long and hard after Roland had left last night, and it was in the early hours of the morning when I finally ran out of tears.

It was in that moment that I realized I'd stopped feeling the crushing guilt and shame I'd carried with me for months. I still felt guilt, but it no longer weighed me down. Baring my soul to Roland had forced me to stop hiding behind the fear of someone discovering my horrible secret.

I'd woken this morning with a lighter soul but a heavy heart. Roland's reaction to my confession hadn't been as bad as I'd feared, but I'd seen the revulsion in his eyes and watched him withdraw from me physically and emotionally. He'd said he needed a few days, but I couldn't see how he'd ever look at me the same. I didn't regret telling him because he'd needed to know the truth, but that didn't make losing him hurt any less.

I stood and took one last look around before starting back to the road where I'd left the Vespa. No one came down this way much, according to Sara, so I hoped it was okay there. I'd hate to tell Nikolas I'd lost his generous gift.

I smiled in relief when I saw the Vespa where I'd left it. A minute later, I was riding the lonely stretch of road back to the main road. Sara's bicycle was nice, but nothing was as fun as a scooter. Nikolas might not smile as much as other guys, but he sure knew the way to a girl's heart.

At first, I thought I was seeing things when a naked woman stepped from the woods a hundred yards ahead of me. I slowed as the tall brunette walked to the center of the narrow road and faced me. When I got close enough to recognize her, I would have sped up to go around her, but she blocked the way.

I lifted the visor on my helmet, trying not to show fear. The last time I'd seen Lex, she'd been in her wolf form and about to attack me. If not for Roland, there was no telling what she would have done.

"What do you want, Lex?"

She put her hands on her hips, completely unabashed by her nudity. "I want what should have been mine."

"I don't have anything of yours." I sounded a lot braver than I felt.

"Don't play coy, Emma. I don't know how you got Roland to imprint on you, but if you care about him at all, you'll end this."

"I didn't –"

"Roland will be the next Alpha; did you know that? He needs a strong female wolf by his side, not a weak human girl who will never be accepted by the pack. You'll only hurt him if you stay. You'll drag him down and make him weak, and no wolf will respect a weak Alpha."

Roland, the Alpha? Why hadn't he said anything to me? There was so much I didn't know about him and his life in the pack.

My chest tightened because Lex was right. It was one thing for a werewolf to take a human mate, but the Alpha? And then there was my past. The pack would never accept someone who used to be a vampire. When Roland had time to think about it, he'd realize that, too. If he hadn't already.

Lex's scowl deepened. "If you'd stayed away from him when I told you to, this wouldn't have happened."

"Roland and I are friends. I had no idea he felt that way for me or that he could imprint on me. I only found out about the imprint on Sunday."

Her eyes widened for a second, and then her voice rose threateningly. "Try again. I saw you with him in the tent, remember."

Fear snaked up my spine. I was alone here with a werewolf who had tried to attack me a week ago. I had to tell her something that would placate her, or I was in real trouble.

"Nothing happened. It rained and we got wet, and Roland put the sleeping bags together so he could share his body heat."

"How convenient. That worked out well for you, didn't it?"

I took a steadying breath. "You're not going to believe anything I say, are you?"

"No."

"Then why are you here? I can't change anything. I can't make Roland's wolf un-imprint from me."

Her smile didn't reach her eyes. "Actually, you can. I talked to some old wolves from another pack, and they said a wolf-human imprint is not the same as a normal imprint because humans have no wolf. If you rejected Roland and refused to mate with him, his wolf would eventually forget you and choose someone else, a suitable mate."

The thought of him with someone else made my heart hurt, but at least he wouldn't have to be bound to someone he didn't want.

Lex began to circle me slowly. "Once you mate, it's forever. Do you really want to tie Roland to you, knowing he'll grow to resent you eventually? Is that what you want for either of you?"

"What makes you think he will imprint on you if I leave?"

She laughed softly. "I can be very convincing when I want to be, and you won't be around to distract him. His wolf is an Alpha, and it will soon see I'm the perfect mate for him."

My grip tightened on the handlebars. "You talk about me leaving for his sake, but you just want to manipulate him into choosing you."

Her voice was smug. "Oh, please. It wouldn't be the first time a woman used her wiles to get a man. I promise you he'll be happy with me...and very satisfied. Werewolves have healthy sex drives, and an Alpha male like Roland needs someone who can keep up with his needs."

Anger throttled my fear. "You don't care about Roland or what's best for him. And you don't know him at all if you think sex is enough to make him happy. He has dreams and plans for college and the garage. One day, he'll be —"

Her mouth turned down. "Tinkering with old cars is a nice hobby, but the future Alpha needs a real job, something more fitting for his position, like taking over the lumberyard from Maxwell someday."

Chagrin filled me on Roland's behalf. "The garage is not a hobby. It's his dream, and he's going to make it happen."

She scoffed. "Look at you, all starry-eyed. I bet he eats that shit up."

"You know what, Lex. I might not be the right mate for Roland, but at least I love him for who he is, not what I can make him into. If I leave him, it will be because that is what's best for his happiness, not yours."

I lowered my visor and moved past her, slowly picking up speed. Glancing in my side mirror, I saw her standing in the road where I'd left her, glaring after me. I looked at the road ahead of me, and when I checked the mirror again, a white wolf stood in her place.

It wasn't until I rounded a bend in the road and lost sight of her that I let out a trembling breath. That girl was crazy and delusional. She truly believed Roland would want her if I was no longer in the picture. And she had no scruples about removing anyone who got in the way of what she wanted.

Lost in my thoughts, I didn't realize I was no longer alone until a growl split the air. I looked at the side mirror and let out a small scream at the sight of the snarling white wolf bearing down on me.

My pulse sped up as I hit the gas. The Vespa shot forward, but it wasn't enough. Lex's stride lengthened, and she began to close the distance between us. I was less than a quarter of a mile from the main road, but it might as well have been ten miles. There was no way a scooter could outrun a werewolf.

The Vespa shuddered as it ran over bumps and ruts in the old road, and my heart lodged in my throat when I hit a rock and almost lost control.

The mistake caused me to let off the gas for a few seconds, allowing Lex to gain more ground. I could hear her claws scraping over the gravel as she ran me down like a big cat hunting a deer.

Don't look back, don't look back, I chanted in my head, needing all of my attention on the road ahead. One more slip and it was all over.

Lex growled again, much closer this time.

I darted a glance at the mirror, and a cold sweat broke out over my body at the savage determination in her yellow eyes. She wasn't trying to scare me anymore. She was going to kill me.

A whimper fell from my numb lips when the wolf's hot breath touched my back. Blood roared in my ears, and darkness touched the edges of my vision.

Fifty yards ahead, a car flashed by on the main road. Hope spiked in my chest a second before claws raked the back of the cargo box.

The Vespa swerved dangerously close to the trees, and I almost spun out on the grass at the side of the road. I somehow managed to get back onto the road, but Lex was waiting for me.

I gunned the scooter again in a last desperate attempt to get away. The main road was so close now. I just had to hold her off for a few more seconds.

A claw nicked my thigh and slashed the seat behind me. The scooter jerked precariously to the side, and I screamed as the road came up to meet me. Tires screeched and a horn blared. I felt the sharp pain of impact.

And then nothing.

23

Emma

I came to slowly as sounds filtered through the dark haze around me. Nearby, something beeped steadily, and farther away, a phone rang.

Where am I? I thought sluggishly, trying to think of the last thing I'd done. Why couldn't I remember?

I moved my hand and moaned as pain shot from my wrist to my shoulder. Tears sprung to my eyes as I opened them to stare at a white ceiling.

Something moved to my right, and a familiar blond head appeared next to the bed, her blue eyes filled with relief.

"Hey, good to have you back, chica."

"What are you doing here?" I rasped, my throat as dry as sand.

Jordan smiled. "The hospital called me when they couldn't get ahold of Sara, and I hopped on the first flight out of LA. Good thing you had both of us listed as emergency contacts."

"Hospital?"

Her brows drew together. "You had an accident. You don't remember?"

I blinked, trying to clear the cobwebs from my mind, but it was hard to think past the pounding in my head. The cliff. I'd left to drive home and I saw...Lex.

It all came flooding back, and I jerked when I remembered the Vespa going down and my shoulder hitting the pavement. I inhaled sharply and another wave of pain went through my ribs.

"Easy there. You're pretty banged up." Jordan laid her hand on mine. "How are you feeling?"

"Like a truck hit me."

"Close. A minivan almost clocked you, but he managed to swerve. You were lucky."

I coughed. "Lucky, yeah."

Jordan went to the table at the foot of the bed and poured water into a plastic cup with a straw in it. She came back and held it so I could drink. The water was room temperature but felt wonderful to my dry mouth and throat. Too bad it didn't do anything to relieve my headache or my other aches and pains.

I fought the tears welling up inside me. "How bad is it?"

"I've seen worse. Your right arm is broken, and your shoulder was dislocated. They fixed the shoulder and put a cast on your arm. You have some cuts and bruises but nothing serious. The doctor said the helmet saved your head, but you have two cracked ribs."

I grimaced. "That explains why it hurts to move."

"I think I can help with that."

She pulled a small metal can from her pants pocket. As soon as she opened it, I knew what it was. Gunna paste was a medicine the Mohiri used for pain relief and healing. I'd never tasted it, but I'd seen Sara's expression when she had to take it after training.

"This will deal with the pain and help you heal faster. Open up."

I dutifully opened my mouth and let her place a glob of the green paste on my tongue. As soon as I closed my mouth, a dry, bitter taste filled it and I had to fight the urge to spit it out. But I knew how potent Mohiri medicine was, and I really wanted to be able to take a deep breath without feeling like there was a knife in my side.

It took about a minute for the gunna paste to kick in, and I sighed as the pain in my head and my right side began to ebb. The Mohiri could make billions if they ever decided to market that stuff. Not that they needed more money.

Once I felt like I could move without pain, Jordan raised the head of the bed so I could see her better. She gave me some more water and fussed over me until I made her stop.

"How long have I been here?"

"They brought you in yesterday afternoon. It's a little after 8:00 a.m. now."

She pulled up a chair and sat beside the bed. "You want to tell me what happened? The police said you were doing about seventy when you hit the main road. And the minivan driver told them he thought he saw a big white dog chasing you."

I shuddered at the memory of hot breath touching the back of my neck. "It was a werewolf."

"What?" Her eyes narrowed. "You better tell me it was a game of tag gone wrong, or I'm going to kick some furry butt."

I pressed my lips together and shook my head.

She let out a stream of swear words that caused a passing nurse to shush her sternly. Quietly, she shut the door and came back to the bed.

"Tell me."

"I don't know where to start."

I hadn't told Jordan or Sara about my relationship with Roland or him imprinting on me. As far as they knew, he and I were only friends. And if I'd told either of them about Lex's aggressive behavior toward me, it would have upset Sara.

"The beginning is usually a good place."

I sighed. "Okay, but you'd better sit again."

Starting with the night I met Roland and Peter, I explained about how I'd kept my distance from the werewolves in the beginning because I'd been afraid they'd find out about my past. When I told her about the two werewolves at the cove and the huge black one who had driven them off, recognition flickered in her eyes. Of course, she knew what Roland looked like in his fur; she'd seen him enough times.

I went on to tell her about Roland coming to see me and how our friendship had grown from there. How I'd felt attracted to him but knew we could only be friends. Then I told her about the party at the lighthouse.

"Hold up, sister." She held up a hand when I tried to gloss over certain parts. "You kissed Wolf Boy? Was he any good?"

"That's not important. And *he* kissed me."

She grinned. "I bet you kissed him back and it was hot. Oh, yeah, I can tell by that twinkle in your eyes. Give me the details."

"It was really...nice." Nice was an understatement when it came to Roland's kissing, but I didn't want to think about that. After our talk the other night, I might never see him again.

"Nice?" She scowled. "You're just like Sara. You never want to share the good stuff. Go on, tell me the rest."

A minute later, she interrupted the story again, her eyes flashing angrily.

"That Lex chick threatened you?"

"She tried to bully me, and I told her I wasn't giving up my friends for her."

Jordan crossed her arms. "What happened next?"

I told her how I'd been determined to keep Roland in the friend zone, but every time I saw him, it was harder to resist him. I talked about the black wolf showing up at my place, night after night, and how I'd come to see him as a friend without knowing he was Roland.

Her voice rose. "That mangy mutt. Wait'll I see him again."

I hesitated a moment before I told her about the camping trip. I left out most of what happened in the tent, skipping ahead to the next morning when Lex showed up. Jordan's expression went from livid to shocked when she heard about Roland imprinting on me.

"Wow," she uttered, finally at a loss for words.

"I didn't know what to do when he told me. I was so happy he wanted me, but he didn't know about my past. I couldn't keep that from him, and I didn't know how to tell him."

"He doesn't know?"

"I told him everything Friday night, and he didn't take it well. Not that I blame him. He said he had to go away for a few days, and I haven't heard from him since." My throat started to close up. "I don't think he's coming back."

Jordan rubbed the back of my hand. "If he loves you, he will. Plus, he imprinted on you. I doubt he'll be able to stay away."

I shook my head. "I don't want someone who's with me because he has no choice. He could barely look at me when I told him."

"He was in shock. Plus, he's a male *and* a werewolf – an imprinted werewolf. The odds are stacked against him handling this well."

She stood and gave me more water. "Now tell me what happened yesterday."

It was hard to talk about my confrontation with Lex, but I managed to get it all out. By the time I got to the accident, Jordan was pacing the room in short angry strides.

"I'm okay, Jordan."

Her nostrils flared. "She tried to kill you. That's *not* okay, and it's against pack law. The Alpha will hear about this."

I remembered what Lex had said about the pack not accepting a human mate. Would they even believe me if I told them what she'd done?

"It's her word against mine."

"You're forgetting the driver who saw her chasing you. And she tried to attack you last weekend in front of witnesses. Trust me, that bitch is going down."

I trembled, physically and mentally exhausted. This past week had been a rollercoaster of emotional highs and lows, topped off by nearly being killed by a jealous werewolf.

Suddenly, New Hastings didn't feel like the safe haven I'd thought it was, and I was forced to think of the possibility of finding a new home. Maybe I should take Marie up on her offer and stay with her for a little while until I figured out what to do next.

"I'm supposed to work today. Can you call the diner for me and tell them I had an accident and can't come in? Let them know I'm okay."

"Sure." Jordan pulled the blankets up to my chin. "Get some rest. We can worry about everything else later."

I grabbed her hand. "Please, don't tell Sara. There's nothing she can do, and it'll only ruin her trip."

"I won't if you don't want me to, but she's going to be pissed when she finds out we kept this from her."

"I know."

She smiled. "We'll deal with that when the time comes. Right now, though, you need sleep. I'll be here when you wake up – to give you some more of that yummy gunna paste."

"Great," I muttered, closing my eyes so I didn't see her smirk. "Thanks for coming, Jordan."

"Anytime, chica."

Roland

Home, sweet home.

Pete picked up the pace when we saw his house through the trees on Monday morning. I would have teased him about rushing to see his mate if I didn't envy him so much. I could be coming home to my own mate today if I hadn't handled things so badly with Emma Friday night.

Her story had floored me, and I hadn't been able to deal with thinking about what she'd been or what Eli had done to her. She'd opened herself up to me, and what had I done? I'd left her there alone. Instead of staying with her and comforting her after all she'd been through, I'd bailed. If she wanted nothing to do with me now, it was what I deserved.

We stopped at the edge of the woods and shifted. Francis grabbed his clothes from the run box first. He yanked on his jeans and set off toward the house without a glance in my direction. It had been like that for the last two days. I wasn't sure what Maxwell had hoped to achieve by sending us out together, but I didn't think it had worked. It was going to take longer than a weekend for my cousin to stop resenting me for being chosen as the next Alpha. I'd give it a decade, at least.

"Catch you later," Pete said. He barely waited long enough to zip up his fly before he followed Francis, eager to see Shannon. I had a feeling Pete was going to be a few hours late for work today.

I hurried to pull on my own clothes. After two long days away from Emma, I was dying to see her, but she probably wasn't up yet. I had no idea what kind of reception I'd get from her, but I'd be outside her place, waiting for her to talk to me.

Pulling my phone from my jeans pocket, I powered it on. The battery was low, but I wanted to see if I had a message from Emma. It was more hope than expectation, and I wasn't surprised to see nothing from her.

There were three voicemails from a number I didn't recognize. When I hit play on the first one, I was surprised to hear Jordan's voice. My surprise quickly gave way to apprehension when I heard her message.

"Roland, I hope you get this message soon. I'm at Mercy Hospital in Portland with Emma. The hospital called me because I'm one of her emergency contacts. She was in an accident yesterday in New Hastings and she's a little banged up, but the doctor said she'll be okay. She told me about you two, so I think you should be here. See you soon."

I stared frozen at the screen for a moment before I set off running for my house. My keys were in my pocket so I jumped into the Mustang and took off. It wasn't until I hit the interstate that I remembered to play Jordan's other messages. Her voice was less friendly on the second one, which had come in last night.

"Roland Greene, where the hell are you? You have a lot to answer for, buddy. Emma said you were freaked about what she told you, but that's no excuse for not being here. Do you know how upset she is? You better get your ass over here because your girl needs you."

"Fuck," I muttered, hitting play on the third message, which I'd received an hour ago.

"Wolf Boy, so help me. You better be lying unconscious somewhere because that's the only excuse you can have for not being here with Emma. Especially since it's your damn fault she's here. Thank God at least one of us cares about your *mate*."

"Oh, Jesus."

My gut knotted painfully. Jordan's anger didn't bother me as much as the fact that Emma had been in the hospital for two days, thinking I didn't care enough to be there. The thought of her in pain created a lump in my throat, and I hit the gas harder. Despite Jordan's assurance that Emma was okay, I tortured myself imagining her in a hospital bed hooked up to machines.

I was a wreck by the time I got to the hospital and found out what floor Emma was on. I spotted someone at the nurses' station and hurried over to ask for the room number. Before I could reach it, Jordan intercepted me, looking like a vengeful angel.

"It's about damn time you got here," she whisper-yelled at me. "Where the hell have you been?"

"I was hunting," I said in a low voice. "I just got back an hour ago. How is Emma?"

"She's asleep. You don't check your phone?"

It was my turn to scowl. "Maxwell doesn't allow us to take phones with us when we hunt."

She pulled me into an empty waiting room. "Why would you go off hunting after what happened Friday night? That was a dick move, Roland."

"I know." I rubbed my face miserably. "Maxwell ordered me to go, and I thought it would help if I got away for a while."

"You mean you ran away," she accused. "That girl's been through hell, and you have no idea how hard it was for her to open up to you. Yeah, the vampire did some horrible things, but Emma was a victim, just like Nate. If you can't see that, then you don't deserve her."

My gut twisted. "Where is she? I need to explain..."

Jordan grabbed my arm. "Hold up. Before you see Emma, I want to know why you didn't keep her safe from that she-wolf. You had to know that female was dangerous after she nearly attacked Emma the first time."

A chill ran down my spine. "What are you talking about?"

"I'm talking about that bitch Lex. She tried to kill Emma on Saturday."

"What?" I croaked.

"Emma was riding her scooter on some old road down by the cliffs when Lex stopped her and told her to stay away from you. When Emma tried to leave, Lex shifted and chased her."

I stared at her. "She caused Emma's accident?"

"She chased Emma to the main road where Emma almost ran into a mini-van. The driver told the police he saw a large white dog behind the scooter. What color is Lex?"

My heart began to pound and my hands curled into fists as I was swamped by rage and guilt. Jordan was right, this was my fault. If I'd reported Lex to Maxwell like I should have, she never would have hurt Emma. I'd thought she'd given up on me when she found out I'd imprinted on Emma.

For Lex to try to kill a human, especially a werewolf's mate, there had to be something seriously wrong with her.

Jordan snapped her fingers in front of my face. "Hey, chill. Your fangs are showing."

I took deep breaths until I calmed down and my canines receded.

"I'll take care of Lex," I said in a hard voice. "But I need to see Emma first."

"Second door past the nurses' station. Fair warning, Wolf Boy. If you make her cry, I'm going to neuter you."

I nodded and went to Emma's room. Easing the door shut behind me, I walked around the curtain blocking the bed. My stomach clenched when I saw her lying in the bed, hooked up to an IV. Her face was pale, and her dark hair was fanned out across the pillow. She had a cast on her right arm from her wrist to her elbow, but I couldn't see any head injuries. Thank God for the helmet or she might have...

I swallowed painfully and walked over to the bed. Her hand felt cold and small in mine, and her fingers twitched at my touch.

"I'm so sorry, Emma. I never should have left you."

I sat on the chair beside the bed, still holding her hand. Seeing her like this scared me. It was a harsh reminder of how vulnerable she was, how easily I could have lost her. And her last memory of us would have been of me walking away from her.

Jordan was right, I'd run away at the time Emma had needed me most because I couldn't cope. She had been through horrors I couldn't even begin to imagine, and she'd confided in me because she loved me. And how had I repaid her trust? In one breath, I'd told her I loved her and nothing would change how I felt about her, and in the next, I'd turned my back on her.

An hour passed before she stirred. Her eyes opened slowly, and she turned her head to look at our joined hands. Her eyes lifted to mine, and the sadness in her gaze gutted me.

"Hey," I said softly. "How are you feeling?"

She wet her lips. "I'm okay."

"I'm sorry I didn't come sooner. I was hunting, and I didn't know about the accident. I came as soon as I got Jordan's message."

She gave a little nod and looked away.

"Are you in pain? Can I get you anything?"

"No," she said in a hollow voice that made my chest ache. I could feel her withdrawing from me, and I was desperate to set things right.

The door opened and a middle-aged doctor entered, followed by Jordan. Emma quietly pulled her hand from mine and looked at the smiling woman, whose name tag said Dr. Elyse Webber.

"Good news, Emma. We're kicking you out of here." She checked on Emma's cast and took some of her vitals. "Everything looks good, but you'll have to take it easy until those cracked ribs heal. The cast will have to stay on for six weeks."

Cracked ribs and a broken arm? My anger flared again. Lex would pay dearly for this. If she were a male, I'd kill her for hurting my mate.

Dr. Webber consulted the chart at the foot of the bed. "I can give you a prescription for pain meds if you need them."

"I'm good," Emma said quietly.

"Okay then. I'll send the nurse in to remove your IV, and we'll get you out of here. If you have any problems, come back to see us."

"I will."

As soon as the doctor left, Jordan took over. She went to the cupboard and retrieved a plastic shopping bag that contained a pair of jeans and a top.

"I picked up some clean clothes for you to wear home. I figured you wouldn't want to put on your old things."

Emma smiled wanly. "Thanks."

Jordan looked at me and pointed at the door. "You want to wait outside?"

"Yes." I turned to Emma. "I need to make a call. I'll be back when you're ready to leave."

She simply nodded, and her lack of response worried me. She'd barely said five words to me since she woke up.

The waiting room was occupied, so I went outside. I didn't want anyone to overhear the conversation I was about to have.

Maxwell's phone rang twice before he answered. "Are you calling to tell me why you're not at work?"

"Yeah. I'm at Mercy Hospital with Emma. Lex Waters tried to kill her."

"What?" he snapped.

I related what Jordan had told me. Then I told him about Lex's pursuit of me and her growing aggression toward Emma, ending with the incident at the campsite last weekend.

"Why didn't you tell me this sooner?" he demanded.

"I thought I had it handled and that Lex would let it go after she found out I'd imprinted. If I'd known she would do something like this, I wouldn't have left town." I rubbed the back of my neck. "Emma could have died. Lex has to pay for that."

He let out a harsh breath. "This is a very serious allegation, Roland. I'm not saying I don't believe your mate, but it will be her word against Lex's."

Anger surged in me. I knew the Alpha had to be an impartial judge, but there was no way Lex was getting away with this. She'd gone too far.

"The driver of the car Emma almost ran into said he saw a large white dog chasing Emma. How many white wolves are in town now?"

He was quiet for several seconds. "Two that I know of. I'll call them in and send Francis to check out that old road. If a wolf has been there in the last few days, he'll pick up their scent."

"What will you do with her?" I asked, confident Francis would smell Lex at the scene of the accident.

"I don't know yet, but if she harmed your mate, she'll be punished. You have my word on that. How is Emma?"

I watched an ambulance arrive at the emergency room, and I shivered. Emma had been in one of those two days ago.

"She has a broken arm and some cracked ribs. They're releasing her soon."

He exhaled loudly. "Take the day off and be with your mate. I'll call you when I know more."

I hung up and went back to Emma's room to find her dressed and sitting on the bed. She was still pale, and she held her injured arm against her stomach. I wanted so bad to hold her, but I was afraid of hurting her.

Jordan came in behind me, waving some papers. "All checked out."

"I'll get the car and pull it up outside for you." I fished in my pocket for my keys.

"Jordan is taking me home," Emma said softly.

Before I could object, Jordan dangled her car keys. "My BMW will be more comfortable for her than the Mustang. You can follow us."

The BMW might be more comfortable, but it was clear in the way Emma avoided my gaze that she didn't want to ride with me. I could feel the distance growing between us, but I couldn't press her while she was in this condition. She was recovering from a terrible ordeal, and I'd give her space if that was what she needed.

A nurse brought a wheelchair for Emma. She protested weakly that she didn't need one, but she soon gave in. I wheeled her down to the front entrance and stayed with her while Jordan went to get the car. Emma didn't say a word the whole time we were alone, and I didn't try to get her to talk. There was so much I needed to say to her, but now wasn't the time.

Jordan pulled up the car, and Emma let me help her into the passenger seat and strap her in. My hand lingered on her shoulder before I made myself step back and shut her door.

I walked around to the driver's side, and Jordan looked up from the cell phone in her hand. "I'll take good care of her."

"I know." There were few people I'd trust with her safety, and Jordan was one of them.

My phone vibrated as they were driving away, and I pulled it out to read the two texts from Jordan.

Give her a day or two. She's been through a lot.

Don't ask me why, but I'm pretty sure she loves you.

I stared at the second text for a long moment before I laid the phone aside and started the car. Jordan's words gave me hope that my stupidity hadn't cost me the only girl I'd ever loved. I hadn't wanted a mate yet, but I couldn't imagine my life without Emma. All I could do was hope she felt the same way about me.

24

Emma

It felt strange to be back in my apartment, even though I'd only been gone for two days. But it was nice to be surrounded by my things and not the constant smells of antiseptic and disinfectant.

The best part was being able to take a shower and wear my own clothes. Jordan wrapped my cast in plastic and helped me shampoo my hair. I was too tired and sore to care about modesty. She even dried my hair and brushed it out for me, prompting me to say I could get used to being pampered like this. And then, she ruined it by shoving another glob of gunna paste in my mouth.

"I couldn't give you too much in the hospital because they'd notice how fast you were healing. If you take this four times a day, that arm will be better in a few days."

I couldn't argue with that. I'd only been wearing the cast for two days, and already I wanted it gone. Thankfully, my ribs were almost healed already.

Jordan's cooking skills weren't as good, so we had sandwiches for lunch. I didn't have much of an appetite, but she wouldn't let me up from the table until I ate at least half my sandwich.

"You've been pretty quiet today," she said after she finished her second sandwich. "Want to talk about it?"

"Just trying to work out some stuff."

She nodded and took our plates to the sink to wash them. "When you told me about you and Roland, I was kind of surprised. He never made any secret of the fact he didn't want a serious relationship. But when he showed up at the hospital this morning, all he could think about was seeing you. He nearly lost it when I told him what that Lex chick did."

I didn't want to talk about Roland, but I couldn't stop from asking. "Lost it how?"

She turned and leaned against the counter. "He started to shift. That only happens to pups or adult wolves in a highly emotional state. That boy has it bad for you."

"He said he loved me before I told him about my past." It was hard to think of that night and how quickly the adoration in his eyes had changed to revulsion.

"You don't think he still loves you?"

I shook my head. "I think he does, but sometimes love is not enough."

Her brows knit. "What do you mean?"

"I mean that some people are not meant to be together no matter how they feel about each other. Roland is a werewolf, and I'm an ex-vampire. I don't think you could find two people more unsuited for each other. I knew that from the beginning, and if I'd listened to my head instead of my heart, none of this would have happened."

Jordan crossed her arms. "There's no logic to love, and who cares how different you are. Obviously, Roland doesn't, or he wouldn't have imprinted on you. So, he freaked out a little when he heard about the whole vampire thing. He also came running the second he heard you were hurt. Give him a chance to grovel and plead his case before you write him off."

"Grovel?"

She snickered. "That's more for my amusement than anything else."

I gave her a small smile. "I don't want to talk about my disastrous love life anymore. Tell me about what you've been up to. You haven't mentioned your Egyptian warrior in ages."

She made a moue. "That one's a lost cause. Last I heard, he was in South Africa."

"That's too bad."

"Yeah." She sighed loudly. "He had a really nice sword."

It felt good to laugh, even if it made my ribs hurt a little. Jordan told me stories about her adventures in Los Angeles, and her face glowed with excitement. She and I were so different. She loved the warrior life, always moving around, fighting, and I wanted a quiet, stable life. She'd never be able to stay long in a place like this, and I could have stayed here forever.

Marie called after lunch, and I was careful not to tell her I'd been in the hospital. Since our reunion, our roles had somehow flipped, and she'd started acting like the big sister. She worried about me living here alone, pointing out that technically I was only eighteen. It still felt strange thinking of my ten-year-old sister as a woman in her thirties, but she was also trying to adjust to our new relationship.

"I've hardly written a word since I came home. Every morning when I wake up, I think it was a dream. And then I look at the pictures of us on my phone, and it feels like I'm going to explode from happiness."

"Same here."

She sighed. "One night wasn't enough to catch up. I want to come up for a real visit. Or you could come here. I know you're not ready to see Mom and Dad, so it can be just the two of us."

"I'll think about it." My life was too up in the air at the moment to make promises.

Half an hour after I hung up from talking to Marie, Shannon called. She'd heard from Peter that I'd been in an accident, but it didn't sound like she knew about Lex's involvement. I wasn't up to talking about it, so I assured her I was okay and promised to talk to her in a few days.

Jordan took the phone from me when I hung up, and she announced it was time for a nap, despite my assertion that I didn't need one. She gave me more gunna paste and tucked me into bed with orders to stay there.

"You're worse than Nurse Ratched," I groused as she pulled the covers over me.

She let out an evil laugh. "Maybe I'll add nurse to my résumé. What do you think?"

"I think the other warriors should be very afraid."

The smell of food woke me hours later, and I was surprised to see how long I'd slept. I found Jordan in the kitchen, taking plates from the cupboard. On the table was a large bag from the diner, and the smells wafting from it made my mouth water.

"Your boss sent dinner. A guy name Scott delivered it and said to tell you everyone at the diner is hoping you get better soon."

I looked at the large containers of fish and chips. My favorite. "That's so nice of them."

"Yeah, and it smells amazing." Jordan picked up the bag by the handles. "I checked out the roof while you were asleep, and I thought it would be nice to have our dinner up there. A little rooftop picnic."

"That sounds great."

I got two sodas from the fridge, and she carried the food and plates. It was a warm evening, and the sun felt good after days in the hospital. I was ravenous after my small lunch, and Jordan nodded in approval when I put a second helping of fish on my plate.

"How long are you staying?" I asked her as we lounged after our meal, too full to move.

Her eyebrow rose. "Sick of me already?"

I smiled. "I figured you'd get bored here soon."

"It's no L.A.; that's for sure."

She made a squawking sound as Harper swooped down to land on the table. The crow eyed the food containers then cocked his head to give me an expectant look.

I laughed at them both. "Off the table, buddy. You want a treat, you go to your dish."

"What the hell?" Jordan sputtered when Harper jumped off the table and strutted over to his food dish. "You have a pet crow?"

I put fries and leftover fish on my plate. "He's Sara's crow, and he drops in for treats every now and then."

"Oh yeah, she told me about him." Jordan watched Harper. "Does he actually understand you?"

"I think so. But then, he is one of Sara's pets, so..."

"Say no more."

I carried my plate over and scraped the food into the crow's dish. When I straightened, my gaze fell on a classic blue Mustang parked up the street.

Jordan came over to stand beside me. "I wasn't sure whether or not to tell you."

I stared at the car as conflicting emotions rose up in my chest. I missed him, and I wished he was in here with me, but I wasn't ready to talk to him. I believed he still loved me, but I couldn't stop remembering the way he'd looked at me and how much it hurt when he'd walked out.

And then there were the things Lex had said to me about how the pack would treat Roland if he had a human mate. I knew she had been trying to drive me away, but there'd been a ring of truth to her words, and I couldn't forget them.

"Why is he out there?"

"He wants to be close to you even if you won't see him." She shrugged. "I guess bonded males are all the same whether they are Mohiri or werewolf. You should have seen Nikolas before Sara finally mated him. Impossible to live with. I bet Wolf Boy couldn't leave if he wanted to."

"Sara and Nikolas are happy together."

She made a face. "Ridiculously happy. I couldn't handle a male all up in my business, no matter how hot he is."

"So, if you were in my shoes, you'd tell Roland it was over?"

"If I was in your shoes, I would've boxed that boy's ears by now. But that's me. If I was in love with him like you are, I'd give him hell, and *then* I'd give him a night he'd never forget."

I turned away from the ledge, my heart heavy. "I wish it was that easy."

"Whatever you decide, make sure you do what makes you happy. Life's too short to waste."

"Says the immortal."

She snorted. "Mohiri mate for life, too. Can you imagine being stuck with someone you didn't like for centuries? It doesn't matter how long your life is; you have to make it count."

I nodded, but I couldn't stop Lex's words from playing in my head. *"You'll drag him down and make him weak, and no wolf will respect a weak Alpha."*

What if the thing that gave me happiness ended up destroying his?

I walked into the kitchen, rubbing my arm where my cast used to be. Jordan had removed the cast this morning, after three days of feeding me the horrid gunna paste. She was a tough nurse, but she made up for that with her entertaining personality. Now she was on a plane back to California, and the apartment felt empty without her.

In two days, I'd be on a plane, too, headed to DC to visit Marie for a week. I was excited about seeing her again, and I hoped the time away would clear my head and help me figure out where to go from here.

Yesterday, I called Gail and told her I couldn't work there anymore. I'd already lost a week of work, and now I was leaving for a week. My future was too uncertain, and I wasn't sure how much longer I'd be in New Hastings. It wasn't fair to Gail to hold on to the job while I figured out what to do with my life.

I hadn't spoken to Roland since the morning I left the hospital, though he came by every day and sat in his car across the street for at least an hour. He didn't try to approach me or call me, except for a few texts to ask how I was doing. Jordan said he was waiting for me to forgive him. The thing was, there was nothing to forgive him for. I couldn't blame him for reacting as he had to something that went against everything he was. Just as I didn't blame him for Lex's actions.

But it wasn't fair to leave him hanging any longer, especially with me going out of town, which was why I'd texted him earlier, asking if he could come over to talk. I still wasn't sure what I was going to say to him, and my heart ached every time I thought about it.

When the doorbell rang, I jumped. I'd been so lost in thought I hadn't heard a car pull up. Sucking in a deep breath, I went to open the door.

"Hi."

He gave me a smile that made my stomach flutter. It seemed like forever since I'd seen him, and my eyes drank him in.

"Hey. You look great. Your cast is gone."

"Arm's all healed thanks to Jordan and her Mohiri medicine."

I stepped back, motioning for him to enter, and he followed me into the living room. I sat in one of the chairs, and he took the couch, looking a little crestfallen at the distance between us.

He looked around. "Is Jordan still here? I didn't see her car."

"She left a few hours ago."

"Oh."

Silence stretched between us. I fidgeted under his gaze and searched for something to say.

"Emma, about what happened. I can't tell you how sorry I am for hurting you, and for what Lex did to you. I'll do whatever it takes for you to forgive me."

I held up a hand. "There's nothing to forgive. I didn't tell you the truth about me sooner because I knew how you felt about vampires. I don't hold that against you."

"But Lex..."

"Lex is the one who attacked me, not you." I could still hear her claws against the back of the Vespa, and I shivered at the memory.

"I promise you'll never have to worry about her again. She took off after she attacked you, and Maxwell tracked her down. She's confined to her family farm and banned from coming to the Knolls. She's lucky she wasn't banished."

I'd known Roland wouldn't let her near me again, but hearing that she was banned from town sent relief coursing through me.

He patted the couch beside him. "Will you come sit with me? I won't touch you unless you want me to."

The hope in his eyes was almost my undoing, but I steeled myself against it. I shook my head. "We need to talk."

His smile wavered. "Okay."

"I'm leaving on Saturday to visit my sister in DC for a while, and before I go –"

"You're leaving?" His body went rigid. "Why?"

I looked down at my hands. "Marie asked me to visit, and I need time away to think."

"About us?"

"Yes." I met his gaze again, hating myself for the confusion and hurt on his face.

"I don't understand. You love me and I love you. What is there to think about?"

I played with the hem of my top. "Relationships are about more than love. There's so much we don't know about each other. You just found out I used to be a vampire, and I know so little about your life in the pack."

"We'll get to know each other. Ask me anything."

"Why didn't you tell me you're going to be the next Alpha?"

He frowned. "I found out last Friday, and I haven't had a chance to tell you with everything else that happened. Is that what's upset you?"

"No, I'm happy for you." I swallowed painfully. "But I can't be a proper mate to you."

"What do you mean?" he demanded. "My wolf chose *you*. You're the perfect mate for me."

I bit the inside of my cheek, trying to stave off the tears until I got through this. There'd be plenty of time to cry later.

"The Alpha needs a strong mate at his side, not a weak human who'll only drag him down. The pack won't accept me, and you'll be stuck with me. I'll ruin your life."

His eyes widened. "Of course, the pack will accept you. Why would you think that?"

"Lex said –"

"Lex," he growled. "You believed her? She'll say and do anything to get what she wants."

I clenched my hands in my lap. "I know she was trying to drive me away, but some of the things she said were true. How can your pack respect an Alpha female who's not even a werewolf? I'll make you look weak in their eyes."

"The pack already knows I imprinted on you and that Maxwell chose me to be the next Alpha. Do you know how many people have spoken out against me having a human mate? Not a single one. Shannon and April love you, and Pete and Paul already think of you as part of the pack. My mother and grandmother keep asking when I'm bringing you home to meet them."

He stood and came over to kneel at my feet. My stomach dipped when he took my hands in his warmer ones.

"You are not weak, Emma. You're one of the strongest people I've ever met, and I love you with everything in me. There will never be another mate for me, and the only way you'll hurt me is if you leave me."

My breath bottled up in my chest. I'd spent the days since the accident thinking he'd be better off without me and trying to prepare myself to end it with him. I was afraid to let myself believe I didn't have to give him up.

Roland gave me a hopeful smile, as if he sensed me weakening. "Let me take you to meet my mother and some of the other people in the Knolls. I want to show you how much you've already been accepted by my pack. Please, say you'll come."

I nodded, not just because I couldn't refuse him when he looked at me like that but because I desperately wanted him to be right.

He rewarded me with a smile that melted the icy lump in my stomach. In that moment, I would have done anything he asked of me.

"I'm going to hug you now," he said roughly. "Is that okay?"

My pulse quickened. "Yes."

His hands moved to my shoulders, gently pulling me against him. I went into his arms and buried my face in the crook of his shoulder, letting his warmth surround me. One of his hands moved up and down my back in light strokes that made me want to burrow against him and forget this horrible week ever happened.

Too soon, Roland leaned back to look at me. "Been wanting to do that all week."

"Me, too."

Smiling, he stood and tugged me to my feet. "Let's go."

"Now?"

"Yes, now. You think I'm giving you a chance to change your mind? Besides, I want to show you something I've been working on."

"What is it?" I asked, taking a detour to the kitchen to grab my keys and phone.

He grinned mischievously. "If I tell you, it won't be a surprise."

"I'm not sure I like surprises anymore."

"This is a good one, I promise."

All the way to the Knolls, he deflected my questions about what he wanted to show me. Instead, he talked about how nice it was now that the gathering was over and most people had gone home.

"Grandma's still here because she wanted to meet you," he said, turning onto a rural road with no houses.

I rubbed my thighs. "I'm meeting your mother and your grandmother?"

He reached over and took one of my hands in his. "You'll love them. But I have to warn you, Grandma will try to feed you until you burst."

My jitters calmed a little. "As long as there's pie."

Roland laughed. "There is always pie."

We passed a sign that said we were entering the Knolls. Suddenly, we were surrounded by rolling fields planted with corn and potatoes, and large farmhouses with ancient trees in the yards. I'd never been to the Knolls, and I think I'd expected it to be more like a bunch of log cabins in the woods.

"It's beautiful."

He nodded, looking pleased.

I watched two young boys chasing each other with water guns, and I smiled, picturing Roland at that age.

"That's Maxwell's house." He pointed to a large white house at the end of a long driveway. It was bigger than the other houses, but I figured the Alpha needed the biggest place.

Two houses down he said, "That's my house."

I looked at the brick ranch-style house that had neatly tended rose bushes and a homey feel to it. Then I noticed we were driving past it.

"We're not going in?"

"Not yet. I thought I'd show you around first."

We drove through the Knolls until we came to a gravel road that looked new. At the end of the short road sat four bungalows in various stages of construction. The houses were spaced well apart so they didn't feel crowded, and the builders had left trees between them for privacy.

Roland pulled the car into the driveway of a pretty gray house with a wraparound porch and a wide chimney. He shut off the engine and looked at me. "Want to see inside?"

"Yes." I unbuckled my seat belt and got out.

The door was unlocked, so we walked in. The interior was done in warm neutral colors and the smell of paint still hung in the air. We walked from the kitchen to the living room, and I saw that the place was partly furnished. It also looked like someone was living here.

"It's cozy," I said, admiring the big fireplace in the living room.

"That's not the best part."

Roland took my hand and led me down the hallway to a closed door. He opened it to reveal a bright room facing the woods with large windows on two sides. There were cupboards and a long worktable with a sink. But the thing that drew my attention was the large easel standing in the corner next to a stack of blank canvases.

My throat tightened as I realized what I was looking at.

"It still needs a little work, but it'll look great with all your paintings and stuff. And there's plenty of natural light for–"

I flung myself at him, my arms hugging his waist tightly, my voice so choked I could barely speak. "It's perfect."

His arms came around me. "A bunch of the guys pitched in to help. Everyone was angry about what Lex did, and they wanted to make it up to you."

There were no words to describe what I was feeling. While I'd spent the week agonizing over our relationship, he'd been building me an art studio in this beautiful little house. Our house.

I waited for the thought of living with him so soon to freak me out. Instead, I found myself thinking how it would be to be able to hold him like this every day. To never be alone again.

Roland released me, smiling like a kid at Christmas. "Come. Let me show you the rest of the place. Then you can hug me all you want."

I snorted softly at his teasing tone and let him go. He showed me a guest room and bathroom before leading me to the master suite that was already furnished with a king-size bed, a dresser, and two nightstands. The bed covers were slightly ruffled and a pair of jeans lay on the floor.

He smiled sheepishly and picked up the jeans, tossing them in the bathroom.

"Sorry. I don't have a hamper yet."

"You're living here?"

"It was easier to do the work that way." He gave me a searching look. "What do you think of the place?"

I nodded approvingly. "Your house is beautiful...even with dirty laundry on the floor."

He came over and cupped my face in his hands, the intensity in his gaze stealing my breath.

"This is *our* house and that is *our* bed, and I won't share them with anyone but you. And if you'd rather stay at the apartment, then I'll move in there, if you'll have me."

"You'd move out of the Knolls for me?"

A werewolf needed to live near the woods so he could shift often. If he moved to town, he'd have to drive out here every time he needed to shift.

He gave me an incredulous look. "I'd go anywhere with you. Don't you know that? I love you, Emma, and wherever you are is home to me."

My heart swelled, and I pressed my lips together as the tears came. I'd been alone for so long, and it was difficult to conceive that someone could love me this much. Since Sara had healed me, I'd been tainted by what Eli had done to me and what he'd turned me into, and I'd felt unworthy of happiness. Roland's love made me feel clean again.

"Don't cry." He brushed away the wetness on my cheeks. "We don't have to rush into anything. I know you've been through a lot, and I'll wait as long as you need me to. All I'm asking is for you to give us a chance." His voice grew strained. "I don't want to lose you."

I reached up to pull his head down to mine. In the breath before our lips touched, I said, "You could never lose me."

His mouth moved tenderly against mine as if he was afraid to push me for more. Impatiently, I swiped my tongue across the seam of his lips, and he opened to me with a small gasp of pleasure. I kissed him deeply, and he crushed me to him, his hunger matching mine and sending fire through my veins.

He was breathing heavier when my lips moved to the curve of his jaw, and I smiled to myself as I explored his throat with my mouth. I released his head to slip my hands beneath his shirt, and he made a small sound when I began running them over his back.

When my fingers traced the hard muscles of his abdomen, he sucked in a sharp breath and his hands tightened on my shoulders. I could feel him tremble as my hands roved over his body, but he didn't move. He was letting me have full control, and it made me love him even more. That was when I knew exactly what I wanted to do.

Roland

I could barely breathe as Emma's hands traveled over my stomach and chest, her soft touch setting my body on fire. I trembled from the strain of not moving, but I was afraid to do anything to startle her. I'd fantasized about her touching me like this, and I'd die if she stopped now.

Her hands slid down to my waist, her fingers snagging the bottom of my shirt to push it up my body. She wasn't tall enough to finish the job, so I gladly did it for her. I tossed the shirt on the floor, savoring the cool air against my heated skin.

She trailed kisses across my chest while her hands continued their gentle exploration. When her fingers dipped inside the waist of my jeans, my body felt like it was going to combust. She ran her fingers along my stomach until she reached the button. My whole body tensed when she released the button and lowered my zipper with agonizing slowness.

"Emma," I said roughly when she hooked her thumbs in the top of my jeans and began to slide them down my legs. No one had ever undressed me like this, and it was the most sensual experience I'd ever had.

My jeans pooled around my feet, and I kicked them off along with my Chucks, leaving me naked except for my underwear. She stood slowly, her hands skimming my legs and sending delicious shivers through me.

A groan slipped from me when her small hand cupped me, and I couldn't keep my hands off her any longer. I lowered my head, and she rose up on her toes to meet me in a smoldering kiss that left me dazed. She clung to me as my lips grazed her throat, and my hands followed the contours of her back and firm bottom. I smiled in satisfaction when she let out a ragged breath and melted against me.

Lifting my head, I looked down into her lovely brown eyes as my hands went to the front of her shirt. She gave a small nod, and I unbuttoned the shirt and pushed it off her shoulders to land on the floor near my discarded clothes.

"So beautiful," I murmured, kissing her shoulder.

She bared her throat to me, and I touched my lips to the spot beneath her ear where her pulse fluttered wildly. My own heart raced as my hands moved over her soft skin, spanning her waist. She was so small compared to me, and I was half afraid of being too rough in my need for her.

As if she heard my thoughts, she took my hands and moved them to the waist of her pants in silent invitation. I claimed her lips again as I unbuttoned her pants and pushed them down over her hips. She took over, shimmying out of them and kicking them aside without breaking the kiss.

The feel of her bare skin against mine drove my arousal to new heights, and I knew there'd be no stopping this time unless she asked me to. When I unclasped her bra and let it join the growing pile of clothes on the floor, she responded by relieving me of my underwear, her fingers stroking me with maddening slowness.

I shuddered and scooped her up in my arms, carrying her to the big bed. With one hand, I held her while my other one pulled down the covers. I set her down gently on the cool sheets and lay beside her. Her fingers tangled in my hair and pulled me to her, and I lost myself in the kiss.

My lips trailed down her throat to her soft breasts, and she arched against me. Her fingers dug into my scalp and pure pleasure rolled through me. No one had ever affected me this strongly, and my body was coiled tight, threatening to explode if I didn't have her soon.

I lifted my head to meet her heavy-lidded eyes. "I want you so much it hurts. But if you're not ready for this, tell me. I meant it when I said I'd wait as long as it takes."

"Even months or years?"

I swallowed hard at the thought of waiting years to make her my mate, but the alternative – not having her at all – was unthinkable.

"Yes, as long as we can be together."

She smiled and cradled my jaw in her hand. "You're kind of amazing, you know that? Must be why I'm so crazy about you." Her other hand went lower, eliciting a growl from me. "Make love to me, Roland."

"Thank God," I breathed, earning a sexy laugh from her.

I quickly divested her of her panties and tossed them over my shoulder, to her amusement. I gave her a wicked grin, determined to replace her mirth with a different kind of pleasure.

Rising over her, I proceeded to kiss my way from her lips to her toes and back again until she was clinging to me and moaning my name. When neither of us could last much longer, I settled between her legs and raised myself on trembling arms.

"Emma Chase, will you have me as your mate?"

Her eyes widened at the sound of her real name, and her smile stole my breath away. I'd never seen anything more beautiful than her, flushed from our lovemaking and her eyes brimming with love.

"Yes," she whispered.

Our bodies fit together as if we'd been made for each other, and I moved slowly to draw out the experience of claiming my mate. Nothing else in my life would compare to this moment. My wolf howled impatiently, but I ignored him, wanting this to be perfect for Emma and me. When she cried out softly, I found my own release, joy filling me as the imprint formed a bond we'd share for the rest of our lives.

When I could move again, I fell on my back and pulled her on top of me. Our bodies were covered in a light sheen of sweat, and I could feel her heart racing as quickly as mine. My limbs were like wet noodles, and my chest was bursting with happiness. No one had told me how whole and utterly content I'd feel when I mated. No wonder Pete couldn't stand to be away from Shannon. If I had my way, Emma and I wouldn't leave this bed for days.

"Comfortable?" I asked her huskily.

She snuggled against me. "Mmmm."

Chuckling, I lifted the hair away from her face. "Are you going to sleep on me?"

She arched an eyebrow. "I *am* on top of you, so that would be a yes."

"Good thing I have a healthy ego." I reached down and pulled the sheet over us then wrapped my arms around her.

"Am I too heavy?" she murmured.

I kissed the top of her head. "You're perfect."

"Are we mated now?"

"Yes."

I had a moment of panic that she regretted what we'd done, especially since there was no undoing a mate bond. As a human, she could walk away, but my wolf and my heart would be hers forever.

"Good." She pressed her lips to my chest. "I was going to say we should try again if it didn't work the first time. I'm sick of female wolves trying to take my man."

A laugh rumbled from my chest. "When I get my strength back, we'll make sure we're good and mated. Better safe than sorry, right?"

"Absolutely."

Minutes passed and I figured she'd dozed off. I didn't mind. I was holding my mate in our bed, and I was more than content to stay like this all night.

"Roland?"

I stroked her back. "I thought you were asleep."

"Just resting my eyes. Although, you do make a nice bed." She lifted her head and rested her chin on her arm so she could look at me. "I really do like this house."

I brushed her hair from her face. "I hoped you would."

She smiled. "I don't have a lot of stuff, other than my art supplies and my espresso machine. You think that'll fit in the Mustang?"

"Are you serious? You want to live here?"

"Yes."

I put my hands under her arms and pulled her up until my mouth met hers in a long, slow kiss. When it finally ended, both of us were breathing faster and I was extremely aware of the soft naked body pressed against mine.

She pushed up to a sitting position, straddling me, and heat shot straight to the place where her body rubbed against mine. Seemingly unaware of what she was doing to me or how ravishing she was in all her naked glory, she rested her hands on my stomach and gave me a regretful look.

"I still need to go visit my sister next week. I want to spend some time with her, and she'll be hurt if I don't go."

"How long?" I asked in a strained voice.

"Only a week."

She wriggled her bottom, and I had to suppress a groan. Her lip twitched. The little minx was trying to kill me.

Before she could blink, I rolled us until she was on the bottom again and I was exactly where I wanted to be.

"Shouldn't we be going to see your mother?" she asked breathlessly.

I pressed a light kiss to her mouth. "If you're going out of town in a few days, we really should make sure the mating took first. You don't want to leave me alone here, unmated, with all these females."

She licked her bottom lip. "You're right. I'm not feeling quite mated yet. We should definitely fix that."

And we did.

~ The End ~

ABOUT THE AUTHOR

When she is not writing, Karen Lynch can be found reading or baking. A native of Newfoundland, Canada, she currently lives in Charlotte, North Carolina with her cats and two crazy lovable German Shepherds: Rudy and Sophie.